CONTENTS

For Rosette Bathish (Teta) and my mother

It is part of morality
not to be at home
in one's home.
—THEODOR ADORNO

GUAPA

I.
CASTRATING DONKEYS

T he morning begins with shame. This is not new, but as memories of last night begin to sink in, the feeling takes on a terrifying resonance. I grimace, squirm, dig my fingers in my palms until the pain in my hands reflects how I feel. But there is no controlling what Teta saw, and her absence from my bedside means that she doesn't intend, as she had promised, to file away last night's mess in a deep corner of her mind.

On any other morning my grandmother's voice, hoarse from a million smoked cigarettes, would pierce my dreams: *Yalla Rasa, yalla habibi!* She would hover over me, her cigarette by my lips. I would inhale, feel the smoke travel to my lungs, jolting my insides awake.

On any other morning Doris would be beside her, pulling up the shutters in my room in a quick and violent snap. Removing a bandage to ease the pain of sunlight. One final *yalla*, then Teta would pull the sheets away and toss them aside. She took particular joy in doing this on cold winter mornings, relishing the way my skin broke out in goose bumps as I leaped across the room to snatch the blanket.

This is not how I wake up this morning. Getting up today involves battling demons more powerful than sloth. There is everything that has ever happened, and then there is this morning. I've crossed the red line with Teta.

My mobile rings. I roll over in bed and pick it up.

"Where the fuck are you?" Basma barks. "You should have

been here twenty minutes ago. I've got to meet a South African journalist who wants to interview some female refugees and the office is empty."

I clear my throat and rub my eyes. "Basma, I'm sorry—"

"Don't be sorry, be at the office. And I suppose I'm your ride to the wedding tonight, yes?"

The wedding. The wedding, the wedding, the wedding.

"Yes?" Basma asks again.

"I'm not feeling well," I croak. "I don't think I should go."

"I'll pick you up at eight."

I put the phone down and reach for my cigarettes. The cigarette will stimulate my brain. Thoughts will begin moving. I light one and inhale. My throat is raw from last night's pleading, and the smoke burns as it makes its way down.

I thought you were doing drugs. It didn't even cross my mind . . .

I had woken up a few times already, but the air still felt heavy. I wasn't ready to leave my dreams, so I plunged my face in the pillow and willed myself to sleep. After three or four or a thousand times I could not do it anymore. My eyes were shut but my brain was wide-awake. So here we are. I have no choice now but to face whatever the day may throw at me.

I sit up. Doris has placed a cup of Nescafé on the floor beside the bed. I take a large gulp. The coffee is weak and cold but lubricates the smoke's passage, leaving only the faint buzz of the nicotine and the silkiness of the tar on my tongue.

Open the door. Open the door right now.

What compelled her to look through that keyhole?

Taymour. He always reminded me of a young Robert De Niro. Those honey-colored eyes, those thoughtful lips. I need to see him again, run my fingers across the soft hair on his forearms. I was so foolish to ignore the signs, to believe in a future that would never exist. Now it's just me here, alone in bed. But I can't part with him this way, on these terms. Last night can't be the last we have together. I need to hold him, whisper in his ear that we can get past this. Can I not turn back the clock, turn that damn key in the lock to block the view?

Against my better judgement I send him a text message: *We need to talk about last night.*

Taymour. The banging. Teta's screams. I can hear it all again. My stomach turns at the thought of his name. In the three years we've been together, this is the first time I cannot bear to think of him. I need to speak to him, to hear his voice, but his name brings back all the shame. I'm an animal, dirty and disgusting, madly hunting after my desires with no care for what is right and wrong.

Repulsed, I jump out of bed and survey the bedroom. I had become careless, and now I've paid the price. I need to get rid of everything to do with him. I lift the mattress and grab my journal and toss it on the bed. I flick through the pages, tearing out the ones that mention his name. But his name runs through the sentences of every page, like a virus through the bloodstream. I rip out page after page until I am left with the last entry I wrote only a week ago. My eyes fall on the words written on the paper.

He's making a mistake. I just know it. He tells me I'm unreasonable, that I am expecting miracles. Maybe it's me who is unrealistic, but I know he can change. Is it okay to force change on someone if it is for the better?

I tear out the final page, crumple it in my hand, and continue the cleansing. Scattered around the room are old mix CDs he made for me, his handwriting scrawled on the silver discs in red and black marker pens: *Taymour summer mix*; *CHILL OUT*; *GOOD music 4 Rasa (4 a change)*. I throw them all on top of the journal. Under my bed I find a postcard he had sent from Istanbul last year. The picture on the front is of a clear blue sky over the Bosphorus. He had sent it in a brown envelope so nobody would read the words he had written on the back:

> *Final day. Bought some shoes from Asian side. Laces snapped as I tried shoes on and shopkeeper said, smiling, that I must be an angry man. Wanted to tell him there is a lot to be angry about, but then thought of you. How can I be angry when I have you? Outside it was raining hard. Looked out shop window and a seagull swooped in, snapped at a cat sitting by the door. Flew off with a tuft of fur. Writing this on ferry. Rain sliding down window, boats navigating choppy waters, an old man sits next to me reading a newspaper.*

I can't get rid of this, of us. Can I? Maybe it's best to just hide all this stuff for now, to not throw everything away just yet. I toss the postcard on the growing pile on my bed. Scooping the pile of Taymour's stuff in my hands, I reach for the top shelf in the closet and dump his things in an old shoe box hidden behind a stack of books. With her bad knee, Teta can't climb on a chair to get to the top shelf, and even if she could, she won't be able to move the books with one hand while supporting herself with the other.

I put on an old T-shirt, some trousers, and some socks from the pile of clothes on the floor. When I'm ready, I open the door and step onto the ancient carpet in the hallway. Teta's door is shut, and the house is still. I start walking down the hall, and when I'm certain no one is around, I turn back to the room, bend over, and peer through the keyhole. There's a clear view of my bed in the middle of the room, like a crime scene. Above it, shards of sunlight pierce the cracks between the wooden slats of the shutters and shine against the dust particles dancing in the air. The white walls are ridden with mosquito carcasses.

Teta could see everything from here. Last night she told me

that after looking in, she tried to go back to sleep but tossed and turned for a while before getting up again and pounding on my door. But what exactly had she seen? Was it when we kissed, or while we were entangled in each other, or maybe afterward? Perhaps she had peered in as we lay naked in bed, forehead to forehead, whispering?

No. I can't think of this anymore.

There's a sound of water hitting porcelain. Doris is washing dishes. She looks up when I walk in. She's wearing an old T-shirt of mine, which has the name of the college I went to in America.

"Good morning, sir," she chirps. Beyond the citrus smell of washing liquid I scan her face for knowledge and allegiance. She must have heard the screams last night, but did she understand enough to know what they were about? There is little I really know about Doris. She has a degree in criminology from the Philippines but has spent the past twenty-five years of her life cleaning our house. How have years of mopping floors and washing dishes shaped her views on love and morality? Where would she stand on what happened?

"Thanks for the coffee," I say, watching her movements for clues that might answer some of these questions. She smiles, adjusts her ponytail, then plunges her arms back into the soapy water. She doesn't give anything away. She must know. After all, aren't housekeepers the bearers of all family secrets?

I walk through the living room, past the portraits and photos of my father hanging on the walls in identical black frames. When we moved here after his death, Teta hung every picture she had of him up on the walls. Every day there was a new photo she found somewhere, and up it went in a black frame. Now the house is a shrine to him. Like a spiritual leader, he looks down on us from every wall. There's a photo of Baba in the seventies, with a large mustache and bright orange shorts, a cigarette in his hand; Baba at his graduation from medical school, his arms around the neck of a friend. Photos shot in studios over the years, one of him and me when I was five, him tickling me, my head thrown up in the air, laughing hysterically. The photos hanging on the left-hand side, where the morning sun hits them, are yellow and faded. There is one of him and Teta, both of them staring solemnly at the camera. He is resting his hand on her shoulder. Another of the two of them, Teta looking straight at the camera with an amused smile on her face, Baba reaching out toward the lens, half his face cut from the shot. Who would have taken that photo? Maybe it was me. Perhaps I intended to conceal my father's face.

The only picture of Baba not hung up in the main rooms of our house is a portrait my mother had painted. In it my father is holding the hose of a shisha in one hand and cradling his chin with the other. He is glancing off to the side, a restrained smile on his face. Teta hated that painting. When Mama had finished painting it, Teta stood in front of it for hours, pointing out mistakes. His hands were painted too delicately, like the hands of a woman. His mustache was lopsided. His nose was drawn too bulbous. The shading of his skin made him look jaundiced. After Baba died the painting plagued Teta with a conundrum: to hide an image of Baba or to showcase a memory of Mama. In the end she compromised by hanging it in a dark corner in Doris's room.

A few times I have entertained the notion of ripping all of Baba's photos off the walls. Not because I hate him. No, I loved my father. I just want to choose to love him, not have his memory shoved at me everywhere I look. Every photo of him seems to be like an order, "Love me! Love me!" Anyway I haven't torn his photos off the wall, not just in fear of Teta's reaction; if I throw away all his photos, leaving behind empty spaces, who would be our leader then?

There are no photographs of my mother in the house.

I step onto the small balcony with its cracked walls that have been weathered by years of sunlight. Antar, Teta's canary, cocks its head and tweets at me from its cage. The city is heaving in the scorching July morning. In my head everything is jumbled. Cars have been honking since dawn, the air smells of jasmine and exhaust fumes. Apart from the faint sense of uncertainty, you would never think that change is brewing. This closed city. It feels too small.

In the building opposite ours, Um Nasser is hanging up the laundry on thin metal wires that crisscross her balcony like an obstacle course. She waves at me and I cautiously wave back.

"Where's your grandmother?" she calls out.

"She's still asleep."

"That's not like her. Is she sick?"

"No, just tired."

Antar tweets, catching me in the lie. I flick at the cage and look down from the balcony onto the narrow alley below, where stray cats fight in the shade of the tall buildings and the sounds of fruit sellers calling out today's prices echo in the air. This part of town, the old city, can be headache-inducing, but at least it has been spared from the mayor's latest project, which was to install flashing pink and yellow lights along the roundabouts of the western suburbs, making the city look like it's throwing itself a deranged party. For that, at least, I am grateful.

We moved to this neighbourhood when I was thirteen, a year after my father died. We had enough savings but no steady stream of income, so we sold our villa in the western suburbs for a fifth-floor apartment in this old building downtown. This left us with enough money each month to pay for our food and clothes, and to just about keep up appearances. The new building overlooks a main road with three mosques that drive me crazy with their wailing, a market, and a kindergarten. Our apartment is not large, only two bedrooms and a small laundry room, which was converted into a bedroom for Doris. The living room has a large window and a door leading to a small balcony, where I now stand. Although most of my friends still live in the western suburbs, I enjoy living downtown. It seems fitting that we would live here, at the point where the sprawling suburbs meet the slums in al-Sharqiyeh.

I sit in Teta's chair and light another cigarette. Teta positions her chair at the perfect angle on the balcony, which gives you a view of both the television and the streets. In her pink-and-white cotton nightgown, her hair blow-dried into a golden bob, she spends the first few hours of her morning on this balcony, with one eye on the news and the other on the neighbourhood's happenings. She drinks a cup of Turkish coffee and smokes two cigarettes as she watches the news programmes on the crackling television set, the same stories told differently on state TV, the foreign-funded stations, those of the different opposition groups—which grow in number as the groups themselves divide and split—and she heckles each in turn. Meanwhile she greets neighbours as they wake up. She watches their comings and goings, eavesdrops on conversations. I swear, she collects gossip like the best investigative journalist you can think of. She then pieces these together into stories, and recounts them to the neighbourhood women during their midmorning *subhiyeh* of coffee and cigarettes.

Imagine if my story makes her *subhiyeh* this morning.

You know that stubborn woman still refuses to congratulate them for the marriage? I saw her sulking on the balcony the other day.

You would think they would have resolved their fight by now. They're not solving the Palestinian issue for God's sake.

We explained to her the wedding invitations were limited. Nabil asked his mother to keep the numbers low . . .

He did marry a beautiful girl. Slightly dark, but . . .

They are swimming in money . . .

He'll probably run off with the maid like his father did.

When is Rasa going to bring you a nice girl?

You would never believe this story, but I caught someone in his room last night.

No! Who was she? Is she from the neighbourhood?

He was with a man!

Ouf! Does the man come from a good family at least?

No, I know Teta will guard this secret far better than Taymour and I had.

Doris comes with an *ibrik* of Turkish coffee.

"Have you seen Teta this morning?" I ask as she pours me a cup.

"Still in room," she says and walks away, her neon green slippers shuffling on the carpet. I take a sip. The coffee is hot and strong and helps me lose some of my empty feeling. I settle into Teta's chair and turn on the television for the 8 A.M. news. A young woman in a pink veil is recounting today's top stories. If Teta were here, she'd be muttering, *Look at her! She wears a hijab but still covers half her face with red lipstick. She looks like a cat that has just eaten her own kittens.*

The woman on TV looks somberly at me as she announces the headline story.

"At dawn this morning a group of terrorists, armed with foreign weapons, occupied vast swathes of land in the eastern side of the city, al-Sharqiyeh." As she speaks footage is shown of masked men with heavy machine guns running through the empty streets of the slums. "Footage released by the terrorists shows them massacring at least fifty army personnel stationed on the outskirts of al-Sharqiyeh." As she says this more grainy footage is shown of a line of headless bodies on a dirt road. One of the masked men points his gun in the air and lets out a series of shots as the others shout, *"Allahu Akbar."*

The president appears on the television now. He is sitting behind his desk and is dressed in military uniform.

"Let me make myself very clear," he says in his military voice, which is slower and more shouty than his other voices. "This attack is further indication that there are terrorist elements in the country that are benefiting from destabilizing the situation. We will do everything in our power to crush these terrorists for the security of our nation and its great people."

My head is spinning with the president's voice, the image of the headless bodies in the dirt, the thought of Teta spying on Taymour and me in bed. I look out from the balcony toward al-Sharqiyeh. A flock of birds hovers over the city, oblivious to the mess us humans are making, to the heavy ball of shame and fear in the pit of my stomach. An eerie quietness cuts through the usual sound of traffic and street vendors. Is this ominous stillness new, or have I only just noticed it?

I switch over to CNN. I can't stand to look at the president's face, and I want to see how the foreign media is covering the events. The television anchor, an older woman with dyed blond hair, has a look of concern in her eyes. "The troubled nation has been experiencing upheaval since protests erupted earlier this year, and the latest development seems to confirm growing fears around the radicalization of the opposition to the president's rule."

Only a few months ago I was on that television screen. My beaming face, along with thousands of others, all crammed together, waving flags and singing victorious songs. The camera panned across our nameless faces and we cheered back. We each had a name, a history, a life. But we were willing to forsake all of that if it meant appearing strong, united, steadfast. For that moment we wanted to be nameless because we were one united mass against the bullshit we had thought was inevitable. No more hypocrisy, no more fear, no more staying put and shutting up and selling our souls to political devils for the sake of "stability." After an eternity of fear and suspicion and disappointment, it suddenly seemed so obvious, as if the opportunity had been staring us in the face our whole lives and all we had to do was reach out and grab it. At one point I was interviewed by CNN, and with a smile on my face I addressed all my friends who had left and vowed never to come back: "You can come back now! We need you to help us rebuild!" We were so hopeful then, so ridiculously naïve.

I turn off the television and pick up my phone. The dark screen of my mobile glares back at me. Still no word from Taymour. I want to call him, just to hear his voice, even though I don't know the right words to say. Instead I call Maj. His phone is turned off so I send him a message: *My grandmother caught me and Taymour last night. It's all a mess.*

Just last night we had been at Guapa: Basma, Taymour, Maj, and me. We drank beer and argued. The subject was, as always, American imperialism and the sad state of our revolution. Taymour had been so insistent that now, more than ever, the president was the only alternative, it was either that or the Islamists.

"Look here," he was explaining to Maj, "think of it this way. We're all starving. The president has knafeh cooking in the oven, and you are standing over his shoulder criticizing his ingredients and methods of cooking, and insisting on taking it out before it's done because it's not to your liking. But there are some people in the kitchen who want to destroy the knafeh, and as soon as you open that oven they'll reach in and throw it all away. What will we do then?"

"That's what the regime wants you to think," Maj said, flicking the ash of his cigarette onto the table, "that you either eat their bitter-tasting knafeh or you don't eat at all. We can't accept that."

"I'm craving knafeh now." Basma yawned, pulling her curly hair back from her face, her eyes glazed over from the hashish we had smoked earlier. I wanted to explain the sad reality that, knafeh or not, we've been kicked out of the kitchen, which is why we were in Guapa drinking ourselves silly. Instead I remained silent, watching Taymour speak, admiring his voice, his conviction, the way the dim red lighting of Guapa cut shadows into his face. As they argued I dreamed of kissing his cheek, because it struck me that to kiss your lover's cheek in public was quite ordinary, and more than anything I wanted for us to be ordinary and in love. Of course then Basma left and Taymour, Maj, and I went to Guapa's basement, danced and drank some more, and then Taymour and I came back here and . . .

I peer into the apartment. Teta's door is still shut. The last time she slept in this late was the morning after Baba's funeral. I could leave now, quickly before she wakes up. But that might tell her I'm running away, that I'm even less of a man than she thought. But if she comes in and I'm sitting here watching television and drinking coffee, she'd think I have no shame, like I am proud I was in bed with a man last night.

I stub out my half-smoked cigarette and walk out the door.

Emerging from the gray stone building where we live, I step out onto the busy road. Street vendors are selling tissues and pink battery-operated mini-fans and arguing over the ever-rising price of apricots. As I turn the corner onto the main road and the cold shadow of the president's statue falls across me, I recall, with perfect clarity, the day this statue was obscured by clouds of tear gas that burned my lungs.

I pass the supermarket across the street from our building. It's the supermarket Taymour and I hid in when the snipers attacked a few months ago. At the time, we crouched in a nook between the entrance and a fridge filled with ice cream and frozen chicken. These days, walking past the supermarket brings back the screams of the crowd in my ears, the image of bodies dropping to the ground reflected in the broken glass of the door, and the feel of my face against Taymour's neck, hot and sweaty. Now the supermarket carries on as normal, except the broken glass is patched up with a piece of old cardboard. Even this early in the morning the sun shines strong and bright and the sky is clear of clouds. Today will probably be very hot.

With the heavy traffic it'll take me at least thirty minutes to get to work. Running to find a cab, I hear the president's voice booming from the speakers of the cars and coffee shops, warning of the imminent threat from those who are seeking to destroy the nation.

"Be watchful, be vigilant. Don't trust anyone," he says over and over. His voice is like alcohol, making everyone drunk, and I am very hungover.

I hail the first taxi I see, a weathered Mercedes that is probably older than I am. The taxi driver looks worn. Like me, I don't think he's had a good night's sleep. The dashboard is covered in ash and plastic cups, stained with the tar-like sludge of Turkish coffee. He greets me with a grunt and a click of the meter. I give him directions to my office.

"Traffic is shit down there," he grumbles as the car sputters forward.

When I first returned from America, I was eager to learn about the challenges of an everyday man's life. I sat in taxis and listened to drivers complain: about the cost of living, the government's failures, the corruption and poverty. My American education had given me a way to analyse my people. I felt I was mixing with the true salt of the earth, the authentic Arab voice. But like an old lover, as the years pass and the complaints remain the same, that rose-tinted vision has cleared. The problems they complain about are now my own problems, and problems are much less glamorous when they are yours. Anyway, today of all days I don't have the energy to bestow sympathy. I have my own troubles to deal with. I need my own space to think. But the driver talks and talks, invading my thoughts. I look out the window to avoid any pretence of conversation.

This strategy is unsuccessful.

"Gas prices are up again," he says, looking straight ahead. The stench of morning breath, cigarette smoke, and resentment poisons the air in the car. "I drive this broken-down *zift* car around the city in this heat, and I get, what, five, maybe six customers. I end up spending more on petrol than I get from customers. It's like castrating donkeys."

He looks at me, expecting a response, but I only look out the window. He is about to speak again, I can sense it. I rummage through my bag and grab my iPod to block him out. The white earphones are all tangled up in themselves. I try to untangle them before he speaks but I'm too late. He is off again.

"Castrating donkeys. You know why that is? It costs you twice as much to clean yourself afterward as you get from doing the job."

I smile at this, put away my iPod. Knowing he is winning me over, the driver chuckles and lights a triumphant cigarette.

We stop at a checkpoint. The soldier asks for our papers. An automatic guilt surges within me, as though I may be dragged out of the car for a crime I have unknowingly committed, within the maze of complicated rules and unspoken regulations that descend from every corner. The government here does not answer to the needs and desires of the people, I think as I hand the soldier my documents. Here, people must answer to the government.

"Where are you coming from?" the officer asks, looking through our papers.

"Downtown," the driver replies.

"Avoid the main road today," he says as he hands us our documents. "There's lots of security because of last night's events."

We're moving again, taking a right off the main highway and onto a crowded side road.

"Soon we'll need to show our documents to take a shit," the driver tells me as the meter rises in regular clicks. He lets out a sigh. "All of life these days seems like castrating donkeys."

The flood of people leaving the villages is reflected in the heavy traffic, which is already showing signs of expansion. The roundabouts heave with the cacophony of honking cars and screeching motorcycles that have maneuvered themselves into intricate contortions that seem as though they would never be able to disentangle from one another. The exhaust fumes wrap themselves around us as we weave between the people and cars. The lights change from red to green, and the procession of cars begins to honk more aggressively. The meter clicks one more time.

Meanwhile the sun is cooking us. Beads of sweat swell on my forehead. The driver leans out the window and spits, then turns up the radio to counter the noise of the cars.

"Tell us your name and where you're calling us from," the voice on the radio says.

"My name is Om Noaman, and I want to thank you for taking our call and thank your program for all the work it's doing for citizens and thank the radio station for airing an excellent show and—"

"Thank you, Om Noaman. Where are you calling us from, my sister?"

"I want to complain about the road that the municipality has—"

"Where are you calling us from, Om Noaman?"

"I'm calling from Beit Nour, sir."

"Om Noaman from Beit Nour, go ahead and tell us your problem."

"As I was saying I am calling to complain about the road that the municipality has destroyed. They told us they wanted to pave the road. They came and—"

"That's what they told you? That they were going to pave the road?"

"That's what they told us and we thought, *yalla*, it would be nice to have a paved road because the current dirt road floods in wintertime, and the past two winters have cut us off from the cities so it's been—"

"And did they pave the road?"

"No, but that's not the problem."

"What is the problem, Om Noaman?"

"The problem is that they dug up the main road to the village and they promised to have it paved. That was six months ago and we are still waiting. This is the main road that takes the children to school. For the past six months the children have had to climb into this twenty-metre ditch and back up again just to go to school."

"Have you tried calling the municipality?"

"You know with the events we are very worried. No way in or out. We have young children, old people. We can't leave. Everyone is scared and—"

"Have you called the municipality, Om Noaman?"

"We used to call them every day but not anymore. They used to promise to fix it, but they haven't done anything and now they aren't even answering our calls."

The driver slams on the brakes as a young boy selling a stack of Qurans and washcloths dashes in front of the car.

"May sixty dicks dance on your mother's pussy," the driver barks, leaning into his horn. The sun, the horn, the voices on the radio. All of this is giving me a terrible headache.

"Okay, Om Noaman, I will give the municipality a call now. Please stay on the line while I find the number. There we go. If you would stay on the line for one moment please, Om Noaman . . . "

There is a click and then a dial tone as the radio host punches in the numbers.

"Office of Mr. Qasem."

"Hello, this is Mohammad Bashir calling live from the radio program *Bisaraha*. Can I speak to Mr. Qasem, please?"

"One second, please." There is a rustling on the line, and then, "He's busy."

"This is very urgent, sir. We're currently live on air and just need to ask him one question. Please let him know we are live on air."

There is more rustling and then a brusque voice comes on the line.

"Yes?"

"Hello, sir, I'm Mohammad Bashir calling from the program *Bisaraha*. Have you heard about us before?"

"Yes."

"We take calls from citizens across the country—"

"I know what you do."

"We have just had a caller from Beit Nour who has told us that the municipality authorized the digging of a ditch for an assessment to pave the road."

"The country is being attacked by jihadi terrorists and you're talking about a ditch in the road? Have I gone mad?"

"Sir, this happened six months ago. Six months ago. Those poor children have to climb in and out of a twenty-metre ditch to go to school. Six months ago, sir."

"We sent someone to take care of this."

"Well the person never arrived, sir. The children are climbing in and out of the ditch to get to school, sir. Twenty metres, sir. *Haram*, sir."

"The Americans funded this project. I'm not in charge of their decisions."

"Please see if you can deal with this today, sir. It's the only road to the village, sir. I'm going to call you back. In twenty minutes, sir?"

"Give me a day or two."

"Thirty minutes, sir? We need to have a guarantee before we go off the air."

"*Tamam.* Give me half an hour."

"Thank you very much, sir, on behalf of the village of Beit Nour and from myself, Mohammad Bashir."

I glance at my phone, hoping for a call from Taymour or Maj or anyone, really. Perhaps even Mohammad Bashir.

Are you saying she caught you, sir?

Yes, she caught me.

Well what were you doing there together in the first place, sir?

It's my life, I can do what I want.

But you're in her house, sir. She does own the house, sir.

It was my room.

Do you pay rent, sir?

No, but—

Is the house in your name, sir?

I'm entitled to some privacy.

If you're living in her house, then you follow her rules.

There's nothing wrong with what we were doing.

Eib, sir. It's a perversion, sir.

There are lots of perversions in our world.

What you were doing is haram, *sir.*

The car jolts as we drive over a pothole. A plastic coffee cup rolls across the dashboard and onto the floor. The sludge at the bottom of the cup seeps into the dirty carpet under our feet.

"Nothing works." The driver spits. "This is a country, they say. What kind of country is this? Do you think this is a country?"

"It was always this way." I look out the window and say nothing more. Why get into an argument about the government with this guy? I've heard enough stories of informants posing as drivers to catch casual complainers. The risk isn't worth pursuing yet another frustrated diatribe.

"How old are you?" he asks.

"I'm young."

"What are you, a woman? Tell me how old you are."

Oh to ignore him for the rest of the ride, or else to tell him to shut up and remind him that I am paying not for his opinions but for his driving! There is no reason to be nice, to believe in anything, when everyone around you holds your fate in their hands. And make no mistake, everyone is to blame for the mess Taymour and I are in, because society is made up of everyone, and it is society's stupid rules that are keeping us apart. But try as I might, I can't ignore the taxi driver. To ignore him would be *eib*, shameful. So I answer his question.

"Twenty-seven."

"You see, you're too young to remember. Things were never this bad. Married?"

"No."

"Why not?"

I look out the window and sigh. "I'm still young. I don't want to get married."

The driver turns to look at me. I continue staring out the window to avoid eye contact. My youth can only get me so far with this question. In a few more years this answer would no longer be acceptable. In fact, this excuse for my permanent bachelorhood is already being met with disapproval and well-meaning advice on finding the right girl.

"Smart man," the driver says.

The smell of the taxi brings me back to my first time, the first time I operated purely on instinct. The memory returns to me so vividly I feel I am back there, at fourteen, in the backseat of that taxi. At the time my father had been dead for eighteen months, my mother had vanished the year before that, I was magically sprouting hair in places I was not expecting, and I was still sharing a bed with Teta.

I was returning from a history lesson at Maj's house. We were both struggling with the material. Our school followed the British curriculum, which meant we had to study the history of Europe and the World Wars: the Kaiser, the Treaty of Versailles, then Churchill and Stalin. It all seemed like another universe to us, so Teta and Maj's mother agreed to share the costs of a private tutor.

I hailed a taxi outside Maj's house and got into the backseat, as Teta directed me to do when riding in taxis alone. The man behind the wheel was young, though I couldn't make out his age: perhaps eighteen, maybe twenty. He was wearing a tight red T-shirt that gripped his body. He drove without speaking. A familiar pressure inside me began to build. It was a terrible choking sensation that had been growing in the months since I lost my parents. I had no control over my destiny, and everything around me could suddenly die or run away.

I rolled down the window and pressed the back of my head against the leather seat. The crisp November air felt cold against my face, releasing the pressure somewhat. Through the streetlights, which lit up the inside of the car in recurring waves, I saw that the driver's forearms were potholed with scars. I admired the way his T-shirt stretched tightly against his chest. His arms broke out in large goose bumps.

"Shut the window, it's cold," he said. I rolled up the window, feeling the choking sensation close in on me once more. I watched the muscles in the driver's arms tighten as he shifted gears. The large veins running under his skin awoke a sensation inside me I had never felt before. I wanted to connect with him in some way, to be closer to him somehow.

"Is this your taxi?" I asked.

"My brother's," he said. His jaw clicked as he chewed a piece of gum. He sighed and put one arm behind the passenger seat while steering with the other. I looked at the hand resting behind the seat. His fingers were decorated with gold and silver rings. Dark black dirt was wedged underneath his fingernails. I glanced down at my own fingernails, which Doris had clipped earlier that day.

I tried to imagine what this man's life was like, outside of this taxi. His rough accent meant he probably lived in al-Sharqiyeh, maybe in a tiny room that smelled of fried onions and cigarettes, because that's what I imagined al-Sharqiyeh would smell like. How much did we have in common, he and I? If I knew then what I know now, I would have put our differences down to a complex algorithm of class and culture. But back then I did not know about any of that, so I stuck to what we had in common: the car we were both sitting in.

"Do you drive this taxi often?" I asked.

"One or two nights a week," he replied, making a turn into the side street that took us off the highway and toward my new neighbourhood downtown.

"Do you enjoy it?"

"Enjoy what?" His eyes flicked up to look at me through the rearview mirror. His eyes were a cool gray, almost silver.

"Driving the taxi," I said, holding his gaze as I played with the dog-eared corners of the history books on my lap.

"It's just a job," he said, turning back to the road.

"Well, what do you like doing when you're not driving the taxi? Do you watch television?" Teta fed me a diet of dubbed Mexican *telenovelas*, American television shows, and an endless stream of news. Perhaps his television set also showed those channels.

"I don't have spare time. When I'm not driving, I work on a construction site."

The next turn would take us to my street. I felt a sudden panic. I wanted to spend more time with this man. We were moving closer to something new and exciting. I wanted to be his friend. And not just any friend, not like Maj or Basma, but a friend who would always be around, someone I could hug and be close to. My insides were buzzing. I wanted him to keep on driving, to take me out of this sad town, far away from that empty apartment with Doris and Teta.

"Is that why you have big muscles?" I scrambled to find a way to delay our separation. He glanced at me, studied my face for a while, clicked his chewing gum. Then his lips turned to form a crooked smile.

"Come up here and sit next to me," he said.

I hesitated. It would be *eib* to say no, although it also felt *eib* to say yes. Stuck between two *eibs*, I left the books in the back and climbed into the passenger seat. We drove past Teta's apartment. He took a right into a dark street and parked the car between two large trees. He unzipped his jeans and pulled out his thing. It stood between us, hard, like an intruder to an intimate conversation. Instinctively, I reached out and grabbed it, and he let out a slight moan. I studied the thing in my hand, feeling it grow in my palm.

"*Yalla,*" he whispered as his eyes scanned the area.

"Huh?"

"Put your mouth on it," he said impatiently.

I swallowed and bent down. He smelled sour and hot. I put his thing in my mouth and looked up for further instructions.

"Wet your mouth, wet your mouth," he hissed. "Your tongue is like sandpaper."

I swallowed a few more times until my mouth was wet, and this time the process went more smoothly. He seemed happy with this and sighed. He pressed down on my neck but he remained alert, his head darting back and forth as if following a game of tennis. I was down for a few minutes when my excitement began to disappear, replaced with a strong sense of guilt that I was making a terrible mistake. I struggled, concentrating on breathing through my nose and not gagging each time he pushed my head down. I wasn't sure how long this would last. He groaned. My mouth filled with salty slime. The warm hand at the back of my neck disappeared.

"Get out now before someone sees," he said, zipping his trousers up. I wiped my mouth, took my books from the backseat, and got out of the car. The man started up the engine, reversed out onto the road, and sped off.

I looked around. There was no one. The awkward feeling slowly disappeared, and the memory of what happened seemed sweeter. I stored bits of it for later: the warm hand on the back of my neck, the sour smell, the shape of his thing in my mouth. I relived those memories as I walked home.

Teta looked up when I came through the door. I was terrified to face her. She always seemed to know everything. This was something she should never know. She was sitting in her nightgown, cracking roasted sunflower seeds between her teeth. On the television the news showed footage of bombs dropping on a busy neighbourhood.

"You found a taxi?" she asked, picking at bits of seed lodged between her teeth.

For a moment I thought she might be able to tell just by looking at me, or that she would smell the taxi driver on my clothes and face. I swallowed hard, feeling the salty slime slide down my throat. It felt scratchy, like I was coming down with a cold.

"Yes, but he took the long way," I said, trying to look as natural as I could. I took a deep breath. This was the first lie I had ever told Teta, and as I said this a part of me split from her forever. The gooey liquid in the back of my throat felt far away from the words coming out of my mouth. I was two people now, in two separate realities, where the rules in one were suspended and different from those in the other.

"Look at this shit," the driver says, bringing me back to the car, which is smoky with cigarettes and summertime. He points to a truck crammed with what seems like hundreds of men and women in tattered clothes. They are crushed against one another like tobacco in a cigarette. Chairs, suitcases, and torn plastic bags are squeezed in the spaces between them.

For so long I thought I was immune to this. I could look at the refugees and feel pity that they have nowhere to go and are reliant on the goodwill of others. Today I feel just as stranded as them. I want to grab my own belongings and hop onto the back of that truck, let it take me wherever it is going. I could probably help these people, share some of my savings, my English skills, direct them to the good NGOs, the right UN agencies. I could be of use to them somehow. They would take me in.

The driver points to a boy tapping on the window of the car in front of us. "What has this revolution brought us? Children have been arrested and tortured, families have lost their homes. Where is there left for refugees to go to? They're still coming but they don't realize we're all going to be refugees soon, just running from place to place. Back to our Bedouin roots." He chuckles bitterly. "We've destroyed the country, and for what? Castrating donkeys, I tell you."

"Things will get better," I say.

He looks at me and lifts an eyebrow.

"You must not be from around here."

Tell me we're okay. I can't lose you to what happened. We might not have our bedroom but we can find new places to be together. We can figure out the logistics later but for now just tell me we're okay—

"Everything is falling apart," Nawaf announces, peeking his glistening bald head through the door of our shared office.

I close down the e-mail I'm writing to Taymour and open the document I'm supposed to be translating. The document is about the need to stabilize the fluctuating exchange rate. I've translated six papers for this company in the past week, liberally misinterpreting sentences I find distasteful.

"Where's Basma?" Nawaf asks, squeezing himself into the chair across from my desk.

"She called me this morning . . . there's a new journalist in town . . . South African, looking for a female interpreter. She should be back soon."

Nawaf pours us each a cup of Turkish coffee from the flask he carries with him. The cheap fabric of his white shirt stretches over his belly. A few stray hairs poke out as the old buttons struggle to keep the material together.

"Cheers," he raises his cup in the air. "The country is falling apart and my love life is in ruins. I really think this is it, Rasa. I really do."

"With the al-Sharqiyeh crisis or with your girl?"

"Crisis? Is that what we are calling it now? A crisis? No, not the crisis, man. The girl! It's all a terrible, sad mess." Nawaf sighs and sucks on his cigarette hungrily. "She's playing games with my poor, weak heart . . . oh, what's the use? You'll never understand. Look at you, tall and handsome . . . the only thing that will ever break your heart is that cigarette you're smoking . . . Take my advice, Rasa, never place too much hope on matters of the heart because women are ruthless."

"What's happened now?" This is not the first time Nawaf has announced that it is all over for him.

"We had plans to go to the cinema—"

"What film?"

"Never mind what film now . . . all week she's playing hot and funky with me . . . phone calls in the middle of the night . . . text messages . . . I can't wait to see you . . . I miss you. Honey. Baby. Fire! Fire, I tell you. We had plans to go to the cinema yesterday . . . all day, morning to night, I try to get in touch with her like a silly donkey . . . telephone, message, e-mail, Skype, Facebook. Nothing. Finally she calls me at midnight . . .

sorry, she says . . . I'm confused, she says." Nawaf coughs and rubs his face with a leathery palm. His head is a good shade or two darker than the rest of his body, which makes his face look like an overcooked pancake. "She says why marry a translator when she can marry a doctor or an engineer. What would people say, she says."

"She sounds like my grandmother." Teta was not happy I had become a translator. Then again, nothing short of becoming Baba would have satisfied her. *Habibi*, she might begin. *Every day you're looking more and more like your grandfather. And you make stupid decisions like him as well. You should never have come back from America. You should have stayed and found a job there but they didn't give you the passport. God knows why. It's their loss. But there we are. What can we do? All this education and you are an interpreter.*

I turn to Nawaf. "You know she still pesters me to get a job in the Gulf. To do what? Work in some soulless air-conditioned office on the millionth floor of some skyscraper and fall asleep bored and horny, without even the solace of alcohol to keep me sane?"

"They have great Russian girls there, though," Nawaf says. "Apparently they organize the brothels like a supermarket. One room has all Russian, one room all Thai, and you even have a room with just African girls if you're in the mood for something spicy. I'd listen to your grandmother if I were you."

"Perhaps," I say. When I returned from America I had thought I could do something more useful than the Gulf. Become an aid worker maybe. Or a revolutionary. I was so optimistic back then, and anyway when I came back I saw that nothing had changed.

I turn to Nawaf. "Anyway, mark my words. When our company starts turning a profit your girl will be begging you to marry. Besides, if she loved you she wouldn't treat you like this."

"Love is never enough, you idiot. Anyway, how is your girl?"

"Fine," I say, perhaps too quickly. I hesitate. I had told Nawaf about "a girl" after his persistent questions.

"You still won't tell me her name? Not even her family name? Is she still insisting on keeping everything secret? Who is she, Rihanna?"

"I told you a thousand times, her parents are very traditional. *Eib.*"

"We stick our heads up our asses and call ourselves traditional."

It pains me not to be able to tell him Taymour's name. I have considered feminizing it, perhaps as "Tara" or "Tamara," but, like picking at a knotted piece of string, introducing a first name would inevitably lead to questions about a last name. Then comes the name of a father and the village they are from. People pick and pick with their questions. Eventually the entire thing unravels.

Taymour's name is embargoed under a cloak of *eib*. The closest word for *eib* in English is perhaps "shame." But *eib* is so much more than that. The implication of *eib* is *kalam il-nas*, what will people say, and so the word carries an element of conscientiousness, a politeness brought about by a perceived sense of communal obligation. *Eib* is an old cloak that Teta draped across my shoulders many years ago. After Baba's death she wove an intricate web for the two of us. In public we were stoic, navigating social obligations like pros. When it was just us, unspoken words rotted in our mouths. Teta hid her grief behind a pinched nose, a tight smile, and her ever-growing list of *eibs*. It's *eib* not to go visit the neighbours during Eid. It's *eib* to miss a wedding, even if you hate every minute of it. It's *eib* to pick your nose in public. Accepting a second helping of food on the first offer: *eib* ("*Shoo*, I don't feed you enough?"). It's *eib* to ask a woman how old she is or to ask someone what religion they are. It's *eib* for a young boy to play with Barbie dolls. I've come to realize that if worn correctly, the cloak of *eib* is large and malleable enough to allow you to conceal many secrets and to repel intrusive questions. For example, it's *eib* to ask me my girlfriend's name if I don't offer it to you first.

I suppose because of this secrecy, Taymour's name holds an unexplainable power over me. It's a name weighed down by secrets and implications, transformed into something much larger than its seven letters. I look forward to listening to people say the name with their unique inflections and tones. I analyse it, I spell it out. Sometimes I even whisper his name out loud when I can be certain nobody can hear. This satisfies me for some time but it's never enough. No, I need others to say his name too. It makes the name real. It makes us real.

"What's wrong with you today?" Nawaf asks. "You're inside your head. I can see the sadness in your eyes."

What can I tell him? That there's a reason I always keep my phone beside me, never faceup on a table? That everything he saw of me before today has been a performance—from the *zalameh* jokes I tell to my throaty laugh and the concerted effort to deepen my voice. That there is no girl and there never was any girl? When I had Taymour by my side it was okay to hide behind all that, because at least I was hiding something. But am I even hiding anything anymore? We all tell lies to protect our solitude. We deny the truth and present a false image of ourselves to blend into society. It's the same everywhere, but here the stakes are much higher. So I put on my mask and let out a roaring laugh.

"Nawaf, you fat bastard, all you're seeing is a reflection of your own miserable life."

"Suck my dick, Rasa," Nawaf says, throwing a pen at me.

Basma walks into the office and tosses her handbag on the desk.

"Finally you guys show up. I've been running around the city all morning with a new client and the office has been empty. How can we start a business if two-thirds of us don't even show up on time?"

"I've had a rough morning," I say, lighting another cigarette. "Don't ask."

Basma pulls a baggie of hashish from her handbag and turns to Nawaf. "And you? Did you correct the spelling mistake on the website like I asked you?" The three of us have just set up a website for our sorry little company, and our home page currently promises "*impaccable* translation services."

"I've been meaning to call them all morning, but I've been busy."

"What are you busy with?" Basma says, sitting down on the table and rolling a joint. "We need to fix that spelling mistake."

"I was with John. Remember him, that British journalist? Rasa went with him to the interview he did with the tribes in the north?"

"How can I forget." Basma laughs. "Walking around like he's Lawrence of Arabia, then he drank some dirty well water and was hospitalized for a week."

"Yes, well, you'll be glad to know he's better now. He called me this morning, last-minute, to translate a few meetings he had. I even went to one meeting with the head of the reform process. He interviewed him about the takeover last night."

"Shami?" I ask. "But he speaks English."

"Yes, yes, but John brought me along anyway as he needed a driver." Nawaf turns to look at me. "You worked for Shami, no?"

"Only for a few months when I first came back from America. I arrived with a suitcase full of dreams and he destroyed every one of them."

"Why?" Nawaf asks, picking up his phone. Basma lights the joint and takes a puff.

"When I applied for a job with him, I sent him my thesis, which was all about the barbaric economic policies of the International Monetary Fund, how they made the rich richer and the poor even more desolate. The next day he called me into his office. You're the one who likes the public sector, he tells me when we meet. I tell him yes and his big mustache, it's like a broom on his upper lip, starts to twitch in excitement. He hired me the next day. My first task was to get a document signed at the ministry of something or other. The next morning I arrive at the ministry at eight thirty . . . the first employee comes in at eleven. Then I'm sent on a treasure hunt through the building . . . up and down the stairs . . . into countless offices and rooms looking for hundreds of stamps and signatures."

"Thieves . . . " Nawaf shakes his head, not looking up from his phone, his fingers texting furiously.

"I spent the next two weeks in the offices of vice presidents and deputy heads and vice deputy president heads, sitting with groups of old men who drank coffee, smoked cigarettes, and took phone calls mid-sentence. Anyway, I will spare you the suicide-inducing details of government bureaucracy in this country, but finally after two weeks, I went back to Shami's office with the signed document. He looks at it and asks me what it is. I tell him it is the document he needed signed. He grunts and tosses it on top of a heaving stack of papers . . . he looks at me and his bushy mustache is twitching like crazy now. Do you still like the public sector, he asks me . . . that was all. Do you still like the public sector . . . I find out later that if he ever needed a document like that signed, he would simply call up his friends at the ministry and get a signature in a matter of hours."

"He was just trying to show you that your American degree is worthless here," Basma says.

"Well, he was right." Shami had sold himself to the Americans as a reformer, someone who would facilitate democracy in our country. Presenting yourself as a reformer is the surest way to get rich here, and I had thought that by working with him I would at least try to meet all this reform nonsense halfway. I delved into the murky waters of the president's agenda, writing reports and briefs about "reform" and defending elections that meant nothing. I was drowning in these words, and the work of transparency and beauty I came back from America to create was becoming clouded. Things I wanted to say were coming out like muddied water on the page. Words that looked so simple on paper concealed more than they revealed, which for words is a cardinal sin. It is like turning on a lamp to see what's in a room only for the light to be so blinding it makes it impossible to open your eyes. What purpose does the lamp serve then? If a lamp only makes it harder to see then it is of no use, and if your words only serve to conceal the truth, then you might as well not say a word at all.

Nawaf reaches for the joint and Basma shakes her head. "Finish the stack of translations first."

"So you can get stoned on the job but I can't?" Nawaf whines.

"I can't work unless I'm stoned."

My phone rings. Unknown number. Taymour must have forgotten his phone at home. That's why I haven't heard from him all morning.

"Hello?"

"Rasa? This is Maj's mother."

"Hi, Auntie."

"Auntie?" Nawaf chuckles. I silence him with a finger to my lips.

"Have you heard from Maj today?"

I tell her I haven't and she asks when the last time I spoke to him was.

"Last night," I say. "I sent him a message this morning but I haven't heard anything."

She sighs. In the background there is a sizzle of something being dropped into hot frying oil.

"He was out late last night," she says. "His phone has been turned off all morning. I'm worried, especially with . . . things in the country not being okay. Was he at Guapa, or whatever that silly bar is called?"

"He was, but I left before he did." I close my eyes as the sound of Teta's screams comes back to me. "Don't worry, Auntie. I'm sure he's fine . . . maybe he forgot his keys and his battery died . . . he is probably staying at a friend's house . . . I'm sure he'll call soon." Maj is probably passed out on someone's couch, or else met a guy and spent the night with him.

"I'm certain he's got himself into trouble with that silly job of his. And for what? Who cares what the police are doing to those terrorists. He's just inviting trouble for himself."

A wave of paranoia crashes over me as I hang up. Maj is perhaps my oldest friend, and I can't bear to think he's been harmed. I've never had many friends. Friendships, especially close ones, are hard to maintain when you have so much to hide. When I was younger I spent most of my time playing with one kid, Omar, who lived next door. He was from a wealthy family who made their money in politics. I was never sure exactly what his father did, what mattered was that Omar was from the sort of family that made Teta happy that we were friends. He went to the American school, which was the best school in the country. I went to the British school, which had been the best school in the country until the American school was built.

On most days during third grade I met Omar at the super-market after school. We bought Slush Puppies and walked home together. Omar traveled to America every summer and would show me all the cool stuff he brought back with him. In the beginning I tried to keep up with his trends, but I was always too late.

"Chicago Bulls?" he would scoff. "It's all about the Lakers these days."

One day, on my way to meet Omar, a boy followed me from school. I recognized him from class and knew enough to avoid him. He was weak and scrawny and would only bring me trouble. I turned around and glared at him for a few moments, then carried on. Still, I could hear his footsteps behind me. I stopped again.

"What's your name?" I demanded.

"Maj," he replied.

"Listen here, Maj. You can't follow me. You understand?"

I turned around and continued walking. Five minutes later I looked back.

"You're still following me."

"We live on the same street."

I sighed. "Fine. Keep some distance then." He took two steps back. "No, farther than that. One more step. Okay, that'll do."

I met Omar at our usual spot by the supermarket.

"Who is he?" Omar asked, gesturing toward Maj.

"Some kid who followed me from school," I said. "Just ignore him."

We bought our Slush Puppies (of course Maj picked the pink one) and went to pay. The old man behind the cash register looked at Maj and smiled.

"Look at you, with your caramel skin and big lips," he said. "So beautiful you could be a girl."

Omar and I snickered, but Maj looked pleased. We left the supermarket and were walking down the street when four boys began to follow us. They cornered us in an empty alley between two buildings. It was the perfect place for them, because the alley was narrow and leafy, so you couldn't see it from the street if you just happened to be walking by.

One of them grabbed Maj by the back of his shirt and threw him to the ground. As Maj tried to get up, another boy kicked him from behind. A third poured Maj's pink Slush Puppie over his face, rolled him over, and rubbed his face in the pool of pink mud that had formed.

The leader of the gang walked up to him. He was in our class. His name was Hamza. He looked like a frog: short and fat, with yellowish skin and a wide nose. He pointed at Maj and laughed, and the other boys followed suit. Omar joined in with the laughter, hoping it would save him, but it only brought him to their attention. One of the boys walked toward him with an angry look on his face.

"Don't you dare! Don't you dare!" Omar stammered. "You don't know who my father is . . . "

The boy backed away and turned to me. I held my Slush Puppie in front of me like a sword, trying to keep my face as calm as possible. I didn't understand what they wanted, so I could say nothing to reason with them. Behind me Hamza whispered in my ear.

"Throw the first punch and I'll be right there with you, Rasa. Throw the first punch and I'll take care of the rest."

I had never been in a fight before and didn't know how I would fare. For all I knew I could have had super strength. I clenched and unclenched my fists. The boy reached over and flicked my ear and then stood back with his arms crossed, an amused smile on his face.

"I can't hit him for you, Rasa," Hamza whispered. "If I do, everyone will think you're a girl. Do you want that? Do you want everyone to say you need another guy to protect you? Listen to me, throw just one punch and you'll have proved yourself. No one can say anything."

I clenched my fist, counted down in my head: three, two,

one—and still my fist remained by my side. Then, just as
quickly as the boys appeared they were gone. I looked around.
Maj was on the ground. Omar was shaking, his face red and
furious. I walked over to Maj and pulled him up.

"You all right?" I asked.

Maj smiled and nodded. He wiped the mud from his
clothes and face, then carried on walking as if nothing had
happened. Shaken, we continued home. Just before we turned
onto our street, Omar bent over and vomited.

"*Ya habibi*, that looks exactly like tabbouleh," Maj said with
a groan.

"Looks the same coming up as it does going down," I
remarked.

I've never really been able to eat tabbouleh since then.

After that Maj attached himself to me, even though he wasn't
any safer with me. In the beginning I tried to ignore him and
hoped that he would go away, but he was always there, prancing a few metres behind.

"Have you heard from Maj today?" I ask Basma as she
scrolls through our work e-mails.

She shakes her head and asks why.

"His mother just called. He didn't come home last night."

"Who's Maj?" Nawaf asks.

"Do your work and don't ask questions," I say.

Nawaf sighs and flicks through the stack of reports on the
desk. "I don't know any of your friends. You guys never invite
me out with you. How am I ever going to meet a nice girl?"

"We don't invite you out because you're a brute," Basma
says. "You're only in this company because you're my second
cousin." Nawaf gives her the finger, and Basma blows him a
kiss and hands him the joint. "I'm joking, *habibi* . . . here, have
a puff."

I look over Basma's shoulder as she sorts through the mail.

"Are we getting any new requests from last night's crisis?" I ask.

"I thought you were calling it a revolution," Nawaf says, blowing smoke up in the air.

Until a few weeks ago I had referred to the events as a revolution. When the protests first began six months ago, I had heard about them from Maj. *This is different*, he'd texted me. *This is huge.* And so we went to the *midan*, clad in our running shoes, flag in hand and chants ready. The first two days there were the usual suspects: the chain-smoking trade unionists, the women syndicates, the bearded Islamists, and of course the younger adults like us, who for the past few years had been hidden behind computer screens, writing increasingly angry anonymous tweets about the regime, the hypocrisy, the façade and hopelessness and injustice. Until then we had all accepted that this was how it was, there would not be anything to look forward to, we either had to get away or die trying. But as I held the leathery hand of a curly-haired trade union activist, I realized that being cold and wet together was better than being warm and dry in the richest country in the world.

Every day for that first week the numbers grew. I stood side by side with people from villages I had never heard of who were speaking in dialects I didn't know existed. The revolution treasured us all with the unconditional love of a mother. She held us close, promised she would always be by our side, and told us to go out and raise a storm. And amid the tear gas and beatings and arrests, we stayed. They arrested Basma one day, but she escaped from the police van and disappeared into the crowd. Thugs infiltrated the *midan*, beating, stabbing, tearing off clothes. We laughed in their faces and sang and danced and shared tips on how to lessen the pain of the tear gas the regime thugs lobbed our way.

Even Teta's threats didn't stop me from going. She yelled and slammed her fists on the kitchen table. Everyone else is going, I explained. I can't just stay at home and read about their deaths on Twitter. I hugged her, kissed the elegant wrinkles on both her cheeks, and promised I would stay close to home.

The eighth day of the protests began like any of the seven that preceded it. I packed my protest bag and headed to the march, following the cloud of American tear gas that enveloped the city centre. I met Taymour a few buildings down from ours and we joined Maj and Basma in a corner of the *midan*. Maj jumped on my back and I carried him as we walked. We locked elbows and marched, singing the old nationalist songs we sang in school, but the words had meaning now and the melody had power. We were singing for us, reclaiming our past and celebrating our future. Everything we thought was for the president was actually ours. We were not just taking back the streets, we were taking back our lives.

The crowd arrived close to our neighbourhood, only two streets down from Teta's building. Then it happened. A lightning crackle of gunfire. I looked at Basma. For the first time in the ten years I've known her, there was fear in her eyes, real terror, but also hope and power and anger. The crowd looked around, at one another, at the dense buildings that lined the streets. Then more crackle, and someone screamed that they were shooting from the roofs, and suddenly everyone was running.

A young hijabi woman beside me tripped over her own feet. Her head made a noise as it hit the pavement, a cracking sound I heard for months afterward. I dropped to the ground beside her, turned her over, shook her body to wake her. She was still breathing but her head was heavy in my hands. I yelled for the people to clear a way, but no one listened. Everyone was shouting too loud, the crowd stumbled over us to flee. I lay on the woman and buried my face in her stomach, my hands over my head to protect against the stampede of boots above us. I don't know how long I was down there, but suddenly there was a violent tugging on my shirt.

"Rasa, *yalla*, get up!" Taymour's voice rang in my ear. "We have to get out of here."

Taymour pulled me up and we stumbled hand in hand through the hordes of people. I chanced a look behind me, but the young hijabi woman was swallowed by the crowd. Maj and Basma were also nowhere to be seen. Rocks and Molotov cocktails flew over the crowd in all directions. Heavy tanks had now blocked all the roads out of downtown, making a death trap of the centre. Crowds of people with blood on their clothes streamed into the alleys. On the ground lay bodies and pools of blood that appeared glossy over the asphalt. Some people were crying, a few were laughing hysterically. We turned around and spotted my neighbourhood supermarket one hundred metres down the road, where I had bought yogurt and cigarettes only a few hours earlier. The supermarket was across from our building but the road was heaving with people running in all directions. I pulled Taymour in the direction of the supermarket. We sprinted down the street, arms over our heads. We pushed ourselves through the packed shop and crouched in a nook between the door and a fridge. My phone vibrated as a text from Maj reassured me that he and Basma were okay. We huddled together in the shop, our heads in each other's necks, for thirty long minutes, until a lull in the shooting allowed us to run across the road and into Teta's building.

"I can't go upstairs," Taymour shook his head. "Your grandmother will see me. I'll hide out by the stairs until I can leave."

"She won't know anything about us. She'll think you're just a friend."

"I'm not just a friend, Rasa." There was blood smeared on Taymour's right cheek. I looked down at my hands. For the first time I noticed they were covered in the woman's blood.

"Listen, just go upstairs, she'll be worried about you. I'll be fine."

In the living room, Teta was pacing under a cloud of cigarette smoke, while state TV showed a documentary about the life of the Prophet. When Teta saw me she burst into tears. Then she hugged me tight. Then she slapped me so hard she split my lip.

"Never go back," she ordered, with the ferocity of the president himself.

I nodded. I was shaken. But as the sniper shots cracked outside, I knew I was going back. I was willing to die for this. We were all willing to die for this. Because this was more important than one single life, more important than ten or even fifteen lives. And when the president appeared on television that evening, scolding us like misbehaving children, I was sure of only one thing: that to stay at home would be to return to the fear and denial that had ruled us for generations.

On that day we had sixty-four dead and more than three hundred disappeared. After that, the casualties only rose. Whenever I tried to leave Teta threatened to throw herself off the balcony, or guilt-tripped me by feigning heart palpitations. State TV warned of terrorists infiltrating the protests to kidnap children and rape women. And though many were convinced it was regime thugs that were responsible, the number of people on the streets began to shrink. And one by one, many of my friends decided they had too much to lose for something so uncertain. The new media production house Basma and I had started to build, which we thought would be the first in a cannon of new local media free from the constraints of the president's propaganda, turned into a measly translation company for foreign journalists coming in to write their own stories of the events. After a while Maj was the only one I knew who kept going to every demonstration. He tweeted and wrote chants and organized a fringe stage for the stragglers who were not backed by the powerful bearded men. He saw the attacks get worse, the bodies burnt to a crisp and mutilated by blunt knives, and he hurled rocks and pieces of concrete at men in uniform. But everyone else stopped calling it a "revolution." Instead it became a "crisis," and when the president declared he was fighting terrorism people eagerly backed him.

Many of those I marched alongside now cheer as they smash the revolution to a thousand pieces, and I don't know what to think any more. Anyway, there are enough opinions about the events that I don't need to form another one. I am not smart enough to find the solution to the country's problems, or the solution to Palestine, or terrorism or peace in the Middle East. I can't even find a way to be with Taymour.

I look at Nawaf and smile. "I don't know whether it was a revolution or a crisis."

"Anyway," Basma says, changing the subject back to work. Since the protests, Basma has stopped talking about politics. She'll refer to it occasionally, only briefly and with an exasperated look, like she is dealing with stupid people. Maybe she's right to do so. After all, it's not like I'm starving or unable to live. I'm simply bored. Is boredom reason enough to rebel?

But we lost so much for this crisis. So many people we went to school with, shared lunches with, and stood alongside in assembly have vanished into thin air in the six months since we first went to the streets that frosty January morning. Nadia is in jail. She played Sandy in our high-school production of *Grease*, which only ran for two nights before it was shut down after one of the parents complained that the hand jive was too provocative. During Nadia's trial last month, they paraded her out in a cage, wearing one of those humiliating white prison suits. While they read out her ridiculous charges she made a V sign with her fingers and smiled defiantly, in what seemed like just another one of her performances. Rami and Shadi, who were the basketball stars of our class, both disappeared on the first day of the shooting, their bodies probably holed up in a prison cell somewhere or else thrown in a ditch by the road outside the city. And Joud, our valedictorian and the smartest girl I knew, simply went to sleep one afternoon and never woke up. When I went to her funeral, her mother pulled me aside and confessed to finding an empty bottle of pills stashed under her mattress.

"Tell me she's going to heaven?" she sobbed, clutching my shoulders. "Please, Rasa, tell me she won't go to hell for what she did."

Taymour's name flashes on my mobile screen. I reach to pick it up and Nawaf bats my hand away.

"Stop looking at your phone like an expectant father. Don't you want to hear my opinion of the events?"

"Since when do you have an opinion?" I say.

"Well," Nawaf says, ignoring me, "the takeover will only burnish the president's antiterrorist credentials, making his crackdown look less severe, perhaps even justified . . . who knows, maybe the regime engineered al-Sharqiyeh's fall . . . "

I reach for my phone. My heartbeat quickens as I open the message: *We can talk but not today. Busy.*

"I'll be back in a minute," I tell Nawaf and Basma as I walk out of the room.

In a cubicle in the bathroom I call Taymour. He picks up on the fourth ring.

"I know you're busy but I just need to hear your voice," I say. "Please?"

"Rasa, nice to hear from you," Taymour says cheerily. I can hear a commotion of excited voices around him.

"Can you go somewhere quieter?" I ask. "Where you can speak more freely?"

"Unfortunately, no," he replies in the same cheery voice.

"Please tell me we're still okay?"

"That's great, that's great. Listen, I have to go."

"Where are you going? Just promise me I haven't lost you."

There's a silence on the other line. Taymour's heavy breathing crackles through the phone. "You haven't lost me," he finally whispers. "I just . . . I just need time. Last night was too dangerous. And we're not out of it yet."

"I know but we can't give up. Give me a bit of time and I'll find a way, okay? I promise I'll find a way we can still be together."

"I have to go, Rasa. We're going to do some preparations . . . then the family lunch . . . really got to go, sorry."

"Just give me a bit of time," I say, but Taymour has already hung up.

I sit on the toilet with my head in my hands, feeling relieved to have spoken to him but also guilty, because the sound of his voice awakens my hunger. It is ravenous, this hunger. It gnaws on my insides all the time. I am like an addict hunting for my next fix. I crave moments when we can be one, even if just for a moment. A stolen kiss and a knowing glance across a sea of guests at a party. Accidentally walking into each other in crowded bars, our bodies pressed together for a brief moment, our fingers touching as he hands me a drink or a cigarette. For a while this was enough. No one questioned these public moments of intimacy. We were simply best friends. In private, we laughed about close calls and covered each other in kisses. I stroked his face, his arms, his body. I lay on top of him and pushed into him, felt the hairs on our chests bristle against each other as I breathed into his ear, desperate for a part of me to infiltrate his tough exterior. I wanted to be as close to him as it was possible to be.

I notice my hands are shaking and there is a ringing in my ears. I feel as though I've knocked over a dish and stained one of Teta's expensive tablecloths. I haven't lost him yet, I try to reason. He said that himself. We can fix this. There is still hope. There's always hope.

A few weeks ago Teta went to visit an old friend who had moved to the provinces. She packed her bags for the night and took Doris with her, leaving me in charge of the house. Taymour immediately came over. It was the first time we had spent the night together and woke up in each other's arms. His morning breath tasted of victory. I made us both coffee while he went to buy some fresh pastries and we spent the morning on the balcony, reading the newspaper, listening to Fairouz, and watching the world wake up. Um Nasser glanced at us suspiciously from her balcony, and I explained that Taymour had come for a morning coffee. It was a glorious day. I wanted to wake up next to him every morning, cook his favorite foods, do his laundry.

"This is what our life could be," I said to Taymour.

He glanced up from the paper momentarily. "In a less cruel world, perhaps."

"Is this world really that cruel?"

Taymour was silent for a while. He looked out across the messy arrangement of limestone buildings that extended to the horizon. "For a long time the world seemed empty to me. Nothing I did gave me any joy. I was resigned to live this way, dead to the world. But then it changed. The night we met. You showed me how to feel."

"And now?"

Taymour looked at me and smiled. "And now I don't know whether I love you or hate you for that."

Sitting in this bathroom now with nothing to show for our relationship except for a pack of lies and a guilty conscience, the realisation that I will never be able to bring him into my bedroom again is sinking in. That bedroom, it's not enough space for us, for the potential our love could be. And to stay like this, ignoring our desires, we might as well be dead.

I wash my face and look at my reflection in the filthy mirror, at the drops of water clinging to my despicable face. Is there anything more pitiful than an Arab who attaches emotions to his homosexuality?

When I return to the office Nawaf looks up from his phone.

"What did she say?" he asks.

"Who?"

"Your girl. That message must have been from her. I can see the hunger in your eyes, *habibi*. What did she say?"

Basma looks at me with an amused expression on her face.

"Basma, can I talk to you alone for a minute?"

She follows me outside the office. As soon as she closes the door behind us the events of last night spill from my mouth in hushed and panicked whispers. When I'm done she takes a breath.

"Are you absolutely certain your grandmother saw the two of you?"

"Yes, definitely. And I don't know what to do or where to go. I'm trying to get in touch with Taymour but he's not really listening to me, and of course he's busy . . . " My voice trails off.

Basma is silent for a moment as she considers the options. Finally she shrugs. "There's only one thing you can do, *habibi*. You deny. What are you expecting, to open up new highways in this poor old woman's mind? Deny everything. She saw nothing . . . that's what happened. If she says otherwise, convince her old age has made her crazy. Because nothing happened, right?"

"But—"

"Nothing happened, Rasa." Basma pats me on the back and opens the door to our office.

Nawaf is rolling another joint. He looks up as we walk in. "We really cannot function like a team if you're excluding me from conversations."

My phone rings, saving me from responding.

"Rasa, it's Laura," the voice on the other line says.

"How are you?" I ask, cautious. Laura is one of those journalists, young, American, ballsy, and desperate to make a name for themselves. They strut around the country with no fear, asking questions that would have gotten them killed if they hadn't had a Western passport.

"I need you for an important interview I've arranged. Can you pick me up?"

"Today's a bit mad . . . " I begin. The last thing I need is to be dragged along on some adventure, and Laura is exactly the kind of journalist who would do that.

"I'll pay you double. Please?" she says.

"What's the assignment?"

"I'll explain when I see you. The meeting's at eleven, and it'll take us at least an hour to get there."

I sigh and tell her I'm on my way.

Although she never outright said so, it was no secret that Teta held my mother responsible for Baba's death. My father got sick less than a year after she left and died six months later, and Teta lay the blame squarely on my mother's deviance and subsequent departure, the heartbreak and trauma of which allowed the cancer in Baba's body to fester.

If my father blamed anyone, he did not make it known. He had always been a private man, who had worked hard for a future that was snatched away from him. That was Teta's mythology of him at least. Most of his interactions with me were driven by his determination to remind me that life was too difficult to waste time challenging things you could not change.

This ideology, a pragmatism that bordered on fundamentalism, was largely driven by Teta. She had always been pragmatic about death, too. Throughout her life she was never far from grief: Her father was struck down by tuberculosis when she was sixteen. Her mother was killed a year later, when a stray bullet flew in through the kitchen window and lodged itself in her neck as she was making coffee. Teta enjoyed four years of marriage before her own husband died of a heart attack, only a few months after she gave birth to my father. Baba was all she had left, and then he died, too. But it was in his death that she developed a hierarchy of mourning. The death of her son was the pinnacle, elevating her suffering beyond that of anyone else, including my own.

"It's natural to see your father die, Rasa," she explained to me a few years after his death. I was in high school then and we had just sat down for dinner one evening. "The human body is prepared to experience the loss of a parent. But nothing can ever prepare someone for seeing their child die."

But that conversation happened much later. When Baba first got sick, I was twelve and Teta said only one thing to me: "Not a word to anyone. You understand?"

The next day I told Maj my father had cancer. "Not a word to anyone," I threatened. "You understand?"

Teta refused to let a doctor see Baba, preferring to create her own healing remedies. She boiled carrots and courgettes and potatoes and asparagus for hours, until they released the most rotten stench in the house. She then mashed them furiously into a gooey brown pulp, added a sprinkle of salt, and took it to his room. Why did my father go along with this? As a doctor, surely he must have known the futility of her potions, but if so he did not say anything. Standing in the hallway, I listened for voices coming from the room, but they both spoke too quietly for me to hear anything other than the scraping of the spoon against the plate and the soft, smacking noises of my father chewing the vegetable mush. I waited with my ear against the door until the creaking of the bed would send me running to my room so they wouldn't know I had been listening.

Meanwhile the country was changing. In al-Sharqiyeh, everyone was angry about the markets opening and the rise in the cost of bread and fuel. They went out in the streets, shouting and burning tires. They stormed downtown and threatened to march all the way to the western suburbs, which quickly split from the rest of the country and were sucked into the global economy. I was oblivious to all this. In my world the only change that affected me was the sudden appearance of some great American chocolate in the supermarket down the road. My favorite was Reese's Peanut Butter Cups. I had never eaten peanut butter before and the taste was sublime. Though they were expensive, Teta was willing to give me the money for one Reese's Peanut Butter Cup a day, if it meant I spent more time outside of the house and less time asking about Baba.

In the western suburbs all was calm, except for the sound of construction next door. Omar's family was building an extension to their villa. It seemed that as the people in al-Sharqiyeh grew poorer and angrier, Omar's house became bigger and more extravagant. Like the cancer growing in my father, Omar's house was experiencing its own growth, with new floors and rooms being built at different angles on the villa, spilling over the rest of the neighbourhood.

"My dad wants to build a games room," Omar explained when I asked about the construction. "We're going to get a Jacuzzi in there, and a snooker table."

Omar's games room became my sanctuary. His family installed a big television that you could watch while sitting in the Jacuzzi, which showed all the American television programs, with no subtitles and no censoring. It was fantastic and I sat there in the bubbling water, eating peanut butter cups and watching *The Golden Girls*. I felt like I was in America, like I was just another character in the movies and none of what was happening was real.

This was a good distraction because when Baba started

getting really sick he refused to see me. Perhaps he did not want his son to see him so weak, the shame of it would only finish him quicker. Though I pleaded with Teta to be able to see him, she remained his fierce protector in the six months he spent dying. She kept him hidden in his bedroom, away from me and anyone else, as if seeing him might ruin any chance of his recovery. Perhaps she thought I had too much of my mother in me, and that simply by looking at him I might make him sicker.

A few weeks into the summer vacation, while Teta was out buying more vegetables, I waited until she was far along down the road and then ran to Baba's bedroom. Peering through the keyhole, I had a good enough view of his side of the bed. He was lying there covered up to his neck by white sheets. His eyes were shut. His chest was not moving.

I opened the door and tiptoed into the room. The shutters were down and only a few rays of sunlight peeked through the slats. The air was stuffy with incense and a sweet odor I had not encountered before, like a cold pancake. I stood by the bed and watched Baba's still body. He looked nothing like the memory I had of him in the months before he got sick. His head seemed shrunken and his hair was as brittle as straw. The bones in his face jutted out so sharply they could cut you. His eyes were sunk so deep in his head they looked like volcanic craters, and his skin was yellow and stretched across his face like a tabla. The man lying on the bed was not my father.

I ran out of the room and slammed the door. In the living room I turned on the television. A cooking show was on, and I stared at the screen. A man in a chef's hat was finely chopping parsley, back and forth, back and forth. My father was dead. My stomach turned, as if the chef was using his knife to chop my insides. I stared at the screen, tears running down my face, the image of my father returning in waves and flashes. Teta walked through the door half an hour later, carrying plastic bags heavy with courgettes and potatoes. She froze when she saw my face.

"Did you go into his room?"

I nodded. She dropped the bags of vegetables and darted across the hall. I tiptoed behind her. She entered his room and closed the door. I stood listening on the other side. For a moment there was silence, and then a heavy wail escaped the room. From behind the door I could hear Teta sobbing as she pleaded with God to bring back her son. I walked down the hall to the living room and sat on the sofa. The chef on television was chopping onions and parsley to make tabbouleh, which reminded me of Omar's vomit from that day Maj got us beat up after school in the third grade. I felt sick to my stomach, a combination of the image of the tabbouleh and Baba's death.

The phone rang. It was Omar.

"Are you coming over today?" he asked.

I peered down the hall. Teta was still in the room. "I can't," I said.

"Tomorrow?"

"I'm not sure."

Omar was silent. "Is your father okay?" he asked.

"Let's hang out tomorrow," I said, and hung up.

An hour later Teta emerged. She walked into the living room and straightened her skirt. She sat on the sofa next to me and lit a cigarette. For a few moments she smoked and stared into the middle distance. Finally she spoke.

"He's gone."

"Did he go where Mama went?" I asked.

"No. Your mother went to hell."

I was twelve.

My father's burial was the only public moment in what had otherwise been a private death. After the funeral Teta refused to have any guests over. Conversations that would begin were quickly diverted. It was a day of shame and secrets, unspoken but hanging in the air.

We returned from the burial to a terrible silence. As Teta unlocked the front door I burst into tears. Teta ignored my sobs and went straight to her room. She did not come out until the next evening. I spent the day walking around the house, examining objects that now appeared in a new, more uncertain light. A fork, a vase of flowers, Teta's ma'amoul tray, the red tassels on the living-room pillows. Items that held an echo of a past that seemed, if not necessarily loud and happy, then at least full of people. Now it was just Teta and me. I picked objects up and turned them around in my hands. I brought them to my nose to catch their scent. The objects were heavy with the absence of my mother and father.

As the sun went down, lengthening the shadows in the house, the wind began to howl and the sky darkened with the threat of rain. The sound of traffic floated in through an open window in the living room, alongside the calls of a neighbour ordering her children back home. Inside there was only silence, and I thought of my father slowly rotting under the ground.

A few weeks after school began that September, the president's father died suddenly of a heart attack. A blanket of despair was foisted upon all citizens. For ten days the country shut down in mourning. Music was banned as the funeral was broadcast on all the television stations and the radio stations played recordings of his old speeches. When we returned to school after the designated days of mourning, every assembly for the next week began with a moment of silence to honor the old man, which often descended into collective weeping that was encouraged by the teachers. To question the tears was to be a heartless traitor, so I joined along. I wept and bawled with everyone else, although I was perhaps the only one thinking not of the president's father but of my own.

"Your car is straight out of the fifties," Laura says as she gets in. She pushes aside the yellowed newspapers piled on the passenger seat. It is just past ten and the thick layer of dust on the dashboard is baking in the midmorning sun. The stench it is giving off is overwhelming. It's what I imagine a long-abandoned dream might smell like. A plastic Oum Kalthoum bobblehead stands in front of the steering wheel. Her head bobs as the engine sputters to life.

I tell Laura it is Nawaf's car and she chuckles.

"Of course it is," she pushes her black-framed glasses up the bridge of her nose. "It's all Nasserite and full of promise."

I met Laura when she had just moved here as a stringer for the *New York Times*. She often quoted me during the early days of the protests, back when she was new to the country and looking for any old "voice from the Arab Street." If you search for me online you'll find my name pops up in one or two articles. To be completely honest, she made me sound much smarter than I really am. But as she got accustomed to the city and worked her way up, developing contacts with opposition leaders, presidential advisers, and other guys way more important than me, she interviewed me less and less, and then not at all.

"Where are we going?" I ask, reversing out of her driveway and onto the road.

"I got clearance to meet with this guy, Ahmed Baraka, who is high up with the opposition," she says. "He lives in the eastern side of the city. Do you know your way around that area?"

"You mean al-Sharqiyeh?"

"Yeah." She passes me a piece of paper with a number on it. "If you call this number they'll tell you where to meet."

"I'm not sure it's safe to go there today. Did you not hear the news?"

Laura laughs. "I am the news. We'll be fine, I've got a good source."

Although my gut instinct is to walk away, even if she's pay-ing double, I grab the piece of paper and punch in the number on my phone. The deep voice of a man picks up on the first ring. I explain who I am and he says to meet at the clock tower in the centre of al-Sharqiyeh.

"Park there and give me a missed call. Don't get out of the car, and if anyone asks, tell them you're with Baraka," he orders.

I close the phone and hand Laura the piece of paper.

"We should get there as soon as possible," she says, folding it and tucking it into her bag. "It's a busy news day and I have three big stories to cover. There's this one . . . then after lunch I've got a meeting with the head of intelligence about last night's takeover. And I also want to write about the arrest of the gay men in the cinema."

"What arrest?" I ask.

"You didn't hear? Last night, maybe an hour or so before the militias took over al-Sharqiyeh, police stormed one of those cinemas downtown and arrested a bunch of gay guys who were cruising there."

Laura is still talking as my thoughts return to Maj. A sense of dread gnaws at the edges of my stomach like a corrosive acid. While trying to concentrate on the road, I pull out my phone and give him another call. His phone is still off. It is not like him to be out of touch this long, with not even a text or status update all morning.

"What do you know about the arrests in the cinema?" I ask Laura.

"Not much," she says, flipping through her notes. "I'm try-ing to find out where they're holding them. There are a couple of human rights groups on that." She looks up at me. "Why are you interested?"

"No reason." I shrug. He's definitely involved in that gay cinema thing somehow, if not reporting on the arrests then maybe as one of the victims. If I hear nothing by this afternoon I'll have to tell his mother what little I know. I turn to Laura. "So the guy on the phone said to meet them at some old clock tower."

"Okay."

We are silent for a few minutes, and then Laura speaks.

"You know," she begins. "I've known you a few months now but I feel like I know nothing about your life."

"What do you want to know?" I ask.

"You don't live with your parents, right?"

"I live with my grandmother."

"Oh. Where are your parents?"

I hesitate. My hands clutch the steering wheel tighter.

"I'm sorry. It's none of my business."

"It's fine." I smile. She must have noticed my discomfort because she abruptly changes the conversation to point out the extra security guards at the entrance of a shopping mall, then returns to her notes.

I take the road that leads us out of the affluent quarter where the rich neighbourhoods merge into a crescent of prosperity along the western side of the city. Empty land awaiting further construction frames the outer edge of this part of town. The land is divided into plots to fit a three-storey villa with a pool, a garden, and a maid's room. Everything outside this area is, as Taymour once put it, "traffic jams and hepatitis."

We drive past the American embassy at the southern edge of the suburbs. The compound is fortified by tanks, armed guards, and large concrete roadblocks that have annexed the sidewalks around it, blocking passages, impeding traffic, and forcing citizens to walk in the street.

"Look at this," Laura scoffs. "Twenty-first-century diplomacy . . . if it were up to the American government every city in the Arab world would have an archipelago of green zones."

She sits back, looking pleased with herself for saying this. On the dashboard, Oum Kalthoum's head bobs as I drive over a pothole.

On both sides of the road there are pictures of the president. There are pictures of him with his family, his elegant wife dressed in an emerald green evening gown, a sparkling tiara on her head. There are posters of him in the dishdasha worn by the northern tribes, photos of him dressed in a suit and tie, some of him with a beard and others of him clean-shaven. Like a Barbie doll, the president comes in different costumes: Tribal President, Business President, Islamic President, Secular President—collect them all.

We stop at a government checkpoint plastered with photos of the president. The flag hangs limply on the barrier blocking the road.

"Where to?" The soldier at the checkpoint leans into the car as I roll down the window.

"We have a meeting," I tell him. He looks about nineteen, with an AK-47 slung over his shoulder and a helmet too big for his head.

"Road's closed," the soldier says, shifting his weight as he struggles to carry his weapon. His eyes scan our faces, moving from mine to Laura's and back again.

"We have authorization," I say. Laura shoves the paper she is clutching into my hand. I give it to the soldier.

"What business do you have there?" he asks, his eyes inching down the page.

"She is a journalist for an American newspaper. She's arranged interviews."

The soldier is quiet for a while, the silence uneasily settling between the three of us.

"Do you have a cigarette?" he asks, finally, breaking the silence.

"For you, three," I say, pulling out a handful of cigarettes. I drop them in the palm of his hand and he nods and waves us forward.

Laura takes out a scarf from her bag and begins to wrap it over her hair. I don't know what this Ahmed guy will be like. How would he react to seeing me, a T-shirt-and-fashionable-jeans-wearing guy from the western suburbs, speaking English with an American accent? Would my haircut offend his sensibilities? Would he smell injustice in the brand-new soles of my Converse shoes? But what about the other thing—would he know I was in bed with another man last night? Would he be able to smell Taymour's sweat on my skin?

Taking a turn off the main road I drive across the bridge that separates the suburbs from al-Sharqiyeh. The familiar signs of McDonald's and Starbucks make way for tattered billboards that crowd over each other, fighting for attention, some advertising Fair and Lovely skin-lightening cream and *baladi* yogurt, others demanding that citizens support the reform process. Tiny shops selling dusty water bottles and kaak and mashawi line the ramshackle road.

We used to drive over this bridge a lot when my mother and father were still around. Back then, on some Fridays when Baba wasn't too tired from work, he would put on a pair of jeans and stand by the door, smiling and jingling the car keys in the air. The sound of those keys made my mother and me so happy, and on cue we would jump off the couch and get in the car. Baba would drive across the bridge towards the hills on the outskirts of the city. My mother always asked Baba to drive through al-Sharqiyeh, and on the days Teta would join us, she would insist we keep the windows rolled up.

"But if we're going to live in this country then we really have to *live* in this country," my mother would say, pushing her Mike and the Mechanics tape into the cassette player. Her favorite song on that album was about an unhappy woman who drank a lot of coffee.

I would watch my mother sing along, so beautiful and full of melancholy, and I would feel helpless that she loved such a sad song, and wondered if I was to blame somehow for her unhappiness. Once the song was over she'd rewind the tape and play it again. And after that song played three or four times it was like my mother had found a companion to her sadness, and we'd stop and eat at a food stall in the centre of al-Sharqiyeh, a feast of roast chicken so tender the meat dripped off the bone.

"You'll get diarrhea," Teta would say, sulking in the car while the three of us stood on the side of the road, licking our fingers from the juices seeping from the meat. Afterward we would jump back in the car. Baba wouldn't stop driving until we were far out into the mountains, away from society.

Before Mama's sadness overwhelmed her, she would wake up every morning, put on her paint-stained jeans, take the public buses (much to Teta's disdain), and get off in al-Sharqiyeh to walk around, paint, chat with the kids and show them her art supplies. No matter how much Teta told her that "people will talk" if her daughter-in-law kept visiting the slums, and regardless of how hard she tried to introduce Mama to other high-society women ("This is so-and-so, she just graduated from a university in London, and this is her sister so-and-so, she is best friends with that famous actress I pointed out to you on TV last night. And this is so-and-so, she lives just down the road and has set up a wonderful jewelry business . . . "), Mama still woke up every morning and made her way down to al-Sharqiyeh.

As for me, I don't go to al-Sharqiyeh anymore. It is mostly journalists who roam these parts, like ants on a piece of rotting fruit.

After we've driven about one hundred metres from the bridge, we stop at another checkpoint. This one is not government-run. The idea that something could be free of the president's control should fill me with excitement, yet the two men standing guard at the checkpoint, their faces wrapped with an olive green cloth so that only their eyes are visible, bring out in me the same old fear. I stop the car and roll down the window.

"*Assalamu aleykum*," I greet them. They say nothing. One of them bends down and looks at Laura, then back at me. I tell him she's a journalist and give him the paper. He reads it over and makes a call on his phone. I close my eyes and breathe in deeply, trying to steady my nerves. Beside me Laura shifts in her seat.

The man is on the phone for a few minutes. When he finishes he puts the phone in his pocket and strolls back to the car. He walks to the back of the car and slams his fist on the trunk. I press the button and the trunk springs open. He rummages inside. I think of what might be in there, what mess Nawaf might have left behind. Dammit, I should have checked this beforehand. I rub my mouth and look straight ahead. Finally the man closes the trunk and walks over to where the other man is standing, right by my window. He whispers something in the man's ear and the man bends over.

"Keep going straight along this road," he says. His breath is sour. "You'll get to a traffic light. Make a right and go up a hill. The clock tower is at the top. Wait there."

"Thank you." Relieved, I want to get out of the car and hug them. Instead I offer them the most grateful smile I can muster as they wave us on.

The road, smaller now, is lined with palm trees. Laura is silent as she rotates between editing her list of questions and updating her Twitter feed, and my thoughts return to Maj. If he is among those who have been arrested, and by now it is probably wishful thinking to believe otherwise, God knows what they will do to him. He's mouthy enough to say something that might piss off a policeman. And if they find out what sort of information he collects, that would be even worse.

I don't feel comfortable sharing these concerns with Laura. I don't want Maj to be just another decontextualized story, another headline on the bottom of the fourth page of some foreign newspaper. Besides, there won't be any protests demanding Maj's release, no opposition groups to fight in his corner. It'll just be me, and what use am I when I can't even voice my worries to an American journalist. Whenever I think things could not get any worse, the universe exposes another layer of darkness.

There's no point thinking of this now. I need all my focus on making sure we get in and out of here alive. The man on the phone instructed us not to get out of the car. It didn't sound like a trap. Why would it be a trap, anyway? What point would killing us make? Would my death advance their political interests somehow? I turn to Laura.

"I *will* actually have to charge you double for this, you know."

Laura laughs, and although I can hear a nervousness in there, her laughter calms me.

"Are you optimistic about my country?" I ask, trying to take my mind off our situation. I've learned to listen to the good foreign journalists, the ones who speak to everyone and get a bird's-eye view of what's happening. The bad ones, those who spend their time in the Four Seasons speaking to people like me, they are useless. But the good ones can be fortune-tellers.

Laura looks up from her mobile phone and peers out the window as we drive by a poster of the president. In this one he is dressed in military uniform. The words "Together we will save our nation" parade across the bottom of the poster in intimidating black lettering. Someone has ripped the president's head off.

"I'm not sure anymore." She sighs.

She asks me for my thoughts about what's happening in the country. I tell her that the political situation is very bad, that we are stuck between terrorism and authoritarianism. She says that most people outside the cities don't have the luxury for such politics, all they think about is how they will feed their children. I tell her that may be the case, but economics is political. She narrows her eyes. She can see my international schooling on my face and hear it in the way I speak English with ease. Although she judges me for it, she also recognizes that she needs me. I am her bridge, her reliable Oriental guide. I speak both Arabic and English and understand how Americans see us.

We continue driving in silence. As we make our way through al-Sharqiyeh, steaming garbage and discarded tires lie on either side of the potholed roads. Everything feels like it is covered in a thick layer of soot. Two barefoot girls push a scrawny donkey along the road.

"Wretched of the earth," I say as we drive past the girls, catching the eye of the taller one.

Laura looks up from her notes and smiles at me. "Welcome to the other half of your city, Rasa."

"Do you think we will have an Islamic government?" I ask her.

"So long as it's the will of the people, does it matter whether or not it's Islamic?" she asks me.

"I left college believing that so long as the government was the will of the people then that would be okay."

"And now?"

"And now I believe that religion is the last refuge of the poor . . . praying five times a day, all that hand-washing and strict rules . . . gives people some structure and purpose. So long as they believe that life has an ultimate meaning, it keeps them from true despair."

"But you have to respect the beliefs of other people," she says.

"Yeah, yeah, respect. Give respect by giving education, a job, a glimpse of a future without everyone breathing down your neck."

The air stinks of diesel fuel and heat. Finally we see the main clock tower perched on the hilltop, red, white, and blue plastic bags dancing in the air around it. I park at the top of a hill. The car slides backward before coming to a tired stop.

"Stay in the car," I tell Laura as I open the car door and step outside. They told us not to get out of the car but I need some air. The heat of the midday sun beats down on me. Sweat is already beginning to form on my back and armpits, darkening my white shirt and making it stick to me like an extra layer of skin. I have the distinct feeling I am being watched. I look toward a small collection of houses that stand on the edge of the hill. A wooden crate of figs lies on the ground. The crate is broken and a few figs have rolled down the hill while the others are baking in the sun. The sound of the noontime *athaan* cuts across the city, the muezzin's voice soothes my nerves. Yes, God is greater than all of this.

I call the number Laura gave me and let it ring a few times before shutting the phone. I turn around and glance at Laura, who is busy looking at her phone. I quickly give Guapa's manager, Nora, a call.

"Have you heard from Maj today?" I ask.

"No, why?" A slight worry creeps into her voice.

My eyes scan the empty plot of land around me. "I'm sure it's nothing, it's just that his mother called about an hour ago. He didn't come home last night. Did you notice when he left? Was he alone?"

"I can't remember. It was crazy last night. Let me make a few calls and get back to you."

I put the phone in my pocket and walk toward the edge of

the hill, looking out over my city, one that keeps on growing, messily and organically. Rooftops with aluminum water tanks and white satellite dishes shimmer under the sun. There is something unsettling about seeing the poverty here after spending so much time in the western district. And yet, it also feels familiar, as if the eastern and western districts are two sides of a coin where one could not exist without the other. Millions of lives are being lived down there, in those houses and roads that heave with traffic. Somewhere down there are Maj and Teta, and, of course, Taymour.

Before I met Taymour I had no reason to tell anyone anything. And then, when I had him, I wanted to share my joy with the world. I struggled to keep quiet about us, and immediately told Basma and Maj. My love for him was too great to be confined to a secret life. I told him I wanted to tell others. Taymour did not want this, and the thought of it made him tremble with anxiety.

"But if we stay hidden like this, it will be so easy to lose you."

"We will always find a way to be together," he replied. "We don't need anyone's endorsement for that."

Now that I'm so close to losing him, all I want to do is stand on top of this high cliff and scream his name. I want to cast the pain out of my body and make sure that the memory of what we had will ricochet across the valley and echo throughout the city forever.

I take my phone out and type out a message: *Do you remember promising that we would find a way to make it work?*

I walk back to the car and lean against the side door. A young boy walks up from behind one of the houses. He looks at the both of us, as if weighing his chances, and then settles on Laura. He holds out his arm and sticks out his bottom lip.

"I don't have money," Laura says, looking up from her phone momentarily. She shakes her hands and says, "*Ma fee, ma fee.*" The boy insists, his bottom lip now sticks so far out it almost touches his nose. Laura sighs and points to the crate of figs. "They're fine to eat."

The boy is startled and his lip returns to its normal position. He turns around and walks back to one of the houses.

"This is the problem with you Arabs." Laura shakes her head. "You are willing to starve for your pride."

Ignoring this—for one is used to ignoring such comments in my line of work—I ask if she is planning to interview anyone besides Ahmed while she is here. She shakes her head, not looking up from her phone.

A dusty jeep drives up the hill and stops a few metres away. Two bearded men step out. They look at me, size me up. I try my best to look harmless. Despite the hot day, the men are wearing heavy jackets with bulges at their hips. The younger of the two, good-looking with emerald green eyes, speaks first.

"Laura," he says, pointing to her.

"That's me," Laura responds, adjusting her hijab. The man reaches out and shakes my hand.

"Sheikh Ahmed is waiting for you," he tells me in Arabic. "Leave your car and come with us. We will bring you back here afterward." I turn around and translate this for Laura, and we both get into the jeep, which has a strong smell that after a few moments I realize is gunpowder.

For a long time interpreting felt like the purest form of bridging worlds. If I couldn't say what is truly on my mind then at least I would be able to mold the words of others, illuminating each world for the other and finding the point where both meet. A bridge is a position of power, and whenever possible I try to use such power for good. But when I see that the words I am asked to translate are blatant lies then it is my job to do something. Because if the lies come out of my mouth, if they pass through me even if they belong to someone else, am I not complicit in them? In those situations, I misinterpret.

There's an art to misinterpreting. It needs to be done subtly so that it doesn't cause chaos, but just enough to leave a lingering sense of confusion. Nowadays, when everything is uncertain, it is easier than ever to misinterpret. Lies are everywhere. They hang from our lips, lies built on more lies until we don't know what the truth is anymore. That is the moment when misinterpreting can do good. But words have power. America taught me that.

We drive down the hill and through an empty street, lined on both sides by ramshackle brick houses. A few children peer through windows as we drive by, but otherwise the only signs of life are the clothes hanging limply on metal wires in front of the houses.

It would be so easy for them to drive us to some ditch and throw us in. An image of myself and Laura, our headless bodies thrown into a sand pit somewhere, appears in my mind. I shake my head and look at Laura, who is looking out of the window, her eyes studying the houses and streets. My eyes are drawn toward the delicate skin above her Adam's apple where the men might place the knife. Shut up, Rasa, I think to myself, shaking my head some more.

The jeep stutters to a stop in front of a two-storey building. A bearded man is standing outside wearing a cleanly pressed beige dishdasha and silver-and-blue tennis shoes. I do not recognize the brand of shoes. Perhaps a cheap knockoff. The man is holding a wooden cane, the varnish gleaming in the sunshine. He introduces himself as Ahmed and welcomes us. When he sees me looking at his cane, he smiles.

"They broke my hip. I'm old now," he explains, though there's hardly a wrinkle on his face. There's warmth in his gaze, but beneath that I glimpse a steeliness that keeps me on my toes. It reminds me that although we are being welcomed, we are also being watched.

We follow him up two flights of concrete stairs. Inside, the building looks like it is still under construction. Or is it destruction? It's hard to say. The stairs have no railings, and metal rods jut out of the walls like rusted snakes.

"You're in luck," Ahmed turns to us as we climb the stairs. Even hobbling there is something enchanting about him, something vibrant and captivating. "We just had a shipment of diesel come in this morning so we've got the generator up and Um Abdallah is cooking us a nice early lunch."

I translate this for Laura.

"Where did the diesel shipment come from?" Laura asks.

I begin to translate and Ahmed interrupts me.

"No need to translate back to me," Ahmed says in Arabic. "I understand and speak English, but I prefer to speak only in Arabic. Please explain to her that in our country the elite speak English to appear sophisticated and differentiate themselves from the lower classes. So for me to speak English in my home would be treacherous."

He pauses while I translate this for Laura, who nods and says nothing, and it occurs to me that the only power I had, the possibility to misinterpret, has been stripped from me. I am left with a feeling of being naked with my hands tied behind my back.

"As for her question," Ahmed continues, "we get shipments sometimes from our friends."

"Do you not normally have electricity?" Laura asks, and Ahmed chuckles.

"The only government services we've seen here for the past twenty years have been the regime thugs patrolling the streets and beating our children."

Ahmed leads us into a modest living room. Red and gold cushions line the walls, and a small television sits in one corner broadcasting the news. Ahmed tells us to sit down. The heavy smell of roasted lamb and rice fills my nostrils, reminding me that I have had nothing but coffee and cigarettes all morning.

"Where do you live, Rasa?" Ahmed asks, watching me. I tell him I live downtown and he seems surprised by this.

"I would have thought you lived in the western suburbs."

"I used to live there," I say, trying to remain aloof. He nods, studying me. I glance at Laura, hoping she will jump in to divert the conversation. Thankfully, the sound of clattering of pots in the other room breaks Ahmed's gaze.

"Um Abdallah is finishing up with lunch," he says. "She's not been well the past weeks. Neither have I, to be honest."

I translate and Laura asks him why.

"Our son disappeared last month," he says. "We organized a protest in the city centre and he went along. He never came back home."

"I'm sorry," Laura says. "How old is he?"

"Twenty-four," Ahmed takes down a framed fourteen-by-ten-inch photograph from the wall. He hands it to Laura. "Abdallah," he says. Laura looks at the photo and passes it to me. The young man staring back at me in the photo is dark, clean-shaven, and unsmiling. His eyes have the same subdued perceptiveness of his father's. I give the photograph to Ahmed and he hangs it back on the wall.

"Did you still protest after your son disappeared?" Laura asks.

"For a while, yes," Ahmed says. From the kitchen we hear the scraping sound of rice being spooned onto a plate. "We have an obligation to the revolution. Abdallah being gone only makes the struggle more personal for me. The hope that arises from despair can be the best hope of all, and my obligations to demand change are as much to myself as to my country. But we are done protesting. Now we'll take what is ours."

Laura writes this down as Ahmed excuses himself and walks into the kitchen. I can hear whispering. Ahmed says something along the lines of "It's okay, you can come, he's as old as your son." He emerges moments later, carrying a steaming plate of rice with chunks of lamb. Um Abdallah walks out behind him with a bowl of salad. She's a short, plump woman with a round face and large brown eyes. She's younger than I imagined she would be, although it is difficult to know. She could be thirty or she could be fifty.

Um Abdallah puts the plate she is carrying on the table and then hurries toward us. She wraps her arms around Laura and kisses her on both cheeks, as if greeting a long-lost friend. She turns to me and clutches her chest, bowing slightly. We sit down at the table and Um Abdallah puts a large helping of rice, lamb, and salad on each of our plates. As she spoons some rice onto my plate she turns to Ahmed.

"Did you tell them about Abdallah?" she whispers.

Ahmed nods. Um Abdallah asks him what we said. He puts a hand on her arm.

"As I mentioned over the phone," Laura begins, "I'm writing a story for an American newspaper about last night's events. Please feel free to speak candidly, and if there's anything you would like me to not attribute to you, let me know."

"We aren't afraid, you can write our names down," Ahmed says. "Please, eat and ask anything."

"This latest move, taking over parts of the city, where do you see this going?" Laura asks.

"We gave lots of chances. We called for parliament to be dismissed and for new, fair elections. We gave the president one more chance. But you have to earn your legitimacy. Now we have our own plans."

Ahmed stands up suddenly and walks into the other room. He returns a moment later with a large sheet of paper that he places on the table. On the paper is what looks like plan for a city. In the centre is a large circle labeled "mosque." Around it, squares with labels such as "house" and "school" and "hospital" are arranged in a circular fashion around smaller circles, "mosques."

"This is what our future city will look like. No more elitist security measures that separate one citizen from another, no more public institutions located in buildings that are falling apart."

"And look," Um Abdallah says excitedly, pointing to the large mosque in the center. "All the homes . . . no, all the buildings even . . . within five minutes' walking distance from a mosque."

When I translate this for Laura, she asks if they want an Islamic state.

"We live in a Muslim country," Ahmed responds.

"But a Muslim country is not the same as an Islamic state," Laura says.

"Everyone wants an Islamic state," Um Abdallah chimes in. I hesitate as I translate this, but neither Ahmed nor Um Abdallah seems to notice.

My mobile phone vibrates in my pocket. The message from Taymour is short: *We made no promises.* His words form a tiny lump at the back of my throat. I swallow the words down with a spoonful of rice.

"Many in the country don't want an Islamic state," Laura persists.

"No, no," Ahmed shakes his head. "They are a very tiny minority. This tiny minority falls into two camps. The first are the enemies of Islam, who purposefully try to drag the masses away from God. And the other camp are those who simply do not know better. And when they see the benefits of such a state, you will see how they will change their minds." He turns to look at me with a smile on his face. "No?"

I don't reply, and focus on translating all this in between spoonfuls of rice and lamb. That "No?"—was it a challenge to me, or am I reading too much into it? I wonder in which group Um Abdallah and Ahmed believe I belong. Would I even be able to disagree with him? I recall a time, a few weeks after the sniper attacks on the protesters, when I could no longer take being away from it all, and Basma and I went to join Maj in the demonstrations. As we tried to enter the *midan* a young man stopped us with a raised arm and the familiar scowl of old times.

"Women's side that way," he told Basma. He pointed to his left, toward a small square surrounded by a plastic blue tarpaulin.

"What do you mean women's side?" Basma pushed past him. "What are you, border control?"

"There's a special square for women. It's for your safety," the man said.

"We're safer together," I told him.

The man looked at me. "Oh, really? Scared you'll get hurt? Maybe you should also go to the women's section."

Instead I went home. I only went back once after that, at the insistence of Maj, who by that point was involved in documenting police abuses for an American human rights group. When I arrived I realized I didn't recognize anything anymore. The beards had grown out, the women were segregated, and the chants had changed. I scanned the faces in the crowd, and they looked back at me in a different way. The walls had returned. The trust was gone, and I felt my own familiar walls rise once again. Looking around, I began to think: If we did manage to bring down the president, and if we tore down every damn picture and statue from the city, what would we replace him with? The protests had felt like the most authentic thing I had done in my life. Now they felt like a martyrdom operation to help a new generation of dictators come to power. Maybe this shift began with the young man telling me to go to the women's section. How could I share my political dreams with those in the squares when I couldn't even share my personal ones? I joined the protests so that I would no longer have to wear a mask. What's the point of risking your life to remove a mask only to have to wear a different one? That would be like castrating donkeys. So I stayed in the square long enough to smoke a cigarette in solidarity and left soon after.

If the revolution succeeds, it will be people like Ahmed who will have my fate in their hands. If that happens, will I still be able to hide behind conversations? For today it helps that the food we are eating is delicious, the lamb is soft and fatty and melts the moment I put it in my mouth. The salad is cool and crisp. I wolf down my food, and Um Abdallah immediately puts another dollop of rice and meat on my plate. I try to protest but she stops me.

"Eat, eat," she insists as she pushes more salad my way. She turns to Laura. "Look at Abdallah, he's the perfect example of a young man who was failed by this regime. He is so beautiful, Abdallah." She stands there, holding the salad spoon, then turns to me suddenly and asks, "*Ustaz* Rasa, can I ask you a question?"

"Of course . . . "

"Do you pray?"

"Pray?" I hesitate. "Sometimes . . . not often."

She shakes her head. "No, my son. That's not right. God created this entire world for you, provided you with this wonderful meal, the clothes on your back . . . the very breath you are taking at this precise moment, God gave it to you. And you do not take five minutes out of your day to thank him? Please, I am telling you for your own sake . . . just twice a day at first, if that's all you can manage . . . I promise you will see the changes in your mind and body immediately."

I nod solemnly. "I will pray," I say, and a sudden image shakes me with the impact of a thought that reclassifies all other thoughts—the idea that Um Abdallah could be my mother. The thought comes to me quickly, insidiously, that now that her son has disappeared I could move out of Teta's house and live with them. I would eat delicious food like this all day, scooped straight onto my plate, and we would pray five times a day and then go out together to protest as one big family. We would rebuild this country starting from right here in this tiny living room in al-Sharqiyeh, and yes, every house will be within five minutes' walking distance from a mosque. It would be nice, really, to have such a mother and father. Plus, I'd finally get out of my bourgeois bubble. Here I'd have some authenticity maybe, and my position on things would be clear.

Laura says something and Um Abdallah quickly replies with something that sounds like "I hope your story can help us find him," but I do not hear her properly. I ask her to speak more slowly because I can't translate at this speed. Again Um Abdallah says this too quickly, and Ahmed repeats it to me.

"She asks if there are any specific questions you need to ask to help us find our son," Ahmed says. I translate this for Laura.

"I don't want to raise your hopes," Laura begins. "My newspaper wants me to cover the wider protests, but I'll definitely mention that your son disappeared."

Um Abdallah stands up and grabs the photograph of Abdallah hanging on the wall. She carefully takes the photograph out of the frame and hands it to Laura.

"You can have this photograph," she says. "If you publish this in your newspaper—"

"Oh, no, I can't do that," Laura says, pushing the photograph away. Ahmed takes the photograph from Um Abdallah's hands and places it on the table.

"What sort of questions do you have for us?" Ahmed says, his left hand resting on the picture of his son's face. "We will answer them."

Laura puts her fork down and wipes the oil from her mouth with a tissue. She pulls out her notebook and begins firing questions at them. I rapidly translate their responses, whispering into Laura's ear until it seems as if they are directly speaking to one another, like I am no longer in the room.

They tell her about the protests, how they organized them-selves and what they are demanding. Um Abdallah describes how, when the tear gas was falling, she could see the angel Gabriel in the smoke ("If that's not a sign from God of the Islamic state then explain to me why I saw him?"). They tell us of the media representation of them as thugs and terrorists, but they are excited. They are convinced they don't need the gov-ernment anymore. They have created their own world, and it can only grow from here.

My own voice rises in excitement as I translate. Ahmed catches my eyes.

"You know what they say about the president's gaze," he says. "How it unpacks your existence bit by bit until you are naked and helpless, your most secret thoughts out in the open for all to see. But we are not scared anymore. We are not blinking."

He continues to gaze into my eyes as he speaks. Is he sus-picious, is he questioning my commitment to his ideals? The look in his eyes reminds me of the president's.

Um Abdallah speaks up, her voice rising. "If it's true what they say, that Abdallah is dead, then he is our martyr in heaven watching to make sure the revolution is completed. We will make the entire country burn so that his death is not in vain."

The conversation turns suddenly, as Ahmed begins to talk about his philosophies. Laura asks him about his thoughts on the West.

"One must avoid the wicked influence of the West on our society," Ahmed says matter-of-factly. Laura scribbles furiously as I translate his words.

"For example, your men look like women and your women look like men. This is permitted in Western societies, even encouraged as equal rights," I hear myself explain to Laura. "So now in your countries you have men who sleep with men who look like women. This is like dressing a pig up as a sheep and slaughtering it so you can have some lamb."

"It's a beautiful thing, this revolution," Um Abdallah says. "Now it's the simple people in the country, the poor and the downtrodden and the illiterate who are giving us an education."

Another thought occurs to me, the realization that we are from the same country, the same city even, yet we never truly knew each other. I want to tell Ahmed some things and to ask his opinion of many more. I want to agree with some of his views and challenge him on others. I want to tell Um Abdallah that my best friend is also being held by the regime for who he is, for who he wants to be, but I cannot find the words to do so. How will they react if I tell them Maj was arrested while at the old cinemas? How can I explain that I am like them, misunderstood, vilified by the regime and the media? I don't have the words to say any of this, and the brief moment of deep solidarity I feel dissipates before my eyes.

Ahmed stands up abruptly. "It's time to pray." He moves to a corner of the room and turns toward me. "Aren't you coming?"

I am about to shake my head but then I realize that he is not asking me a question. There is no more disguising my opinions in translations, no more hiding in the shadows. I am either here or there, with him or not. Surely a true fundamentalist would be confident enough in his own beliefs not to force them on others.

I stand up and follow him to the corner of the room. Ahmed puts his hands to his head and kneels down, and I do the same. I fight a sudden urge to grab him by the arm and pull him away from his prayer. I want to take his hand and dance the tango with him in his living room. No more preaching and fighting, this side over that. Let's choose ambivalence; let's just dance to the beat of this nonsense. Or if not dance, let's make love. I would like to make love to Ahmed, force his dishdasha up, grab him by the thighs, and take him in my mouth. Show him a good time, help him loosen up.

When we return to the table I notice Nora has left a message on my phone: *The bartender says he saw Maj leave alone. It's not looking good . . .* I put the phone in my pocket and take a seat at the table.

"I hope you will present the truth about us," Ahmed tells Laura.

Um Abdallah takes the photograph of Abdallah from the table and pushes it into my hands. She looks at me as she does this, in a way that makes me feel that if I refuse the photograph I am complicit in his disappearance. I put it in my bag.

"You will help us find him," Um Abdallah says.

Laura says nothing, and I find myself both hating and respecting her for refusing to make promises she cannot keep. I want to tell Um Abdallah that Laura will mention her son in her article, assure her that we will find him. But I'm stuck, as Laura isn't saying anything and Ahmed will certainly notice any attempt to alter the exchange. Instead I remain silent and stare at Um Abdallah and Ahmed. Their faces look like an empty home whose inhabitants had gotten up, gathered their things, and walked away.

After I've dropped Laura off I drive aimlessly through the western suburbs. The streets are wide and leafy, a far cry from the noise and crowds downtown. Even the heat feels different here, less urgent, more playful. I'm in no hurry to go home, to Teta and Doris and that bedroom. I try Maj's phone again as I drive by his house, but it's still turned off. Driving through the roads of my old neighbourhood I am reminded of our last months here before we moved, just before I turned thirteen. Those months following my father's death nearly killed Teta. She spent most of them in her room, emerging only to go to the toilet or refill her jug of water. Ever since my mother left I had wanted to die, so at the time I had felt that at the very least Baba's death brought Teta and me to the same level of mourning.

We did not speak of his death at the time. The only way to understand the implications of his absence was in the facial expressions of teachers, classmates, and old family friends. Like a detective, I stole glances through doors and windows, hoping to catch Teta in an unguarded moment. More often than not all I caught were glimpses of her putting on her creams and make-up, or the sound of her blow-drying her hair. Every now and then I would catch her staring out a window or at the photos of Baba that increasingly cluttered her bedside table.

For the first few months after Baba's death Teta put into me what she could no longer put into her son. All the food I craved, she cooked. She rubbed arrack on my belly when I had an upset stomach and shoved spoonfuls of tahini down my throat when I woke up with a neighing cough. I was the last thing she had left. I was not just her grandson now. I was also her son and her husband.

This did not last long. Soon enough I was back inside the citadel of Teta's rules. "Don't walk barefoot on the cold floor or you'll get diarrhoea. Don't turn the television off if you see me sleeping on the sofa, it will wake me up and I won't be able to fall asleep again, and God help you if I lose my afternoon nap because it will disrupt my sleeping schedule for weeks. Don't greet the guests in your pajamas. Use the same damn glass for drinking water, you don't need to use a new one every time. What are you, a prince? Just put the glass on top of the water cooler so you won't forget you've used it. Be a man. Don't eat rice after eight, your stomach doesn't work in your sleep and you'll have indigestion in the morning."

The week before school began that year I decided I would run away. There was nothing left for me at home, and I needed to find my mother. Unlike Teta, my mother might be able to speak to me about Baba's death, to answer difficult questions and explore uncomfortable subjects, with no regard for shame.

I felt certain that the best way to find her would be to do as she had done and simply walk out the door, and I would naturally find myself following in her footsteps.

When Teta went into her bedroom for her afternoon nap, I carefully packed a bag with things I might need for my journey. I put in my plastic water bottle, a banana, two books, my Discman and a couple of CDs, a box of Band-Aids, a spare T-shirt, and my favorite sandwich—*halawa* in pita bread microwaved for exactly thirty seconds until the *halawa* was soft and melted. When Teta's snores drifted down the hall, I tiptoed to the front door and quietly let myself out.

Outside, I took a left and walked down the road, sprinting past the giant monstrosity of Omar's house before anyone could see me. At the end of our street I took a right and walked in the direction of the supermarket. The late-summer sun was beating down on me. It would be a good investment to buy a Slush Puppie to cool me down, I thought, stepping into the shop.

Slush Puppie in hand, I walked toward the main traffic light. The road widened and eventually would merge with the highway leading downtown, then on to al-Sharqiyeh. It wouldn't be easy to walk down the highway, but if I stayed close to the edge I'd be fine. As the highway came into view, a terrible loneliness overcame me like vertigo. At home Teta and I had grieved, but it was only out in the quiet, leafy streets that I realized how on my own I was. I was free, yes, but I was also terribly alone in my freedom. And what would Teta do when she woke up and realized I was no longer there? There would be no going back. If she were to know I had tried to run away she would never forgive me.

I sat on the sidewalk and peeled my banana as I contemplated my options. Even though my mother had always been the one I could talk to, she was never a good listener. This was not for lack of trying. In fact, she always tried to listen, but her mind could never focus for too long, or else she would push her own thoughts into my head, taking my words and twisting them to suit her mood. Still, I could talk to her more than I could talk to Teta. With Teta there was little to be discussed apart from whether I was getting good enough grades, what I would study at university, and what I would name my first-born.

On the other hand, my mother had walked out the front door two years ago and had not been in touch since. Teta—stoic, reliable, and oppressive—had always been by my side. Mama was as loving as she was unpredictable. How could I be sure she would not leave me again, this time to die? Besides, I had already spent most of my money on a Slush Puppie, had already eaten my only banana, and I had only been gone for half an hour. What would I do this evening, or tomorrow, or the day after that? But to return to Teta's house with its oppressive silences would be a different sort of death . . .

Teta was still in her room when I came back. A cool breeze flowed through the house and down the hall. I walked to my room. The door to Teta's bedroom was ajar. Peering through the crack, I saw Teta sitting on her bed. She was in the process of dressing herself. Her large breasts hung down until they touched the tips of the light brown *gain*, an old body shaper she wore to push in the bulge of her stomach. Teta always wore her *gain*, long after it had been replaced by more effective corsets. She wore it as a uniform, paired with a light sweater and a fifties pencil skirt. Her hair, which she washed once a week, was always blow-dried into a tidy bob, her roots dyed monthly since the eighties to maintain that golden sheen.

There she was, sitting on the bed, the silky fabric of her *gain* stretching across her rounded stomach. I watched her study her hands thoughtfully. I was about to turn away when she looked up. She caught my gaze, and in her eyes was a flash of panic. Or maybe it was vulnerability? Whatever it was, I ran to my bedroom and shut the door. I stayed there for the rest of the afternoon. When I emerged in the early evening, we sat down for dinner and did not speak. After that Teta made sure to lock her bedroom door before removing her mask.

All at once I am aware that I am driving by the old supermarket. I park Nawaf's car, go inside, and buy an orange-flavoured Slush Puppie, and walk through the fields of asphalt toward where our old house used to be. On the way, I see what was once Omar's enormous villa. It's now a gym and fitness centre. On the top floor a number of women run on treadmills. A few months before graduation, news spread that Omar's father was implicated in a corruption scandal. In response he had taken all he could and fled the country. Omar's now somewhere in Europe, making films. His father apparently lives on a yacht on the Mediterranean Sea. I suppose he might still be there, on his yacht.

Our house was one of a number of houses that have been torn down and replaced with a glitzy shopping complex. This does not make me sad. Rather, I feel an inevitable emptiness. I take a seat across from the shopping complex, on a bench under a leafy orange tree. I enjoy the shade and watch the chic-looking women in oversized sunglasses, shopping bags hanging from their elbows, their high heels clicking on the paved road as they complain about the departure times of flights to London. I catch snippets of conversation around me, pleasant, meandering, pointless. After a while the calmness begins to annoy me, the voices grate on my nerves.

In a café next door, a young couple is having lunch in the sun. The man, dressed in a smart business suit, is telling a story while the woman, picking at a quinoa and feta salad, listens intently. At the punch line, she throws her hands in the air and lets out a boisterous laugh. Bits of quinoa from her fork fly in the air behind her, landing a few feet away. Two pigeons immediately descend on the crumbs.

The sun's burning rays on the ground and trees, combined with the fruity smell of the Slush Puppie, create a familiar perfume that brings back more memories of my childhood. Suddenly I feel like I am back there myself, as if it was only yesterday that I was twelve years old and had just lost my father.

His death changed everything. I was now the man of the house and completely unprepared. Alongside this, other feelings began to creep up on me, dangerous feelings that challenged Teta's rules. On the outside you couldn't tell what was happening. But in private I created a secret cage in my mind where I stored these dark thoughts. Like birds, I captured them as they flew by and put them in my cage for a time when I may need them. In that cage I stored secrets I could not so much as whisper to myself, for fear they might escape into the world. They were free to roam in the cage but unable to escape, lest they be discovered by Teta. With no words and no diagnosis, I could neither understand nor treat my symptoms. My dreadful misfortune remained nameless. Until George Michael.

"British pop star George Michael, formerly a member of the hit duo Wham!, revealed to the world that he is gay on Friday night during a CNN interview," a blond woman on the television announced one evening in that cheerful American voice, as I lay on the living-room carpet doing homework. "It was the thirty-four-year-old singer's first interview since his arrest for allegedly engaging in a lewd act in a Beverly Hills park restroom."

Gay. That's the word, I thought. Suddenly everything was clear. I checked to make sure Teta was still busy cooking dinner in the kitchen, and then inched toward the television to get a closer look. I wanted to take it all in, to study the screen like it held the secret to my survival.

"I don't feel any shame," Michael was now saying on television, his face obscured by large black sunglasses. "I feel stupid and reckless and weak for having allowed my sexuality to be exposed this way. But I do not feel any shame."

I got up and went to the bathroom. I turned the faucets on to let the water drown out any noise and stared at my reflection in the mirror. When I gained the courage I mouthed, then, ever so softly, whispered two words to my reflection: "I'm gay."

As the words rolled off my tongue I watched the way my mouth moved to see how the phrase fit. I said it again and again. Sometimes I was distracted by my own reflection, by my teeth, or by a smudge on the glass mirror. My mind momentarily turned to Doris and whether Teta would yell at her for not cleaning the mirror well enough. But my thoughts inevitably refocussed on the contours of my mouth and how it moved when I spoke those two words, what the reverberations of my breath felt like against my lips, how the words fogged the mirror as I exhaled, warping my reflection. I said those two words in the lowest of whispers so that I could barely hear myself. I said them first as a question, then as a statement, and finally as a sad sigh.

I'm gay.

There was a release in the first time I said it, the first time I had put those thoughts and feelings into words and let them escape from the secret cage. It was not yet a confirmation. But it was the beginning, the teasing out of the possibility of what my strange affliction might be.

I was different from everyone else.

I was doomed to be alone.

I was going to spend eternity rotting in hell.

But the word *gay* wasn't good enough. It was too far away, too intangible. Other than George Michael, there did not seem to be a whiff of gay in the air. Did this disease not exist here?

How had I become contaminated? Had all the American television I watched infected me with gay? The word, destined to be confined to foreign lands and chance headlines in English newspapers, seemed to be both a fantasy and also wholly unsuitable to my life, an otherworldly identity that jarred with who I was.

I collected similar words, trying them all out in the bathroom mirror to see how they fit. The bathroom became my favourite room in our new apartment. Heavy blue tiles decorated the walls, and apart from a small fan in the corner that looked out onto the alley below, there were no windows into the outside world. It was contained, enclosed, controllable. I spent hours in there, or as long as I could get away with before Teta began banging on the door. I feigned constipation and was consequently stuffed with prunes and yogurt, but it was worth it.

The first word I came across was in religion class. On normal days the class would degenerate into a question-and-answer session that consisted of our teacher giving bored pronouncements on whether things were *haram* (plastic surgery: not *haram* if for medical reasons; going to the gym: *haram*, one should not distort the body Allah gave you; oral sex: *haram*, but it's complicated and she wasn't going to discuss it).

One day someone from the president's office was visiting the class so the teacher was forced to give us a lecture. She told us the story of Sodom and Gomorrah, whose sins—which included homosexuality—had called down the vengeance of God, who punished them by raining fire on the cities. God ordered the Prophet Lot to escape and never look back. But as Lot and his wife escaped, his wife took one last look at Sodom and immediately turned into a pillar of salt.

"That's why the Dead Sea is salty," the teacher explained.

Basma raised her hand.

"Is that where *louti* comes from?" she asked. "From the Prophet Lot?"

The teacher glanced at the official from the president's office, who nodded his head. "Yes, *louti* derives from the name of the Prophet Lot," she said.

"What does *louti* mean?" Maj asked.

The teacher paused and looked at the official again. Once again he nodded his approval. She cleared her throat, opened the Quran, and began to read: "'Do you commit such indecency in a way that no one has preceded you in the worlds? You approach men lustfully instead of women. Truly, you are a nation who exceeds in sin.'" She looked up at the class triumphantly.

The students groaned.

"Maj, are you originally from Sodom?" asked Hamza.

The class snickered. I raised my hand.

"So that means it's *haram*, right?" I asked.

"Are you trying to be funny, Rasa?" the teacher said.

"No—" I began.

"Don't be a clown," she snapped.

Louti. I went back home, turned on the faucets, and said the word in front of the bathroom mirror: "*Ana louti.*"

Sodomite. No, it was too religious. All it did was remind me I was going to hell.

One morning a few weeks later, we sang the national anthem in assembly and then filed into a neat line to march back into the school building. Hamza was shadowing me from behind, treading on the back of my shoes with every step I took.

"*Khawal,*" he snorted in my ear whenever I tripped. I ignored him and kept walking. He tripped me again. "*Khawal.*"

This continued for some time, until my curiosity got the better of me. I turned around.

"What does *khawal* mean?"

Hamza caught my eye and mouthed, "*Baneekak*"—I will fuck you. He did not say this like it was a good thing. The look in his eyes made my cheeks burn with shame. *He* will fuck *me*. I quickly looked away.

At lunch I went into the office of Mr. Labib, our history teacher, an older man with kind eyes who always had two white blobs of dried spit at the corners of his mouth. I asked him what *khawal* meant.

"Where did you hear that?" he asked. He spoke very slowly, as if studying each word before letting it out. I shrugged. He sighed and licked his lips, the dried spit gleaming. "*Khawal* refers to effeminate men. A long time ago the word referred to male belly dancers. But it's not used for that anymore."

"Is it used for gay?" I asked.

"What . . . what did you say?" he stammered.

"Gay."

"Don't use that word here," he said, eyes narrowing. He licked his lips, stood up from behind his desk, and ushered me to the door.

I went back home and stood in front of the bathroom mirror.

Ana khawal.

"Rasa, the water's been running for ten minutes," Teta warned from the other side of the door. "You're going to bring a drought on this country."

Maybe I was a *khawal*. I recalled my actions leading up to Hamza calling me a *khawal*. Was it my wrists, which often hung limply under my chin when I was engrossed in what the teacher was saying? Or was it my voice, which, when I forgot to control it, would escape from my mouth in a higher pitch than what was normal for the other boys in school?

Perhaps *khawal* was an aspect of who I was. A sissy. A girlie-boy. But it didn't encompass everything.

My obsession with finding the perfect word continued. It was funny that both English and Arabic have so many words that explored every dimension of what I was feeling, and yet not one word that could encapsulate it all. I suppose it's no surprise I became an interpreter, given my early days spent deciphering the meaning behind words in front of a foggy bathroom mirror.

In the end, it all boiled down to the fact that I did not want to be different. I needed to belong somewhere, even if it was between the syllables of an obscure word in the dictionary. I needed to belong and I needed our lives to return to being the same as everyone else's. I needed to be back in the western suburbs, with Maj and Omar. I needed Baba and Mama to come back and bring with them everything familiar that they had taken away: the smells of apple-flavored shisha and Mama's heavy perfume, the Ramadan soap operas and the sounds of excitable sports commentators shrieking "GOAL!" reverberating through the apartment, the parent-teacher meetings where Mama would ardently defend my bad handwriting by explaining that "Einstein also had bad handwriting." Now it was only Teta, at home and at those parent-teacher meetings, her hair tucked behind her ears as she quietly maneuvered through the crowds of younger parents, her slim brown cigarette hanging from her wrinkled lips, a cigarette she insisted on smoking in the classrooms, ignoring the teachers' objections.

For a while my secret cage contained only the taxi driver, stored away like an exotic bird. By the time I was sixteen the cage had stored secret crushes and fantasies and obsessions and the images of various body parts of male classmates that were etched into my mind. I captured these thoughts until I was alone in the bathroom and could take them out to fly for a few hours before Teta began banging on the door and I would have to carefully lock them back inside.

Nightmares of marriage traumatized me. While I felt affection toward many women, I could never imagine myself with one. Whatever attraction I felt was due to the social acceptance that courting a woman might bring. I resigned myself to the inevitable prison sentence of marriage. I would marry and have children and live every night in fear, curled up in the far corner of the bed, anxious at the thought of touching my wife. I would be unhappy and alone, and any future children would be nothing more than a gift to Teta for her years of hard work.

In my final year of high school, I discovered POLSKASAT. It was Omar who, in excitable whispers over the phone one day, first told me about the obscure Polish channel that you could get on the satellite if you knew the exact frequency. That Saturday night, after Teta yawned and announced she was going to bed, I waited until her snores travelled across the quiet house and then scrolled through the channels until I arrived at POLSKASAT.

The channel was broadcasting a Hollywood movie, *Thelma and Louise*, except the voices of all the characters were dubbed by a bored-sounding Polish man. After what seemed like an eternity, Thelma and Louise finally drove off the cliff. The credits rolled on and on. When the final name scrolled by, the screen flickered for a few seconds, and then a woman in a pink dress appeared. She was an icy blonde with perky breasts. A number rolled across the screen, surrounded by flashing Technicolor words: CALL ME, SEXY GIRLS, PARTY. European techno music blasted from the television as the woman, her face plastered with makeup and desperation, made a "Call me" sign with her hand.

In the back of my mind I knew this was only sending me further into the harshest levels of hell, but I couldn't stop. I watched, transfixed, as these women appeared one after the other, each of them urging me to call. One wore a long red dress, a few appeared to be at a slumber party, playfully hitting one another with pillows. While walking a fluffy white poodle in the park, one woman was wearing nothing but a pair of knee-high boots, her breasts glistening in the sun. I divided my attention between watching these women and listening for any noises coming from the house. Every time I thought I heard something I flipped to the next channel, which was broadcasting a Turkish game show.

An hour later the screen flickered again. A dark-haired man in a suit sat in an office, his feet resting on his desk as he leaned back to read a newspaper. I inched closer, my nose nearly touching the television screen. A woman with bright red hair walked in. They spoke, their voices dubbed by the same Polish man who spoke on behalf of Thelma and Louise.

The man began kissing the woman's neck as my eyes darted between the screen and the dark hallway. He took off her shirt and began gnawing at her breasts as she leaned back and moaned. I watched the man closely as he explored her body, his excitement amplifying my own. When he was done she turned toward him and began to take off his shirt. The man unbuckled his belt. I held my breath as he dropped his trousers, waiting to catch a glimpse of what was beneath it all.

Except the camera panned out in perfect timing and refocused on a new scene where, by now, the man was plowing into the woman. The cameraman skillfully navigated their gyrating bodies to avoid the man's nakedness. I pleaded with the cameraman to give me a glimpse of a bit more of the man, tilted my head to the right, upward, to see if maybe the editors might have missed something. That damn cameraman, we were locked in an eternal battle, he and I.

POLSKASAT became my ritual and my education. The excitement would begin on Saturday morning and grow over the course of the day. I would spend the afternoons lying on the floor in my bedroom listening to George Michael on my Discman and counting down the hours until POLSKASAT came on. The excitement would be almost unbearable in the final few hours of Teta's wakefulness, when she would be watching the evening news.

Once she was safely tucked away, I would flip to POL-SKASAT and watch, fixated, the volume turned so low that I had to strain to hear the barely audible moans, and my finger preemptively on the Channel Up button of the remote control, listening for the sounds of footsteps coming down the hall. Occasionally I would close a door or put a chair in the way to alert me when Teta was coming. On most nights, however, her midnight forays were only to get a glass of water or to deliver a slumberous complaint about my late-night TV habits, which rarely delved into any sustained interest in what it was I was staying up late watching in the first place.

One Saturday evening a few months into this habit, I had become cocky and my impatience began to show.

"It's getting late," I told Teta after the evening news had fin-ished and she had poured herself another glass of arrack.

"I'm staying up tonight," she said.

"What for?"

"I wasn't born yesterday, *habibi*. What channel is it? Don't make me go through all the channels."

"I don't know what you're talking about," I persisted, nerv-ous now.

"It's those dirty Soviets, isn't it?" she asked, scrolling through the Eastern European channels.

My protests were futile so I gave in and told her. She flipped to POLSKASAT and we sat watching the last thirty minutes of *Ghost*, dubbed into Polish. To calm my nerves I busied myself with trying to explain the film's story line to her.

"He's a ghost? Really this is stupid," she insisted. I explained to her that it was a sad movie but she could only see the humor in it, which wasn't helped by the bored-sounding Polish man who dubbed all the characters.

"She's very pretty, but she's so stupid to cut her hair like a boy," Teta noted, as Demi Moore said her final goodbyes to Patrick Swayze.

Finally it was time. The credits rolled, always to the very last name. Then the familiar flicker, that brief pause, the black screen, and finally the first woman appeared.

"Oh, Rasa." Teta sighed as she lit a cigarette and watched a blond woman in a Lolita uniform suck on her thumb. "Is this *sharmoota* what you stay up all night for?"

The next clip featured a woman on a bench. She pursed her lips as she gave us a knowing smile. The camera zoomed in and out of her skirt as she opened and closed her legs. I watched Teta from the corner of my eye, hoping she would get bored before the movie began, when suddenly the woman's legs opened and something happened that I had never seen before.

"Is she?" Teta gasped, leaning forward in her chair. "No! She is. Oh my God, she's pissing." Teta's mouth gaped open and then she began to cackle. "Look at her, look at this *sharmoota*, like a dog, opening her legs and pissing on the park bench."

"It's really not usually like this," I explained, jumping up and turning the television off. The screen went from a pale yellow stream of urine to an abrupt blackness.

"Is this what you stay up late to see?" She cackled, laughing so hard she had a coughing fit. "Pissing in the park like a dog . . . a bitch!"

I could not really watch POLSKASAT after that. I knew that if I were to ever stay up late, Teta would know exactly what it was that I was up to, and the shame of it sapped any enjoyment I may have felt. It was not just that I was going to hell, but now Teta knew I was going to hell. But at least, I secretly thought, Teta believed I was a healthy young man.

After a few months, someone somewhere in the Ministry of Culture must have heard about POLSKASAT. Perhaps the minister himself had walked in on his son watching a POLSKASAT movie and demanded something be done, I don't know. All I know is that one night, out of curiosity, I flicked to POLSKASAT and sat through until the Hollywood movie had finished. The titles came up and then the channel suddenly went down, leaving a gray static. The glorious days of POLSKASAT were over.

"Pardon, do you have a lighter?" a young woman asks me, half of her face hidden behind gold-and-silver sunglasses. She has shoulder-length black hair ironed so straight it plunges like daggers down the sides of her face. She is cradling a phone between her ear and her shoulder.

I noisily slurp what is left of my Slush Puppie and hand her my lighter.

"He told me this over dinner last night," she speaks into the phone as she lights her cigarette. "And I am so tired of it all. The agony of waiting . . . No, no, I'm not that kind of woman. Either you marry me or you don't." She returns the lighter to me and walks away.

It's one thirty in the afternoon. I've been trying to ignore the fact that Taymour is having his family lunch in a restaurant just across from the shopping complex, but before I know what I am doing I have walked there. It is one of those fancy restaurants, with a huge hall filled with tables that fit thirty to forty people. Some are slowly clearing out as families finish their meals. I hover by the entrance, looking for him, when a waiter dressed in a sharp suit comes up to me.

"Can I help you?"

"A table for one, please," I say. He gives me a strange look, confusion transitioning toward disdain, but I repeat my request in English and he is more receptive. As he leads me down the hall I scan the tables for Taymour. Finally I see him, sitting in the centre of one of the large tables. There are at least twenty others with him, his family, midway through the meal.

Taymour is wearing a white shirt. Their waiter has just placed a large platter of barbecued meat on the table and the family digs in, unaware of the tall, pitiful figure watching them. Taymour carefully hangs an orange napkin from his collar and grabs a few pieces of shish taouk from the platter. An older woman (his mother, or perhaps an aunt?) leans over and puts a barbecued tomato on his plate. Taymour shakes his head and feigns anger, his mouth, those beautiful lips glistening with oil, mouthing "No, no," but he does not make any attempt to remove the tomato from his plate.

"Are you coming?" the waiter asks impatiently, a few metres ahead.

"Yes, sorry." I follow him to a table. I sit down and position my chair so that Taymour's view of me is blocked by a marble pillar and the plastic branches of a fake tree. Regardless, the family is so consumed in their meal, laughing and talking and clinking glasses, that they would likely not notice me if I were to stand at the end of their long table like a lonely ghost.

"What do you want?" the waiter asks.

"An apple shisha and some Turkish coffee, medium, please."

"That's it?" he asks tiredly.

"Some baklawa, too."

After the waiter leaves I return to watching Taymour. My view is restricted by a fat bald man sitting across from him, who moves his head too quickly and too often for me to settle into one position. Taymour is clean-shaven, his hair gelled and combed to one side. His shirt is stretched across his shoulders and arms. How I love getting lost in his arms. I thought seeing Taymour might make me feel better but it only makes me feel worse, because the Taymour sitting across the room from me is the Taymour that society wants, the one who is responsible and hardworking, the good citizen who would never disobey his family or the government. And I would never be invited to sit at the table with that Taymour, to meet his family and share a meal with them, laugh alongside them as I force a barbecued tomato onto his plate. I feel so far away from him, and to think only last night we had our arms around each other.

The waiter brings me my order. I inhale on the shisha and the smoke further obscures my face. I take out the photograph of Abdallah from my bag. His eyes stare back at me, challenging me to find him. In which prison cell in the city are these eyes locked away? There is sadness in those eyes, of a life that did not come easy. Or am I reading too much into his gaze, drawing out lives where they do not exist? I turn the photograph over and grab a pen from my bag. If I cannot say what I want to say to Taymour, if I cannot walk up to him and blurt it out, then I will write it by hand, so that at least he will know how I feel. I will record our history on the back of this photograph and it will stay with us. I'll give him the picture of Ahmed and Um Abdallah's son, with my words scrawled on the other side, and as he reads my words, his hands touching the same photograph I touched, the same photograph Um Abdallah and Ahmed touched, Taymour will recognize that we are worth fighting for, and we will all be connected somehow. As I begin to write, in tiny letters to fit it all in, Taymour's table bursts into a roar of laughter, clinking glasses and cheering.

Habibi Taymour,

I know you don't like me to call you that, to call you habibi. But if there is one time I can do so let it be in this letter, which you can burn after reading if you wish. No one will ever know that you are my habibi. And you are, whether you like it or not, my habibi. I want to write to you because I do not know if you will let me speak to you again after last night. I do not mean it in the sense that you would not speak to me at all, no, no, I mean that I am no longer sure if you will allow us to be truthful, if we will ever have our barriers down as we did last night, and the night before that, and on that first night we met three years ago. How can I begin to tell you what it meant to meet someone who finally understood me, someone I could talk to and confess everything?

Do you remember that first week we met, how you came over every night? Teta had no idea. All day I would long for you. My heart would jump when you'd miss-call me to let me know you were outside. I'd stand by the dark stairway listening as your footsteps came closer, my stomach in excitable knots. Then, after letting you out, I would get back into bed, stick my head deep into your pillow and savor the way your smell mixed with Doris's orange blossom laundry detergent. I'd lie there and wish for sleep to come, not just to dream of you but also to forget you.

And although soon society got in the way, and you insisted we see each other less, you remained my days and my nights, my only thought and source of pleasure. In public I'd watch you walk with ease through a crowded room, and then watch you do the same in my bedroom, naked. You would cross the length of my bedroom, knowing my eyes followed you, hungrily gaping as you strolled to pick something up, seemingly at random, and move it from one side of the room to the other. It was a performance, in as much as your swagger across a vast wedding hall or a crowded bar was a performance. But this performance was only for me. I was your only audience. Only I will see you this way, in here, I'd tell myself. When Doris came in to clean the room the next day she would never know that you had been here, naked, your bare feet leaving invisible footprints on the floor.

When we were alone in my bedroom, in our bedroom, you would sing to me. Did you know that when you're singing your face appears different? It is a rare moment where you do not seem too concerned with society. A vulnerability, sad and nostalgic, would emerge. In my bedroom you would strum *your guitar and start with a gentle hum, and when you sang your voice would expand like a sunrise, awakening something in me that felt dormant all my life.*

"Promise you will sing only to me," I would beg you, and you would smile and kiss my forehead. And our foreheads? Oh, our foreheads were the gateway into each other. Don't forget all the times we sat in bed silently, forehead to forehead, for what seemed like hours. It was as if we were connecting to each other, our thoughts flowing through the point where our heads touched. In my entire search for more space, the space between you and me is the only one I wanted to squeeze out. My thoughts have nowhere to go now. They're just swimming in circles in my head, jumbled up and locked in that damn cage in my mind.

Perhaps I had been dreaming too carelessly. Too boldly. Perhaps you had sung a bit too loudly. And so now? Will we ever re-create what we had? My room was our sanctuary. Otherwise it was rushed, in moving cars, as we struggled to drive with one hand and fool around with the other, always on dark streets. It was an exercise in logistics that settled cravings, rather than indulged them. Our last sanctuary of indulgence is gone, and today of all days . . . is this crazy? If I am crazy, then I am crazy. Crazy and furious. Not at you, no. At myself, for letting my guard down, for expecting that we could get away with what we were doing. I never held back. I gave you my all, sacrificed everything for us.

Anyway . . . this letter is not meant to indulge in these memories, even if that's all I have. E-mails deleted, text messages deleted, no photos. Nothing can be left to chance, to the curious eyes of a stranger. Only my memories are left, and here I am remembering it all . . . Listen, I want you to play an important part in my life, even though I still don't have the words for what this part could be. I want you to assure me

that you will always be there, somehow, that you won't just
get up and leave one day.

  But even as your instinct might tell you to run away from
us, remember how good I've been to you, how cleanly and
honestly I've treated you, how much I love you . . . and we
don't have a choice but to believe that love is greater than
anything else. And if it means running away and starting
over again, then maybe that's just what we have to do . . .

I look up from the letter, breathless, clouded in shisha
smoke. They are clearing plates, a nearly empty platter of fruit
sits in the centre of Taymour's table. A few of the diners have
lit cigarettes. I study Taymour's movements, as if examining
the tricks of an award-winning actor, looking for moments
where he might slip, a feminine flick of the wrist, a dramatic
gasp, or a camp roll of the eyes. Someone reaches over and
claps him on the shoulder and Taymour turns and smiles. The
turn, yes, slightly feminine, maybe? But barely noticeable.
Even in the little imperfections, the tiny giveaways that are
imperceptible to anyone but me, his performance is flawless.
For a long time I was learning from him. I began to go out with
him to his social events. At dinner parties we sat beside each
other. At the table he paid me no attention, but under it I
would feel his foot brush mine. It would withdraw, but soon
enough it would be back. I admired the way he conducted
himself, flitting between roles so naturally. He had that cool
disinterest and controlled boom of a laugh that all successful
society men have. He could be among a crowd of admirers and
one quick glance my way would remind me where his heart
was.

Through trial and error I learned his rules. In public there
would be no hand-holding or inappropriate touching. We
would greet each other with a firm handshake and maybe a
kiss on one cheek. I was not to refer to him as my boyfriend,

my *habibi*, even in private. He would come over once a week, on Thursday nights, and would leave during the muezzin's call to prayer at dawn. I was not to act too feminine, even as a joke, but if I approached him from behind and tried to take control he would tense up and quickly move away. He asked if I was willing to let him enter me, but I refused. My refusal was instinctive. There was no logic to it. I felt that if I let him enter me, I would have jumped off the cliff, and there was no guarantee he would follow. If he didn't try so hard in public, if he was just comfortable being a man and doing man things, then perhaps I would have agreed. I would have let him take me however he wanted and enjoyed myself in the process. But his public performance of manliness felt like a competition, and I couldn't let go or else I would lose. But what would I have lost exactly? I could not say but I felt the threat of the loss viscerally. I could not open myself to dishonour, did not trust him enough with my shame.

He was right when he told me once that he had one foot in and one foot out. It was a balancing act, and he navigated it so effortlessly. But I was his one foot out, wasn't I? In fact, he made sure I never met his mother. He introduced me to his father once, a few years ago at the wedding of one of his distant cousins. I remember being surprised at how tall his father was, but like Taymour he was very handsome. The way he held himself, his gestures and manners of speech, reminded me so much of Taymour that I fell in love with him even more, because I realized I was not just falling in love with Taymour but also with generations of him that connect through history, traits that had been passed down from one generation to the next. I was in love with his ancestry that stretched out for centuries.

After I met his father I was so happy I wanted to return the favour, to show him that everything in me would be open to him and only him. I took him to our old neighbourhood in the western suburbs. It was late afternoon, and the streets were empty. I showed him the site of our old house and told him about my father and mother. As we walked down the old streets, I mentally introduced my father to Taymour and told him everything that had happened between us. I asked him to forgive me, that there was nothing I could do. This was just how I turned out, I explained. I promised him that I would protect Teta from this secret, but that I owed it to myself to live an honest life. A sense of calm settled over me, and I took it to mean that my father had given me his blessing.

The shame hit me as we drove back from the area. I thought of how Teta might react if she knew what I had done, visited my family's grave with Taymour, my secret lover. I couldn't help but feel that I had tainted my father's memory. I had thrown away the dreams Teta and Baba had for me and had taken their source of shame to my father's ghost and demanded his acceptance. I began to cry in the passenger seat. The more I tried to stop myself, the harder the tears came. My shame was revealed to him now, I thought, as I buried my face in my hands. There was nothing left to hide.

He reached over to touch me and I quickly pulled away.

"Please don't," I sobbed, and he squeezed my leg, as if to say that it was okay.

But still he never introduced me to his mother. He withheld the person to whom he is closest. Was there a reason? Did he think she would know, once she looked at me, the true nature of our relationship? He would never let me sit at the table, by his side, among his family. My role is to stay here, hidden behind smoke and pillars.

One of the women at the table gets up. She walks toward me, quickly passes by my table without giving me a second glance, and enters the bathroom. Although I don't know what she looks like, I'm convinced the woman is Taymour's mother. So convinced that I get up and walk toward the bathroom, hovering by the doors. When the woman comes out again we are face-to-face. She looks at me with the same honey-colored eyes as Taymour's. There is that same melancholy in her eyes, but also a flicker of shrewdness. She shifts her head to the left, slightly, studying me. I look back, unsure what expression I have on my face. Does she know? Can she see it in my eyes?

"Do I know you?" she asks, hesitant. Her voice is much deeper than I imagined.

"No, Auntie," I reply, swallowing.

"What's your family name? There's something very familiar about you."

"You don't know me, Auntie," I insist.

She nods, although not with belief. She maneuvers around me and walks back to the table without looking back.

I return to my seat. The encounter has shaken me more than I imagined. What was I expecting? That she would welcome me, invite me to sit at the table with them, introduce me to the rest of the family as her future son-in-law?

I fold Abdallah's photograph into a small square and put it in my pocket, then leave a few bills on the table and sneak out before anyone notices me. As I get into Nawaf's car, my phone rings.

I almost don't recognize his voice.

"I'm in the prison downtown," Maj mumbles, in a tone that instructs me not to ask any questions.

I drive Nawaf's car back to the office and walk the fifteen minutes to the police station. The weather is stifling but I feel the need to clear my head. I tell myself that Maj is okay and soon he'll be free. There's still Teta, and Taymour, but those problems seem less immediate. Shame and lost love are bourgeois worries, I tell myself. Metaphorical prisons are no match for the real thing.

Walking along the main road, I navigate the traffic and

bustling market stalls. During the first protests I had felt as though I was seeing everything for the first time. My senses were alive. This was my city, and I was finally in control of my destiny. I experienced this feeling so intensely that I would appreciate the scent of jasmine and the feeling of cool springtime rain on my skin. Even the smell of the diesel from the cars used to make me nostalgic. Nowadays I don't smell the jasmine, the sounds of downtown give me a headache, and the diesel stinks. My vision is once again grey.

Cars are honking and fighting for right-of-way in the busy roundabout. Some cars are blasting pop music from crackling speakers, the songs merging into one another until they are just a cacophony of shrill *habibi*s and *yalla*s. In the centre of the roundabout a circle of trees surrounds a statue of the president. You can measure his popularity in certain neighbourhoods by how many posters of him the government has put up. The less popular he is, the more posters his thugs hang in defiance.

My headache is worsening, as though someone is hammering a rusty nail into my skull. Maj is okay, I tell myself again. He's okay. I've heard his voice. But his voice . . . he has never sounded like that before. At least he's alive, at least he is well enough to speak. For now, that counts for something.

Maj is always getting himself into trouble, and ever since we became friends I have inevitably been sucked in. When we were younger, anytime I was outside with Maj we were at risk of getting chased, so I made sure that we hung out in my room as much as possible. We were about nine then, and in my room he always wanted to play bride and groom. He insisted on being the bride, prancing around draped in a white sheet. He took great joy in mimicking the poise of the real-life brides we saw at weddings. Begrudgingly, I would stand next to him in my suit, all square and *zalameh*-like. He would take my hand and lead me back and forth across the length of the room, waving and gushing over the imaginary guests that surrounded us.

One day my mother walked in on us. I froze, with the inexplicable feeling you get when you are young and think you have done something wrong, although you are unable to explain why.

Maj didn't skip a beat.

"I'm so glad you came, madam," he said, showering her with hugs and kisses. "Please, please, have a seat."

"*Mabrook*." Mama laughed, a confused look on her face. "You look beautiful, Maj."

"Why thank you, thank you, madam," Maj gushed. "It took the coiffeur hours to get my hair. Just. Right."

"You're a beautiful bride now," my mother said. "But as soon as you take that dress off you'll spend your life chopping onions."

"That's why I'm never taking it off, madam." Maj pranced around the room. "They can't make me work if every day is my wedding day."

"Enough!" I grabbed the veil off Maj's head and threw it on the floor.

My mother looked annoyed. "Rasa!" she gasped.

"It's *eib*," I explained.

Mama, a lover of all freaks and outcasts, placed the veil back on Maj's head. Then, as she walked out of the room, she turned around and looked me in the eye.

"I've lost you to your grandmother, haven't I?"

One of my main goals in high school seemed to be to keep Maj from getting us both beaten up every day. His femininity offended the sensibilities of everyone, which only made him more adamant to flaunt it. He'd flirt with all the boys and bat his long eyelashes at them, his arms and legs like tentacles, coiling themselves around his conversations. Then when they chased us, I had to drag him along to keep him from falling behind.

Even after college, after he had grown his nails out and

painted them first in a subtle French manicure and then later a deep red, even after he began to pluck his eyebrows into a dramatic arch, even after he began performing in Guapa's underground parties, even then I stayed by his side. It is rare to find someone who has such an unwavering faith in humanity, while maintaining such a blissful disregard for what other people think of him. I feel shame for many things, but my friendship with Maj is one of the few things in my life I am proud of.

I take a shortcut between two derelict buildings. A man is playing a grand piano in the middle of the alley. The piano is mounted on a vegetable cart. A group of children surround him, rolling him down the alleyway, laughing and singing. The man is banging on the piano keys, and every so often he throws his head back and roars with laughter. I catch some of the lyrics to the song they are singing:

> *Destruction is bad, but when it's from within it's terrible*
> *We've been waiting for electricity and water*
> *But the world only sends delegations*
> *They come and go, blocking sidewalks and stopping traffic*
> *What is it with this world? I swear to God it's terrible*

The young pianist smiles when he sees me coming. Deep dimples pierce both cheeks. "Sing along," he says.

I shake my head and carry on walking. My mind drifts to last night at Guapa. As with most things in this city, there was the public Guapa and then there was the *real* Guapa. After the main bar closes and most of the patrons leave, usually to friends' houses or to drunkenly drive around the city's empty streets, a dim red light in the basement of Guapa switches on, and after a few minutes of screeching feedback from the microphones, the show begins.

Apart from the red light, there's a small, crescent-shaped

wooden bar, a few tables and chairs on one side, an old sofa on the other, and a set of speakers blasting trashy Arabic pop music. The basement room, about half the size of a tennis court, is also where Nora, Guapa's manager, lives. That's the reason it's safe from the authorities. So long as it is in private, they do not care if a few men wear dresses and dance to silly music.

Guapa was livelier than usual last night. As soon as we walked in Maj rushed off to get changed, so it was just Taymour and me. I worried all the people would scare Taymour off. Although he regularly drank with us upstairs, he hardly ever came downstairs and so was noticeably uncomfortable, shifting and glancing around the room, and I felt obliged to act cool and confident to make up for it. A couple of knife-blade-lean boys with a faint lick of eyeliner smiled at us.

"Are you *boyfriends*?" one of them asked with a trace of awe. He looked about sixteen and like he might be from the provinces, but he spoke in a perfect American accent.

Taymour stiffened at the question.

"I *really* want a boyfriend," the boy said.

Taymour leaned over and whispered in my ear, "Do you have any idea the shit I'll be in if someone recognizes me?"

"Relax. We'll just stay for a quick drink and see Maj perform."

There were two stylishly dressed women I didn't recognize, who sat at a table in a dark corner surrounded by a few of Guapa's regular butch girls. The butch girls were, as always, dressed in black T-shirts, old jeans, and scowls that appeared terrifying if you didn't know them. The two women seemed happy to just sit there looking pretty, smoking their cigarettes and staring at their phones.

There were of course the regulars: the older men, taxi drivers mostly, who sat by the bar, their worn-out eyes looking up from the tip of their whisky glass across the sea of thin young boys, who were squealing and jumping from corner to corner, scrounging drinks from naïve newcomers. These boys seemed to change their outfits in unison; some days they were in leather vests and the next they'd be sporting chiffon scarves around their necks. But their fake designer handbags always hung from their elbows as they spoke to one another like middle-aged housewives, their hands flapping about like a fish out of water.

Then there were the muscled guys, like peacocks in their open-neck shirts, with comically inflated arms and chests, standing in a serious line along the outskirts of the room, shuffling their feet to the music like robots. Most were too self-conscious to speak lest a feminine turn of phrase fall from their mouths, and from what I heard some don't even call themselves gay because they would never bend over for another man (although Maj insists you can get them to roll over like a dog doing tricks if you ply them with enough drinks).

Many of the best-looking men only had eyes for the foreigners, because they were a get-out-of-jail-free card. The reality is that the get-out-of-jail-free card only materialized for a lucky handful over the years, so much so that I don't understand why those poor men even bother. But you could immediately tell from the type of foreigner that came in what goods he wanted to purchase. Some of them were slight, wearing expensive suits and constantly touching their coiffured hair. The manly men, the taxi drivers, banking on a piece of ass and a foreign passport, would rush over, light the foreigner's cigarette, and puff out their chests. When a foreigner strutted in with his balls hanging like two footballs, the younger boys would clamour around him, batting their eyelashes, their butts up in the air for the foreigner to take a sniff and make his selection.

Behind the bar a couple of al-Sharqiyeh boys served

drinks. They were the usual bartenders at Guapa, tall, dark, with lean bodies that moved swiftly as they shook cocktails and poured pint after pint. They were mesmerizing, but everyone knew those guys were off-limits. Nora always made sure the men she hired only had eyes for women, so as to not mix business with pleasure. If a newcomer were to foolishly make an offer to one of these men, they were swiftly banned from coming again.

A handful of the boys clacked around in heels, and Taymour was looking at one of them in particular, a potbellied older queen with bright orange hair and tropical green eye shadow, who was leaning against the bar as he painted his lips with stubby fingers.

"Are you sure there's no one here who will recognize me?" Taymour asked.

"I'm positive. And even if they do, that would mean you would recognize them as well, so your secret would be safe."

"That's not the point," he snapped. "It's not that I want my secret safe, it's that I don't want anyone to know. No matter who they are. Really, this was a mistake."

"I wonder where Maj is," I said, trying to change the subject.

The skinny boys who had admired Taymour earlier were now closing in on us. They formed a circle around Taymour, squeezing his cheeks and arms. Taymour staggered into a corner, wide-eyed. In my pocket my phone vibrated.

I'm in the bathroom getting dressed!

I looked up in time to see the bathroom door open, and Maj's heavily made-up eye peered out from the crack. I grabbed Taymour's arm and dragged him away from the boys. As we pushed through the room an anarchist boy crashed into us. He had long curly black hair, pulled back from his forehead by a bandanna. I recognized him from a demonstration a few months ago, but as the Arabic music blended into a bass-heavy techno beat he didn't seem to notice me. The sight of him twirling around the room with closed eyes, a wide smile, and a blissful look on his face was a glorious antidote to the unimaginative God-worshipping slogan chanting that had become routine at the demonstrations these days.

Maj opened the door just wide enough to let us in. The bathroom was tiny, the sink dirty with smudges of black eyeliner. He pointed to the empty bathtub and Taymour and I perched on the edge. The bathroom was hazy with smoke. Maj, a cigarette in his hand, was dressed in a Princess Jasmine costume: a turquoise bra, genie pants, and a long black wig. The bra straps hung loosely off his shoulders, the tattoo under his neckline in full view. He got the tattoo after the first violent attack on the protests, a simple statement in Arabic along his collarbone: If you won't let us dream, we will not let you sleep.

When Maj first started doing drag he would dress up as Madonna on some nights and other nights as Cher. One day he walked into Guapa and declared he did not want to perform as Western divas any more, explaining that "the appropriation of queerness into the capitalist system, it's happened in the West to such a terrible extent. And we're next. What we have, we're next in line."

So he performed as Arabic pop princesses instead. He painted his lips thick and juicy like Haifa, put on a blond wig as Elissa, and only lip-synched to Arabic songs. I found that while the lyrics had changed from English to Arabic, everything else remained the same. But more recently he had changed once again. "War-on-terror neo-Orientalist gender-fucking" was what he liked to call what he did.

Maj gave me a hug and took a swig from a glass on the sink.

"Are you ready?" I asked.

"I'm always ready," Maj said. "You'll be watching, right?"

"Of course!"

"That's the spirit," Maj said. "We will always have fun. If there's a bomb on the right, we'll dance to the left." He looked at Taymour with an expression of distaste. "Isn't that right, *Monsieur*?"

Taymour cleared his throat. Maj and Taymour never saw eye to eye and tolerated each other only for my sake. I suspect Maj didn't like Taymour because everyone else was so enamoured with him, and Maj wanted to make sure Taymour knew that he was lucky to have me. Maj threw his cigarette in the sink, blew out the smoke from one side of his mouth, and pointed his thumb toward the door. "*Yalla*, go, I'm on in a minute."

We left and stood in the crowd. Then, as the first chords of "Genie in a Bottle" began to play, Maj stepped out of the bathroom. He was wearing a full niqab, but the cloth covering his face had a print of Marilyn Monroe's face. The crowd roared. I remember Taymour chuckling next to me, and we watched Maj slowly take off the niqab and begin belly dancing in the centre of the room, lip-synching to the music. The crowd danced and sang along.

The song ended and was quickly followed by a deep tabla beat mixed in with nineties techno music. Maj jumped on the coffee table, spilling a plastic cup of beer on the floor. Two younger boys crawled up beside him. The three of them wrapped shawls around their waists and swayed their hips furiously to the beat. You could tell the boys were from al-Sharqiyeh because they always put in more effort and seemed to dance harder than those from the western suburbs. They had more to lose by coming here, and their hips jutted this way and that, bouncing to the music, as if this might be the last time they would ever dance.

Taymour pointed to his watch. I should have ignored him and kept on dancing. But I was hungry for him and nothing else mattered. I grabbed his hand and we stumbled out of the door like fools, sweating and laughing. We grabbed a midnight shawarma from the place around the corner. We ate our platters in his car in a dark alleyway under a large lemon tree. He was pensive, dipping a piece of chicken in and out of the garlic sauce in sad, hopeless gestures.

"What's on your mind, *habibi*?" I asked him.

He looked surprised, but I wasn't sure if I startled him by talking or by calling him *habibi*. "I need to get out of this city," he said.

"But if you want to get out, then why are you—"

"I don't want to talk about that," Taymour interrupted. "For tonight at least, let's act as if tomorrow isn't happening."

"Fine by me," I said, dropping a pickle in my mouth.

"I don't even care where I go," he snapped, throwing his chicken into the pool of garlic sauce. He turned to me with an intense look in his eyes. He leaned toward me, sucked the oil from his fingers, and ran his thumb along my lips. "If I leave," he whispered, "would you come with me?" His hot breath smelled of garlic and alcohol. "Or would you just stay in that apartment with your grandmother for the rest of your life?"

I swallowed as his thumb made its way across my lips. "I want to be with you. Isn't that obvious already? So if you want to go, I'll go, and if you want to stay, then I will stay in that apartment with her until the day she dies, or I die, or the day this city truly falls apart."

Taymour sighed and leaned back against the seat. "Nothing ever falls apart just like that," he said bitterly. "This city has been decaying for decades now, and it's going to keep on decaying. Unless we leave, we'll rot along with it."

I laughed to ease the tension. "Well, that's optimistic."

The conversation exhausted me. I looked out into the narrow street, at the overflowing silver garbage can where a family of cats was tearing through the black bags. I loved Taymour because he was from here, because everything in him reminded me of everything here, because to love him was to love this city and its history. And yet I couldn't love him because he was from here and so held ideas of how to be and how to love, which would never fit in with the love that we shared.

But I did not tell him any of this. Instead I laughed and kissed him in the darkness. He kissed me back, hard, and as the engine roared to life I didn't want to ever let go. It was only last night and remembering it now I can't help but think how naïve we had been, how full of hopes and dreams. We were playing with fire, Taymour and I, as we pushed and pulled, not knowing how to get somewhere we weren't even sure we wanted to go, all the while unknowingly dragging each other to the desert to be shot.

The police station is an imposing brick structure with hardly any windows. As soon as I see it I feel like a fool, as if I am offering myself up for slaughter. The heavy metal doors are manned by two police officers with oily hair. I tell them I am here to pick up a friend, and as I say this it occurs to me that this might be a trap. Maybe they forced Maj to call everyone who was at Guapa last night. No. Maj might not feel any shame about wearing a dress, but he has too much pride to sell anyone out.

The police officers point me toward a dark hallway that smells of sweaty feet. I walk through, the floor is sticky, and I come out at what looks like a waiting room. The room is sparse, with a large desk at the front, a green metal bench along one side, and a row of chairs in the centre, their blue paint chipped to reveal rusted metal underneath.

Along the bench, two women and one man sit. The man is tall and slim and in his forties. He is nervously smoking a cigarette under the No Smoking sign. As his eyes scan the room he gets up and paces for a few moments on his long legs before sitting back down again. One of the women, a Filipina maid, stares at the floor. The other woman, probably a prostitute, is wearing a short skirt and silver stilettos, her face painted in shades of lilac and green. She picks at the lavender-colored nail polish on her fingers before letting out an unimpressed sigh as I walk in.

I approach the uniformed officer behind the desk, a small balding man in his fifties with a hairy mole on his forehead, and tentatively explain my situation. I give him Maj's name and tell him that he is due to be released.

"Sit down," he says without looking at me.

I take a seat on the bench next to the Filipina woman. The officer at the desk stands up.

"Not there," he barks. He points toward the blue chairs.

I stand up and take a seat on a chair in the centre of the room. I take out my phone and type a message to Taymour to distract myself. *You promised we would always find a way to be together. We can still meet in hotels. See, that's just one idea. There will be others, if only we choose to look at the positives.*

"Put that phone away or I'll break it over your face," the officer shrieks. I quickly press Send and slip my phone back into my pocket. I can feel my heart pounding in my chest.

The officer sits back down, lights a cigarette, and flicks through his phone until another officer comes out of one of the rooms behind the desk. The two officers speak to each other for a moment before going back into the room together. The woman in the short skirt coughs and lets out another heavy sigh.

Jagged cracks run down the glossy beige walls. A portrait of the president in an ugly gold frame stares at me from behind the officer's desk. In this one he is dressed as a police officer. Beside that is a portrait of the president's young son, who is also dressed as a police officer. I stare at the picture for a while before looking away, trying to unthink the angry thoughts that are beginning to form. A slapping sound reverberates from a room down the hall, like a butcher slamming a slab of meat on a table.

An ongoing fear of mine is to be arrested and taken to a

place like this. Perhaps for something I might say or think in a careless moment. Having seen the records of police abuses Maj has collected over the past months, my mind often returns to the images of killing and torture, the slashed thighs and pulled fingernails and burned flesh. What compels the feasting on death and fear that takes place within prison walls? Ideology? Power? Pure sadistic enjoyment? Or fear? The walls close in on me. I feel helpless again, there is nothing I can do but be here and accept whatever comes. I look at the man pacing nervously by the bench. He stubs out his cigarette and immediately lights another one.

The officer comes out of the room.

"You. With the ugly haircut." He is pointing at me. "Yeah, I'm talking to you. Don't look so surprised. Your haircut is ugly, you didn't know that?"

I stand up, follow him into the room, terrified and yet relieved that something, anything, is happening. Inside the room there's a metal table, which is bare except for a notepad, an ashtray, a half-empty glass of tea, and a large folder. I am not sure how to behave. Cocky, as if I have protection, or shall I be friendly, present myself as an unflinching ally of the regime? Maybe apologetic, but apologetic for what exactly? What mask shall I put on for this performance to get me and Maj out alive?

"Sit down," the officer with the mole on his forehead says as he shuts the door. He remains by the door, while the other takes a seat behind the desk.

I sit in the chair opposite the desk and put my hands on my lap. No sooner have I done this than the officer behind the desk jumps out of his chair.

"UNCROSS YOUR FUCKING LEGS!" he roars. I look down at my legs, the right one resting on the knee of the left, and quickly uncross them.

"Why are you here?" demands the officer.

My hands are shaking now. I steady them on my knees,

mumble something, can't remember which mask I decided to put on.

"Speak up," the officer says.

"I'm here to pick up someone I know. Maj . . . Majdeddin. I received a call earlier."

"How do you know the prisoner?"

"I . . . I went to school with him."

The officer picks up the folder on his desk and pushes it toward me.

"This is your file," he says. "You understand?"

I say nothing. For a moment all three of us are silent. They stare at me and I stare at the folder on the desk. It is black, with papers and documents spilling out of it from all sides. My life, or everything the regime deems relevant about my life, is in that folder. Twenty-seven years of events. What have I done in the last twenty-seven years that would be a cause for punishment? Anything I have ever done could be taken as a threat to the regime, if that's what they wanted to prove. There is nothing I can do except sit and take it, speak logically, and hope that logic might, for once, be enough.

"You used to work for Shami," the officer says.

"Yes. Can I ask why you are questioning me? What crime have I committed?"

"Suspected terrorism."

I laugh. "Excuse me?"

"Shut up!" the officer yells. "You were at the protests."

"Some of them." My mind races through my meager list of friends who might be able to get me out of this, assessing the power each of them might have in case things get nasty. Laura might have enough voice to help, and Basma has an uncle who works for the government . . .

"Why?" the officer asks.

"Huh?"

I've angered him. "Why. Were. You. At. The. Protests?" He

spits each word out as if I have tricked him into eating a bitter almond.

"Everyone was at the protests," I reply.

"I wasn't," he says.

"I wasn't either," the officer by the door chips in.

"I thought it would make the country better," I explain.

"This is what you think?" the officer says with a raised eyebrow.

"I don't know what I think anymore," I say.

The officer pauses for a moment. He reaches across and opens the folder. He picks up the paper at the top of the file and examines it.

"You sent a message to the prisoner this morning, is that correct?"

"I can't remember." The officer pushes the paper toward me. A single sentence is typed at the top of the otherwise empty paper.

My grandmother caught me and Taymour last night. It's all a mess.

"Did you send this?" the officer asks again.

"Look, I'm here to pick up my friend. I've done nothing wrong."

The officer looks bewildered, like he is speaking to a monkey. He turns to his colleague.

"She protests, she sends vague messages to a criminal, then she says she's done nothing wrong." The other officer chuckles.

"I'm sorry," I say. I hate myself as I say this, and I think of what Laura said, about how Arabs kill themselves for the sake of their pride. Fuck my pride. What is my pride worth if I am dead? But this is not about pride, this is about dignity, and I feel myself losing any shred of it. I would like to think I would die for my dignity, but in this room all I am thinking about is how to get out.

The officer takes the paper from my hand and smiles. He

sits back, the folder in his hands, and begins to flip through the papers.

"Four years university in America," he says. "Did you do anything in America?"

"I studied."

"Did America send you to protest?"

"No." I can't help but chuckle. I do not add that we could only be so lucky as to have America on our side.

"But you speak good English, you travel around with foreigners all the time."

"I'm an interpreter."

"What are you interpreting for them? What are you saying?"

"I can assure you, everything that comes out of my mouth are the words of others." I smile as I say this, though I don't know why.

The officer pushes the folder away and looks me in the eye.

"Do you believe in God?" he asks. His cold eyes bore into me, demanding a frank answer.

I swallow, shrug, and hold his gaze. "I'll believe in what you want me to believe in."

Suddenly the mood in the room changes. The air feels lighter somehow, and I know I am safe. The officer sighs, looks at his papers, and shoos me away with his arms, as if I am a waste of his time. The other officer opens the door. I walk out into the waiting room, not sure if I have ever felt so relieved to be deemed pathetic. The Filipina woman is no longer there. The other two people look at me curiously, as if to glimpse their fate in my eyes. I sit back down in one of the blue chairs and wait.

I close my eyes and try to focus on my breathing, in and out. In and out. Sounds drift to my ears: the voice of someone shouting in a room down the hall, the scurrying of cockroaches on the floor by my feet. After what seems like an eternity I open my eyes again and nothing has changed. My thoughts drift to Taymour and being in bed with him, but this gives me no comfort. Today thoughts of Taymour bring to mind Teta's screams, Ahmed's unflinching gaze, the threats of the police officers, and the fear and shame return.

Taymour was right. We have to get out of here. With the brutish thugs of the regime or the head-banging fundamentalism of the opposition, Taymour and I would always be forced to wear masks, to bend and mold ourselves to their image. Teta is only the first of many. Here, Taymour and I will never be anything more than a dirty secret waiting to be uncovered. The only option we have is to get as far away from this damn place as possible.

As soon as the thought enters my mind I push it out again, hide it away in case the hope that thought carries shows on my face. But my mind is working against me now, and as I thrust the thought away more thoughts come. I want to kill the president. I want to plant a bomb and blow up this entire city, watch it burn to the ground. Trying to get rid of these thoughts is pointless, the more I try to avoid thinking them, the more they come to me, each thought more destructive than the last. I can't pollute my mind with these thoughts here. I half expect the security officers, having read my thoughts, to barge in to take me to a dark cell in the basement. I'm going crazy. Really crazy. I close my eyes. When I open them again my eyes fall on the portrait of the president and his son. I quickly shift my gaze. Perhaps someone might not like the way I am looking at them.

The next time the officer comes out of the room he has Maj with him. I stand up as they walk in, but neither the officer nor Maj makes eye contact with me. Maj shuffles to the desk and the officer makes him sign a release form, which Maj signs without reading. When he turns around I notice one of his eyes is swollen shut. His hair clings to his forehead in matted clumps. He has a bruise on his cheek and his bottom lip is puffed up to twice its size. His mascara is streaked down his sunken cheeks. I think of Maj last night, dancing with his arms in the air, triumphant. Now he makes brief eye contact with me before looking back down at his shoes.

The officer shoves Maj toward me and I catch him. The officer wipes his hands on the back of his trousers, as if he has been handling a dirty rag. Looking at Maj up close I can see a crust of blood has formed around one nostril. Holding him by the arm, I walk him outside. Maj winces as we emerge into the midafternoon sun. I give him a bottle of water and he drinks it thirstily. We walk down the road for a few minutes, not saying a word. When we are far enough away that it feels secure to speak, I ask Maj if he's okay. He nods and grabs a cigarette from me, which he places in between his chapped and bloodied lips.

"What happened?" I ask, once we have put the police station at a safe enough distance. I try to lighten the mood. "The last time I saw you, you were grinding against two skinny boys in a Princess Jasmine costume. Was it the cinema?"

"Is it on the news?" he takes a drag of the cigarette and coughs.

"I'm not sure. I heard it through Laura."

"So it will be news." He sighs and runs a hand through his hair.

We walk to where Maj parked his car. People are staring at us, Maj stumbling like a zombie. On our way we pass the cinema where he was arrested. The doors are now boarded up and sealed with red wax, a sign that an immoral crime has been committed. A notice stuck to the red wax reads:

To whom it may concern,
This door has been stamped with red wax enforced from a

decision issued by the presence of a judge dealing with urgent matters in the city. The claim was submitted by Fawzi Basha and founded under claim number 080537 and is enforced for a period of one month from the date above, open to extension. It is prohibited for anyone to remove the red wax from the door without prior review by the court that authorized this decision.

I tell him to go to the hospital but he shakes his head. He hands me his keys and I unlock the car and help him in.

"Is there someone we can tell about this?" I ask.

"Who can we tell? The police?"

"What about documenting your injuries and reporting them to the human rights group you freelance with?"

Maj puts his sunglasses on and lets out a bitter chuckle. "The only purpose those reports serve is to make the West feel better about themselves for selling our regime weapons."

We sit in the car smoking our cigarettes, neither of us in a rush to go anywhere. I am smoking a lot today, but it is only in the act of smoking that the worries subside. My problems take on the form of smoke escaping from inside me and dissipating in the air. But when I stub the cigarette out they are inevitably back, like an endless well of shame and fear, so I must light another one. I am slowly killing myself like this. I have already smoked a pack of cigarettes today.

An angry knock on the car window jolts me back to reality. A clean-shaven man in sunglasses is staring at us. I lower the window.

"*Yalla*," the man grunts. "You can't stay here."

"What do you mean we can't stay here?" I ask him. There is a rudeness in my voice, an attempt to reclaim some of the dignity I lost in the interrogation room.

"I mean," the man huffs, "for security reasons you can't sit in a parked car. Either get out of the car or start driving."

"What kind of security threat do we pose, sitting in a car?" I ask. "We're just having a cigarette before we drive. Do you want me to drive and smoke?"

"Get out of the car if you want a cigarette. You can't stay in a car that isn't moving. New regulations."

"That's okay, we're just about to leave," Maj tells the man.

"Donkey," I mutter, starting the engine. The clock on the dashboard says it's almost four-thirty. Taymour should be getting ready for tonight, with no idea of how my day has gone. Maj leans back into the passenger seat and sighs.

Neither of us wants to go home so we stop at a supermarket and buy an ice pack and some tomato and mortadella. I put the ice pack on Maj's eye, and we eat the tomato and mortadella in the car while drinking Turkish coffee. I watch as Maj slowly wraps a slice of tomato in a piece of mortadella. He winces as the acidity of the tomato touches his lips.

"What did they do to you in there?" I ask.

He shrugs and says nothing. I bite into a slice of mortadella and wash it down with a sip of coffee. I look at Maj's face, trying to read his bruises. A punch in the mouth, definitely. Maybe also another one below his eye. The scrape on his cheek looks like an abrasion, as if he was shoved up against a rough wall or else pushed to the floor. Did they do anything else to him? Was there something else that did not leave a physical mark?

"Did they rape you?" I blurt out.

Maj pauses, then shakes his head, then shrugs. "They roughed us up. Called us names. Satan worshippers. They pulled out my file and showed me the records they had on me . . . what I did for a living. I couldn't tell if they were more angry about my day job or my night job. Anyway, they pushed me around some more. They put us in this concrete room and hosed us down with freezing water. They told us we were dirty perverts and needed cleaning."

I close my eyes as I try to process this. I want to drive back to the station and stab both the officers with the rusty leg of that blue chair they made me sit in. And then I'll kick them really hard. In their kidneys or their balls. Then I remember I have never been in a fight and I feel helpless all over again.

"The water was so cold," Maj says, shaking now. "They stripped us down. They lined us up against the wall. Then these men came behind us. Their hands were so cold. They pulled apart my legs and put something in there." As he speaks I notice something has happened to him. Something I've never seen before. For the first time, I hear shame in his voice and can see it settling in his features. "It felt like an egg. They had such cold hands. And rough too, like sandpaper."

I think of the taxi driver from many years ago. *Your mouth is like sandpaper.* I look at Maj but he does not say any more, his eyes drawn to his fingers as they fold and refold a piece of mortadella.

"Do I have ugly hair?" I ask him suddenly, trying to lighten the mood. "The officer said I had ugly hair."

Maj laughs so hard he chokes on his food. "It's true. I'm sorry, Rasa, but you really have to stop getting haircuts from your grandmother." His black eye, bruised shut, begins to secrete a liquid that looks like a single teardrop.

II.
IMPERIAL DREAMS

I return home at five P.M., gloomy and terribly tired. The door to Teta's bedroom is still shut. By this time she should be lying on the sofa, the remote control resting on her stomach as her faint snores accompany the string of afternoon news programs. But the cushions are pristinely fluffed, the TV is off and cool to the touch. Teta's purse rests on the coffee table. I've grown up thinking of that purse as a treasure chest containing a bounty of gifts—sticks of gum, hard-boiled sweets, thin brown mint-flavoured cigarettes—all hidden among tissue papers so old they disintegrate in your hands. She has never slept this late. Perhaps I have humiliated her to death.

Doris makes me a Nescafé and puts lots of ice in it. Usually I would drink this in front of the television, watching Oprah tell me to live the most honest version of myself. That's how I usually spend these long, hot, boring afternoons with nothing to do but dream of Taymour. But today I take my iced Nescafé to the bathroom. I take off my clothes and hang my underwear on the doorknob to block the view. I've learned my lesson. Let them peer through the keyhole. I call Taymour but he does not pick up, so I send him another message: *We will find a way. We'll find a country where we don't need visas and we can live our lives away from all this* ihbat, *all this depression*. I don't expect a response, but I send it anyway. I'll plant the idea in his mind, and then tonight I'll give him the letter. It will remind him of everything we are fighting for and will convince him to run away with me. Once he sees me, he won't be able to forget what we have. He'll leave it all in a heartbeat.

I sit naked in the empty bathtub and sip my iced Nescafé, smoke Marlboros, and play Candy Crush Saga on my phone. If I win with one star it means that Taymour loves me, and if I win with two it means he will never leave me. If I win with three stars then it means that we will find a way to be together.

I play Candy Crush and dream of America, of a world where no one asks what you're doing and you are free to do what you like, kiss and love whomever you want and be the person you were meant to be. Before I went to America I had thought of it as a place where it didn't matter who you were or where you were from, all that mattered were the ideas in your head.

I was wrong.

"Dreamers from all over the world go to America," Teta had warned. "But the dream is simply bait. America is like a fisherman's hook that can catch you and either cut you up and eat you or, if you are not to its taste, toss you back in the water with a hook-shaped hole in your cheek."

I chose not to listen to her warnings. Even now, as I sit in the empty bathtub with a hook-shaped hole in my cheek, the memory of America's possibilities remains strong.

The decision for me to study in America was made before Baba got sick. With the money he had saved up, Baba made Teta promise that I would get an education abroad. When he died, Teta and I had no source of income. Despite that, she refused to touch the money Baba had saved for my education. She stashed his money in the bank and became a hairdresser for the neighborhood women. Soon enough on every street within a twenty-kilometer radius from our house women began to sport Teta's golden bob. To top off her wages, on Fridays Teta wore her hijab and black abaya and went to the mosque down the road to collect donations, and on Sundays she wore a crucifix and drove to the nearest town. She hid among the churchgoers, stood up and sat down when they did. She knew when to say "Kyrie Eleison," and she even took communion. Then, as the charity box was handed out, she reached in and took her weekly stipend.

Our income was dwindling but our social standing remained the same. We were saved by pity and a sense of obligation. We held our heads high as we watched a new elite emerge, a fresh breed that discussed "construction projects" and "real estate investments" and "import-export initiatives." We were an aging Chevrolet surrounded by brand-new Ferraris racing around the city.

My desire to go to America was compounded by the mythology that surrounded the place. Beyond the television, movies, and books, America was the place where my father and mother fell in love. My father was completing his final year of medical school. Mama was an art history student at the community college. She spent her mornings in class and her afternoons in galleries, sketching in her notepad. In the evenings she went with friends to a French café in the city. That was where she met my father.

He fell in love with her instantly. She was beautiful, with long charcoal hair, large green eyes, and olive skin. Even later, at her worst—sobbing into a pool of blood and broken glass on the living room floor—I could see why my father fought so hard for her.

After six months of stalking and pleading, my mother agreed to meet my father for a coffee. He won her over on that first date. Six months later, Baba found the courage to bring her home to meet Teta. When my father first came back, with my mother at his side, Teta could not have been happier that he had found an Arab woman in America.

"What was she doing in America?" Teta asked her son, eyeing my mother with a forced smile on her face.

Baba explained that Mama's family moved there when the president took power.

"My father did not even wait for the president to come to power," Mama corrected him. "At the first sign of disturbance he packed up the house and left."

Teta narrowed her eyes disapprovingly. "Why are you so proud that your family ran away so quickly? And so you grew up in America, yes? That's not the right environment to raise a girl. In any case, you get married *here*. You live *here*."

Mama's parents did not take kindly to this news.

"After all the mess we went through to leave, you want to go back?" her father screamed on the phone from thousands of miles away.

"But I love him," Mama said defiantly.

"You love him more than you love your own freedom?"

But my young parents were of the idealistic generation that saw potential wherever they looked, and they returned hand in hand to build a new pan-Arab nation.

It rained the night Teta dropped me off at the airport. I hugged her and sensed that she was holding back tears. We had never been apart for longer than a few hours, and the prospect of not seeing each other for a year felt like the end of the world. We both knew that once I boarded that plane something was going to change inside of me, the boy who hugged her goodbye would be gone forever, and neither of us had any idea of the man who would take his place.

"Call me as soon you arrive" was all she could say. I tried to ignore the tears that hung behind her every word, knowing that if I thought too much about them they would trigger my own, and I wanted to be a man, a real *zalameh* with no emotions. As I walked through the terminal Teta waved until she was just a speck in an ocean of people. When I could no longer see her I ran to the bathroom and burst into uncontrollable sobs. I did not stop crying until I fell asleep on the plane, when I was exhausted and felt there were no more tears left to come out.

The immigration queue was long. I stood in line with my papers in hand, letters from the university, bank account statements, visas, and immigration forms that Teta and I had neatly filed in a color-coded folder. I made it through after the sun had set, and took the airport shuttle bus downtown, followed by the train to my new home, a student residence on the west side of the campus, a high-rise brown brick tower with curved façades and vaulted archways.

In the winding halls, students were laughing and talking in strange accents I had only ever heard on television, the walls so thin it was as if they were in my room. I had nothing with me except a suitcase of clothes, mental images of American college campuses that I gleaned from movies, and my expansive collection of Now That's What I Call Music! CDs. Having grown up on its television and books, America was a part of who I was before I even set foot there, but the reality of America was grittier and more alien than I had imagined it to be. My boxlike room on the ninth floor was empty except for a hard bed, a wooden desk, and a lightbulb that hung from a sad-looking plastic cord. I pulled up the blinds to take in the view. The glowing lights of the city extended far out to the horizon, and just below I could see the leafy courtyard, the freshly watered grass shimmering under the light of the streetlamps.

I had thought that by setting foot in America I would immediately transform into someone else, like one of those people on television, and I was saddened by the realization that I was still the same person here as I was back home.

I dropped my suitcase on the bare mattress and called Teta. Her voice seemed far away, it was as if she was speaking to me from another world.

"*Hamdullah*, Teta, the trip was very smooth, very easy . . .

The subway wasn't too expensive . . . No, I didn't have to bargain, they have the prices on the wall . . . Yes, it's very organized, you know, there's even a shuttle bus from the airport that's free if you show them your boarding pass, and as soon as I arrived at the university I registered and they gave me the keys . . . No, just a deposit . . . Yes, it's fine, I paid with the cash you gave me . . . They gave me a receipt, yes . . . Of course, first thing tomorrow I will go buy a good coat, I promise . . . My room is very nice, I have everything I could want really . . . a bed and a desk and a closet with coat hangers . . . There's a lightbulb . . . I'm very excited."

There was a silence.

"The apartment feels very empty," Teta whispered.

The tears came and there was nothing I could do about it. "I want to come back," I sobbed into the phone.

"Be a man, Rasa. Don't you want to make your father proud?"

Yes, yes, I did. But in coming to America I had another goal in mind: to explore this unknown world of gayness, to observe it and try it on for size and see if it really was for me. I had arrived in America as me, but I was determined to transform into something better, like someone from the television, and in that first week I studied and observed this new world: the girls in tiny shorts parading down leafy streets, punks with piercings and tattoos and rainbow-colored hair checking out dusty vinyl records in second-hand shops, burly frat boys drinking gallons of beer on couches perched on front yards, with barbecue grills so large they could cook a human body. I studied the rules, customs, organisation, precision, I observed with a degree of excited trepidation the gluttonous celebration that existed within it all, and as soon as I could I bought myself a George Michael poster and hung it above my bed to remind me of the real reason I was here.

The money Baba had left us was enough to get me to

America but not enough to keep me there, so my first objective was to get a job. The university library was hiring, so the day before school began I walked into the large, menacing limestone building and handed my application to the head librarian, a bald man with a beach-ball belly.

"You don't have any previous work experience," he said as his eyes scanned my application. "No work in high school?"

I shook my head.

He looked up from my application and pursed his lips. "You're foreign aren't you?"

I nodded.

"Well . . . we do have a quota to fill . . . "

The next morning I found myself in the basement, two floors underground, shelving volumes of art history journals dating back to the late nineteenth century. The job was menial but required concentration. The head librarian had warned that a misplaced volume might never be found again, and the fear of forever losing something so old, weighted with history and memory, meant that I took longer than most to shelve the stacks of books. The bookshelves in the basement, particularly the old and disused periodical shelves, were so dusty I had to take regular breaks to wash my hands and eyes. Occasionally I flipped through them, feeling their brittle pages worn down by the years and the students who had consumed their knowledge.

I emerged from the library by midafternoon as if from a deep tomb. I squinted in the sunlight. The campus was deserted. I walked to my afternoon class as a peculiar disquiet settled around me. The class was empty. On the chalkboard someone had scribbled a note in white chalk.

DUE TO TODAY'S EVENTS THIS AFTERNOON'S CLASS HAS BEEN CANCELED

I walked across the empty campus back to my dorm, my mind deep in thought about whether I would have the courage to attempt the washing machine in the basement laundry room. I was so dazed from the hours of shelving books that I nearly walked straight into the chunky girl who lived in the room next door. She had pale skin, jet-black hair, and a ring that looped through her nostrils. I could almost hear Teta whisper in my ear, "Ring through the nose, like a cow."

"I'm sorry," I mumbled, taking a step back. Her eyes were red and wet. "Are you okay? What happened?"

"What do you mean what happened?" The girl sniffed. She looked at my confused face and let out a surprised guffaw. "You really don't know what happened? Oh my God. You of all people should know."

Another person who lived down the hall from us, a wiry guy with black nail polish, came up behind her and wrapped his arms around her. I watched as they held each other in silence, his chin nestled in the corner of her neck, thinking to myself that I had never seen a man wear nail polish before. What would people say?

After a few minutes they were still holding each other. I became bored so I headed toward the common room. A crowd had gathered around the television watching the news. Footage of smoke and fire, only a few seconds long but shown on a loop. I watched it about six or seven times. No one spoke. I went into my room and phoned Teta.

"Maybe you should come back," she suggested softly, her voice faraway and afraid.

"Why would I come back?"

There was a knock on my door. A girl popped her head into my room. She had long blond hair like in the movies.

"I'm collecting blood donations for the victims of the attacks. Would you be up for donating blood?" she garbled through her braces.

"No," I said. She flashed me an awkward smile and shut the door behind her.

"What are you doing?" Teta screamed from the other side of the phone. "Make up an excuse if you don't want to donate! Don't just say no! They'll think you're a terrorist."

"People here aren't like that."

Another knock on my door. It was the girl again.

"Look," she said, "I just want you to know that no one blames you for what happened."

Unsure how to respond, I nodded and thanked her. She gave an apologetic smile and left.

"Listen to me, boy," Teta said on the line. "If you feel something is not right you come back immediately, okay?"

"What do you mean 'not right'?" I asked. Everything felt not right.

I did not leave my room for the rest of the day. That night I dreamed the police came to get me. I heard the sirens blaring through my bedroom window, the flashing red-and-blue floodlights lighting up my dark room. The girl with the blond hair and braces flung open the door and pointed to my cowering figure in bed. "That's the one," she cackled, her silver teeth like knives in her mouth. Policemen with large machine guns burst through the door and dragged me away. They threw me in a giant barbecue in the front yard of one of the frat houses. The hot coals burned my skin. Frat boys surrounded the barbecue. They watched me burn and chanted the college football anthem as they cheered one another with red plastic cups full of beer.

In the morning I woke up with a fever. I stumbled to the dining hall for breakfast, my bones aching. The mood in the hall was somber, the few people who were there walked like zombies through the hall. Avoiding eye contact, I grabbed a green tray and headed toward the food shimmering under the halogen lights. Limp fried cubes of potato, sickly yellow scrambled eggs, oily pink bacon. My stomach lurched. I dropped my tray and scurried back to bed.

I woke up in the late afternoon with a pounding headache. My forehead was still burning but I did not want to go to the doctor. Instead I headed to the campus pharmacy and walked through the aisles aimlessly, not recognizing the packaging of all the products, a million options for the same thing. I turned to the cashier, a pasty-skinned man with a pencil mustache.

"Do you sell any antibiotics?" I struggled to get the words out.

"You'll need a prescription for that," he said, not looking up from the crossword puzzle he was doing.

"Do you have *any* medicine?" I asked. "I've got a fever, sore throat, headache . . . "

He sighed, reached behind the counter, and dropped a series of different-colored boxes in front of me. Without looking at them I bought them all, spending two weeks of my allowance, but it was worth it to not be in there one more moment trying to choose between thousands of products all claiming to address the same ailments. I returned to my room and swallowed a combination of the pills and went back to bed, only to wake up an hour later and vomit it all.

The next morning, feeling even worse, I finally went to the campus clinic.

"You have the flu," the nurse said. "Go back home and get some rest, honey."

"What flu?"

"*The* flu."

"Is it serious?"

"Get some rest and drink lots of fluids. If you're not better in a couple of days come back and see me."

"Listen," I rubbed my face. This was a terrible dream I was in. "I've never felt this bad in my life. I think I'm dying. If you'll just prescribe me some antibiotics—"

"You don't get antibiotics for the flu." She chuckled, drawing out each syllable in the word *antibiotics*. "Besides, we don't just hand them out willy-nilly. Humans will build a resistance to them and soon we'll need truckloads of that stuff to cure a paper cut."

"But I'm sick now," I said. This was not the time for a biology lesson. "I'm not asking you for willy-nilly, I'm only asking for one prescription for a few days."

"If you're not feeling better in a few days, come back. Bye."

She was right of course, and after sweating through my first experience of the American flu, I emerged from my room fully recovered three days later. Stepping into the cafeteria for breakfast, the eyes of the other students followed me as I piled food on my plate. Something was different.

Over the next few weeks there were rumors of Arabs and Muslims being taken away for questioning and then deported. Headlines appeared in campus newspapers, stories of Muslims chased off campus by rowdy students. I looked at my dark skin, watched the worried glances whenever I rolled the *r* in my name during class. For so long I had felt different from everyone else. Now I was lumped together with an anonymous mass. An Arab. A Muslim. I was one of "them."

"You're from the Middle East? Super jealous," remarked a girl in one of my classes. "Your life must have been so interesting."

"It wasn't, really."

"I grew up in Ohio," she said by way of explanation. "We don't have war and politics and all that stuff. Where you grew up must have been ten times more interesting than where I grew up."

Those first three months in America I did nothing more than go straight to class and then straight back home. On some days I worked shifts in the library shelving books, and in the evenings I tried to make sense of how others reacted to me. I began to understand events in my life as plot points in a narrative of war and oppression, painted across my history with the brushstrokes of innocently asked questions and pointed statements. Why do *you* force women to wear the hijab? Why is *your* culture consumed with hate? Why do *you* produce terrorists? Do *you* wear Jesus sandals? Why? Was it an Islam thing? Was it because *you* didn't have freedom or was it because *you* hated freedom? And why did *you* hate women so much? Why did *you* do this to *us*, they asked. Why do *you* hate us, they lamented. Why why why?

Like piranhas in the water the questions picked me apart, picked "us" apart. In the evenings, exhausted with these questions, I sat in front of the television in the common room and watched pundits scream at one another as they discussed my home in ways I had never heard of, as if squabbling over puzzle pieces while looking at the wrong picture.

Oftentimes I would not be able to handle the television for very long, choosing to pace my tiny dorm room as fuzzy thoughts somersaulted in my head like the linty tumble dryers in the basement. I was terrified to set foot outside lest someone ask one of their questions. I tiptoed everywhere, lost in my thoughts. This *Arabness*. This *Muslimness*. This was all new. A new marker of difference. A "thing" I had been my whole life. A thing to which I had previously not given a second thought. But this was not just any old thing. No. This was a thing that killed and maimed and destroyed. I was no longer someone with thoughts and dreams and secrets. I was the by-product of an oppressive culture, an ambassador of a people at war with civilization.

I had come to America preparing myself to be like a character on those television shows. I was going to be Blossom's best buddy. I was going to have a coffee-shop gang like in *Friends*. More than that, America was going to offer me the space to examine myself in something clearer than the foggy mirrors in Teta's bathroom. At the very least, I had hoped America would give me the space to set free the birds in the cage in my mind, to sift through the memories of taxi drivers and POLSKASAT images that I had been diligently filing away. But I was instead confronted with something completely new: my Arabness. I wanted to scrub my skin off, my name off, my accent off, anything to deflect the suspicious looks.

The secret cage in my mind remained locked. I watched as men held hands on campus and students discussed their sexual escapades with ease, and felt even farther away from them than I had felt when I was a young boy watching George Michael on television.

Stuck in my head, I paced around my tiny room, listening to the drunken laughter of the other students in the halls outside. I thought about my life, digging through my roots to understand the way my branches grew. My Arabness, this new identity foisted upon me. Was that also kept hidden from me, like my father's death and the whereabouts of my mother? Was there more to being Muslim than I had been told?

One evening, walking home from the library, I passed a homeless man sitting on a corner. The man was dressed in black jeans and a dark blue hoodie. He had long, straggly black hair and an unkempt beard.

"Got any spare change, buddy?" the guy asked.

I reached into my pocket and handed him a few dollars.

"Bless you, my man."

"You're welcome," I said, beginning to walk away.

"Where's your accent from?" the man called out.

"Not from here," I said.

"Hey, hey, I get it. We're on the same dance floor, baby."

On the rest of the walk home I thought hard about the differences between home and America. One of the most obvious ones was that at home I spent months visiting and revisiting the video store down the road from Teta's house, checking to see if pirated copies of the latest Hollywood movie had arrived. Those movies secretly filmed in a cinema far away. The shaky footage often had people getting up and walking across the screen right when the action would begin. In America, cinemas screened complete, uncensored, up-to-date movies. Instead of just reading the reviews I could actually go and watch the movie.

Here, the television beamed the latest episodes of all my favorite shows straight into our dorm's common room. There were hundreds of channels, with clear schedules that never changed. All the comedy shows you could dream of were only a click away. Back home I had spent countless summers fiddling with the antenna of the television set, hoping to catch a glimpse of Miss Universe competitions so that Doris and I could cheer for Miss Philippines, and even when I was lucky to have stumbled onto Omar's games room, the episodes aired were still at least six months behind the real thing.

But perhaps best of all, in America there were books. Shelves and shelves of them. Any book you could ever dream of! All at the tip of your fingers. No more begging visitors from abroad for obscure books, or obsessively scanning the four shelves of English books in the bookstore downtown.

And it was the books that helped me understand. By the end of my first year I had read all of Amin Maalouf and Karl Marx and Partha Chatterjee and Edward Said. If America and my part-time library job gave me anything, it was the solitude to explore these texts, interrupted only by the odd student looking for coursework or needing to check out a book.

The first time I read Marx felt like the first time I watched POLSKASAT. Marx was a taboo I had heard about but never had access to, and reading his words stirred new parts of me I didn't know existed. Reading the first lines of *The Communist*

Manifesto, the imagery and assuredness of Marx's voice spoke to me in a way that other authoritative texts had not.

Maalouf spoke of identity as malleable and subject to the whims of society. According to him, an individual identified most strongly with the aspect of their identity that was under attack, and indeed in America it was not my gayness but my Arabness that was abject. Edward Said taught me how to think. His writings were compassionate and honest, patient and powerful. His words conveyed the intensity of an intellectual who had dedicated his life to speaking on behalf of the underdog and unmasking the deceptions of oppressors, like a vigilante opening the back door to a magician's cruel tricks.

Chatterjee made the theories of some Western writers seem like the wild ideas of a science-fiction story presenting fantasylands as if they were fact. The identity of a nation, what was that if not Western imagination exported to the colonial world? If so, what is left for us to imagine? If the students I encountered imagined a fantasy world where we hate with all our hearts and have dedicated our lives to terror, what is the alternative to such an illusion?

In the past I had worried that with the option of being happily married denied to me I might not have a reason for living. And now, confronted with my American isolation, I felt very close to nonexistence. With no one to speak to me of familiar things, there was nothing to stop me from sinking into a bottomless well of loneliness. Yet to have come upon these powerful ideas was like having a group of mentors guiding me out of my despair.

With my nose in dusty old books, memories returned. I recalled dinner parties my parents held in our living room when I was seven. For a year these parties were a weekly occurrence, bringing together artists, writers, and intellectuals— doctors from the hospital where my father worked as well as university professors and journalists. In the late afternoon

Mama would begin to prepare food as Baba lit candles dotted around our house. Our living room was all deep reds and browns and golds, the centerpiece a giant Persian carpet that boasted symmetrical patterns of flowers and branches. Guests would arrive just as the sun would begin to set. They'd sit on pillows around our mahogany coffee table, smoking cigarettes, sipping arrack, and munching on roasted mixed nuts from bowls placed around the room.

On those nights I would be called to greet our guests and then quickly retire, either to my bedroom or to keep Doris company in the kitchen. A dizzying concoction of smells and sounds, fried sausages and pastries stuffed with cheese and spinach, alongside the fragrance of perfume, whisky, and shisha, and the sounds of boisterous laughter and debate and the music of Pink Floyd, Samira Tawfik, and Abdel Halim all wafted in from the living room. I was occasionally invited to sit with the guests for some time. I would squeeze myself between the warm bodies of my mother and father on our brown leather couch, and pick out the roasted almonds from the bowls of mixed nuts until my father scolded me with a quiet stare for not leaving any for everyone else.

I recall one night six of them were furiously debating under a cloud of smoke. At the time what they were saying meant nothing to me, they were simply words thrown around above my head, but through my readings in America my memory of those words began to form thoughts and ideas, and I started to understand the world of my mother and father. It was after the Berlin Wall had fallen, and Mohammad, one of my parents' friends who worked with an international company, was laughing at another friend, Nadeem, the head of the lawyers' syndicate.

"Oh Nadeem-o!" Mohammad sang as he threw a handful of mixed nuts in his mouth. "Where are your Soviet friends now to come save you? You realize this is the beginning of the end, don't you? Capitalism has triumphed."

Nadeem scoffed and made noises about Western imperialism and the evils of the free market. Sima, a journalist with thick curly hair and smoky eyes, nodded her head as she sucked on a shisha that Baba ensured was never without fresh coals. "Arabs should not settle for being a citizen of some imaginary country the colonizers have set up on make-believe borders," she said. "After all, we are all one Arab people."

"And what do you propose we do with the non-Arabs in our region?" Nadeem asked. "Burn them at the stake? No, no, the solution is socialism."

"You are all looking outside for solutions," interjected Hassan, an old friend of my father's who had kinky black hair and wore a pince-nez on the bridge of his rounded nose. "The answer is within."

"And what are you suggesting exactly?" Sima asked, blowing so much smoke through her mouth that for a few moments her head disappeared behind the white cloud.

Hassan took a sip of his dark red tea. A piece of wet mint stuck to the top of his beard, and he sucked it into his mouth. "We were Muslims before we were Arabs. Our true path is to follow the teachings of the Prophet, to live as he did and re-create the *umma*."

"*Ya*, Hassan, *ya habibi*." Sima jumped in. "You work in the oil fields for a few years and you come home wanting to drag us back to the seventh century. Drink some arrack and relax."

Hassan laughed and raised his glass. "Enjoy it on my behalf, sister. I'm happy with my tea."

My father spoke up. "Fundamentally, the primary affiliation of the Arab is his family, his tribe, his community. Yes, we can speak of one shared Arab culture. But family is the core of who we are as a people. Without his family, an Arab is nothing."

Throughout this discussion I would gaze at my mother's large glistening eyes as she took it all in, smiling, her glass never far from her lips, only moving so she could take a drag from her cigarette. Mama drank a lot on those nights, sometimes so much that she would remain seated until the guests all left, when Baba would have to help her up and walk her to bed. I look back at that time as one of the happiest periods in my life, and I would fall asleep blanketed in the sounds and smells of those parties that continued well into the night. But then a knock on our door one morning by two men from the government put a stop to those parties. The only thing that remained of them was my mother's glass, which never again strayed too far from her lips.

And so what did it mean to be Arab now, under America's harsh gaze? What is Arab or Muslim if not a fabrication, one invented and reinvented by politicians who engineered meaning behind these words to suit their history. The American pundits screaming at each other on television seemed only too happy to play along in constructing this fiction.

I knew a lot about lies and fabrications. I saw the insidious intentions behind the white lies told in the shared histories of both my country and my family. I thought of an incident two decades earlier, when a group of rebels attempted to overthrow the president's regime and install a socialist government. The revolt was quickly crushed and, to push his point home, the president massacred the rebels' families in the centre of town.

Of course, if you want to read up on this incident you will not find it easy to do. It won't appear in history books or school curricula. The event exists only in the minds of the surviving family members of the rebels, thought of but never spoken about. In class we were taught with texts that glorified small, ancient victories that happened hundreds of years ago. The chink in the armor of the regime was erased from history. To speak of the rebellion—no, even to think of it—was a great betrayal, not just of the president but of the nation.

Teta ran our house much like the president ran the country. She had a tight-fisted control over memory, liberally erasing the past to control the present. It was no coincidence that Mama's photographs were taken down from the walls of the house when she left, replaced with even more photos of Baba. The few times I asked about my mother, Teta would take a deep breath and turn her head in the other direction. I would be punished by hours of cold silence. Soon enough, to bring up Mama, even so much as mention her name, was equivalent to staging a coup. It was a betrayal of Teta and most of all of Baba.

The solitude of America and the books it contained helped me uncover the secret to the hegemony of both the president and Teta. I explored my newfound freedom by finally thinking about my mother. I tried to uncover what had happened in those first eleven years of my life, bringing any memories I could muster to the surface to subvert Teta's rule.

I remembered Mama telling me that when they returned from America, Teta insisted that Mama and Baba live in separate houses until they married. Mama was given the guest room, and Baba was sent to live with the neighbors. Mama moved in, set up her art supplies in the corner of a room, and began to paint. She saw the world as if new, and Baba, who fell in love with the ways in which Mama saw the country, took her to the villages to meet with the farmers and the women who embroider traditional clothes. She painted them working in the fields, surrounded by orange trees and braying brown donkeys.

At first, Mama's arrival filled my grandmother with excitement. Teta set about moulding her into the high-society woman she imagined her son should wed. In the mornings, after Teta checked my mother's bedsheets for blood—to make sure Baba had not snuck in at night—she invited the neighbourhood's best women for *subhiyeh*. But my mother didn't care about any of that.

"We'll set up a clinic in al-Sharqiyeh, and maybe a few in the villages," she explained to Teta one afternoon, before turning to my father. "You'll treat people, for free of course, and I will teach the children art."

"Let everyone be responsible for their own liberation, *hayati*," Teta replied. She turned to my father. "There's a new private hospital that has opened up on the way to the airport. I play cards with the general manager's wife. I'll have a word with her."

And so she did, and so my father worked in the private hospital. "Just for a few years," he explained to my mother. "Save for our own house, and then invest in the clinics."

My father worked night shifts, then he worked day shifts, and soon enough he worked both on the same day. And the money came pouring in and it was just my mother going to the villages and to al-Sharqiyeh. But this remained unacceptable to Teta. She was not going to see her future daughter-in-law painting with street children in the slums.

"This isn't America, *habibti*," she would say. "You can't walk around like you're Mother Teresa. People talk here."

But if my mother understood this, she was not concerned. The dresses Teta bought for her hung unworn in my mother's closet. And each time she slipped into those paint-stained jeans, my grandmother's resolve only strengthened. The family's standing was on the line, Teta warned my father. "Be careful. You only have one life, one reputation. Don't make a mess of it." And if Mama had no intention of becoming a good wife, then Teta would shame her into being one.

"You are not ironing along the lines, *ya binti*. What's the point of ironing if you are not following the creases? Anyway what does this old woman know? Maybe wrinkled clothes are in fashion. I'll just shut up. Do it as you like, *habibti*."

That was how it became. "I don't mean to interfere, but . . . I wouldn't think of cleaning it like that, but . . . I suppose if that's how you want to be dressed . . . But maybe I'm the stupid one . . . I'm the donkey . . . Maybe I'm the one who doesn't understand . . . Do it however you like, *habibti* . . . I'll just shut up, it's better." And so on.

On the morning of my parents' wedding Teta burst into my mother's room to find an empty bed. Frantic, she called up my father.

"Your wife has run away," she said, near tears. "The girls are coming in a few hours to begin preparations and she's run away!"

Baba assured her that Mama must have gone out to do some last-minute errands, or else needed a few hours to reflect. Teta, terrified of my mother never returning but desperate not to tell anyone about this embarrassment, paced the living room, drinking coffee, smoking cigarettes, and tutting to herself.

My mother returned by midday, an hour before the celebrations were to begin. Teta heard her before she saw her, for there was loud drumming and singing coming from down the road. Peering out the window she saw my mother, riding on the back of a donkey, surrounded by a procession of Gypsies who roamed the empty plots of land by the airport road. The Gypsy women were trilling and dancing barefoot, while the men banged on animal-skin tablas and sang wedding folk songs. They pulled up in front of Teta's house and stood there, dancing and singing. Teta watched them from behind the curtains, shamed and furious.

After the wedding, my mother begged my father to use his savings for the new house he had promised her, so they would be out of Teta's grip.

"What do you mean buy another house?" Teta snapped when Baba raised the idea. "Don't waste your money. Save it for your child and just build another floor here."

And before she had even finished her sentence, Teta was on

the phone to a construction company to make plans. When the extra floor was complete, that was where Mama and Baba moved. This allowed Teta to keep a watchful eye on Mama, and every morning Teta let herself in, carrying a pot of food she had cooked the night before.

"Your cooking is fine, *habibti*, but my son is very picky, you know. He prefers his food to have flavour."

The battle lines were finally drawn over my name. Mama wanted to call me Rasa. Teta, perhaps out of spite, insisted that I be called anything but.

"I like it," my mother said. And for once, my mother did not need to explain herself. Being pregnant with me, she had the upper hand.

"I just told her I would keep you inside me until I got my way," Mama explained, a triumphant smile on her face, as she stroked my back in bed one evening.

I was born the day after Valentine's Day. When she first saw me, Teta took one look and burst into tears.

"*Allahu Akbar!* He looks just like his father." Teta kissed the hospital-room floor. She clutched her chest and turned to my mother. "You see I was so scared, *habibti*. Not that he would turn out like your side, but, you know . . . "

It didn't stop at my name, and the fact that Teta had been defeated on such a crucial battlefield only increased her resolve.

"You stopped breast-feeding him? He's only two. I breast-fed my son until he was four, you know."

"Please let me do it my way."

"Fine, fine, I'll shut my mouth. Maybe *I'm* the one who doesn't understand," and as Teta walked away she would mutter, just loud enough for my mother to hear, "Her breasts are too precious for her own son. That's why he cries whenever she's around."

When I was three Mama caught Teta struggling to stick

almonds up my ass to relieve me of constipation. (As I recall it now, I wonder whether the almonds played a part in my desire for men.)

"What the hell are you doing?" my mother said, snatching me from Teta's arms.

"Two days and nothing has come out," Teta muttered, picking up another almond.

"That's not how you treat constipation," Mama snapped, pulling my trousers back up. "And I told you to stop smoking next to him. His clothes are covered in ashes."

"What do I know, anyway? After all, I raised your husband and look who he ended up marrying."

By the time I was four the primary battle was over language. Teta only ever spoke to me in Arabic. Mama insisted on speaking English to me, because she said it was the language of power. So I spoke both, navigating the two languages like a combat zone.

"Where are you going?" my mother would ask.

"To school," I'd say.

"Say it in Arabic," Teta would bark.

"To al-school," I would reply.

As I grew older, I became frustrated with my mother's heavily accented English, which jarred with the accents I heard on television. "Snake" became "essnake," "orange juice" became "oranjuice," "mirror" became "mirrow."

"There is no *e* at the beginning of snake," I recall telling her once. I tried to get her to say it without the *e*. She humoured me, repeating "snake" over and over, but she could not rid herself of that *e*.

At the time, I despaired. Why couldn't she say it like the television mothers do? Why must that vulgar accent remain? It was disgusting, that treacherous *e* at the beginning of the word. My mother, who had spent more than half her life in America, was still somehow unable to be truly American. She was a half-formed thing, a freak and an outsider, neither American nor Arab, stuck somewhere in between. I wanted nothing more than for our family to be normal, and even in her pronunciations my mother was adamant in keeping us different. But now that I was in America, where the *s* hissed with ease from the mouths of everyone I met, the perfection of it so sterile, I longed for that unwelcome *e* in all its vulgarity.

By this point, memories of Mama were hazy in my mind. They were like old photographs that had yellowed and faded over time. And yet, slowly, forgotten memories floated to my consciousness as I began to search for them. That first year in America I would go to bed in the evening, my mind racing with ideas of Arabs and Islam, feeling an alienation that struck to my very core, and in my dreams I would reach for memories of the one true outsider in our family, and hear the distant voice of my mother begging my father: "This is not what we agreed. Talk to her. Please."

"What do you want me to do? She's my mother—"

"I'm your wife!"

"She's only trying to help," I would hear my father say, before he returned to work, or turned the television on, or prepared the coals for his shisha.

Whether I was recalling events that really happened or simply making up history as I went along, all I could do was weave the memories together into a story, to build a nation of Mama inside me.

For months I searched for my mother in phone books and on the Internet. Although I was not certain she was in America, the resurgence of my mother, if only in my memories, made me believe that she was closer to me somehow, if not in geography then perhaps in spirit. Despite my searches, there was nothing conclusive to draw upon. Did she not want to be found? And even if I did find her, I would arrive as this confused mess of a boy, with stupid questions about Arabs and

Islam. Would her own freakishness console me or only drive me even further outside the norm?

In that first year in America I did have a brief respite from my isolation. After spring break I met two pre-med students at the library. The girls were from Tennessee, and almost every day for a month I spent many hours in their dorm room as they played Southern gospel music at a deafening volume. I clapped and sang along with them, not knowing the words but open to learning, an eager smile on my face. Quite simply, I was happy to be invited to a party for the first time. One day I casually remarked that they looked like Venus and Serena Williams. They gave me a long lecture about American racism, about slavery and Martin Luther King and the struggle of civil rights in America. Then they stopped inviting me to their dorm room. I was left with a feeling that race in America was a story passed on through generations. I also began to understand that now I was inevitably a new chapter in this story, although as of yet I did not have a Martin Luther King to help me field off the stereotypes and lies about my race and religion that were being formulated before my eyes.

I thought of Islam. Although our family did not have time for religion, Baba discovered God in his cancer. Before he became too sick to go anywhere, he took me along to Friday prayers. I went with Baba and we prayed. We took our cue from the row of men in front of us, the new ritual fascinating in its oddness. When they knelt, we knelt; when they crossed their arms, so did we.

But then the strange feelings appeared. I watched the broad backs of the men as they knelt in front of me, their backsides inches from my face. As thoughts of the men infiltrated my brain, I fought with myself. God can't catch me thinking these thoughts in his house, I remembered thinking. I had closed my eyes and focused on being in the present moment, to be one with God. But the temptation to open my eyes, to catch one more glimpse of the men's bodies, snatched my focus away soon enough.

When Baba died so too did that brief foray into the mosque, and for that I was thankful. I couldn't face having to deal with the confused feelings I had. And it was tedious, the public spectacle of communal prayer. There was nothing to stop my mind running off to admire the mass of bodies in front of me. And in the end all I took away from it was the memory of the sight and smell of the men's bodies that surrounded me. I tucked the memories away in my secret cage and continued to beg for God's mercy.

By the end of my first year at university, aided by long periods of self-reflection amid the library's dusty shelves, it dawned on me that maybe Islam was the source of the contradictions I felt inside. Not just Islam but religion as a whole. After hours of doing exercises to rid myself of the limpness in my wrists, after years of late-night prayers furiously demanding, negotiating, and then pleading with God to make me fall in love with women, he failed me. They all failed me. So I turned to Marx.

I came back after my first year in America to find that a barrier had formed between Teta and me, like film on Turkish coffee. I immediately informed her that I had ceased to believe in God and declared myself a communist.

"If you don't believe in God then you can't eat any more kaak during Eid," she threatened.

"If I can't have any kaak I will spit on the Quran," I threatened back.

I didn't budge. All the anger and betrayal I felt was put into the class struggle. I insisted Doris needed to have one day off to leave the house.

"One whole day every week," I insisted during that warring hot summer.

"What else? Would you also like the girl to sit at the head of the table during lunch?"

"I'm sick of 'the girl this' and 'the Filipino that.' For God's sake, you talk about her as if she were some kind of slave that doesn't deserve even the most basic labor rights."

I also brazenly taped an old photograph of my mother on the wall above my bed. Teta did not allow any pictures of her, and I had secretly held on to that photo for years. Throughout high school I had kept it hidden in a shoe box under my bed. Occasionally I would take the photograph out to examine it. The photo was old, taken in the eighties, and the colors had yellowed over time. Growing up, I had looked at that photo many times, at least once a week but usually every two or three days. I had always been so careful with it, keeping it out of the light and regularly wiping off any dust that might gather on it. But more than that, I was careful not to gaze at the photograph for too long, even if I wanted to, because I didn't want the photo to lose its power.

In the photograph I am wearing a straw hat and sitting on my mother's lap. I am happy, my finger in my mouth, giggling, showing off my few teeth. My mother's lips are pursed, her fingers positioned like claws around my sides, as if she might be tickling me. Her lips were large and juicy, and her kisses were desperate and wet. When my mother closed in on me and covered me in kisses, tickling me with her mouth, I would howl with laughter. Her lips looked like they might be painted on, accentuated, but as far as I can remember she never wore lipstick. In the photograph she is wearing large dark sunglasses so I'm not able to see her eyes but I remember them very clearly, because they are my own. When I look in the mirror and see my sad face, the big green eyes staring back at me are my mother's, and I feel sad all over again.

My mother only wore make-up around her eyes, black kohl that accentuated the greenness. I remember this because when

I was eight, Mama returned from one of her trips to al-Sharqiyeh earlier than I had expected. Usually she would be back by midafternoon, and I would spend the hour before waiting by the door like a puppy. If she was ever late I would pace the living room worrying that I had lost her. But then I would hear her keys jingle as she approached the front door, and I would run into my room so she would not know I had been waiting for her.

That day she came home earlier than usual, heavy on her legs, carrying four or five canvases wrapped in clear plastic. I was lying on the sofa watching television, and as I turned to look at her, she lifted her head. The kohl was all messy around her eyes, like a raccoon, wild and dangerous. She glanced at me and then quickly looked away, dropping her bag and keys on the floor and running into her bedroom, slamming the door behind her.

When Baba came home a few hours later, I followed him as he opened the bedroom door to find my mother, a large bump curled under the white sheets.

"What's going on?" he asked.

"I can't take it here anymore," she said from under the sheets. "You can't walk down the street without bumping into a religious nut or an authoritarian one."

Baba was quiet for a moment. He motioned for me to leave, but I ignored him. He leaned in to her and whispered, "I can smell the drink on you. What happened?"

My mother pulled the sheets away and sat up in bed.

"I took some of the paintings to be exhibited in the art space. A few men came in and pointed to that one I did of two women picking olives in a field. They said it showed the women uncovered. Uncovered! They said it was *haram*, that I painted their hair with sexually suggestive brushstrokes and I'm devaluing their women. For God's sake I've been painting al-Sharqiyeh and the villages for years. No one has ever said anything about *haram*. How can something suddenly be *haram* when I did that painting ten years ago? But what could I say? I just took my stuff and left."

"Good for you," Teta's voice boomed from behind us. She had appeared seemingly from nowhere. "When you play with stray dogs, don't be surprised when they bite."

"Mama, please," my father began.

"No please, no nothing. Her emotions come too easily, *ya ibni*," Teta interrupted. If there was one thing my grandmother despised more than my mother's sentimentality, it was my father's attempts to, if not understand her moods, then at the very least console her. "It was fine when you were young and had dreams of saving the world, but you've got the boy now. It's time to stop the painting nonsense." She turned around and left the room.

Teta's casual mention of me, "the boy," filled me to the core with a heavy guilt. I was partly responsible for my mother's slow unraveling, one more chink in the crumbling armor protecting her dreams. The deeper truth, that I was merely a weapon in the war between Mama and Teta, was not something I understood at the time, and even now the thought feels intellectually sound but emotionally hollow.

Later that same evening, I sat across from my mother at the kitchen table as she prepared dinner. She was increasingly agitated, sighing and muttering to herself as she minced bulbs of garlic. Finally she pushed her chair away and stood up. She walked past me and I caught a whiff of sour alcohol and rose perfume as she reached over and grabbed a knife from beside the sink, which was still dripping wet. She turned to her painting of the women in the field and slashed the canvas diagonally, starting from the top right to the bottom left, and then the same thing across the other direction. She dropped the knife back in the sink and returned to the garlic bulbs.

Ten years later, I gleefully smiled when Teta gave death

stares to the photograph of Mama tacked above my bed. And after that hellish summer battle with Teta, I headed back to America for my second year of studies, taking this newfound freedom with me.

I filled out the landing card while I stood in line at immigration. Jotting my name on the form felt like writing a political manifesto. It was no longer simply a name my mother had fought hard to call me. The name reeked of Islam. I wrote down my place of birth and no longer thought of the city with the ripest peaches and watermelons. Looking at my city scrawled onto that white card became a red flag for interrogation. My fate was marked on me by these unchangeable realities. I was branded like a cow arriving from an infected farm that had been designated a hazardous zone. I was a threat waiting to happen.

"Where do you live?" the immigration officer asked me as I handed her my landing card.

"Here," I replied.

"Sir, you don't live here," she said. "You study here. Where do you live?"

"Just write down I'm a Muslim. That's what you want to know, yes? Write down: I'm a Muslim."

"Sir, are you being smart with me?" She grabbed my passport. "I'm just going to check this through the system. Don't run away now."

One evening, a few years after the painting incident, just as we sat down for dinner, Teta turned to my mother and asked, "You're not going to run away like your father did, are you?"

She asked this many times after that, always finding the perfect moment when my mother least expected it. Mama began to spend a lot of time in the kitchen. The religious nuts had found an ally in Teta, and together they succeeded in forcing my mother to drop her paintbrush. She took up a number of secretarial jobs that she was never able to hold for very long. When she was working, she would be gone all morning and when she arrived home she'd fetch another bottle of her medicine from a drawer in her dressing table and go into the kitchen to cook. She'd pour herself glass after glass until there was not a single drop left in the bottle. The more upset she was, the longer she'd spend in the kitchen, cooking up a storm. She would joke with Doris as they cooked, or else if she were really upset she would chop onions at the kitchen table.

Chopping onions made Mama cry. But not like they made everyone else cry. No, onions made Mama cry so hard she sobbed. Sometimes Doris and I would watch her and laugh, and eventually she would laugh along with us. She would sob and shake with laughter, the fat teardrops rolling down her face and into the chopped onions. The tears always added a special saltiness to the meals she cooked. Other times she remained in her own world, and even as I told her about my day at school, about the teachers I liked and disliked and the subjects we were studying, she'd nod her head and smile but her eyes would be far away. Sometimes she would interrupt me to mutter something under her breath.

"What is it, Mama?" I asked her once. "What did you say?"

My voice brought her back for a moment. "I'm sorry, *habibi*, what were you saying?"

"It doesn't matter," I said angrily.

"I did it all wrong, didn't I? I'm a horrible mother."

"No, Mama. You're the best mother anyone could ever ask for." But that would make her cry even harder and so after a while I stopped saying that, too.

On bad days she spent hours chopping onions. She chopped enough onions for the entire month, which she would then freeze in clear plastic bags. We all knew why she was doing it. Teta knew, Baba knew, Doris knew. And Mama knew we knew. Still she chopped, and nobody said a word, because we also knew the second someone said something the façade would crumble. And if Mama started to cry without the bucket of onions in front of her, everyone would know everything and we'd have no choice but to talk about it. So it was better that Mama just took those onions out of the cupboard and chopped.

Because Mama was upset a lot there were onions in everything: with our stuffed grape leaves, our bamia, our morning eggs, and our fresh fish on Fridays.

"You're going to gas me to death with all this onion," Teta said one evening as we sat down to eat. "Is that your plan for killing me off?"

Mama stood up to leave the table.

"You're not going to run away like your father did, are you?" Teta said, passing me the rice.

Baba poured himself a glass of arrack. Mama sat back down and took a sip from her glass.

I moved out of the dorm and into a studio apartment. In defiance of what it meant to be a good Muslim boy I grew my hair shoulder length and began smoking. The cigarette was my confidant. I grew into my looks and for the first time felt glances of appreciation from women. I transformed myself from a wide-eyed, fresh-off-the-boat Arab into a tall, dark, mysterious foreign student, always deep in thought, who smoked cigarettes outside lecture halls and stared into the middle distance with an air of authority.

And it was on one of these smoke breaks, as I lit a cigarette and thought of the class struggle, that a girl with thick auburn curls and a deep tan rode across the courtyard on a bright yellow bicycle. She tore through the grassy area and screeched to a halt inches from my face.

"Please give me a cigarette," she said in a thick French accent. She had a yellow flower tucked behind her ear and a brashness that, as a newfound communist, I found incredibly sophisticated.

I gave her a cigarette. She leaned on her bike as I lit it for her. She inhaled deeply and blew a cloud of smoke from the corner of her mouth. I watched the smoke mingle with the lush tangles of her curly hair.

"I'm Cecile," she said, giving me a quick hug. I could smell the papaya body lotion on her silky skin.

"I'm Rasa," I said.

"What frat are you with?"

"I'm not a member of any."

Cecile looked shocked. "Really? It's the only way to have a social life. Like everything here, you've got to pay for your friends. Anyway, where are you from, darling?"

I told her and her blue eyes brightened.

"I have many Arab friends in France. I mean I am not pied-noir, but I find them endearing somehow."

I did not know what to say to that and so we became friends. Cecile was—and I would only later come across the perfect word to describe her—fabulous. She helped me navigate the crazy world of America, providing me with both company and a steady supply of marijuana. The latter, in particular, turned the hours of shelving books from a dreadful chore to a thrilling adventure. I floated through the musty shelves of the library, finding words of incredible depth in even the most mundane of corners. In return I provided her with an ear, upon which she could deposit her daily musings about herself.

Compared to many of the Americans I met, who'd had little contact with Arabs and looked at me with mistrust and fear, Cecile was from France, a country, she explained, that was "heaving with Arabs." Thus she treated me with a familiarity bordering on contempt. The familiarity was based on this new Arab identity of mine that I had not come to fully understand. Still it was a welcome change.

On the whole, our friendship took place on a plain separate from her wider socializing. She had her life in America, with keg parties and sororities and girls' nights out and dates at pizzerias and art exhibitions, and then she had me.

This was fine. I quickly discovered that I did not excel in social environments, with their concentration of belligerent students who were always a sentence away from making drunken comments about my Arabness. Instead I met Cecile in wood-decorated coffee shops, dusty second-hand bookstores, or the apartment she shared with four other girls, where we watched Bergman films she discovered in her film studies courses.

I grew fascinated with the way in which Cecile divided friends into boxes, picking and choosing among them depending on her mood. I envied her ability to compartmentalize her social life, organizing it to suit her needs. When she wanted to see a friend, she would make time for them. If she did not, she would not. Teta, on the other hand, taught me that if someone wanted to see you, then you saw them. What you wanted did not matter, because the certainty of *eib* trumped the ambiguousness of desire. Because of this, there was something appealing about Cecile, who did and said what she wanted with no concern for what others thought of her.

One day Cecile introduced me to someone she had been dating.

"I should probably warn you," she said over the phone, "Ray is a bit eccentric."

When they arrived at my studio apartment, Cecile barging straight in and Ray lumbering behind, it took me a moment to recognize him. The last time I had seen him he was hunched in a corner, a hoodie covering most of his face. Now he was wearing dirty jeans, a large black cowboy hat, and oversized sunglasses. But the long, straggly beard and hair helped me put the puzzle pieces together.

"I know you . . . " I began.

"Awesome, man," Ray said. He reached out to shake my hand. His fingernails were chewed up and black with dirt. I made a mental note to wash my hands as soon as I could.

"Yeah, we met last year . . . I gave you some cash—" I stopped myself. Did Cecile know that he was homeless? I turned to her. "How did you guys meet?"

"Very funny story. Ray was sitting by the bank downtown, and he asked me for some spare change. We started up a conversation *et voilà*!"

"Great," I said, as casually as I could. What would people say to this? They would mark Cecile for life as a harlot who chases after street boys. I tried to formulate the best way to break this news to her as Ray opened my mini refrigerator.

"Wow, hummus," he exclaimed as he started to make himself a sandwich, a musky smell following him around the room.

"Cecile—" I began.

"Listen, Rasa," she interrupted, lighting a cigarette and perching on the tiny table in the center of my room. "I need a huge favor, yes? Ray, he will stay with you for a short time, okay? You know, my housemates are so uptight and . . . " She waved her arms. "It won't be for long . . . he's going to be a chef you see. Lots of interviews lined up, but you know he needs a base, and it's getting colder . . . for only the next few weeks, yes?"

"Of course, of course," I said. How could I say no? The gods would rain down a tsunami of *eib* if I were to deny Ray my house. "I mean my apartment is tiny, you know. It's just a studio . . . I don't know where he would sleep . . . but I guess he can have my bed and I can take the floor, and—"

"*Merci*, my love, I know it is not easy. I promise, maximum two weeks."

That evening, as I was speaking to Teta on the phone, Ray tapped me on the shoulder.

"Hey buddy, you got an extra towel or shall I just use yours?"

"Use mine," I whispered, placing my hand on the receiver so that Teta would not hear.

"Nice one," Ray said, nodding.

"Who was that?" Teta demanded.

"No one, Teta." How would I even begin to explain to her that I was now sharing my studio apartment with a homeless man?

"That voice . . . who was that man?" she asked.

"I've got the mayor's son staying with me, Teta. His house is being renovated so I'm doing him a favor."

"Good boy. You're treating him well, yes? Give him your bed and sleep on the floor. It's good to have the mayor's son on your side . . . "

One morning I woke up and realized it had been months since I had spoken Arabic to anyone but Teta. Speaking only English made me a different person, I realized, someone less easygoing. But I was nervous to try and start speaking Arabic again, fearful that the rust of the language on my tongue might throw me in a pit of despair. There were some things I could only say in Arabic, and without the language I felt I had been stripped of a set of core emotions. Speaking Arabic I felt like a kinder person somehow, more passionate and human.

The feeling was very different from how I felt growing up, where one of my major concerns had been to find new ways to avoid attending Arabic class. In English class we read the Famous Five, Judy Blume, *Lord of the Flies*, *Robinson Crusoe*, all that stuff. I saw myself in the characters and could feel what they were feeling. Arabic, on the other hand, was like a dead world. We only had one large textbook, which had short vignettes of Quranic verses and old nationalist poems that were boring as hell, and the grammar was too damn difficult.

It wasn't even the Arabic I spoke, which was free-flowing and malleable. The Arabic that was shoved down our throats was rigid and alien. So Maj and I would feign illness or else spend the hour hiding in the bathroom cubicle, which smelled of piss but at least we could joke and speak however we wanted.

It was around that time that we became friends with Basma. That was good for the both of us, because Basma was popular. She had chocolate skin, dangerous eyes, and a mess of curly hair. She had a keen eye for playing the system and was not afraid to do so, and that made her powerful.

Basma hated Arabic class, too, so the three of us ditched it together. We hung out in Smoker's Paradise, which was on the top floor of an abandoned staircase. The high-school kids spent hours there smoking cigarettes and kissing. No teachers ever went up to Smoker's Paradise, especially in the winter. The staircase was exposed and smack in the middle of a wind tunnel, so it was damn cold.

For the most part the high-school kids left us alone. We were harmless. We just sat there in Smoker's Paradise giggling at Maj, who was obsessed with Madonna and would stage-whisper performances to us while we huddled together for warmth.

On Valentine's Day, the day before I turned eleven, we spent three whole hours in Smoker's Paradise. When we finally stepped back into the school hall our faces were flushed and our hands were like frozen fish fingers.

Valentine's Day was nothing special to anyone except Maj. He was also hooked on American television and so knew exactly how to celebrate. Every year he would send himself a secret card or a bouquet of flowers. That year he had gone all out. He bought himself a dozen red roses and some red balloons. Of course he was beaten up during lunch for that. There was Maj, clutching his balloons as the boys kicked him, squealing, "I'm a lover not a fighter!"

Anyway it was just our luck the principal caught us. Miss Nadwa was a foul old lady with straw-like hair and a bad eye. She looked like a cross between a scarecrow and a pirate. She was always walking around the halls, peering at us with her one good eye, barking orders.

"Tuck your shirt in, boy. *Ya ayni aleyk* . . . where do you think we are—the jungle?"

"Take your hand off his shoulder, *ya binti*. This is not a disco."

As soon as we stepped out of Smoker's Paradise, Miss Nadwa popped her head into the corridor.

"Run!" Basma screamed.

We turned on our heels and bolted. We ran to the other end of the hall and took a right. Basma was in the lead, and Maj and I were trailing. At the time Mama was really unhappy, chopping bowls of onions every night. She stayed up all night but in the morning she had produced no new paintings or sculptures. She just sat there chopping onions and whispering to Doris. When Mama was unhappy, it meant that I was bloated and gassy. Running down the hall, my stomach like one of Maj's red balloons, I struggled to keep up.

"*Yalla*," Basma urged us on. "Faster!"

I waddled along behind her, clenching my butt with all the strength I could muster. My stomach gurgled. I felt sick from holding all the farts in. Sweat began to form on my forehead from the strain. I felt that if I let it all out now I might gas the entire school to death. A fart holocaust.

"Where are we going?" Maj yelled.

"Basement! Basement!" Basma shrieked as she bolted down the stairs. I stopped and crossed my legs. If I ran another second I was sure I would pass out.

"What are you doing?" Basma yelled as she ran down, three steps at a time.

"I need a minute." I groaned. I looked back, hoping Miss

Nadwa had given up. But there she was, panting behind us. And only a few metres ahead of her was Maj, tripping over his Valentine gifts. A trail of red petals followed him down the hall.

"Drop the flowers," I yelled.

"No!" He clutched his bouquet tighter. The red balloons bounced in the air behind him as he ran.

I caught my breath and hobbled down the stairs. Basma was two floors ahead of me. Her quick footsteps echoed through the stairwell. When I was one floor down, I looked up. Maj had just reached the staircase but Miss Nadwa was right behind. Just before he went down she made a lunge for him. She grabbed him by his shirt collar and pulled him back into the hall.

"Save yourselves!" Maj shrieked, squirming under Miss Nadwa's iron grip. "For the sake of the Prophet, just keep going!"

"Enough!" Miss Nadwa screeched. "Basma and Rasa, I know it's you."

We stopped running and turned ourselves in.

Miss Nadwa grabbed Maj and me by our ears and dragged us to the office, while Basma danced around her. "I'm calling your parents. Then suspension."

"But I'm a girl!" Basma shrieked, flailing her arms. "You want to destroy my honor, miss? You want to bring shame on my family? Let me warn you, miss, if you do this, it will be on your head! You hear me?"

As usual this worked, and Basma blew us a kiss as she walked out of the office. As for Maj and me, well, they called our parents, honor be damned. Maj tried to reason with her.

"Look, miss, it was my fault. I urged them to come with me. And I would do it all over again, you see. If I could I would propose the entire school accompany me to Smoker's Paradise to ditch that silly Arabic class. You see, miss, the teaching is all wrong. How can we fall in love with this language when it's being taught from that stupid book by that silly donkey? Hear me out, miss, I will give anyone my attention. But only if they earn it. No one is simply entitled to it just like that." He snapped his fingers and put his hands on his hips. "You get my attention if you entertain me, *ya* miss."

In a single move Miss Nadwa reached behind her desk, unplugged the black cord connected to her radio, and whipped it across Maj's side.

"Owww!" Maj howled. "Well, that won't make me want to go back to that class."

My mother stumbled into Miss Nadwa's office. She caught my eye and pointed her finger at me.

"You are in deep SHIT," she slurred.

"What's this language?" Miss Nadwa shrieked. "We are not in a marketplace, *habibti*!"

Maj burst into a fit of laughter. He bit the insides of his cheeks to stop but it only made him snort. He shook in his chair, snorting like a pig, and that set me off. I laughed and laughed. I clutched my stomach and squirmed to keep all the farts inside. But it was useless. They ripped through me like a trumpet. Maj was rolling on the floor now. Tears were streaming down his face. Miss Nadwa shrieked and shrieked. I turned to look at my mother, who could not hold it in any longer and let out a squeal of giggles.

One night, a month after Ray had moved in, while he was out drinking with money he borrowed from me, Cecile and I ordered Chinese food and watched a film in my studio. We divided the cost equally. Cecile handed me the plastic fork and gave herself the spoon, and with the knife she scraped a line down the thick red sauce in the circular dish of the Kung Pao chicken.

"Eat up until this line," she instructed. I stared at the crescent-shaped ration in front of me. In minutes I had wolfed down my portion. I was about to go in for another bite when Cecile smacked my fork away with her spoon.

"Already you ate your portion," she said with an annoyed look on her face. "Shit, already you ate over the line. The rest is mine. See?" She pointed to the now half-eaten line that snaked down the middle of the dish like a sneer. "Always so greedy, Rasa."

Ten minutes later, long after she had turned her attention back to the movie, I realized I was still staring at the Kung Pao chicken, feeling increasingly angry and ashamed. I was a greedy Arab, scolded for eating more than my share. But the meal cost six dollars, and it was obvious that Cecile did not intend to eat all of her portion that night. Who cares if I ate a bit more than my share? The more I thought about it, the angrier I became. Her street-rat lover had spent most of the fall semester sleeping in my bed without so much as lifting a finger, and she throws a tantrum because I ate an extra spoonful of rice? What a typical capitalist move. Even food, the most sacred of gifts, is sliced up and privatized. Cecile really is a petty bourgeois European, I thought, lighting a cigarette. But what could I say, really? There was nothing. Besides, forget about capitalism. More than anything, negotiating over six-dollar Chinese takeout was *eib*. It was the *eib* to end all *eib*s.

"I'm going to break up with Ray, by the way," Cecile said, spooning a piece of chicken into her mouth. "He scrounges off me too much."

What an utter little bitch you are, I thought, still fuming. Instead I told her that I thought it was about time she get rid of him. And after the movie Cecile wrapped up the remainder of her portion of the Kung Pao chicken and took it home with her, saying she would eat it for lunch the next day.

So this was how it was going to be, I thought. Cecile's actions—from sorting her friends the way a little girl arranges dolls to intricately breaking down restaurant bills and dividing and rationing food like we were in a famine—were nothing more than a microcosm of America itself. Everyone had their space, fiercely protected, their plot of land, their books and their meals and their money and their laws and their rules and their rights. They divided everything into manageable parts that only they owned, and everything seemed orderly and operated under a law that was immune to any appeals to *eib* or *haram*, as such actions would have called for back home. There was no *eib* here. There was only the law and human rights.

When Ray returned home drunk later that night, I put the chain on the door and didn't allow him in.

"You've got to go, Ray," I said.

"You can't just kick me out without notice," he slurred, banging on the door.

"I've been asking you for weeks. Now I'm telling you."

Ray kicked the door a few times and fell over.

"This is really triggering me, you know? It's bringing back memories of my father kicking me out of the house."

"Always so greedy, Ray," I said, enjoying how much I sounded like Cecile. "Get off *my* property or I'm calling the police. I have rights, you know!"

I never saw Ray again, and after the incident with the Kung Pao chicken I kept my distance from Cecile, spending a greater deal of time on my own. With the exception of being alone in the bathroom, there was little time for myself in Teta's house, so having this time in America allowed me to continue reading and exploring imaginary worlds I didn't know existed. More important, it allowed me to think of my mother.

As much as possible, I needed to bring her back to life, to delve into our history and discover what had happened to her. Although she had made a decision to stop painting, Mama was not able to put the paintbrush down for long. She floated between secretarial jobs during the day, and stayed up many nights, bottle in hand, working on pieces she never finished. She often worked all night, barely sleeping. Our kitchen came to be littered with half-finished paintings and melting clay sculptures that—like a teenager hiding cigarette butts—she desperately tried to conceal from Teta. But her ideas came to her on a whim and fled just as quickly, leaving behind a carnage of crumpled papers, multicolored stains, and jars of paintbrushes with crusted stems soaking in dirty water.

I recalled these memories while lying on my bed in America, staring up at the white walls of my studio apartment, blasting George Michael's album on repeat, the album that got me through the worst of my teenage loneliness. It finally dawned on me one evening, as I stared at my bare walls, that if I could not find her in the directories, I might be able to locate the details of her parents.

I had never met my mother's parents. When she lived with us she barely spoke to them, so I knew they were not close. They spoke once every eight or nine months, and afterward my mother would be nervous and distracted, pacing under a cloud of smoke and talking to herself. One time she had announced that they were finally coming to visit that summer, but the summer came and went and nobody ever arrived. Still, I knew their names, and it didn't take long to find my grandfather's number. He was a retired doctor and professor at one of the colleges on the other side of the country. Tentatively, I wrote down his number on a piece of paper and picked up the phone.

He answered on the third ring. As soon as he said "Hello," sounding both more American and more dignified than I expected, a combination I had not thought possible, I realized I had made a terrible mistake.

"Hello?" my grandfather repeated.

I remained silent, my sweaty palm clutching the phone. I

willed the words to come out, but they remained lodged in the back of my throat.

"Hello?" he said for the third time. I did not want to see my mother. I was terrified at the thought of it, of being consumed by her again, of being probed and eaten alive. Would she be able to see what I was hiding in my secret cage? And how would she react? More terrifying was the thought that she might accept me for who I was, and expose my own guilt and shame in the process. With Teta it was easy. Yes, she could sometimes be sadistic and fickle, but we had an understanding of the red lines that neither of us breached, and together we allowed our shame to grow. In Teta I had an ally who would help me hide my shame. But meeting my mother again, the woman who had worked hard to ensure there was not a single stone of our family's shame left unturned, no shadow left unexplored—what would she uncover from my cage of secrets? She would expose all my secrets with a single glance.

I hung up, my hands shaking. I slid back against the wall, defeated yet relieved that my shame remained undisturbed. Coming this close to reaching out to my mother, I knew, was an ultimate defiance of Teta's rules. This one phone call was the equivalent of ten million viewings of POLSKASAT, and when Teta called me that evening for our nightly chat, I feigned sickness and hung up after a few minutes.

As I was falling asleep, I recalled a morning not long after my mother had come running back from al-Sharqiyeh in tears, vowing never to paint again. On the days when Teta was around, Mama would wake up late and spend the morning drinking Nescafé and smoking cigarettes by the kitchen window, silently looking out past the single palm tree in our front yard. But that morning Teta had gone to visit some friends, so it was just the two of us, my mother and I, free to dream up crazy ideas without the fear of Teta's disapproving judgements. If I had known that such moments would soon end I would have taken advantage of them, appreciated them more per-haps. That day Mama woke up early and went straight to the bottle. Afterward she danced around in her nightgown listen-ing to Remi Bandali songs. She grabbed me in her arms and I sang along with her, and after breakfast we sat on the kitchen table and Mama, cigarette in hand, began to plan my birthday party.

"We can't have too many people," she said. "Twenty?"

I nodded solemnly. "Sounds about right."

"And for food, mini-pizzas of course . . . "

"Lazy cake?"

"Yes, yes, absolutely." My mother nodded, paused to take a puff of her cigarette, and looked out the window at the garbage collectors picking up our trash. "Don't you think peo-ple look funny when they walk? The way their arms move around as they move, almost like aliens. Why are we so scared of aliens when we are such aliens ourselves?"

"Mama, focus please! We need to organize my birthday," I pleaded.

"Sorry, yes, your birthday. Where were we? Do you want a clown?"

"I'm ten, Mama. I'm too old for a clown."

"Well how about an elephant? We can dress him up like in *Dumbo*. You know, when they went to the circus?"

"Where would we get an elephant? They don't have any here. Besides, we'd never be able to fit an elephant in the house."

My mother stubbed out her cigarette. "Yes," she clapped her hands, her smile so wide it was almost a grimace. "An ele-phant. Perfect. Absolutely perfect."

My second winter in America was the coldest in recent his-tory, and as the snow piled up around the brick houses and the streets iced over, my questions became bitterly frosty. Why had my mother not been in touch with me in the first place? In fact, why did she have to leave at all? Was it because of the state of the Arab world, where we treated mental health and addiction with the same reckless disdain we had for everything else? Perhaps Cecile was right. And those pundits on television, they were right, too. Why was everything done with little planning, just a bunch of haphazard *inshallah*s thrown around? Was I angry about the state of the Arab world? Yes, I was angry. I was furious at the lost potential, at the millions of young people who have no opportunities because of structural impediments that ought to be challenged. I was angry about the lack of law and order. I was angry for myself, about my lost childhood spent navigating this confusing maze of chaos and loss. I was angry about my education, with its ancient and rigid teaching methods peppered with false truths and blatant lies, where the only goal was to make us forget how to criticize and ask challenging questions. And most of all I was angry about my mother, that she had to go so far and leave me behind like I was just another one of her abandoned paintings. And that was the fault of our society. We needed more damn lines in our Kung Pao chicken.

By spring Cecile was once again back in my life. She seemed gentler and more giving now, cooking lasagnas and casseroles for me and inviting me to museum exhibitions.

"You're funny," Cecile said once, halfway through recounting the events of a party she'd attended the night before. It was April and by then my questions had darkened considerably, but spring made Cecile optimistic. She was draped across the stained brown couch in her living room. The white skin of her legs, which hung over the arm of the couch, glowed in the sunlight streaming in from the window.

"Why?" I asked.

"You always have this pained expression on your face."

"Really?"

"Yeah," she said, "and you walk in a funny way, like you're carrying the weight of the world on your shoulders. Like this." She jumped up from the couch and walked heavily across the room, shoulders slumped, arms hanging loosely by her sides. She looked like an ape. "Lighten up."

Lighten up. As if it was just by a click of your fingers that you could remove this weight.

When I returned after my second year, Teta gave me a long hug, covered my face in kisses, then ordered me to take off my clothes and jump in the shower.

"You smell like them," she said.

"Like who?"

"Like them"—she gestured in the vague direction of the bulky laptop I had purchased at a discount from the university's computer store—"*al-ajaneb*."

"Really? What do foreigners smell like?"

"I don't know," she paused. "Like butter."

She threw the contents of my suitcase into the washing machine, bought me a special shampoo that smelled of rose water and olive oil, and ordered me not to spend too long in the shower as we were running out of water. And as the last drops of water from the tank fell on my head, I rinsed the shampoo from my hair and for a brief moment felt at home.

It was during my third year in America that the attacks began. The Americans had invaded one country and were itching to stick their dicks in another. The piece of paper with my grandfather's phone number taunted me from my bookshelf. Every morning I'd promise myself that I would toss it out, forget it even existed, and every evening I would decide to hold on to it for one more day.

Having discovered my Arabness in America, and then quickly finding it first under scrutiny and then under attack, I felt I needed somewhere to channel some of my feelings. I enrolled in an elective course called Politics of the Third World, taught by a collective of lecturers. Each lecturer had his or her own unique expertise in an esoteric corner of the globe. They were young, with deep tans, rolled-up sleeves, and battle scars from recent adventures in faraway countries with unfamiliar names.

It was in this class one morning that—from across the mass of half-asleep students slumped in their chairs—my gaze rested on the most beautiful person I had ever seen. He had a week-old beard and his hair, the color of burned eggplant, flopped across his face and into his eyes. A silver stud in his bottom lip sparkled in the harsh lights of the lecture hall. His concentration was focused on the lecturer, who was making a structural link between diarrhea in Africa and the legacy of colonialism.

I couldn't take my eyes off him. Besides his physical beauty, there was a softness in how he held himself. I could see it in the way he coolly brushed his hair behind his ears as he concentrated, the way his eyes flicked down every so often to examine his nails, and the way he bit his bottom lip, making the silver stud dance from side to side. I wanted to be near someone who existed in this world with such ease. At the very least, I felt I could learn from him.

It was months before we spoke. During this time I inched, seat by seat, closer to him in class. I stole glimpses of him around campus. I waited. Waited for what? I don't know. I was stuck in a terrible limbo of wanting to speak to him but petrified of doing so. I had no experience of actively pursuing somebody.

I began to follow him. It became my mission to find out as much about him as it was possible to know. His favorite coffee shop was Café DuPont, which specialized in organic coffee and vegan cakes. DuPont was decorated with reclaimed wooden benches, Zapatista artwork, and antiwar leaflets. Bearded men in corduroys and women in dreadlocks who smelled like wet earth spent their evenings at DuPont reciting spoken word poetry and listening to folk music. Even though the coffee was twice the price of anywhere else, I visited DuPont whenever possible to catch glimpses of him. I learned his habits and the schedule of his classes and modeled my own routine around it.

Finally we met. It was the evening of the Politics of the Third World final exam before the winter break. The atmosphere on campus was giddy with the excitement of a long holiday after weeks of stress. By then my feelings had reached a fever pitch. I knew that after tonight I wouldn't be able to satisfy my cravings for him until classes reconvened in the New Year.

I searched the crowded exam hall but could not see him anywhere. Afterward, I walked through the bitter blizzard that had enveloped the city like a snow globe. The exam had been easy, yet I walked to the bus stop with a profound sense of failure. I stopped to tie my shoelaces, my hands red and numb from the cold.

When I stood up, he was there. Just like that, we were face-to-face. For a moment in that blizzard he appeared to be a mirage. His winter coat was unzipped, and underneath he wore a blue sweater and khakis. Up close, I noticed imperfections in his face: the mole on his neck, the slight crookedness of his two front teeth, minor blemishes on his skin.

He spoke first.

"I don't think we've met." His voice was softer than I had imagined.

"I'm Rasa," I croaked. The sound of my voice was unfamiliar, like I was hearing it for the first time.

He smiled. "I know. I'm Sufyan."

"That's an Arab name," I said, stiffening. Revealing my secret to an American was one thing, but if an Arab found out then by tomorrow every Arab would know about me. Then

Teta would find out about me. The thought was too terrifying to consider for very long.

"I'm originally Arab," he said, pronouncing his *r*'s as *w*'s, like Elmer Fudd. "But I was born and raised in the States."

He asked me where I lived and what I was studying. He explained he was majoring in philosophy and Arabic, and that he wanted to travel to the Middle East after graduating. As he told me this he stretched and a small bit of light brown skin on his abdomen, patchy with fine black hair, peeked from under his jacket. He smiled and watched me closely as I told him about home. I studied the way he flicked his wrists as he spoke. Slightly feminine. There was hope after all. And he knew my name.

I practically skipped all the way home. The blizzard took on a dazzling beauty. The snowflakes were like falling embers from fireworks that had shot up in the sky the moment Sufyan approached me.

For the next month I thought about him. Locked up in my apartment, the memory of the few moments we shared kept me warm from the blistering cold outside. I closed my eyes to recount the memory as vividly as possible, reimagining everything down to the minute sensory details: the snowflakes on my face, the beer-soaked cheers of students cutting through the frost in the air, Sufyan's brown eyes and shy smile. I remembered exactly where I had been standing and how Sufyan had leaned in when I spoke, tucking a strand of his hair behind his ear, how his jacket rode up his hip and, for a few exhilarating moments, a strip of caramel abdomen exposed itself to my sight. I was a master of time, drawing out those minutes when Sufyan had been mine, when his attention was on me and nobody else, to hours and even days. I dissected each image and scent and sound and emotion so that I might expand the time we'd spent together.

I imagined him in bed with me. I cuddled the pillow and

convinced myself it was him. I pictured him waking up and turning toward me, bleary-eyed and smiling. I thought of kissing him, navigating that silver stud under his bottom lip. I lay in bed with a smile on my face and, as I looked up at my George Michael poster, felt I finally understood why other people seemed so carefree.

It was easy after that. I knew his habits and routines, so I made sure I was always where he was. I learned to prepare my talking points well in advance of our encounters. I read up on current events and looked up the CDs of obscure bands I glimpsed in his bag. The library database provided me with a list of all the books he had ever taken out, which ranged from early philosophers like Plato, Aristotle, and Ibn-Khaldun to more modern political theorists like Antonio Gramsci and Rosa Luxemburg. I followed his book selection like a reading list, flipping through them, reading them not as Rasa but as Sufyan. It was my way of bringing us closer together, because if I could think his thoughts and truly understand him, and if that felt *right*, surely this was meant to be.

The Sufyan project was a great distraction from the declarations of war that had poisoned the air in America. The American regime gleefully bombed countries that were similar to mine, countries that shared the same religion and language. One by one the countries fell and then they were no longer countries. I discovered that when America chooses to go to war, the invaded country becomes a situation. History and people and songs and art are swept away, and the country becomes a political event that takes on new dimensions that tell a story. An American story.

I was waiting for my coffee at DuPont on a wintry Tuesday morning when I felt a tap on my shoulder. Sufyan was smiling at me when I turned around.

"Well, hello," I said, thinking that it was not even nine in the morning and already this day, with its low sky and grey clouds, was bound to be a good one.

Sufyan opened his mouth to speak but was interrupted by the barista, a tall white man with yellow dreadlocks.

"Americano for Ross," the barista yelled, holding up the white paper cup. I grabbed my drink and turned back to Sufyan.

"Did he just call you Ross?" Sufyan asked, his eyebrows closing in.

"It's easier this way," I said, pouring in a sachet of brown sugar. "Otherwise they'll ask me where my name is from, want to talk about how awful it is about 'what's happening over there, bro,' and then they'll write 'Ross' on the cup anyway."

Sufyan's eyes softened and he let out a chuckle. "Next time I'll tell them my name is Osama. They won't get that wrong."

I laughed and waited as he ordered his drink.

"Are you going to the antiwar protest this Saturday?" Sufyan asked.

"I wasn't planning to go. Is it really going to make a difference?"

"All things in life, no matter how small, have some level of significance," he said. He curled his lower lip into his mouth and played with his silver stud, rolling it from side to side with his teeth.

"Maybe I'll go then," I said, and he squeezed my shoulder.

Days later I thought of what he said. Even the smallest things are significant. I was certain this was a sign, that there was something important in our knowing smiles and coy conversations. He had a reason for inviting me to the protest. He wanted me closer. I could feel it. He wanted something from me and I wanted him to know that I wanted something from him, too. Oh but to say it out loud, we couldn't. There was too much at stake. All we could do was inch closer until that moment when neither of us could deny it, when we were standing together at the edge of the cliff. We were inching closer now, and I promised myself that the next time I saw him I would push us so far out on the edge we would not be able to return.

The next day, as Cecile and I browsed for clothes at a charity shop, I asked her if she'd like to come to the antiwar rally.

"I don't believe in protest," she said, picking up a straw hat that was frayed at the edges. She placed the hat at an angle on her head and examined her reflection in the mirror. "Most of those people out protesting are usually just projecting their personal demons into political outrage. It's not healthy."

"I feel like it's important we go," I insisted. "People are dying out there in the world."

"Then go, darling," she tossed the hat back on the pile of clothes. "Go."

I went. It was raining. I followed the crowds holding antiwar signs with photos of the American president with devil horns, until I arrived at the location Sufyan told me would be the epicenter of the protests. Tens of thousands of people were surrounded on all sides by riot police. I watched the crowds talk and chant excitedly. As my eyes drifted across their faces—some angry, some jubilant, and others simply cold—I understood that running into Sufyan by chance was not going to happen.

The wind was bitter and slapped against our faces as the crowd marched through the city. An antiwar coalition handed me a sign to hold, which said NO BLOOD FOR OIL in angry red letters. I held it awkwardly under my armpit as I marched, rubbing my hands together to keep them from going numb. I kept to myself, holding the sign but not chanting, my eyes darting in search of Sufyan.

I had been there for fifteen minutes when I noticed a young woman wearing a long black raincoat watching me from underneath a red-and-white polka-dot umbrella. She had round black glasses and dark curly hair. For a while I ignored her attempts at eye contact, but finally her eyes caught mine and she walked up to me.

"Are you Arab?" she asked. She carried her bag with incredible seriousness, and inside I could see a heavy book titled *The Postcolonial Exotic*.

I hesitated. "Yes."

"I had a feeling you were," she said, shaking my hand. She had chewed-up stumps for fingernails. "I've seen you at the library. Then I saw you here and thought I might as well ask."

I told her where I was from.

"Me, too. Do you live in the suburbs?"

"I used to. I live downtown now." I paused. "Well, I live *here* now. But before—"

Her eyes lit up. "I love downtown. It's so authentic. Really I hate living in the western suburbs. Whenever I'm back home the thought of it makes me so aggressive. Want to walk together?"

Leila was two years older than me and was enrolled in a master's program in postcolonial women's literature. We marched together and talked about our lives back home. Leila turned out to live only a few neighborhoods from where Teta and I had lived back when Baba and Mama were around. We spoke in Arabic. It had been so long since I had spoken to anyone in that language. Our Arabic was rusty, but we persisted, throwing in English words when needed. Speaking Arabic in America made me feel like I was creating a home for myself on the cold windy evening in this crazy foreign city. We delved deep into conversation, and soon I found out Maj was her second cousin and we knew many of the same people, and only after twenty minutes did it occur to me that finding Sufyan had slipped my mind. I thought of how many Leilas I might have overlooked while being so fixated on him.

"I'm glad you're political," Leila said. "Most of the Arabs

who come to America spend their days smoking weed and getting drunk in casinos. It's very problematic."

As we marched it became apparent that Leila had a well thought out critique of everything from reality television to the international feminist movement. Her conclusion was often that everything was problematic.

"Are you speaking Arabic?" A middle-aged American man with a scruffy beard interrupted us. In one hand he held a megaphone and in another a sign that read STOP THE WAR.

"Yeah," I said, and before I knew what had happened the man shoved the megaphone into my hand.

"Chant something. In Arabic."

I looked at the megaphone. I came to this protest to see Sufyan, and here I was holding a megaphone and about to chant to thousands of people.

"What should I say?" I asked Leila.

"*Bil roh, bil dam, nafdeeki ya bilad,*" Leila said, taking the black-and-white kaffiyeh she was using as a scarf and draping it across my shoulders.

"*Bil roh, bil dam, nafdeeki ya bilad,*" I said into the megaphone. The air was bitterly cold and I tightened the kaffiyeh around my neck.

"Louder," Leila urged. "Chant."

"*Bil roh, bil dam, nafdeeki ya bilad!*"

"That's it!" Leila clapped her hands.

"*Bil roh, bil dam, nafdeeki ya bilad!*" Pellets of cold rain hit my face.

A TV camera rushed toward us. I stared into the camera's blinking red dot.

"*Bil roh, bil dam, nafdeeki ya bilad!*"

"What does that mean?" a man with a microphone asked Leila, who had begun chanting alongside me.

"It means with our souls and our blood we will sacrifice ourselves for the homeland. It's what people used to chant for dictators, but we're subverting it by replacing the dictator's name with 'homeland.' " She seemed very pleased with herself for the chant. The camera shifted back to me as the crowd began to form a circle around me.

"Bil roh, bil dam, nafdeeki ya bilad!"

I raised my voice, hoping my chants would lead Sufyan to me. I chanted again, louder and louder, my fists pumping the frosty air above my head, looking through the crowds for him. But all I could see was an endless stream of people bundled up in parkas and raincoats, holding signs and shaking their fists in the air. The people who had come out in the cold for an idea and a principle, their faces wet and red, their bodies huddled together for warmth. And soon I was not thinking of Sufyan anymore. I was thinking of my teachers, of Marx and Chatterjee and Said. I chanted and I thought of power and imperialism, and I realized that it was all linked, that challenging lies and oppression was also fighting on behalf of love. And my love for Sufyan was my fuel. My feelings for him gave me the energy to blast the words out of my mouth. I pumped my fist in the air and chanted and Leila stood chanting beside me until we were lost in a daze of love and resistance.

"Thank you for being the voice of your people," the middle-aged man said, taking the megaphone from my hand.

But I was fired up now. I wanted to stay and protest for as long as it took. I felt that if we were to give up now and go back home as individuals, then we would destroy the power of the collective we had created when we were united. But the drizzle quickly turned into a heavy downpour of freezing rain. We tried to take shelter under Leila's polka-dot umbrella but my clothes were drenched through to my underwear.

"Let's get out of here," Leila said. "I'm meeting up with some activist friends at a bar nearby. Do you want to come?"

I nodded. I was up for anything that might delay the inevitable loneliness that would sink in when I got home.

As we ran toward the bar, our soggy shoes smacking against the wet streets of the city, my phone began to ring. It was Cecile.

"You were just on the news," she squealed. "You were up on a podium chanting. I couldn't believe it was you. They're showing it everywhere!"

I thought of Teta, and whether the footage of me would be broadcast on her television screen tomorrow morning. I'd get a telling off, for sure. But even if she was to chance upon the footage of me leading the chants, there was nothing she could do from over there. After all, I was resisting an imperialist invasion. What was she doing? Playing cards and watching the news, and as the war worsened her charity would not extend beyond heckling the television set.

I had agency, I told myself. My boots burst dirty puddles on the street like I was crushing American invaders with every step. I had a voice, goddammit. I wasn't going to take any of this war business, or any of Teta's *eib* business, any more.

The bar was noisy and full of Arabs. They were Arabs, yes, but they looked unlike anyone else back home. None of the women had straightened their hair, choosing to leave it in a tangle of curls. The men all had unkempt beards and kaffiyehs wrapped around their shoulders. The atmosphere was buzzing, and I was riding the wave.

We took a seat at the table where, among melted candles, packs of cigarettes, and half-drunk glasses of beer, heavy books were strewn. Books written by Noam Chomsky and Edward Said and Norman Finkelstein, chastising the wars and occupations. The activists spoke hurriedly of "drafting statements" and "building solidarity." It was as if all I had read since arriving in America, about Marx and resistance and all that, was being played out here in the smoky haze of alcohol and debate. I felt comfortable enough to come out of my head and thoughts. The dizzying conversations reminded me of those parties my parents used to throw many years ago. I drank beer and flitted between discussions, catching snippets of heated debates and excitable whispers. My mind buzzed with theories and beer.

"We must build more solidarity with Native Americans," said one man with long curly hair, leaning into a pretty girl with black-framed glasses.

"Arundhati Roy's fiction is very problematic," Leila explained to a group of younger women.

"The statement shouldn't make reference to the Zionist lobby's pro-war memo. That just acknowledges and empowers them," a tall man said, shaking a piece of paper.

"You cannot single out one instance of oppression in the region without unpacking the whole system," said a woman who was smoking a thinly rolled cigarette, her eyes the color of olives.

"Are you telling me in all seriousness that the Quran is not anti-women?" came from another conversation that was taking place behind me. I turned around and saw a short, pear-shaped woman pointing her beer at a man with a bulbous nose.

And just behind the man with the bulbous nose, sitting on a stool in a corner of the bar, among the group yet separate, was Sufyan. He stared thoughtfully into his half-drunk bottle of beer. He had cut his long, beautiful hair short and his beard was trimmed. The excitement of seeing him overwhelmed any other nervousness I had, and before I knew it I had walked up to him and tapped him on the shoulder.

"What are the chances of seeing you here," he said when he turned around. I studied his face. He seemed pleased to see me.

"I'm just with some friends," I said, enjoying how casual the sentence sounded. "I was at the protest but I didn't see you."

"Well, it was only the biggest protest to have ever taken

place in America, so . . . " He chuckled. He looked down at his drink, and I watched the way his delicate fingers traced loops around the mouth of the frosty bottle. "Actually I saw you on the podium, chanting in Arabic."

"Oh, really?" I leaned in closer. "What did you think?"

He smiled. "It was cool. Well they asked me to chant as well, you know . . . "

The woman with olive eyes leaned into the conversation. "Yeah, but you can't speak Arabic for shit. Pronouncing your *eins* like an American." She laughed.

Sufyan looked annoyed.

"You cut your hair," I said, changing the subject.

"It was getting too long," he replied, running a hand over his head.

"Why are you sitting alone?"

"I'm bored. I'm drunk. I want to leave. But I don't want to go home."

"I've got some weed at my place, so . . . " The beer had given me a newfound courage. The possibility sparked in the air between us like lightning bolts of electricity.

We said goodbye to the others and walked back to my studio. We were not talking much. The rain had stopped and the air seemed quiet and still after the excitement of the bar. Our footsteps echoed around us, filling in the silence.

When I opened the door of my studio apartment, I took in the state of the room as if through Sufyan's eyes. My jeans and T-shirts were strewn across the bed. A large ashtray with overflowing cigarette carcasses sat on top of a heavy stack of books that functioned as my bedside table. My poster of George Michael half hung on the wall, the edges beginning to droop. The sink was overflowing with dirty dishes and cups.

"The clothes are clean," I explained, pushing the T-shirts and jeans to one side. "I just didn't have time to put them away. Have a seat."

Sufyan sat on the bed, his eyes taking in the contents of my room. I took a seat on the floor next to him and began to roll a joint.

"Do you smoke often?" he asked.

"Depends how bad the news is," I said, licking the joint closed and offering it to him.

"It's been a while since I smoked," he said, eyeing the joint. "I'm trying to be a better person, to get away from all this shit, but I guess tonight is as good a night as any to let go." He lit the joint and inhaled deeply. A smile appeared on his face as he relaxed into the bed. I took two beers from the fridge and handed one to him.

"Is your family affected by the war at all?" he asked suddenly.

"We're all affected in some way. The entire thing is very *problematic*," I said, enjoying using the word for the first time. "Aren't yours?"

"If they are they don't say so. These days my parents cling to American patriotism with an intensity bordering on paranoia. They feel that if they don't, they might be kicked out or something," he said and smiled.

"What about you?" I asked. He was lying back on the bed now, staring at the ceiling. "Do you sometimes feel alienated from it all? That's how I feel sometimes. I feel stuck between everything. Sometimes I feel that I don't want to be Arab any more. It is causing me too many problems. Instead I wish I were a cloud. I mean that. Or a bird, so I could opt out of all this, this history of our people."

He leaned up on his elbow and looked me in the eye.

"Me? I'm fucking sick of the hypocrisy of white liberals." He paused, as if to consider how he might appear having said this, and then, seemingly pleased with himself, lay back on the bed with one arm against his forehead and continued to stare at the ceiling, which seemed to fascinate him so much.

Meanwhile, my attention drifted to his feet. Well, one foot in particular, which hovered shoeless a few inches away from my face. I examined the contours of that foot, the shape his toes made through the grey cotton socks. I caught a whiff of them. They smelled of laundry detergent and a day's worth of walking. The scent awakened an urge in me. I wanted to get close to his feet. I felt the smell would soothe something in me, somehow. I leaned my head in to catch more of the scent. I breathed in deeply. The smell traveled inside me, making my head feel airy and my fingers tingle, awakening more of that hunger. I felt scared. How deep would I have to go? How much of this smell would I have to take in to satisfy these feelings? Or would my cravings grow the more I fed them?

"Everywhere I look there is violence," Sufyan continued, distracting me from his foot. I looked up at him. Both arms were behind his head now as he stared at the ceiling, but he kept his foot inches from my face. "It seems to be a competition over who can upload and send out the most violent images. Children being slaughtered, people being killed in disgusting ways. I mean, children. Who kills children? So much of it is indiscriminate. I saw this video, they said it was in some Arab country but turns out it was filmed in Mexico and had something to do with drug cartels. But anyway, in this video, two men were lying down and this man brings a chain saw and just chops the head off one of the men. Just like that. His head falls off and it was over. The other man sitting next to him, waiting his turn. What was he thinking, knowing he would be next? What does it feel like, to know that in moments you'll have your head sawed off? I feel bombarded with all of this and I don't know what to do with it or how to make sense of it all any more. I'm left with this . . . this sinking nausea that is closing in on me."

"Crazy," I said, taking another puff of the joint and passing it to him.

"The Internet, man," Sufyan said, inhaling. "Suddenly everything is so accessible. Everything is just . . . here, you know?"

My attention drifted back to Sufyan's foot and, without thinking, I reached out and grabbed it. I held his foot in my hands for a moment, unsure what to do with this newfound treasure. I stared at the grey sock, which looked clean and fuzzy and perfect, and thought of how I wanted to be the one who washes these socks, hangs them up to dry, and then folds them delicately back in the drawer. I would do it every day to make sure Sufyan was living well. I gently ran my finger around the contours of his toes, tracing each toenail as I went along. I began massaging his foot, softly at first and then harder. I pressed my fingers deep into the soft skin beneath his sock. Sufyan sighed heavily and relaxed back into the bed, his arm dropped by his side.

I let go of his foot and picked up his hand, examining the light olive skin. His skin was soft but the veins on the back of his hand were thick and I traced them with my fingers. I could almost feel the blood pulsing through them. I wanted to consume every part of him, his flesh and blood and soul. I gently kissed his vein.

He sat up and looked at me. He had a strange smile on his face. "So we're really alone now," he said. Saying this out loud gave our privacy new meaning. He leaned in and stared at my face. I looked at his smile and realized that what I had been dreaming about for months was about to happen. I was terrified, desperate to stop before we went too far. But his lips were so close, the silver stud just within reach and coming closer by the second. The final second came and went before I could do anything to stop it.

He kissed me softly at first, like a lamb grazing in a field. Then, when he realized how much I wanted him, hungrily, savagely. He fell on top of me on the floor and I felt the weight of his body, its heaviness, pressing down on me. It was unlike any other feeling I had ever felt or could have imagined. His weight pushed me into the ground as he clawed at my arms and hungrily kissed and licked my face and neck. I ran my hands through his thick dark hair and wished that they might become entangled there, so that we would be connected forever, he and I.

Except that wasn't what happened. Perhaps it happened in an alternate universe where Sufyan and I worked out better. It is how I choose to remember it sometimes, because at least with memory I can control it, I can mould it into my truth like Teta and the president do. But in the cold reality of the universe I was living in, I gently kissed his vein and then . . .

"I'm really drunk. I should probably get home." His voice punctured my hazy thoughts. I dropped his hand. He stood up and rubbed his face, and then looked down at me with half-open eyes.

"You can spend the night here if you want," I said. I reached out to grab his hand again but he pulled it away. He ran that beautiful hand through his hair and burped softly.

"Thanks, but I should probably go home."

He walked out the door and down the stairs. His footsteps grew fainter until they were drowned out by a police siren down the street. And then there was emptiness. I locked the door behind him and stared at the empty room. The silence closed in on me. It was well past midnight, but it was already morning back home, so I called Teta.

The next evening I listened to the American president's solemn declaration of war. I watched the footage of bombs dropping on a city that looked like my own, and realized that from now until the day I died that city would not be what it had been. It had become shorthand to describe an event. The country that once existed was no more. It had changed the moment the first bomb fell through the dark sky. Before the war had even claimed its first human life, the first victim was the city itself. A concept, a history, a culture.

Your life must have been so interesting. I grew up in Ohio. We don't have war and politics and all that stuff.

I had been so naïve. So naïve for so long. I wanted to stop this terrible movie. I wanted to stand up and block everyone's view and yell, "Enough! Enough with this! It's all wrong and this has gone too far. Everything is wrong and you've misunderstood it all!"

But I was trapped inside the movie. The only way to stop this mess would be to stand in the streets and hold up a sign that said: THIS ISN'T REAL. YOU'VE MISUNDERSTOOD EVERYTHING. But if I had learned anything from America, it was that while we may be allowed to hold up a sign, it was very easy to simply shift the eye of the camera until you and your sign were no longer in the shot.

After that night I didn't see Sufyan for ten days. For the first few days I feigned illness and missed our shared classes. I avoided DuPont and his usual routes. When I felt ready to face the possibility of running into him, I agreed to go for lunch with Leila. We met at a restaurant called Damascus Express, where we ordered a fantastic mezzeh, some sweet peppermint tea, and shared a slice of knafeh.

"The last time I went home I was surprised by how many women were wearing the hijab," Leila said as we ate. "Had there not been as many in the past or had I just not noticed them before?"

"Come to think of it, a lot of women in our neighborhood downtown wear a hijab," I said, dipping a piece of bread in the hummus. I had probably eaten more than my share of the fattoush, but Leila didn't seem to care. "I never thought of it too much before I came here."

"Precisely, the hijab meant nothing until America decided it did." Leila shook her head. "This country is fucking with my head."

"Are you going back home anytime soon?" I asked.

"*Inshallah*. I need to get to the camps to do a bit more field research." Leila visited the camps whenever she returned home. She was studying the oral histories of the displaced women there. She spoke often of these women, and in particular of a group of housewives she had spent many long afternoons with, drinking piping-hot tea from thimble-sized glasses. The women gushed over Leila, hugging her and feeding her and asking when she was going to find a husband and advising her on how to dress. Leila laughed it off when she told me this, but I could tell they haunted her. They were her moral compass, her superego, and no matter how many books she read or essays she wrote, they were always there in her mind, asking her when she was going to finally settle down and find a husband and dress more womanlike.

We ate like kings that afternoon in Damascus Express. We shared our food haphazardly and didn't split the bill. The owner, a fat man who smoked cigarettes by the cash register, made small talk with me as I paid.

"Where are you from?" he asked. I told him and he smiled. "*Ahlan wa sahlan*, discount for our family. I knew you were from the *bilad*. The pain in your eyes is different from the pain of those of us living on this side of the world. Let me tell you, brother, here or there, us Arabs will always carry some kind of pain."

I didn't know how to respond to that, so I thanked him and walked away.

Without the possibility of running into Sufyan I felt I had no purpose to my days. I reexamined our time together, trying to figure out what went wrong. Everything had appeared to be moving in the right direction. Perhaps he wasn't ready to confront his feelings. Or could it be that I had hidden myself too well? I was safe from society. But at what cost?

Of course then I saw him. I was sitting at my usual table in Damascus Express, drinking Turkish coffee and reading Gramsci's *Selections from the Prison Notebooks*. I looked up and saw him placing his order at the counter. His back was to me but I knew it was him. I had memorized the shape of his head and the way his broad shoulders angled sharply at the edges. His water bottle hung from his bag, the afternoon sunlight reflecting off the maroon plastic and the water that sloshed inside. It was him.

I buried my face in the book. My heart thumped in my chest. My eyes tried to focus on the words on the page but my mind was racing too fast to understand anything.

> *Kant's maxim "act in such a way that your conduct can become a norm for all men in similar conditions" is less simple and obvious than it appears at first sight. What is meant by "similar conditions"? Therefore the agent is the bearer of the "similar conditions" and indeed their creator. That is, he "must" act according to a "model" which he would like to see diffused among all mankind, according to a type of civilization for whose coming he is working—or for whose preservation he is "resisting" the forces that threaten its disintegration.*

I read the paragraph three or four times, Gramsci lambasting the intellectual who believes his particular thinking is universal for all mankind. Sufyan's eyes found and then rested on me. I didn't even need to look up, I could just sense it. The energy in the room shifted. Slowly he began to walk toward me, as if a magnetic field was pulling us closer. Feigning engrossment, I refused to look up. My fingers trembled as I flipped the page, the adrenaline pumping through my veins like an alcoholic who had just tasted a drop of vodka after months of sobriety.

He stopped at my table.

"Funny seeing you here," he said. I looked up. He was carrying a cup of hot chocolate and had a half smile on his face.

"You, too," I said, forcing a smile. I closed the book. His eyes drifted to the front cover. "Do you know Gramsci?" I asked, even though I knew he had taken the book out of the library a few months earlier.

He laughed. "His name is pronounced Gram-shi, not Gram-ski. He's Italian, not Polish."

"Oh."

"Do you like him?"

"I love him," I gushed. His face twitched. "Not in that way, but—"

"Yeah."

I asked if he liked Gramsci.

"He's all right," Sufyan said. He shifted on his feet, his gaze travelling across the room.

"Sit down." I pushed out the chair opposite me with my foot. He looked at the chair but remained standing.

"I never thought I'd see you in a place like this," he said.

"What do you mean?"

He smiled but said nothing.

"Come on, what do you mean?" I persisted.

"You never struck me as the kind of guy who would spend time in an Arabic café." There was an edge to his voice.

"How so?"

He shrugged. "Forget I said anything."

I should have taken the hint and forgotten about it like he suggested. But a part of me was flattered, flattered that I had provoked any reaction in him, that he had given me enough thought to make an assumption about me.

"Well, I'm an Arab so I don't know why it would be odd that I'm here."

"Yeah, you're an Arab I guess . . . but you're like a Westernized Arab."

I let out a nervous chuckle. "What do you mean, Westernized?"

"Like the way you're dressed . . . "

"I'm wearing jeans and a shirt." I looked down at my clothes. "You're wearing jeans and a shirt. Everyone wears jeans."

"Yeah, but you speak English all the time," he said.

"You don't even speak Arabic!" I laughed, but he didn't laugh along.

"Look, I can tell you've got some sort of contempt for Arabs and Arab culture."

"I don't understand," I said. My hands trembled underneath the table. I rested them on my thighs to keep them steady. I felt my face turn red.

"I mean, look at yourself, with your TV American accent and posters of George Michael on your wall. George Michael." He laughed. "You get on a podium and chant for Arab freedom and then a few hours later say you wish you were not Arab. And even here, reading all this Western theory, hanging out at DuPont with all those white people. You've been colonized, dude."

I was aware my jaw was hanging open but I struggled to maintain composure.

Sufyan shifted his weight again. A drop of hot chocolate spilled down the white mug and kissed the top of his index finger. Ten days ago I was kissing that hand. Now we were here. How did we get here?

"Is this about the other night?" I asked.

"What night?"

"The night you came to my place."

"I can't remember what happened that night," Sufyan said quickly. "Besides, I've stopped drinking."

I looked down at my dog-eared library copy of the *Prison Notebooks*. The English letters seemed to jar with me in a way they hadn't only moments before.

"I can tell I've pissed you off," Sufyan said. "I think I'll leave you with Gramsci." He turned and walked to an empty table in the corner.

Feeling sick with shame, I watched the Arab waiters dance between the mess of plastic tables and chairs, using their fingers to pick up half-drunk glasses of red tea. A sweaty-faced man sliced strips of meat off the shawarma. The atmosphere seemed to switch from familiar and comforting to something alien and threatening. Was I a fake, a fat bourgeois cockroach who couldn't succeed at anything, even something as straightforward as being Arab?

I left the café, walked through the smoggy midday traffic, feeling increasingly irate. The rage I felt was conflicted: Was I angry because I expected more from Sufyan? Or was I angry because in a warped way he had pointed out something that contained a sliver of truth? What was it that I had said that gave him the impression I had contempt for Arabs? Had I internalized that much from the pundits and from Cecile? I tried to recount every conversation Sufyan and I had ever had, which was not difficult considering I relived them in my mind until I had memorized each in great detail, in the same way we were forced to memorize the Quran passages and old nationalist poems that appeared on the first page of those damn Arabic textbooks in those classes I spent my high-school years running from. Could that be it? Maybe it was all those times I ditched Arabic class. I missed out on the lesson about how to be Arab. Maybe there was an ingredient somewhere there, a lecture we were given that I missed. Damn Maj and damn Smoker's Paradise. All those times we ran away had now come back to haunt me.

I walked home, head down and lost in thought. I crossed the road and failed to see the traffic light had turned green. A car screeched to a halt in front of me. I fell backward on the road. A black man popped his head out of the driver's window.

"Watch where you're going, asshole," the man yelled, as I picked myself up from the ground and dusted off the gravel from my jeans. "Stupid white bitch thinks he owns the road."

"I'm not white, I'm Arab," I shouted. The man looked surprised. I ran away before he could say anything else.

Sufyan's accusation settled uncomfortably in my conscience. I studied myself in the bathroom mirror. My clothes might be too fashionable to be authentically Arab, I thought. The T-shirt was just a little too tight, the jeans a tad too ripped. Also, I over-enunciated my English letters. Did my *r*'s roll too smoothly now? Was there not enough of an Arabic hint in the way I spoke English? Was my beard too scruffy? Not scruffy enough? Was my homosexuality responsible? Or was it something deeper, something foreign in my soul?

Whatever it was, I needed to reverse the transformation. Sufyan's accusation left me in a no-man's-land, alienated and fearful of the English books that had kept me company for so many years. I kept away from Damascus Express, spending my days studying in my apartment, away from any possibility of running into Sufyan. Of running into anyone, really. I couldn't face Arabs in case they saw through me, and I couldn't spend time with Americans lest they rub off on me. When I ventured out, I did so in a hurry. Head down, I chased pavements until they led me to dark corners of the library or damp computer labs in the basements of campus buildings.

And yet, I had never felt closer to my mother than I did during this time. For once I understood why she might have left, why she needed to get out from under Teta's rules.

I had only just begun to settle into that thought when I ran into Cecile in a damp computer lab in the basement of one of the campus buildings. When I walked in, I should have known that something was wrong—that damn room had not seen sunlight in years, yet Cecile looked radiant. She had a big smile on her face. I should have turned around and gone home and never spoken to her again. Instead I tossed my bag on the table opposite hers and asked her how she was doing.

"Amazing," she gushed. There was a sparkle in her eye.

"Why?"

Cecile looked coy. "Can I trust you?"

"Yes . . . "

"Not a word . . . "

"Of course."

"I was at that crusty coffee shop you always go to, DuPont, yes? You're right, the coffee there really is good. Anyway, I met someone there . . . someone very special. I just saw him sitting alone at a table and I knew I had to have him."

I don't recall what words she used to tell me about her and Sufyan. I only remember her saying Sufyan's name, and the way she pronounced it, it wasn't like it should be pronounced. The *u* was too hard and the *yan* was clipped and it was all just wrong. As she told me what happened an image burned itself into my brain, of Sufyan and Cecile gyrating against each other in the bathroom of DuPont like wild dogs in heat. I pictured Cecile with her black skirt hiked up above her waist as Sufyan's powerful body plowed into her.

I didn't ask who made the first move. I didn't want to know. I preferred to imagine it was Cecile who pushed herself onto him. Of course it was Cecile who, like her ancestors, felt entitled to the world and everything in it. Like another Western conquest, Sufyan was no longer a person. The poor man had become a situation in the bathroom of a fair-trade coffee shop. I thought of what he might have whispered in her ear, but I struggled to picture him whispering anything to her. They were not right for each other.

"Did you guys mention me?" I asked. The back of my neck burned and my skin felt clammy. I wanted to vomit.

"Why would we mention you? Anyway, I'm seeing Sufyan tonight," she continued. "We're going for a date . . . at DuPont, of course."

I closed my eyes. The caged birds were flying in dizzying circles in my mind. Kung Pao chicken. Kung Pao chicken.

"That's not how you pronounce his name." I tried to sound calm but my voice trembled.

"Pardon?"

"I said," I repeated, "that's not how you pronounce his name."

"He's American—"

"No, he's not fucking American," I snapped. "He's Arab. He has an Arabic name. You can't just decide how you're going to pronounce names. It's pronounced *Souf-yaan*, not *Suf-yen*. If you're going to fuck us at least get our names right."

Cecile looked at me like I had just told her I was about to detonate a bomb.

"And stop introducing me to people as your Arab friend."

"Rasa, it's a JOOOKEE."

"It's not funny. You're not funny. How could you sleep with him? You barely even know him!" I shouted. "You . . . you just slept with this . . . this guy you don't know anything about? Are you a prostitute? What if he has a girlfriend? You don't know anything about his life. What is it with you? You just do things without thinking of the consequences . . . this stupid entitlement . . . this . . . this individualistic freedom to act as you please means you act like an animal, a slave to your whims and impulses. Don't you have any shame? What kind of way of life is this?"

I looked down at my quivering hands. For a few minutes neither of us spoke. I turned back to the computer to work.

"What the hell is wrong with you?" Cecile finally asked.

She looked at me like I was crazy, and maybe I was. I felt fucking crazy.

"I'm sorry."

"So you think I'm a whore now? Some kind of loose woman?"

"That's not what I meant . . ."

Cecile stood up. She grabbed her bag and stormed out of the computer room. Before she left she turned around.

"You know, Rasa? Sometimes you can be so. Fucking. Arab."

I sat in the empty room. The computers hummed around me. Thoughts raced through my mind. How could all this happen at DuPont? That was *our* favorite coffee shop. Only a few weeks ago, after he had left my room, I had been in agony. But even then, there was a sliver of hope. Now, there was nothing.

I should have been with Sufyan in that bathroom. I closed my eyes and pictured it, Sufyan and I grabbing at each other in a bathroom stall as the whooshing sound of the hand dryer concealed our moans. Against the hum of the computers, which sounded more and more like an irritable buzz, I pictured myself wearing the black pencil skirt Cecile might have been wearing. I thought of Sufyan hiking the skirt up in one violent tug and pressing himself against me.

The image of me in a skirt turned my sadness into rage. The computers were roaring now. I wanted to stand up and push them to the floor, smash them into a million pieces and scream into the empty room. There were no answers to any of this. In all the books I had read, there were no answers. I was aware that my thoughts were darkening, and that if I did not leave the computer room soon I would grow more bitter with each passing second, like an abandoned cup of DuPont coffee.

So I left. I stepped out into the chill of the spring evening. I speed-walked through the city. The air smelled fresh from the afternoon rain, and the familiar loneliness fell upon me. I embraced the feeling and wrapped myself in it. The buzzing in my head subsided and the thumping in my chest slowed to a dull ache.

A man in a military uniform approached me.

"Any spare change for our heroes?" he asked, shaking a plastic bucket that jingled with coins.

I shouldered past him without responding. I took great joy in doing this. I could never walk past such a soldier back home without being arrested, or worse. But here, let him try and stop me.

I arrived at my apartment and climbed into bed. I pulled the covers over my head and lay in the stifling darkness. I wanted to cry but there was nothing tangible to cry about. I hadn't lost anything. I was back to where I always was, because I had never left. I cocooned myself in my feelings, breathing in the stale smell of the duvet that reeked of sleep and cigarettes. All around me I smelled loneliness and rejection, and it smelled like butter.

Under the covers I am eleven years old again. It is the night before Eid. My father has an overnight shift at the hospital. My father had always accepted the burden of supporting my mother. An emotional wife was a hand he had been dealt, and Mama swallowed up all the love he gave her and demanded more. But when Baba had his night shifts Mama would appear extinguished, like a punctured balloon. Tonight she is more agitated than usual and spends the entire evening chopping onions. It is the largest bowl I have ever seen. She chops furiously for hours, her face swollen and red.

"Mama, are you okay?"

"Yes, *habibi*, I'm fine."

"Please no more onions," I beg. "I can't eat another onion." She looks up just as a teardrop rolls down her nose and drips onto her forearm. She sniffs, her eyes watery, and rubs her nose with the back of her arm.

"You're right," she says. She puts the knife down and takes a drink from the glass by the chopping board. "After tonight no more onions."

She is quiet and sniffly when she puts me to bed. The sour smell of alcohol envelops me as she lies beside me, a wet tissue wedged inside the palm of her hand as her long fingernails stroke my back. I can tell something is wrong by the way she scratches me. The long, lazy loops she makes with her fingernails are more hurried this evening.

"If I write you letters, will you write back?" she asks.

"Why? Where are you going?"

"I'm not well, *habibi* . . . "

"Mama, you're scratching my back too hard."

"I love you so much." She leans into me for a kiss. "One day you'll understand that sometimes loving someone too much can keep you from becoming yourself."

I wake up a few hours later to the sounds of loud sobbing and Teta tearing through the house. The room is pitch-black. I stumble, bleary-eyed, out of my bedroom and down the dark hallway to the living room. My mother is on the floor, crouched on the Persian carpet with the symmetrical designs of flowers and branches. There is a broken bottle and a pool of blood by her hands. Doris is kneeling beside her. Teta is standing a few feet away. In her arms she has a box of chocolates, an envelope with *eiddieh* cash in it, and a plastic bag filled with marbles in various colors. I stand there silently in my Fido Dido pajamas. Mama is sobbing into the pool of blood. She looks up at me briefly and then buries her face in her chest. Her wailing intensifies.

"Mama's sick, *habibi*. Mama's sick," she says over and over again.

Teta turns to Doris. "What happened?" she booms.

"I don't know," Doris says.

"You whisper in her ear all these years and now you act stupid?" Teta roars.

Teta turns to me. The look on her face releases a terrifying blackness that comes plunging down on me like a vulture. I rub the sleep from my eyes to deflect her unyielding gaze.

"Do you know what's going on?" she asks in a calm voice.

I shrug and begin to cry. I don't know why I am crying but the tears come and I cannot stop them.

"Stop crying," Teta screeches. I cry harder. "Be a man for God's sake!"

I try to hold back my tears but they burst from me.

"Go into your room," Teta demands, pointing with one red manicured finger. I drag myself obediently back to my room, crying, feeling a sorrow that seems to stretch for the rest of my life.

I shut my bedroom door as my mother lets forth a wave of hysterical sobs. I jump inside my bed. I am terrified—terrified and furious. Terrified for my mother and also furious at her. Furious that I am caught up in this, furious that my mother has ruined Eid, furious for all those damn onions she's been making me eat. I bury myself under the covers, farting and weeping and thinking furious thoughts.

"Leave me alone," I can hear my mother screaming from the living room. "Get out of my house!"

"Do you see what you are doing to your son?" Teta yells. Upon hearing this, a wave of self-pity roars through my body. I burst into the loudest sobs, making sure I am heard throughout the house. I want my mother punished for this, for making me feel this way. The sound of Teta's footsteps makes its way toward my bedroom, piercing the silence with each step. I smear my tears and snot across my face for added drama, and hold my breath so that my breathing comes out heavy and desperate. The bedroom door swings open. Teta's large figure rushes toward me like a storm.

"*Habibi*," she takes me in her arms, smothers me with kisses. "Don't cry. Don't let her make you cry."

I burst into exaggerated sobs. My nostrils fill with the smell of her rosewater perfume. I am aware I have finally taken Teta's side against my mother. But is that such a surprise? There was never any doubt about it. I am Teta's child. Everything my grandmother tried to teach my mother, I had swallowed up in her stead. It was down to me to ensure we functioned as a proper family, and although I wasn't sure exactly what a proper family was, I could only take Teta's word for it. In the hallway my mother bursts into a fresh round of moans as Doris consoles her. The sound makes me cry even harder.

The next day my mother is gone. If it were not for that, the day would have been like any other, and my memory of it would have faded into obscurity, like all the other unremarkable days before and since. But of course every single thought, feeling, and event of that day remains seared into my mind. Baba returning from his shift that morning, whispering into the phone for hours, dialing number after number. The grey February sky hung low, threatening rain, until finally, just before I went to bed, the skies opened up and drenched the city with loud, heavy raindrops, and I thought of where my mother might be, whether she was caught under the rain or whether she had made it farther than that, somewhere where the weather might be different.

That night, as Baba and Teta put me to bed, I asked them where Mama had gone, and if she would come back, and whether we would look for her. In response my father said only one thing.

"*Habibi*, the one who knows God most is the one who accepts whatever God has given him."

"And God gave us your mother," Teta added.

My father didn't say any more, but those words stayed with me for a long time. My father only talked about important things. The unimportant things, the trivial things, the obvious things, had always been left to my mother. With my mother gone there was no one to talk to about all the other things, and I took my father's response to mean that my mother's sudden disappearance was an obvious thing that didn't need to be discussed.

After that there were no more questions, even if the longing for my mother grew inside of me with each passing year, a longing that broke out of every secret cage I put it in. Teta had taught Baba and me that our privacy was our way to keep the shameful parts of our life from the public eye. For the longest time it had seemed that my mother was determined to consume as much of our private side as possible, to take up as big a portion of our shame, ensure it was spent on her and no one else. Perhaps as a provocation, or else to force our family into a conundrum—to either confront our shame or relegate her to a secret corner of our minds. But shame was stronger, and in her absence there was at least some relief that our shame would remain undisturbed.

The morning after finding out about Cecile and Sufyan, I woke up with a newfound fury. To hell with America and everyone in it, Sufyan, Cecile, and even my damn mother if she was here. I was finished with assuming the best intentions in those who abandoned me, done trying to assuage my loneliness in barren places. Ultimately, I was filled with rage at myself. I had deluded myself all this time into thinking that there was something there, when in fact I was only chasing my tail and losing myself in the process.

And life moved on, oblivious to my pain. The depth of my loneliness was beautiful, and years of hiding my inner turmoil came in handy. All throughout the spring Sufyan and Cecile hung out. I tried not to pay attention but they were there, in my classes and in DuPont. I ignored them and hung out with

Leila. Because Leila was serious. She was responsible. She was reliable. She would never do what Cecile had done. What America had done. She would never betray me that way.

"Do you think I'm too Westernized?" I asked Leila as we walked back home from the library.

"What do you mean?"

"This guy, Sufyan, says I'm too Westernized."

"The American guy? You're letting an American guy tell you whether you're Arab enough?"

"He's originally Arab—" I began.

"Oh, please. Arab Americans are even worse than white people. They look at you like they know you, as if they have an idea of what you're like from stereotypes and their parents' ancient memories. And when you don't conform to their image it terrifies them, because they wear their Arab culture like window dressing but underneath they are as white as snow."

"I suppose so," I said.

"*Mouajanat*, I call them."

"What do pastries have to do with it?"

"Because they're obsessed with the stuff," Leila continued. "I once went to a dinner organized by a group of Arab Americans. They ordered a plate with four *mouajanat* and divided them among twenty people! They would pick at the *mouajanat* like pigeons and sit there so satisfied in their perceived authenticity."

I bought a black-and-white kaffiyeh and wore it with pride, wrapping it around my neck like a protective shield. I chastised the West for its colonial history. My culture was complex and different. Our *inshallahs* were not a lack of commitment, they were a recognition that rules and regulations can only get you so far. If I could not live like a human in America, if I was to have this stereotype foisted upon me, why not run with it and use it to my advantage? I walked down the street flaunting my kaffiyeh, daring passersby to antagonize me. Instead they just crossed to the other side of the street and kept on walking.

Being gay, that wasn't for me. My homosexuality would leave me alienated wherever I went. In America the gay world touched my life at the margins, through references and images and occasional conversations with men and women who celebrated their homosexuality with pride. As far as I could see there was nothing to be proud about. There was only pain, humiliation, and shame. If I were to join this group, I would have to act proud and hide my feelings of rejection and loneliness. If I were to show these men and women that I was terrified for my future, I would be regarded as misguided or a victim of Islam and Arabness. But if there was one thing I was certain of it was that there was nothing misguided about my feelings, and I did not feel that Islam or my Arabness was to blame. If I were to join this group, I would simply go from the repressiveness of secrecy to the repressiveness of pride. I didn't despise my shame. I had no reason to do so. My shame illuminated my intense attachment to the world, my desire to be connected with others.

I took all my rage and channeled it into activism, into human rights and justice and things that were clear and simple. I was passionately angry about the unjust wars, the brutal occupations, the massacred children, and the exploitation of people for profit and the pursuit of new markets. The angrier I became, the less time I had to think of how lonely I really was. I would never have admitted it to myself at the time, but underneath it all I wanted nothing more than to satisfy an inherent feeling of the unfairness of the world in my own life.

A few months after I had terrorized Cecile in the computer room there was a knock on my door. I opened it and there she was, drenched from the rain and holding a casserole dish, the tinfoil on the top dented and collecting rainwater into a little reservoir. Cecile was crying, her usually vibrant curls plastered against her cheeks as she wiped the tears and rainwater from her face with one hand.

"I made him a vegan lasagna." She held up the dripping dish and burst into tears.

"Come in." I brought her a blanket and sat across from her at the kitchen table. The casserole dish sat in the buffer zone between us.

"I've never cooked a vegan meal in my life," she explained in between sobs. "I thought it would be sweet to do that for Sufyan. I put all my energy into it because he hasn't been well these past few weeks and I wanted to chu-chu-cheer him up."

"Go on." I lit a cigarette and watched her. For the first time she appeared weak. Was she so involved in her own issues she failed to see the world was going to hell around her? But a part of me felt that familiar rush at the mention of Sufyan's name, even if she still managed to mispronounce it.

"He wasn't taking my calls. I hadn't seen him in almost two weeks. He's been hanging out with this Muslim Society group on campus that is full of these serious men. He said I would never understand. So when he didn't answer my call today I just went over to his house. I knocked on the door and he comes out looking like he hasn't shaved in weeks. He looked at the lasagna and told me not to come around his house any more and that we were over."

"So you came here?"

"I don't know what's got into him." She blew her nose, leaving in her wake a trail of white tissue carnage.

I walked over to Cecile and gave her a hug and a puff of my cigarette. She burrowed her face in my shoulder, soaking my kaffiyeh with her imperialist tears. I looked at the cold lasagna, wondering at what point it would be appropriate to ask her if I could have a bite.

After that we found ourselves picking up where we had left

off. Cecile got over the pain of losing Sufyan soon enough, finding new emotional crises to satisfy her.

As for Sufyan, he quietly withdrew from the activist circles and spent more time in closed rooms with bearded men. His own beard grew out, from a light, carefree stubble to a serious, fuller Ikhwan beard. In the end neither Cecile nor I could keep him. I was filled with sadness that his new beard had covered up the tiny scar under his lip where the piercing once stood. The silver stud was the first thing that had caught my eye, and its disappearance seemed like a confirmation that everything about those times was now hidden under a thick mound of hair.

After graduation I made a half-hearted attempt to stay in America. But as Leila and I searched for jobs, it dawned on us that without the right contacts, we would never get work. And soon enough the kaffiyeh started popping up everywhere, worn by fashionable hipsters in a variety of colors. What was once feared was now saturated to irrelevance. The kaffiyeh had lost its significance, so I took it off. It was time to go home.

I did one thing before I left America, and that was to tell Cecile my secret. During my last summer there, I rented a room in her house. We smoked weed in the mornings and cycled through the city's parks, reading all the beatniks and listening to Bob Marley. It was like the knowledge that I was soon to return home allowed me to relax and let her into my world, and gave me the courage to step into hers.

The day before my flight home, Cecile and I went to the park, where we spent all day lying on the grass clearing by the crystal blue lake. We had smoked enough weed that we were no longer high but retained a permanent buzz that enveloped us like a blanket. Our skin tingled from the sun as we watched cloud formations and the gentle swaying of the trees above our heads. We watched the sun set on the warm summer evening.

I was not intending to tell her. Our conversations that day

had been lazy and calm. But I knew I had to tell someone before I left America, someone who was far away from home, so that the secret would be out, yet kept at a safe enough distance. And Cecile seemed like the perfect person to tell: She would not hide her emotions from me, or soften her words to spare my feelings. I would get her judgement swiftly and honestly, and if I was to confess this to anyone, I could not stand to question the sincerity of their response.

There was a lull in the conversation as we watched the sun set, our bare feet caressing the blades of grass, our bikes lying next to us. She seemed unsurprised by my confession and was quiet for a while.

"Why are you telling me this now?" she finally asked.

"I don't know. I suppose I owe myself this. I can't say I came to America and left without telling anyone about it. I would go back home and regret it too much."

"Would they kill you over there?" she asked.

"I don't think so." I paused. "Listen, people don't just kill each other like you hear on TV."

"In any case," she squeezed my leg, "I'm glad you told me."

III.
THE WEDDING

I don't realize I have fallen asleep until the door to Teta's bedroom creaks open. Thrust back into the present, I rub my eyes and look around. I'm in a pitch-black room. I try to get up and slip. I'm in an empty tub, naked. The toilet bowl smells of dead cigarettes. My phone says it's just after six P.M. I know it is not a good day when I have spent much of it in the bathroom. I lie back down and stare into the darkness. How long have I been here, dreaming of a time that seems so long ago? Why am I so stuck in the past? Because the present has spun out of my control, so my thoughts are often spent in times where I have the power to change things, even if only in my memory.

I pull myself out of the tub and stand naked in the center of the bathroom. The sound of Teta's footsteps shuffling across the carpet fills me with an inexplicable sense of disappointment. Disappointment that she has woken up at all, perhaps, as shameful as such a thought is. Ever since returning from America, I have found living with her to be a nightmare. She is a difficult woman, always sitting in her chair, watching the news and my movements, asking a million questions every time I leave the house. When I tried to move out once she accused me of abandoning her. I can't leave her now, not unless I get married or she dies, and God knows I'm not getting married anytime soon. So I suppose I will have to continue to avoid her for what's left of our lives together.

I have studied the sound of Teta's footsteps for so long that

I can tell by the number of steps she has taken that she has paused by my room. To listen or snoop, maybe. This old lady and her antique beliefs. Her ideas should have died a long time ago, yet they hang in the air like a fart. It is her and people like her who keep Taymour and me apart. Does this ancient woman not know what love is? Have old age and her stagnant sense of shame dried out her heart? *Eib*, she would say. *Eib*. This obsession with what people will say has stripped her of her humanity.

Her shuffling begins once more and stops just outside the bathroom. I hold my breath. Who knows what she saw last night? Before the screams it had been a night like any other summer night. The slight breeze brought some cool air and the smell of jasmine through the cracks between the shutters. On the bed Taymour and I had been lost in each other. He lay on his back and I fawned over him, stroking his hair and kissing his neck and cheeks. I wasted it. No, not wasted. Ruined. Because all I can think about is how disgusting we must have looked together. All I can picture is Teta watching her grandson, the man of the house, fawning over another man. I'm a pervert, sick and diseased. I've strayed down the wrong path, and it's taken me here, to the point where I seduce men in Teta's house.

I rest my head on the cool tiles of the bathroom wall. I wait but I don't know for what. For her to knock on the door, kick it open, or perhaps scream and bang on it as she did last night. She'll drag me out of the bathroom by my ear, throw me out of the house, and if I don't leave, she'll call the police or the neighbor's son to remove me. I don't know. I am not sure of much, except that I am alone, and that it's unbearably hot.

Instead she stands there. She is on one side of the door and I am on the other, two heavy souls separated by the flimsiest of wooden doors. I bend down and gently move the underwear hanging on the doorknob. I peer through the keyhole, half expecting to see her brown eye staring back at me. But all I see is her white nightgown and nothing more. Her body shifts and the nightgown rustles in the gentle breeze of the early evening. She lets out a deep sigh and lumbers toward the kitchen.

"Doris," she calls out. And then, quieter, but still audible: "How long has he been in there?"

I don't hear Doris's response, but I imagine Teta sitting at the kitchen table while Doris fills her in on my movements. I had noticed Doris look behind me to see who had dropped me off from work earlier today. Perhaps they were in this together, Sherlock Holmes and Watson, out to make sure my movements are not connected in any way to Taymour.

I move away from the door and flick on the light switch, on and off, on and off. Nothing. Another damn power cut. My hands fumble in the darkness, feeling for the lighter. I find it, flick it, and look in the mirror. I look like shit. There are heavy bags under my eyes. My hair is disheveled and my skin is grey. There is no escape from here. I've wasted my opportunity in America. It's gone from me now, like Taymour, like Teta.

I look at my body, like a prison. I live within this prison of contradictions that fight one another like stray cats in my mind. I'm neither here nor there. Not in America and not here. Each forms a part of me, and when they all add up, all that is left is *shaath*.

Ana shaath.

If said in the right way there was a ring to it. *Shaath*, allowing the breath to ride the *aa* in the center of the word like a lazy wave. *Shaath*. It wasn't perfect but it was something I could work with, if on inflection alone. *Shaath*: queer, deviant, abject. Is it just my homosexuality that makes me *shaath*, or something more than that?

I tear myself from the mirror, light the candle by the bidet, and turn on the shower. No water comes out. I suppose I'll have to go to this joke of a wedding in my filth. Besides,

Taymour has seen me at my worst: naked, hysterical, pleading with Teta to stop screaming. If he still wants to run away with me then a bit of filth certainly won't put him off. I get dressed and unlock the door.

The hallway is dark and quiet, but there is movement in the kitchen. I tiptoe to my bedroom and carefully shut the door. The night table is filled with empty coffee cups, their shadows lengthening in the dying sun. I light a candle and place it on the dresser and lie down on my bed.

This bed, this room, is Taymour. Everything in my life is Taymour. When I returned from America and moved back in with Teta, I installed a lock so she wouldn't keep barging in all the time. She threw away my clothes, my ironic American T-shirts, and my perfectly ripped jeans (which she said made me look poor), and she took me shopping in the old city and bought me the frumpiest clothes she could find. I reconnected with Maj and Basma, and it felt like old times except we were drowning in that feeling everyone got when they came back but no one dared mention, of having been surgically removed somehow and realizing that the wound had closed up, leaving us outside. And then there was my first Ramadan back, when I spent the entire month locked in the house watching *Oprah*, smoking cigarettes, and playing countless games of bridge with Teta (honestly, I've never met a person who cheats so much in my life). Then after Ramadan the bars opened again and I got so drunk at Guapa I threw up out the window of Maj's car as we raced through the streets with Radiohead blasting from the speakers. Then I visited the dying museum downtown and wrote a scathing blog post about the government's lack of care for cultural artefacts. Then I met a man online for the first time and we drove in circles around his house until his parents left and we snuck in and had sex so quickly that in a moment it was over and I walked home in shame. Then another wave of violence brought a mass of refugees flooding into the city. Then Maj drunkenly tried to kiss me one night and the next day played it off as a joke. Then I slept with a man from al-Sharqiyeh who wore skintight jeans and told me he dreamed of going to America and getting a dog, and afterward I felt so guilty about my life and my chances and how I had spent the last four years in America doing what, nothing, that's what. Then, after calculating that my monthly paycheck would only buy me thirty beers at Guapa, after a thousand miserable taxi driver conversations and a million paranoid Internet chats with strangers (no name, no face pics, masc4masc), after walking by a policeman beating a teenage boy and looking the other way, after friends started to get married and started to ask me when I was going to get married, after Teta started to ask me when I was going to get married, after women started to ask me questions about my last name, my income, and what neighborhood I lived in (and, of course, whether I was married), after I began to date women out of a lack of any other options, after all of this I met Taymour. He became my world.

I had been casually seeing a girl. She was a close friend of his, but I did not know it then. She was the last one, I decided at the time. We had been on a few dates and were approaching that point where there would be no turning back. We would either be together or not. I had stalled for too long, so that what was left was a husk of what could have been marriage, kids, Teta's approval, all those things.

We were in Guapa, bored, our courtship hanging between us like a sick dog that needed to be put down. I asked her if she wanted to go to the cinema and she said, "I don't know," and sighed. We were all bored then, before the protests. Deflated and resigned to the fact that we would remain like this forever. We sat in Guapa watching the mood darken. I had drunk enough beer to maintain a conversation but not to feign interest in one, and I worked to sustain this level, a faint buzz that kept me mellow. There we all were, the entire country and me in that never-ending prerevolutionary resignation, like sexually frustrated adolescents who have had their POLSKASAT disconnected. And then Taymour arrived.

He was wearing gym shorts, a baseball cap, and a University of Virginia T-shirt. He shook my hand firmly and sat at our table. I was taken by his legs. They were muscled and hairy. He caught me looking at them and I quickly looked away. He looked fresh and sweaty and I could tell from the way his eyes scanned the room that he saw the world the same way I did. I realized then why everything in my life had happened, because it was all leading me to that moment. I saw Taymour and felt that it was true what they say about fate, that in the infinite possibilities we had found each other against so many odds.

After he ordered a beer I asked him what he did. He said he was a doctor.

"Don't just tell him that," the girl urged. "Tell him what you really like doing."

Taymour said he played music, piano, violin, guitar, and that he sang as well.

"A musical doctor," I said, and he smiled. I felt so proud of myself for making him smile, because he smiled in a way that showed he didn't give out smiles for cheap.

I didn't learn much about him until later that night. In Guapa he was so quiet. He nodded at the appropriate points in the conversation and coughed when our cigarette smoke blew in his face. But even then I could tell he was from a good family and had been groomed to behave in a manner deemed acceptable by society. At the time, I had thought to myself that if he were a woman I would have taken him home immediately and paraded him in front of Teta. She would have been thrilled for me to have found a girl like that.

That night I was so happy I drank and drank to delay our separation. By the time we were ready to leave I was ensnared in a blissful drunkenness. Taymour offered to drive us both home, and after dropping the girl off he turned to me and asked if she was my girlfriend. It was so cute, him asking me this, trying to be casual, and yet I could sniff out the curiosity underneath the question.

"I suppose so, yes," I replied.

"And yet you're in the car with me?"

I asked if he had a girlfriend and he chuckled. We were silent after that. But within that silence a more serious conversation was brewing. Until then, we couldn't afford to resort to small talk. We relaxed into the stillness and then he began to hum, and then quietly sing, his voice soft and nostalgic.

When we arrived at my house I invited him in. He accepted. We were both unsure but we were following each other, leading each other into this secret world. He stood beside me politely as I unlocked the front door. In my bedroom I grabbed the bottle of whisky I keep hidden under my bed, a bottle Teta knows about but acts ignorant of, as if to allow me that one vice. I turned off the lights, lit a few candles, poured us each a glass of whisky, and turned the radio on, softly, so as to not wake up Doris or Teta. Taymour asked if I lived with my parents and I told him the truth, immediately, which I never do. About my mother and my father. I hid nothing. We were looking into each other's eyes and to lie would be to blink and ruin what we were creating. On the radio Oum Kalthoum's voice floated through the room.

Oh my heart, don't ask me where the love has gone . . .

Taymour picked up the book sitting on my bedside table. *Seasons of Migration to the North*, he read the title out loud, put the book to his nose and flipped through the pages, breathing in the book's musty scent. I wanted to be the words in the book, to have him breathe me into his body. He turned to me and, tracing his fingers along the book's cover, asked, "Do you feel like you don't belong here?"

"I don't feel I belong anywhere."

Taymour looked down and smiled. "I almost didn't come back after university. The thought of coming back, and having to fit into society's mould, it was too much."

"Even if people like us never fit in?"

He shrugged. "At least we know the game here. We know how society works. We can play by the rules, one foot in and one foot out. It's the only way to be, because if you get sucked too deeply into society you get stuck in the throes of something that simply doesn't exist. But if you're too far away then you are lost."

"My father once said that the most important affiliation for the Arab is his family and community."

"I agree with your dad," Taymour said. "If you don't have society, what else is left?"

We chatted for a long time that night, stifling yawns and chasing away moments of silence, fearing they would lead us toward an ending where we would have to part. We were creating a new world, our own society, in my room. We were populating this world with our unfiltered thoughts and fears. It was all our doing, we knew we had to make sure everything we put into our world was authentic and real, and it felt so good, to finally live and speak from the heart.

The muezzin started his call to prayer, which brought us back to the outside world, gently, like a bridge between our world and theirs. Taymour said he had to go home, but it was in the "had to" that I felt I could hold on.

"The bed is big enough for two," I said, as casual as I could, fielding off the implications that buzzed around us like mosquitoes waiting to strike. He appeared to consider this for a moment and then nodded. I gave him a T-shirt, some clean shorts. I looked away as he changed, but not before catching a glimpse of his strong chest, peppered with brown hair. I took off my jeans and T-shirt, blew out the candles, and climbed into bed. We lay side by side, staring at the dark ceiling. Suddenly his phone rang. It was his mother. He answered and spoke to her in a hushed tone. I turned on the light and fiddled with my own phone. He listened patiently as she spoke, a seriousness returned to his features, and for a moment I assumed a terrible accident had occurred. When he got off the phone he looked disappointed. I asked if everything was okay.

"Everything is fine. I just . . . I have to go home. She sounds worried." He let out a long sigh and lay back down on the bed, the phone resting on his stomach. I did not say anything until the light of his mobile screen went out and we were once again shrouded in darkness.

I lay beside him and turned to face him. "Tell me about your family."

And he did. He told me about his mother, his father, the maid. How they all live together. On the surface everything appears as it should. His parents attend social gatherings, smiling and holding hands. But when they return home his mother goes upstairs to her bedroom, while his father goes into his bedroom. He told me how his mother discovered his father having an affair with the maid. How she ordered an extra floor be built on the roof of their villa. How she moved there once it was built, and every night the maid creeps into his father's bedroom. And how not a soul knows, not his uncles or aunts, his cousins or his grandparents. And it's him, only him, whom his mother has, and she is terrified of losing him.

"It makes me so angry, to be part of this secret. How a series of incidents has forced me into a situation where nothing makes sense and yet everything appears as it should."

Oh, how right he was. It was as if he were foretelling our own story, although at the time neither of us could have predicted everything that was to happen. And then he looked at me and said, "I didn't realize how lost I had been until I saw you tonight. Did you feel the same? That we had been lost for years and had only just found each other again?"

He put his hand on my hip as we lay in the dark. His hand was like an intruder from a parallel universe. I studied the expression on his face as his hand began to move in soft circles on my lower back. I could feel his warm breath on my hand as I reached out and touched his cheek, running my fingers along the contours of his cheekbones and jaw. I was leaving my fingerprints on him, so that if we were to be found there would be no escaping the evidence. I was terrified of what this meant but I also knew that he was right: We had been lost for so many years but now we had found each other, two souls suffering the same pain. I could feel his body trembling. It was as if he had expended all his courage to get himself to this stage, in bed with me, his hand on my back, that he had nothing left to give.

"It's okay," I whispered.

And then we descended on each other. We ripped off our clothes and masks and delusions until there was nothing left, just the two of us, raw, skin on skin. We were completely bare and utterly whole. Two abandoned souls, we wrapped our arms around each other, tried to become one again. We felt unbreakable. Afterward we lay for a while, maybe fifteen minutes, and then he turned to me with a mischievous look in his eyes. He pulled me toward him, harder now, and this time we were rougher, wrestling and pushing against each other, as if through violence we might drown out the shame we felt. We came one more time and lay side by side, panting and sweating, for a few minutes more.

The sun was rising when he left. I unlocked the front door and he touched my hand. His face looked so serious. I gave him a quick, hungry kiss, relishing the softness of his lips for one last time that night. Watching him walk to his car, I felt light as air, as if the weight that had been bearing down on me for years was gone, and I was now like everyone else.

When I returned to the bedroom I noticed his red boxer shorts on the floor by my bed. Had he forgotten them, or did he leave them there for me? I looked for my own underwear but could not find it. Surely he must have noticed, as he pulled on his gym shorts, that he was wearing not his underwear but mine. Maybe it was a message, a promise that he would be back. I put his underwear on, felt my dick touch the soft cotton where his dick had rested only a few hours ago. We were one now.

But then the sunlight crept through the shutters and I began to worry. The birds were singing and at any moment Doris would leave her bedroom and prepare the house for breakfast. Then Teta would wake up and barge into my room. *Yalla ya, Rasa, yalla, habibi.* I felt the danger palpably, intimately. I cleaned up, hiding the glasses of whisky under the bed. As the sunlight crept in through the windows, the shame inside of me began to awaken.

By breakfast I was longing for him again. I sat across from Teta as she complained. I couldn't even tell what was annoying her this time, I just nodded along and picked at the halloumi and radishes Doris had placed on the table. I wasn't concerned with anything that day. I had everything I could ever want. I realized I could be happy without changing myself in the process, and Taymour had shown me how. Was this what all the couples at the weddings I've attended feel?

That damn wedding tonight. I would much prefer to spend the rest of the evening here in my underwear, smoking cigarettes and dreaming I was somewhere else, some other time when there was hope. But if I miss the wedding I would be inviting too many questions.

I open the closet and pull out my suit. I have only ever

owned two suits. The first one Baba bought for me many years ago. I needed something to wear for his burial, and he had the foresight to buy one for me. He didn't tell me what the suit was intended for, but one of the first things he did after he found out about his illness was to take me to a tailor downtown. We parked the car and walked into a quiet shop in the attic of an old building. As the tailor—an elderly man with a salt-and-pepper mustache—silently measured the length of my waist and inseam, I was dimly aware that my father's eyes were red and moist. Looking back now, I'm not sure whether there actually were tears in his eyes or if I had added them in later in my memory of that moment. Maybe I wanted to solidify the atmosphere that surrounded us at the time, the grief and sadness for all that we were to lose, manifesting those feelings into solid, round teardrops in my father's eyes.

That day my father picked out a classic black suit. I wanted a gray one but there was no arguing with Baba. He also picked out a tie that was dark, almost black, except under the sun the color turned a deep blue. When we got back home he knotted the tie for me and said, in a very serious tone, "Don't undo the tie. You won't be able to knot it again."

I only wore that suit once, on the day of his burial. After that it hung on a metal hanger in the corner of my closet, the blue-black tie hanging over it, the knot still in place. When I returned from university after my first year the suit was missing.

"Where did it go?" I asked Doris as I rummaged through the shirts and trousers that hung in my closet.

"Teta throw," Doris said.

I ran to the living room and asked Teta what she did with the suit.

"That tiny thing? I threw it out, it was too small."

"What do you mean you threw it out?" I bellowed. I had never raised my voice at Teta before. But the thought of losing the suit and that tie, which had remained firmly knotted and carried Baba's touch and breath within its knot, was too much to bear.

"What are you yelling about?" Teta snapped.

"Baba bought that for me," I said.

"He bought it for you to wear at his funeral. For God's sake, why would you want to keep that? If you loved your father so much, why not hang on to happier memories?"

"I don't want to pick and choose memories," I said. "We're worse than the government with the way we rewrite history. I am sick of hanging photos of him smiling when I know he's rotting in the ground somewhere."

She slapped me, almost impulsively. When she withdrew her hand, her palm was red. She held on to her wrist, as if using one hand to stop the other one from taking another strike.

"Shame on you," Teta said. "Shame, shame on you."

I bought another suit, years later, when I had come back from the States and my friends started to drop like flies into the cesspool of marriage.

I put this suit on now, and stick the photograph of Ahmed's son—my letter to Taymour—in the shirt pocket. Looking at myself in the mirror, there is nothing special about this suit. There was no tailor, no measurements or anything like that. I simply picked a suit hanging from a rack alongside hundreds of identical suits. I only wear it to weddings, which makes the suit even more distasteful to me. Weddings are perhaps the most cynical of events, so reliant on how much money you earn, what family you come from. Weddings are the most unjust of exchanges dressed up in the language of beauty and love. Each wedding adds a stain of hatred to this suit. It's summer now, wedding season, and tonight's wedding, of all weddings, is the pinnacle of this façade. Given the amount of bullshit tonight's wedding will smear on the cheap fabric, I will probably have to throw this suit away tomorrow morning.

Dressed for the wedding, I step out of my bedroom and walk toward the kitchen. My heartbeat quickens and I resist the urge to run back inside. They can hear my footsteps now. There is no turning back. I stamp down the hall to make sure they hear me coming, to make sure I won't chicken out at the last minute and lock myself in my bedroom for the rest of my life. I arrive at the kitchen door. Doris and Teta turn to look at me, their faces partially hidden in the dark blue shadows of dusk. The flame from a single candle flickers in a corner by the oven.

"You're awake," Teta says. She is sitting at the kitchen table in front of a saucepan of carved courgettes and a neon green plastic bucket of stuffed ones. An unpeeled onion sits in the middle of the table. A warning that things might get ugly. She looks at me. I feel naked under her gaze, as naked as I was when she peered through the keyhole last night. She sits there looking at me, surrounded by the courgettes, the neon green bucket, that damn onion. I want to snatch the onion away and demand that she just cry without it. But in fact she's doing us both a favor, isn't she?

"There's no electricity and no water," I say.

Teta sighs and returns to stuffing a courgette while Doris stands over a frying pan by the stove. I pour myself a glass of water from the water cooler. I can feel Teta's eyes on my back. When I turn around her gaze returns to the courgette in her hands. She stuffs the courgette with a lifetime of experience. First she spoons the rice and meat into the courgette with a quick jerk of her thumb, and then pushes it deep inside before dropping it back into the plastic bucket. Her long fingernails are crusted with dried meat and sauce.

There is silence as Doris and I wait to see what direction Teta intends to take, and whether she will mention anything about last night. If she has watched the news today she would know about the arrests, which may provide an entry point to the subject. I consider asking her but decide not to mention it for fear of inviting a discussion. I stand in the kitchen, paralyzed by the fear that anything I may say could tangentially be related to the events of the night before.

"I don't understand this girl," Teta finally says, pointing toward Doris without looking up from her courgette. "I specifically told her not to clean the floors every day because it's a waste of water. Now we don't have water and need to wait until Friday for the delivery. Clean the floor maximum every other day but at least once a week. Tell me, is that difficult to understand?"

"Teta—" I begin.

"There's no need to clean every day. There. Is. No. Need!" Teta throws the courgette she is stuffing back in the bowl to drive her point home. Doris looks up from the pan for a moment then, shoulders slumped, lowers her head.

"*Ma'alesh*, Teta, just let it go."

"It's a waste. I don't understand why she does it. Why is it so difficult to follow simple instructions?"

"Teta, if she cleans you say she wastes water. If she doesn't then you say she is lazy and dirty. Don't you see that she can never win with you?"

"Don't start acting like a human rights lawyer. My God, we sent him to study in America and he comes back and tells us we are slave owners. The real problem is that you spoil her. Look at her, she's become a *daloo'a*. You joke and laugh with her and she thinks she doesn't have to work. Are we paying her to clean the house or to be your friend?"

I look at Doris. How would Teta react if I told her I was in love with Doris and we wanted to marry? Would she find that preferable to me being with Taymour? On the scale of public humiliations, which would shame her more—that I have fallen in love with a man from one of the best families in the country, or that I have fallen for our maid?

I need to get out of here.

"I'm going to meet Maj," I say.

"Just Maj?"

"Yes."

"Where?" she asks.

"Guapa."

"You're always at Guapa. Aren't there better places than Guapa?"

"I like Guapa," I say, downing the water and putting the empty glass in the sink.

"If only you liked your studies as much as you like Guapa. And why are you dressed like that?" she points a courgette at me. "Are you planning to get married in Guapa as well?"

"I have a wedding later."

"Whose wedding?"

I hesitate. "A friend from university."

"Then why are you going to Guapa?"

"The wedding is not until later, Teta. I will leave straight from there."

"Do whatever you want." She drops another stuffed courgette into the bucket.

"Can I use the car?"

"I need the car."

"What do you need the car for? Are you going somewhere tonight?"

"No," she says. "But I don't like not having a car. I feel like a prisoner. Can't Maj pick you up?"

"It's fine. I'll just take a taxi."

"Don't get yourself in trouble. There are problems out there. The last thing we need is for you to get caught in them."

"I won't," I say, grabbing my wallet and keys.

"It's a republic of shame we're living in these days."

"*Khalas*, stop worrying." I begin to walk out of the kitchen. At the door I pause. If I mention nothing now, will we ever discuss last night? In another family I may have been thrown out with nothing but the clothes on my back, or at least received a beating I would never forget. But that won't happen, because Teta needs me as much as I need her. Perhaps more. And if I'm out of here then she can't control me any more. She'll be on her own. Last night all she could do was wave her arms in the air and scream incomprehensibly. And now? Nothing. Denial. I turn around and look at Teta's back. She is still stuffing courgettes, although her shoulders are now drawn in. She knows I'm standing behind her, watching her. If I leave it like this, she will have won. She'll have had her way, and Taymour will be relegated to the dustbin, just like Mama.

"Is there nothing you want to say to me?" I ask. Her back stiffens. She drops the courgette she is stuffing into the bucket. I hear it fall on top of the pile of courgettes with a wet thud. She turns in her chair to face me. We look at each other, and I can see in her eyes she knows I am challenging her. She licks her lips, like a cat that has just caught a mouse by its tail.

"When is Maj going to get married?" she asks in a sweet voice. She's played her card skillfully. When is Maj going to get married. So she has given up hope on me now, is that what she is trying to say? That there's no use for me any more, so let her start on the next person in line.

"So now you're working on Maj?"

"He'll miss the boat soon."

"Oh don't worry about him," I say. "He has his own mother to do the nagging."

"*Haram.* He's a wonderful young man. What a shame if he doesn't start his own family."

"What is it with us Arabs?" I snap. "Our only goal and dream in life is to get married?"

Teta turns back to the courgettes.

"Go to Guapa," she says, victoriously.

I go to Guapa, drink ice-cold beer that costs twice as much as it does in America, and eat salted watermelon seeds. I sit at the bar and watch the crowd of intellectuals smoke cheap cigarettes and stare into their phones. It is just after seven, and the wedding begins at nine. I don't want to speak to anyone and I don't want to go home.

Guapa is tucked in a quaint alleyway in the old quarter, the roads leading to it are small and narrow, and you often have to drive around the area three or four times before finding a parking space, but it's worth it. The entrance is concealed by two low-hanging jasmine vines that attract bees in the springtime. These vines emit a wonderful smell and, during nights so muggy that walking into Guapa feels like stepping into an inferno, Maj and I often sit underneath the jasmine, the sweat on our skin glistening under the streetlights. We drink red wine, smoke cigarettes, and talk until the idea of going back home becomes bearable.

On the inside the bar is dark and grimy and stinks of beer. Posters of Arabic movies from the sixties hang on the walls. A decaying pool table forms the centrepiece of the room and provides a space for people to congregate in order to drink and watch each other. The bar isn't air-conditioned but there are rickety fans that blow the stale air around in circles. On the margins people stare into the glare of their laptops and smoke. Every night the staff plays the same playlist from the old MacBook perched on the bar. The laptop belongs to Nora, and the playlist is so her: somber, angry, real. I like that.

Nora specializes in setting up bars for disgruntled people to congregate in. These places are difficult to find. Sometimes when the Mukhabarat are bored, they bring Nora in for questioning. They ask her why her clientele are not happy, and eventually they close the establishment down for a few weeks or months or until they've lost interest.

It is surprising Guapa has lasted this long. When Nora took

over the management six years ago she transformed it from an unknown dive into a semi-known dive. Her army of lesbians, in their uniform of black T-shirts and jeans, always comes with her. They play pool and have long, whispered discussions with their confused girlfriends, who are torn about whether or not to leave this secret life for a husband and status in society.

Despite the stench of sweat and stale beer, the atmosphere in Guapa is warm. But it is in the basement that the real fun happens, and where Maj really shines. The moment Maj puts his heels on he becomes someone powerful. He stands in the centre of the room, his bright red lipstick glinting under the lights, head tilted slightly upward, and he commands your attention without even trying. He is so good at dressing up you'd never know he was a boy. I'd only recognize him by his big brown eyes and that deep crease between his eyebrows. For some reason I was always afraid that if I stayed in Guapa too long, I might be stuck with such a crease. From being forced to think too much, to rebel all the time. I don't want to be so outside of everything. Even without a crease I am different enough. I can't do with any more marks of abnormality.

On a nearby chair someone has left a copy of yesterday's *New York Times*. I pick up the paper, and just for something to do with my hands, leaf through the pages. On page three there is an article Laura contributed to, discussing America's growing concerns with instability in our country. I put the paper back down. I still haven't heard from Taymour, although I don't know what I want to hear from him any more. I stare at my phone. It sits there smugly on the table. It's no longer my phone but rather Taymour's, and they are both conspiring against me with their silence.

When I see you at the wedding will you act like what we had never existed? I text, not expecting a response.

I've grown used to the agonizing wait for Taymour. One evening last year he called to tell me that we would have to be apart for a few weeks. His father had caught him creeping into the house at dawn. I told him to lie, but Taymour could not disobey his father's wishes. So I waited for two weeks, checking in every day to see if the embargo was over.

Since then I've spent hundreds of hours like this. Wondering if he will reply, or whether he will come by or not. Then, hearing the sound of the phone vibrating seconds before it lets out a ping. That ping will give me a heart attack one of these days. Sometimes it would say *On my way*, but more often his response would be a simple *Can't tonight*. That *Can't tonight*, always pinging its way into my phone. Why could he not do tonight, exactly? Did he not have legs that could walk him from his house to my bedroom if he so desired? No, can't tonight. So casual. As if it was fine whether we saw each other or not. Whatever. Maybe we will both die and never see each other again. It's okay. No big deal. Can't tonight.

I slam my pint down. Beer sloshes on the wooden bar. The spilled beer bubbles and hisses on the table like a giant protest. I watch the bubbles in the foam pop. Each bubble is like an angry, hopeful face in the crowd. I feel in control, like I am a God creating a revolution from the concoction of spilled foam and beer. When the liquid settles, I drag my finger across the middle, splitting the ocean of protesters into separate camps. My finger is a tank, and I destroy one of the protest camps, dragging my finger along the table to create a vast sea of rebellion. I trace battalions on the wood and imagine they are attacking one another. I make another battalion and then split it into two.

In a corner of the bar a lean man with a mustache tries to catch my eye. Finally I look at him and he smiles, but I quickly look away. I have no desire for sex. My dick has shriveled up ever since I heard Teta outside the bedroom door last night. It's hidden away in shame, like a dog caught chewing the carpet.

It was only a matter of time before I would lose Taymour.

For a long time I was stuck between wanting him near me and feeling terrified: terrified of losing him, but more terrified that I would not lose him, that we would be stuck in this predicament for the rest of our lives. And how would I explain that to everyone? How would I explain that to Teta? My feelings swung between wanting to kidnap him and lock him up in my room forever, so that he would be mine and mine alone, and wanting to kill him so he would be out of my life. A crime of passion, a crime of honor.

I had thought that as time passed I would grow more comfortable with my emotions. Instead, as we fell deeper into each other, I found myself locked in a battle with my feelings. What would happen if I let myself fall? Whenever Taymour came too close I pushed him away with a backhanded insult or accusatory text message. The possibility of abandonment colored what we had. The fear of it lingered between us, so that rejection became an ever-present threat. We were in competition, Taymour and I, over who would leave first. The threat of abandonment is worse than to be abandoned, I think. I couldn't stand the waiting, so I introduced Taymour to Leila.

Well, not at first. I began by telling her that there was someone she should meet, someone very special. I enjoyed talking about Taymour like this, to sing his praises and say nice things about him. When I introduced them, she smiled at him with a funny look in her eyes. Later that day I asked what she thought of him.

"Don't start with me." She laughed. "I get enough pressure from my mother." But even as Leila said this, her eyes registered a flicker of curiosity, and the housewives in the camps who had embedded themselves in her mind many years ago were nodding their heads furiously in approval.

At the time, I told myself that I wanted to see if she loved him for the same reasons I did. It would be nice to hear someone say those reasons out loud, even if it wasn't me.

When I told Taymour of my idea, he laughed it off.

"That's a ridiculous thought," he said. "Why would I do that?"

"It would help us be together. Make people suspect less, no?"

"Something bad is going to happen tonight," a woman seated next to me says, snapping me away from the revolution of spilled beer I've drawn on the bar.

She is in her late twenties, with hennaed hair and lips so chapped they look like gravel. She is sitting alone.

"Every night feels like that in this city," I reply.

"Perhaps. I haven't been here long enough to find out." She doesn't look at me, choosing to stare at the pool table instead. Two men are playing pool with cigarettes hanging dangerously from the tip of their lips. There are only a few balls left in the game, and soon it will be over. The green fuzz of the pool table is ash-ridden and stained with dark patches.

"Where are you from?"

"The camp." She takes a swig from the glass of whisky that hangs loosely from her chewed-up fingertips.

"What brings you here?"

She shoots me a look that tells me I have asked the wrong question.

"What brings me here? What brings *you* here? Am I not allowed to be here?"

"That's not what I meant." For God's sake, how does one disappear in this country without killing oneself? I am tired and don't want to argue, so I turn around and send Taymour another message instead.

Don't give up on us. We always said we would find a way . . .

I want to fight for us, but I am fighting alone. I am hanging at the end of a broken string, like the cigarettes in the mouths of the pool players or the drink from the angry woman's fingertips.

It's as if he has resigned himself to our failure. The part of me that is true and authentic, a part deep within my core, is gone. Now everything is reduced to a single impulse. To see Taymour. To kiss him and run away with him, get out of this shithole.

The woman beside me flicks open a Zippo and a flame shoots up. She brings it close to her face, almost to her curls, and lights a cigarette.

"I'm here because I was outside when the blockade happened," she says, exhaling a thick cloud of smoke across the bar. "I couldn't go back to the camps and my permit expired so I'm stuck."

"I'm sorry to hear that," I say. I stare at my drink and hope she won't pursue further conversation.

"I hate it in this city," she continues. "Nothing works and no one wants to admit it. It's like walking onto a theater set. I feel like if I turn a book over I may realize it's only a cardboard box with a title painted on it. Everyone is in denial . . . keeping up appearances and trying to ignore the fact that everything is falling apart. This entire damn city is schizophrenic."

"Life can't be better in the camp. You're stuck in there like zoo animals waiting for handouts from the UN."

"At least people have souls in the camp. At least people are resisting, they have a purpose."

"So do you support the opposition?" I ask.

She downs the rest of her whisky and laughs bitterly.

We sit in silence for a while, smoking cigarettes, surrounded by the shells of watermelon seeds. I turn back to my beer-soaked revolution on the bar, tracing a few refugee camps with my finger.

Looking across the room that is slowly filling with people, I am all at once overcome with an aching longing to go home. Not to Teta's house, with its heavy silences and shame, but to another time entirely, when my mother and father were around, when Mama was still painting and I would sit by the door waiting excitedly for her to come home, to the time of onions and Jacuzzis and Reese's Peanut Butter Cups and Slush Puppies.

"You're making a mess," someone behind me says, and with one sweep of a dirty cloth wipes away the uprising of beer I've created on the table. Only a few trickles of liquid remain where an entire revolution once stood. I turn around and find myself face-to-face with Nora.

"You left early last night," she says, pulling up a stool next to mine and lighting a cigarette.

"I was tired."

"You see that guy there?" Nora points her cigarette to a young man who is laughing drunkenly with a group of foreigners. "That's the son of the Canadian ambassador. I let him drink here even though he's only fourteen. A few months ago I told him that since he comes here almost every night, the least he could do is give me a visa to Canada. It doesn't even have to be a permanent one, just a visitor visa for a few months, maybe I can find a nice Canadian girl." Nora smiles and takes a sip of her beer. "'Sure, sure,' he says. Nothing so far. I'm giving him another week."

"And to think only a few months ago we thought we'd go out in the streets and suddenly the world would open up and we'd never need visas anymore."

Nora laughs. "He says he wants to write an article about me, a lesbian who runs an underground bar in the Middle East. I told him I'd kidnap him if he did. That's all I need right now. Imagine if he knew what goes on in the basement. He'd be on the phone to the BBC."

I force a smile and drink my beer.

"By the way, I got taken in today," Nora says.

"Again? What now?"

"I've been a good girl, man." Nora throws her arms in the air. "I've deleted all the pro-revolution groups from my

Facebook and told people no more activist meetings at the bar. Head down, you know. But they came in around noon today. It was just me cleaning up. They wanted to talk. They said it was a routine conversation about the bar. Five hours later, I step out of their offices and the sun is setting and I'm thinking, What the hell just happened?"

I catch the bartender's eye and indicate for him to bring more beers our way.

Nora continues. "This time they told me they have footage of me walking into a supermarket and throwing my passport on the floor and calling for an Islamic government." She chuckles and shakes her head. "They should make a movie, these guys, with this active imagination of theirs."

"Did they ask about downstairs?"

"They asked some questions, but very vague, about the people who come here, that sort of thing. I just let them say what they want, *ya zalameh*. They close us down, we'll open somewhere else."

I light a cigarette and sigh, blowing a cloud of smoke above my head. My phone lights up. The glare of the backlight sobers me up as I read the message from Taymour: *I'm sorry. Last night changed everything. Maybe it's better if you don't come tonight . . .*

Please don't deny me, I reply. I put the phone down and then immediately pick it up again and send another message: *If you do then we are both doomed.*

"You look like shit," Nora says. "What's wrong?"

For a moment I consider telling her about what happened last night, but then decide against it. Nora probably hears stories like mine every day. They hang from the walls of Guapa like sad family portraits.

"I'm fine. It's just been a long day." Perhaps one day I will hang my story on Guapa's walls, but for now I prefer to keep it with me.

The woman from the camps has left and in her space two young men with long hair are discussing a new collective of DJs who make underground music.

"It's like a mix of electronica, traditional Arabic music, and sounds captured in sieges and battles," one of them says, while the other nods in appreciation.

From across the smoky room I see Maj walk in. He is wearing black jeans and a tight black vest over a white T-shirt, his black duffel bag thrown across one shoulder. He runs a hand through his bangs and looks around. I wave my arms until he sees me and makes his way through the crowd. Even from here I can see the swelling under his eye.

"How did you explain the bruises to your parents?" I ask Maj as he drops his bag on the floor. A few strands of long brown hair from his wig poke out from one side of the bag. He kicks the bag under the bar and lights a cigarette. He looks better without the dried blood on his face, but up close I can see a cut on his lip and his right eye is colored an angry purple.

"I told them I got into a fight. I got a lecture but now they're over it. Maybe they know, but if they do they didn't say anything. We danced the familiar dance of denial."

Nora comes over to give Maj a quick kiss. She touches the bruise under his eye and smirks, then goes behind the bar to fix us some drinks.

I look at the bruise. "It looks bad. Have you seen a doctor?"

"It looks worse than it is, really," Maj says casually. "My libido always gets me in trouble. We should have invested in that apartment we talked about. We'd have had all the privacy in the world. We wouldn't have needed any furniture, really, except a mattress and some sheets. Instead we've wasted all our money here."

"How can you have wasted it here when you never pay for your drinks?" Nora barks from across the bar.

"Never mind," Maj says.

"You really should stop going to those cinemas," I tell him. "They're not safe."

"You know that's not why this happened."

"Why then?"

"Because of my work," he says. "They knew I was collecting evidence of police abuse."

"Regardless, they would not have anything to hold against you if you weren't cruising."

"They would find something else to hold against me."

"Well, maybe you should find a safer job, then."

"You're sounding like my mother. Besides, it would be more dangerous if the evidence of regime abuses I've collected were actually generating even a bit of outrage from someone . . . "

Nora comes back with a tray of six shots of whisky.

"Drink up, they're watching us tonight and they like us drunk," she says. "It's better for the stability of the country."

We take two shots each. The alcohol burns as it makes its way down my throat. My stomach feels like it's on fire. I grimace and light a cigarette.

"So, Maj," Nora says. "A good night at the cinemas?"

"They got me in the bathroom stalls. I was with this guy, lives in al-Sharqiyeh, gorgeous cock. Then the fuckers storm in. Not dressed in uniform or nothing. Looked like every other guy there. Lots of yelling, people running away. I guess they closed off the exits because they rounded us up like sheep. Up against the wall. Frisked. Said they were looking for 'satanic paraphernalia.'"

Maj appears more confident and alive than I have ever seen him. His voice is like a machine gun, *ratatat tat taratatat*. The arrest, humiliation, and anal exam to "check his sexuality" seem to have given him a boost of confidence. He is carrying the experience of having an egg up his ass like a badge of honour. Doesn't he care what could have happened to him? If he doesn't, I certainly do.

"I'm going to have to find a way to incorporate the black eye into my act tonight," he says, giggling.

"Let's hope we're still open by then," Nora says.

"We are attacked everywhere for being gay," I say.

"We're not attacked for being gay," Maj replies. The crease between his eyebrows, which is now much deeper than I have ever seen it, twitches as he spits out his words. "This is a regime that preys on the angry and the weak. On the down-trodden and oppressed, on the poor, on women and refugees and illegal immigrants. Today they released me in a matter of hours. And why is that? Because I speak fluent English and live in the western suburbs. Politically, I'm too costly to kill."

"Absolutely," Nora says, raising her glass. "To the resistance!"

"To the resistance that is now dominated by religious nuts who hate gay people," I say. "How can you toast to that?"

Nora raises a finger in the air. "Just because someone is religious does not make them against gay people. Many are simply against a rigid framework of sexuality imposed by the West. Those who oppose homosexuality without distinction are misreading the Quran."

"That's not true," I argue. "Remember the story of the Prophet Lot? Islam explicitly condemns homosexuality, and any so-called progressive cleric who suggests otherwise is delusional."

Maj laughs. "By the very nature of being a religious cleric they must be delusional. Besides, Islam or not, there is a long acceptance of homosexuality by Arab society that stretches back to the pre-Islamic period. It was those prudish Victorians who spoiled the party."

"And you're wrong, Rasa," Nora says. "When God destroyed Sodom and Gomorrah, it was not because of homosexuality, it was about lustful acts in general, and criminality, and general debauchery, really . . . "

"Much like Guapa . . . " Maj quips.

"Yes, much like Guapa. Make no mistake, if there's a hell we're burning in it."

"This conversation is my idea of hell," I say.

"Anyway," Nora says. "I'll raise my glass to anyone who opposes the regime."

I shake my head and start on the brand-new pint of beer that has magically appeared in front of me. I'm not sure whether this is my third or fourth but I am starting to feel less inhibited. I wish I could place the blame for what happened to Taymour and me on the regime. Then I could be angry as well. I could wave my cigarette in the air and call for the downfall of the regime and an end to imperialism. But really, what can I do? Call for the downfall of Teta?

"I wish everyone would just sign on to the reform process," I say. "Everyone should negotiate but, like, *really* mean it."

"The reform process," Nora scoffs. "Please, it's driven by the West, which has no desire to see us make our own decisions. They have given us a pen to sign our own death warrant and we're arguing over the color of the ink."

"Besides," Maj says, speaking more quickly now, as if struggling to catch up with his thoughts, "should they negotiate with the criminal regime that has made our lives hell for decades now? Blood on their hands, blood on their hands, all of them, to hell with them all."

"Who doesn't have blood on their hands?" I say. "These days if you don't have blood on your hands, then you don't have any power. Let everyone with blood on their hands come to the table. I don't care. I don't want to make love to them, I want them to stop all this stupidity."

"The resistance will prevail," Nora says, "and I will stand by them until every last regime rat is gone."

Neither of them seems to notice that my head is now in my hands. I suppose revolutionaries have more important things to worry about. I'm feeling hopeless and don't want to say anything else, so I get up to go to the bathroom. I walk down the rickety stairs until the music becomes a series of thumping beats. I stand at the urinal and look at the chipped walls. My phone beeps in my pocket and I pick it up with one hand while I'm pissing.

I know it's hard . . . Taymour's message reads.

I return to the bar and see Maj sitting alone. He watches me as I take my seat next to him.

"I just read the message you sent me this morning," Maj says. "Did your grandmother really catch you?"

"Yes."

"Why didn't you tell me this earlier?"

"You had your own problems to worry about."

"I'm sorry," he says. "And last night of all nights. Have you spoken to Taymour yet?"

"A few messages." I don't tell Maj about going to see Taymour in the restaurant. "What if he just acts like nothing has ever happened between us? As if the past three years were simply my own crazy delusions. Maybe it was all in my head . . . "

"You know that's not true." Maj puts a hand on my shoulder.

"Do I?" A moan escapes from my mouth, a heaviness sinks into the pit of my stomach. I am seconds from crying. "Even you can't say for certain. For all you know I could have made up this affair, dragged you along in my fantasies. Right now Taymour and I are a secret, and when it's gone there's nothing left. Just thin air, as if nothing ever happened. All that's left are memories. And I can't trust my memories."

"You don't need him to validate anything for you."

"No, but I need to speak to him, if only to make sure that last night wasn't just a bad dream."

"Don't go to the wedding."

"I have to go. It's *eib* not to go."

"The tyranny of *eib*." Maj sighs.

I rub my forehead and turn back to what's left of my drink. There are a few ashes floating on the surface of my beer like dead fish. In the background Sheryl Crow is singing about every day being a winding road, and that we all get a little bit closer to feeling fine.

"You know," I turn to Maj, "there's a word in Japanese, *tatemae*, which refers to what a person pretends to believe, or the behavior and opinions people must display to satisfy the demands of society. But at least in Japanese the word acknowledges that it is a pretense. For us, only *eib*. There is not even the recognition that this is all for show."

"But you still buy into it. Still you cry over the biggest coward in the city . . . he's a regime supporter and why? Out of fear. That is the worst kind of regime supporter."

"You don't understand his situation."

"Then you're the coward," Maj says. "Because you're too scared to let go of him. You know people say the opposite of fear is desire, where we presumably run away from what we fear and toward what we desire. But fear and desire are more complicated than that. There's fear at the heart of every desire and desire at the heart of fear. So I wonder, by desiring Taymour, what exactly are you afraid of?"

"You know, Maj, I'm not like you. I can't just feel no shame. I can't walk around acting like a freak."

"What the hell does that mean?" Maj spits, pushing his chair away from the bar.

"I don't mean it that way," I begin. "It's just that I can't afford to let go of him. Because Teta, Taymour . . . they're all I have to work with."

"And what do you think I have?" Maj snaps, the crease in his forehead twitching furiously. "You're always talking about being alone. We're all alone, and everyone in this country is giving an Oscar-winning performance to try to belong. How is a woman with her Armani bag, or a man who slams his bruised forehead down on the floor five times a day, or a police officer who walks around with his baton, puffing out his chest like a gorilla, any less of a performance than when I wear a wig and dance? We are all performing." He points a finger at me. "The problem with *you*, Rasa, is that you want to integrate. But look around. There is nothing *real* to integrate into."

Before I can respond Maj stands up and puts his packet of cigarettes in his back pocket. He picks up his duffel bag and storms down the stairs to get ready.

Basma picks me up from Guapa soon after Maj goes downstairs. She's straightened her springy curls, so that her hair flows in orchestrated waves down each side of her face. She drives us to the hotel where the wedding is taking place. The car races through the streets. Loud techno music blasts from the radio. Basma has one hand on the steering wheel and is rolling a joint with the other. I am slumped in the passenger seat.

Every minute that passes is a minute closer to seeing him. As soon as I see his face I fear my heart will throw itself at his feet. I always knew the dangers of a secret love affair. Such a love is not palpable. It's like a whiff of the sweetest-smelling rose, at any moment it may dissipate, leaving behind not even a trace. If Taymour and I are really over, no one will know our love ever existed. How can I wake up tomorrow morning and put on a mask to hide the empty hole in my life? Forget tomorrow, how can I do that tonight? How can I speak to anyone about anything without discussing how everything has fallen apart? I don't have any energy left to put on my mask. I can't bear the thought of letting my emotions rot inside of me, all for the sake of an illusion. That would be too much sorrow. Too much loneliness.

"I can see a checkpoint," Basma says. "Quick, duck so they don't see you."

I curl myself into a ball and drop into the space between the seat and the dashboard. Make-up kits and bottles of perfume poke my side. Basma slows the car for a moment and then accelerates again.

"No stopping at checkpoints. The perks of being a woman." Basma cackles. "You can get up now."

"I hate society," I say, picking myself off the floor.

"Society hates you back. Here." Basma hands me the joint. "You'll need this. It's a dry wedding."

"But they're not religious." I am already approaching unacceptable levels of drunkenness but I could do with a few more drinks.

"They don't want to offend anyone."

"Well, I'm offended it's a dry wedding," I say. "Doesn't offending me matter?"

"No, it doesn't. Anyway, the manager of the bar next door is a friend of my uncle. I struck a deal with him so he'll sneak us some drinks."

I light the joint and inhale. So that's it, then. After today I'm on my own. But I don't even have all of myself. My public self will be somewhere else, laughing and mingling with others, participating in a façade, while my heart is left to mourn alone.

The hashish hits me. Everything begins to take on a numbing fuzziness. If I can feel like this all the time, things might not be so bad. I take another drag.

"I can't believe this wedding," I yell over the sound of the radio. "It's a façade. I knew Leila in college. Back then she was fiercely political. And now—"

"And now she's marrying into one of the richest families in the country. So she's still political," Basma takes the joint from me and holds it between her fingers like a cigarette. Her fingernails are painted a deep burgundy color.

"Such a façade," I mumble to myself. The car is filling up with smoke and the music is giving me a headache. I reach over to turn the volume down. Basma smacks my hand away from the radio dial.

"Were you with Maj?" Basma asks.

"Yeah. You heard?"

"Heard what? You think I have time to hear anything, *habibi*? I just work and work and then take a fucking sleeping pill and go to bed."

We stop at a traffic light. A car pulls up next to us. The driver, a middle-aged man with a Salafi-style beard, motions for Basma to lower the window. She debates this for a moment and then does so. A cloud of smoke seeps out of the two-inch gap and into the air outside.

"What?" she says.

"It's evening prayer time," the man says. "Have some respect and turn off the music. *Haram*."

"*Eib* on you for interfering in a woman's affairs," she says, playing her *eib* like a trump card. "Mind your own business." She rolls up the window and hands me the joint.

"*Eib eib eib*. What isn't *eib*?" I mutter. The light turns green and we carry on driving. We turn right onto the road that leads to the hotel where the wedding reception is taking place. The hotel was built five years ago with Gulf money. The building looks like an Arabian nights theme park, all sandy and dome-like. Bright yellow spotlights shine against the walls and pillars of the hotel, which gives the sandy walls the appearance of being gold-plated. On most nights, blue lasers shoot from the roof of the hotel's minarets toward the horizon, like a force field protecting the hotel from the rest of the city. It's Aladdin meets a Las Vegas laser show. You can see it glowing from everywhere, like a spaceship that landed in the centre of town and decided to stay. It's one of the only buildings that remains lit during electricity cuts. Apart from the interrogation center, of course.

Basma pulls into the parking lot, which is in an enclave surrounded by tall palm trees decorated with fairy lights. The hotel has three stages of security. The first consists of metal spikes that rise from the ground to prevent any cars from driving through. Basma idles the car in front of the spikes. An armed guard circles around us with a flimsy metal pole with a mirror stuck to the bottom, while the other does the same with an antenna-like stick pointed at the car. The scene reminds me of a sign I saw once while going through airport security in America. After going through the X-ray machine, I was pulled to one side and frisked by a security guard. As his gloved hands roamed over my body, I saw a sign taped to the desk behind him. The sign, in large Times New Roman type, read: REMEMBER! YOU ARE THE FIRST LINE OF DEFENSE! At the time I couldn't help but feel it was me everyone was trying to defend themselves against. I wonder how often these guards think of themselves as being the first line of defence.

We pass through the checks and Basma hands her keys to the valet. We step inside the entrance and make our way toward the metal detectors and X-ray machines. With each layer of security I feel myself descending deeper into a protective shield of privilege. As I approach the metal detector I place my mobile phone and belt and lighter and cigarettes in the plastic basket. I imagine taking out my politics and placing them neatly in the basket. I also imagine taking out my underlying resentment about being subjected to security checks and placing it in the basket. I take out my anger at this wedding, my sadness about the fact that I will never have a wedding like this, and the hypocrisy I feel for going to a wedding in the first place when I should be out protesting or organising or releasing a statement. I place all these feelings in the basket and walk through the metal detector.

I step into the dazzling lobby. A man in a sharp suit is playing a grand piano in the center of the hall. I glance down at my own suit, the front of which is now covered with a layer of dust from crouching on the floor of Basma's car.

"Everything is golden," I tell no one in particular.

"Where's the wedding?" Basma barks at the doorman. He leads us down a red carpet toward some large doors. I stare at the floor as we walk. Red and white rose petals have been tossed on the carpet. Some of the petals have shoe marks on them. The doorman pulls open the heavy doors to the banquet hall.

The wedding hall is a monstrous sight. The smell of perfume is suffocating. Men in Italian suits and women with painted lips and bourgeois hair blow air kisses to each other and talk about how happy they are. Some people stand in a line waiting to greet Leila's parents, as if they are standing in front of a firing squad waiting to be shot. A band is setting up in the corner and excited chatter drowns out the classical music. In the center of the room there is a fountain with a sculpture of a heart that bears the initials L and T. A camera hovers on a pulley, catching panoramic bird's-eye views of the enormous hall. I am about to say something but a bulb flashes in my face and I recoil. For a moment my ears are buzzing and all I see are stars.

"So this is what we have to work with," Basma says, tapping a burgundy fingernail to her lips.

Beside us a group of women are chattering excitedly. They are all wearing open-toe shoes and their toenails are immaculately painted in various shades of pink. I stare at their sun-kissed toes, admiring their impeccable pedicures, until Basma tugs my arm and points toward a crowd of men.

"There's the groom. Let's go say hi."

"He looks busy," I say, suddenly nervous. "Let's say hi later."

"Rasa, you can't arrive and not say hi to him. *Eib!*" She clutches my hand and tugs me toward the crowd. The group of men are huddled together. As we walk toward them they burst out laughing, as if one has just shared a crude joke with the others. I wonder what it must be like to socialize with such confidence and ease. When we approach them the group breaks up and I find myself face-to-face with Taymour.

"Congratulations," Basma sings as she wraps her arms around his neck. He is wearing an expensive-looking suit. His cheeks shine under the lights. I've always preferred him scruffier, but I suppose he is not dressing for me tonight. He looks at me over her shoulder, a hollow smile plastered on his face. When Basma lets go, he shakes my hand firmly. I search his palm for a sign but there's nothing, only a quick, strong handshake and then my hand is empty again.

"Where's Leila?" Basma asks.

"She's upstairs getting ready," Taymour replies. "She's having problems with her hair." Oh, Leila, even after embracing the ideology of the wedding mafia she still finds something problematic, even if it is just her hair.

"I should go help," Basma says. "Rasa, why don't you find us a table?"

When Basma walks away and it is just Taymour and me, his smile disappears.

"I'm sorry about today."

"It's all right. Congratulations," I tell him.

"I'm a lucky guy."

"Oh, please."

"You look nice, Rasa."

"Thanks, Taymour. It was between this and a wedding dress, so . . . "

Taymour grabs my arm and pulls me to one side.

"If you aren't going to behave then you shouldn't have come," he hisses in my face.

"I wanted to see you. I need to talk to you."

"There's nothing to talk about," he whispers, his eyes flitting between me and a group of women heading our way.

"Fine, I'll go." I walk away and he grabs my arm again and pulls me back.

"You can't leave now. People will talk."

"Let them talk."

"Please. Leila wants you to stay. I want you to stay."

"Okay. Listen, I've got something to give you," I reach into my pocket for the photograph of Abdallah, on the back of which I had written my letter.

"What is it?" he asks. The girls are only metres away now and he flashes them that hollow smile.

"Not now. When you have a minute come see me and we can talk."

Before he can reply the group of girls descend on us. They close in on him, forming a circle, and I'm now standing on the outside. I try not to look out of place, glance up at the ceiling, with its colossal glass chandeliers. This society does not feel like it's mine, with its beautifully made-up women and high-fiving men. I feel wooden, afraid to speak lest a skeleton pop out of my mouth, afraid that if I move around too much the stench of my secret may permeate the room like the foul odor of a rotting corpse.

The band has set up now and I walk over to where they are playing a jazzy version of "Here Comes the Bride." Beside the band Taymour's mother is greeting some guests. I consider walking up to her to offer my congratulations. Would she recognize me from the restaurant this afternoon? Perhaps I could drop into the conversation details about exactly who I was, and where her son was last night. If Taymour loses his family, we will be on the same footing again. He won't have anything except me and he'll have no choice but to be with me. It'll be the two of us against the world.

Instead I walk toward the sleek glass tables arranged around the fountain. I recall a few years ago, Taymour and I were dancing the tango in my bedroom. It was just the two of us, bored, with nothing better to do. As we marched, hand in hand, back and forth across the room, I asked him if he ever thought about having children.

"If I get married to a woman, which I don't suppose will happen if I can get away with it, but if I do, then I will have children."

He put his arm around me and I leaned back.

"What about if you were with a man, would you adopt?" I said, watching him hover above me.

"Absolutely not." He pulled me back up in one clean swoop. "It's unnatural."

"It's unnatural for two men who love each other to adopt a child? Why?"

"I don't know, it just is," he said. "It's against society." We tripped on each other's legs. "It's one-two-three-turn, right?"

I nodded. "What is society, though? I mean what are the rules of society?"

"It's just against society," he repeated, and gave me a kiss.

And so the next day I told Maj that I felt that two men should not be allowed to adopt children. I tried the argument on for size and heard myself say it, just to see what it was like. To my surprise Maj agreed with me, saying that adopting children was a heteronormative performance that sought to castrate queerness.

I look around the wedding hall. This is society, I tell myself. My phone buzzes in my pocket. I pull it out and read the text from Maj.

I'm sorry about tonight. Let's meet later and talk, okay?

"What would you like to say to Leila and Taymour?" a voice behind me says. I put my phone back in my pocket and turn around to see an overenthusiastic woman in a red gown interviewing two other women on camera. She is holding a white fluffy microphone that looks like a Persian cat.

"Oh my God, *mabrook*, you guys!" squeals one of the

women in a royal blue dress. Her long hair is blow-dried to within an inch of perfection.

"*Mabrooook*," purrs the girl beside her with noticeably less enthusiasm. "Have lots of sex."

The two women giggle and walk away. The woman with the microphone catches my eye and rushes over, her cameraman struggling to keep up without tripping on the cables.

"What would you like to say to Leila and Taymour?" she says, shoving the white microphone in my face.

I stare at the camera and say nothing.

"This will be put on their wedding video," the woman prompts.

"I don't know," I say. "I wish you a happy life together."

The woman is not impressed. "Anything else?" she asks.

"No."

"Not even some words of advice?"

I catch a glimpse of my reflection in the lens of the camera. My hair is disheveled and my eyes are tiny black pebbles. I look like some wild animal drawn to the light. I take a deep breath.

"It makes me happy to see two people who love and care for each other be together. It gives the rest of us hope that one day we'll all be as lucky as them."

The woman seems satisfied with this and the camera zooms out in search of more guests.

A few months ago, on the night of his engagement party, I was helping Taymour get ready. On nights like those, when he was playing his role for society, he often appeared nervous or distant, his thoughts far from the little world we created. At first this used to worry me, that he might one day never return to our world. After a while I accepted that this was just the way he was, and I loved him regardless.

That night, however, as I showed him how to knot his tie, he suddenly grabbed my hand and looked me in the eye.

"Rasa?" His voice sounded pleading.

"What?"

"Why am I doing this?" There were tears forming in his eyes. "I look around at my family and see how happy they are. Everyone is celebrating and all I can think is that my joy is a lie. Everything in my life is a lie."

I let go of his tie and touched his cheek. "But we're not a lie."

"Then what are we? Are we anything? I sometimes feel like we are just inside my head, and not out here, not a reality. I don't know how we can ever be real."

"Do you mention me to others?" I asked.

"Sometimes," he said, looking down.

"What sort of things do you say?"

"You just come up in conversation. Why wouldn't you? You're all I think about."

"Keep doing that, okay? Just keep mentioning me."

I had wanted to cook him his favorite dishes. I had wanted to introduce him to my family. Even after Taymour and Leila got together, I had believed their courtship would keep our secret safe. I watched as Taymour juggled his public life with our private moments. From my position as his dirty secret I could see how much of society was a performance. I was surprised by how brilliant this performance could be and how high the stakes were. Society can take you high up but very quickly you can lose it all. I realise now we have descended deep into the lie we created for ourselves, as deep as we can possibly go.

I kick a red balloon next to my foot and look around for a table to join. I eye the first table on my right, but females already occupy four of the six chairs. I enjoy the company of women. I share their humor and emotions and being among them allows me to be carefree, but I do not want to be the only man at the table. It would only invite questions: Why is he sitting with the women all the time? Is he looking for a wife? Oh no, not Rasa.

"Rasa, come sit here," someone behind me calls out. Mimi, an old friend from high school, waves me over to a table next to the fountain. She is wearing a strapless turquoise dress. Her bare shoulders shine like sparkling diamonds.

"Where've you been these days?" Mimi asks. "Why don't you call me any more?"

Here we go with these questions and investigations. Why don't you call? Where are you going? When are you getting married? Why is your door locked? Who are you with in there? Everyone in this country is an investigative journalist. Am I to blame for these questions? Do I have a face that invites others to interfere in my affairs? Do I lay myself at their feet and allow them to tread on my neck?

"I've been busy," I say, kissing her cheek. "How've you been?"

"So busy with fashion week. Do you know Lulu and Dodi?" Mimi introduces me to the couple sitting on her right. Dodi has a thin black goatee that appears to be painted on with a needle. Lulu has big lips and velvety eyes. They look like every other couple here and so I don't recognize them.

"I think we may have met at Mimi's wedding," Lulu says. "This is my husband, Dodi."

"Nice to meet you," I turn to Mimi. "Basma is joining us."

"*Très bien*. We'll save her the final seat. Hamza's also sitting with us."

"Hamza who?" I ask.

"Hamza from high school."

The only Hamza I remember from high school is the Hamza who terrorised me relentlessly. The Hamza who cornered us in the alley and kicked Maj into the mud on the day we met. The Hamza who introduced me to the word *khawal*. That Hamza, with his muscle-bound henchmen who took great joy in torturing us whenever they had the chance. Hamza had made sure I spent most of high school with my head down, not drawing attention to myself. I was terrified of sticking out, careful not to laugh too hard but to always blend in, in the hope that they would never notice. When they did they would often push us against the walls of the school halls, moaning in our ears as they rubbed their crotches on us. Sometimes I would masturbate to the thought of Hamza finishing the job one day.

"Are you okay?" Mimi asks.

I nod and take a seat beside her. The thought of having to spend the night sitting at the same table as my tormentor makes me want to curl myself into a tight ball and disappear.

"What's new?" I ask Mimi.

"It's been awful," Mimi says, running a finger around the edge of her glass of water. "Turns out all the business trips my father was making to Italy were because he has another family there. Please don't tell anyone."

"I'm sorry." All I can remember about Mimi's family is that her father is an import-export connoisseur, one of the big families in the city. He imports both cigarettes and respiratory machines for hospitals, thereby ensuring a constant stream of supply and demand.

I glance around the room in search of Taymour. I see him speaking to Leila's father and uncle. He shakes their hands and then walks out of the room. I consider following him to give him my letter, but a hand grabs my shoulder. I turn around to see Hamza. He's looking down at me with a menacing smile. I half expect the smile to turn into a sneer. He shakes my hand firmly, nearly breaking my bones in the process.

"Rasa, how are you, *ya zalameh*?"

Now I'm a *zalameh*. If only he knew what this *zalameh* does behind closed doors.

"*Hamdullah*," I mumble.

"I haven't seen you in years. Are we friends on Facebook? Let me friend you now." He reaches into his pocket and digs out his phone. Moments later there's a ping on my phone. *Hamza has requested to add you as a friend.* His profile picture is a shot of him in military uniform, stepping out of a helicopter. He's wearing Ray-Bans like some James Bond prick.

I really need a drink.

"The fountain is such a nice touch," Lulu says to her husband. "Don't you think, babe?" She pronounces "babe" like it rhymes with "dweeb."

Basma arrives and takes the empty seat next to me.

"They're about to come down," she says.

The music stops and the chandelier lights are dimmed. A spotlight shines at the top of the white marble staircase that snakes its way onto a balcony on the far side of the room. Three men wearing white sharwals emerge onto the balcony. Holding tablas under their arms, their large hands bash the animal skins stretched over the tablas as they begin to walk down the staircase. As the drumming intensifies four other men follow behind them. They stand in pairs, stomping their feet to the drumming.

Behind them the curtains shuffle. Leila and Taymour emerge onto the balcony and look over the crowd. There is a gasp among the guests, followed by a satisfied sigh.

"She's beautiful," Mimi whispers into my ear.

The bride and groom scan the crowd from above. Leila's hair is woven through a crown of white gardenias and arranged in a large bun. She bites the insides of her cheeks as she pats her hair nervously. Beside her Taymour has a tight-lipped smile on his face. He holds on to Leila's arm with one hand, and clenches and unclenches the other hand.

"You know the good thing about not fitting into society?" I whisper into Basma's ear. "I'll never be put in such a silly situation."

"Don't you want to wear a crown of white flowers some-day?" Basma teases with a smile.

Leila and Taymour descend the white stairs as the dancing men begin to sing. Family and friends walk behind them, trailing them like a snake. Some of the women put their fingers to their lips and let out a chorus of *zaghareet*.

"*Lilililililililililililililiiii*"—the trilling sends a chill down my spine. The procession moves toward the dance floor, where the guests converge around Leila and Taymour in a tight circle.

"Let's go clap," Basma says. I begin to protest but she stops me. "Come on. I have to clap. Leila danced at my brother's wedding."

She drags me into the circle on the main floor. Everywhere there are smiling faces, white teeth, squinting eyes, hands clapping furiously to the music. Dazzling circles of red, gold, and white lights race across the walls and floor and faces of the guests. The crowd stomps to the beat of the drums so that the ground begins to tremble. With the music and the lights and the drums and the shaking ground I feel as if I am in the middle of an earthquake.

Somehow, as the stomping intensifies, the trilling *zaghareet* turn into chants of support for the president. "The people and the president are one hand!" the crowd chants in unison. Someone begins to pass out sparklers and they are waved in the air like sizzling sticks of dynamite about to explode. The crowd presses against me and with every breath I gulp in the sickly-sweet taste of perfume and cigarettes. I feel I am going to collapse, but even if I do the celebrations would not stop. The crowd would simply tread on me, oblivious to the sick man being trampled to death under their celebrations. They would stomp until all that is left of me would be a few specks of dust.

Leila catches my eye. She looks concerned when she catches a glimpse of my face. I give her a smile so wide and full of teeth I feel as if I am a crazy person. When she turns around I stop smiling, but then she glances at me again, so I give her another big smile and this time, like a maniac, I keep the smile plastered across my face as I clap and chant the president's name.

Finally the drumming ends and the ground stops shaking. The crowd begins to move away. The air feels cooler and I can breathe easier now. The lights go out and in the darkness my smile quickly fades. A white spotlight shines on Leila and Taymour. They move close, hesitant at first, until they settle into each other. Taymour wraps his arms around Leila's waist as she rests her head on his chest. Their silhouette appears as one.

The opening guitar riff to Roxy Music's "More Than This" begins. Already I can hear Mimi bawling behind me.

"I love this song," Basma says. I take her hand and lead her to the dance floor. She rests her chin in the crook of my neck as we sway to the music. From over her head I observe Taymour dancing with Leila. I try to catch his eye but he doesn't look at me. Perhaps he cannot afford to see me. He leans down and whispers into Leila's ear, and I realize he is singing the words of the song to her.

Did he forget his promise to sing only to me?

When the demonstrations first started we spent an evening at Guapa: Basma, Taymour, Maj, Leila, and I. We drank beer and discussed the merits of different transitional justice processes as I wrote down the names of powerful regime figures who should be tried for corruption. Leila took out a large map and, with a red marker, circled all the villages we would need to visit as part of a symbolic tour that would bring the country together. We talked for hours, over one another and hurriedly, as if there was not a moment to spare. There was so much to do. We were young and on the verge of changing our country. More than that, we were going to change the world.

Later that night, after Taymour had dropped Leila home,

he came to see me. I took him into my room and we cuddled and kissed and laughed, and suddenly it didn't matter that he would marry Leila, because everything was about to collapse and soon anything would be possible. And for the first time I let Taymour enter me. We used Teta's hand cream for lubrication. The radio was broadcasting announcements from the reform process, which we all knew was just a performance put on by the government to distract the people from demanding the truth. He came inside of me, his body shuddering in my arms, and I couldn't help but feel that in a strange way Taymour's gasps and Teta's hand cream were intimately connected to the future of the revolution.

What we felt that night, was it youthful idealism? Reckless naïveté? Whatever it was, seeing Taymour and Leila dance, I realize that feeling is now dead and buried. I am sad and angry and also, in an odd way, relieved. The last bit of hope is gone. And perhaps this is a good thing.

Suddenly Taymour looks up. His eyes scan the room until they find me. Over the shoulders of Leila and Basma we look at each other. Then Leila whispers something in his ear and Taymour looks away. I close my eyes and press my cheek into Basma's, and imagine I am dancing with Taymour.

The night begins to flow more smoothly. Conversations take place in fits and bursts, often starting in Arabic before eventually making their way to English, the language like an abusive boyfriend none of us are able to tear ourselves away from. Basma keeps the stream of alcohol coming my way through hand gestures with waiters who loiter around our table. The more I drink the more the conversations merge into one another, and I descend deeper into a pit of drunkenness that is both reckless and satisfying.

"My mother-in-law is driving me crazy," Mimi whispers in my right ear. "The woman is over all the time, judging my cooking, what I feed the baby. I tried speaking to my husband about it, but he says she's not doing anything wrong. Please don't tell anyone."

"Two gin and tonics," I whisper to a waiter, discreetly passing him a fifty-dollar bill.

"And you know, I've been having such horrendous trouble with the new maid. You know how my mom insisted on sending our old maid back to Sri Lanka after the tsunami to help out with the situation? I understand it's my mother's way of giving back but it really was the worst decision. Ever since, we have had zero luck with maids. We just got a new maid who has been absolutely useless. Indonesian. I know, don't get me started. Anyway, I had enough, so last week finally I sent her back and got someone new."

I smile and nod but I'm distracted by Mimi's nose. She used to have a very hooked nose. Her nose used to be the pièce de résistance of her face. Just before graduation she shaved half of it off, and what is left is a comical upward arch that defies the laws of gravity and has given her a permanently pinched expression. Tonight the upward tip seems even more pronounced.

"Hey, is it true about Maj?" Mimi snaps me back into focus.

"What about him?" I ask, slurring my words.

"I heard he was arrested last night, that he was with the men in the cinema."

"Of course not. Maj isn't like those men," I hear myself saying.

"*Hamdullah*, I was worried for a second. Those places are dirty."

"I sometimes feel like I look like a koala bear," I hear Lulu say. I look at the foundation caked around her eyes.

"Maybe, but not in a bad way," Basma replies.

"They're not dirty, they're just human," I find myself saying, still staring at Lulu's eyes.

"So what are you doing with yourself these days, Rasa?" Hamza asks from across the table as the waiters bring us plates of lamb stew and grilled meat.

"Basma and I've started a translation company."

"A translation company? That doesn't pay much, does it?" he says.

"They probably have a lot of foreign clients," Mimi jumps in. "Don't you, Rasa?"

I nod and ask Hamza what he does for a living.

"I work at the Ministry of Interior," he says. "Good job, free lunches."

I laugh at Hamza's joke, a knee-jerk reaction to stroke his ego. After all, men like Hamza respond well to admiring door-mats, so the role becomes a survival mechanism for those of us who choose not to fight such brutes. But really, I'm terrified. My high-school bully is a regime thug.

"Your voice changes when you to talk to men," Mimi says to me.

"How so?"

"It becomes more manly, more *zalameh*."

I down my drink. There is a beautiful floral arrangement at the centre of the table. Leila makes her way over to us and we all stand to congratulate her.

"You look stunning," I tell her as I kiss her on the cheek, and I mean it. She does look stunning. I have never seen Leila with make-up and an expensive hairdo. Her fingernails, which in college she would chew until they were raw stubs, were now long and immaculately groomed.

"Thanks," she says. "I feel kind of awful. Like, I don't think I've ever been this stressed out. I kind of just want it all to end."

"Everything looks great, relax." I take a sip of my drink. "Are you happy?"

"Right now I'm just in excruciating pain. I've, like, literally got pins stuck in my skull to keep this hairstyle in place. Seriously my skull is kind of bleeding right now. I'm kind of pissed off that it ended up being a dry wedding. It feels so démodé. And I've just found out the caterers have used Lurpak butter in the wedding cake and I'm boycotting Denmark so that's kind of a disaster. And then the attacks this morning made some people kind of scared of coming, which is ridiculous really because, look around, everything's fine."

At university Leila's words were firm and decisive. She used to pride herself on giving committed answers, on delving into her thoughts and feelings and trying to put them into clear words. These days her language is peppered with "like"s and "kind of"s, as if she is uncertain of what is true and what isn't, so assumes everything is all performative anyway.

"Stop problematizing everything," I say, and Leila smiles and gives me a hug.

"How've you been?"

"I've been better. You never come to Guapa anymore."

"I've been so busy with this," she says, waving her arms around the room. "Taymour's mother wanted everything to be perfect and, like, suddenly it just got out of control."

"I can see that," I say, pointing to the heart-shaped sculpture with their initials.

Leila laughs.

"So apart from the hair, you're happy? Is this what you wanted?"

Leila smiles a sad smile. "Life is hard for a single woman, and I'm not getting any younger. You know . . . this will be good. It'll get my parents off my back at least, which will make me happy."

"Do you love him?"

"I suppose so, whatever love is." She lets out a laugh, which is more like a snort, and grabs my arm. "Did Taymour tell you? We're thinking of moving to the Gulf."

I swallow hard. "No, he didn't mention it." Of course he wouldn't mention the possibility of leaving. Or was that what his conversation was about last night, about wanting to get away? What would their life be like in the Gulf? Perhaps they would be happy on the beaches littered with cranes and construction equipment. They would buy their milk and bread from the dazzling shopping malls and fall asleep every night in front of a box set of DVDs.

"Taymour only just brought the idea up for the first time today, really."

"What about your work with the women in the camps?"

"The situation is not good here, Rasa," Leila says. "We need to just kind of get away for a while and ride it out."

I say nothing. What can I say? I had known from the moment Taymour decided to live among society that I would be cementing my own position as one of society's dirty secrets. I am nothing more than an empty shell in public. I suppose it was my choice, but the alternative would be to banish our love and I could not do that. I'd rather live in the world where our love is sacred, within the comfort of the dirty secret. I can at least be with our love and keep it company. Down here, in the underbelly, I can see the magician's trapdoor that reveals society's tricks.

No sooner have I settled into this thought than I am overcome by a sudden urge to grab Taymour by his collar and yell and scream and demand the truth. I want to burst the bubble, reveal the trapdoor. I would grab the microphone and tell the world that Taymour is mine, that he can never be happily married. I'll bring our love into the glare of the spotlights and chandeliers and force the men and women to stare at this ugly baby they've hidden in the basement. Maybe then they will leave us alone and we can live together, happily, without society trying to tear us apart.

"I need to say hi to the others," Leila says, interrupting my thoughts. "Listen. Let's grab a drink at Guapa sometime. It's been ages." Even as she says this I can see in her eyes that we both know it will probably not happen. She squeezes my arm and walks away.

The waiter arrives with my drinks and I take a big gulp of mine and hand the other to Basma. As the waiter leaves I remember I had given him a fifty-dollar bill and didn't get any change back. Two drinks should cost no more than fifteen each, so I would need at least twenty after ordering two. Or maybe twenty-five, but definitely at least twenty, and that is certainly too high of a tip, even in this hotel.

"Hey," I call out, but the waiter is already halfway across the room, serving another table.

"People don't appreciate barbecues here," Dodi is telling the table as he chews on a shish taouk. "There is sun every day, that's the problem. When I was in London people appreciated the sun, they appreciated a good barbecue. They didn't take the sun for granted."

"It's the same with children here," Hamza says. "Go to a village and a woman has ten kids and so, *yalla*, it's okay if one of them goes and blows himself up."

Oh, I loathe weddings. I loathe sitting down and participating in inane conversations with proud parents and smug couples who all look like they might secretly hate each other. Make-up applied to women's faces with the precision of a classical painting, foundation caked to lighten skin tones, hair large and flowing and put together like an intricately constructed bouquet of flowers. And the men with their roaring laughter and crude jokes and boasts about profits and markets. They're all wearing masks so elaborate you can't see what's inside any more. I loathe it all and I am piss drunk and need to get the rest of my change back.

I look around for the waiter. There are two of them hovering near our table. I can't remember whether it was the short fat waiter or the tall skinny waiter who had taken my money. The guy I recall was both short and skinny. Perhaps they have morphed into one thief to steal my change. I catch the eye of the fat waiter and motion him over.

"I gave you or your friend a fifty-dollar bill for two drinks. I need the change back."

"It wasn't me," the man says. "Let me check with the other guy and get back to you."

"How many of you are there anyway?" I ask.

"For your table it's just him and me, unless there's someone else. Do you remember what he looked like?"

I shake my head and he walks off with a promise to return.

"Keep this to yourself," Mimi whispers in my ear, her breath smelling sour of gin and tonic. "Sometimes I wonder whether I made the right decisions in life. I ended up coming back after university because that's what my parents wanted. I got married because that's what they expected of me. I don't think I've ever done what I want to do. Please don't tell anyone."

"Did I tell you I'm opening a cake shop downtown?" Lulu says, grasping Dodi's arm and leaning into the table. "I'm going to call it Muffin Top."

I look around for the fat waiter but he is nowhere to be seen. I call the tall skinny waiter instead.

"Where's the other guy?"

"I don't know."

"I need my change. I gave you guys a fifty. I think. I don't know. Listen, I need my change back."

"Okay, let me check and come back to you."

"What's going on?" Basma asks from behind her drink.

"I gave them a fifty-dollar bill. I need my change back."

"A few of us are going to Sage after this," Lulu says with a cigarette in her mouth, clapping her hands lazily to the music. "It's a new club that opened on the rooftop. We're on the list."

"Siege?" Mimi asks.

"Sage, not siege. Like the herb, not like the war. Sage."

The fat waiter darts past our table. I call out to him but he passes us in a rush.

"Isn't it cute how we're all couples now?" Lulu remarks, looking around.

Mimi sighs. "That's just the way it is. I had to marry because how else was I going to hang out with people."

"When do you think you'll get married, Rasa?" Lulu asks.

"What is it with these waiters?" I snap. "Honestly, the service is terrible. They're thieves."

"You ought to settle down and find yourself someone," Lulu says. She turns to Dodi. "Things just get better when you are married, don't you think, babe?"

Dodi halfheartedly agrees that there is "nothing like it, beeb," and that it is "actually really great, *ya zalameh*."

First the conspiracy of the waiters and now Lulu's questions. They're all conspiring against me.

"Are you seeing anyone?" Mimi asks. "You can tell us, we won't tell anyone."

"I don't have the time," I say. I want to tell them I'm in love. I want to yell and scream about it. I do have a special someone. He's getting married tonight. Drinks on me!

"Why buy a cow these days? Everyone is giving out their milk for free," Hamza chuckles.

I glance at Basma, who rolls her eyes and looks down at her half-eaten plate of lamb and rice. There is a sudden buzzing in my ears and everything feels like it is closing in.

"Rasa will marry when he's ready," Basma jumps in. "He's still building a career. Now get over it, you're worse than an Arab mother."

Meanwhile the conversation continues. While Lulu is joyously talking about the stability that marriage brings, I look at Taymour laughing onstage and hide behind a fresh cigarette.

Another waiter rushes past Leila's mother, an anguished-looking woman who is scanning the crowd like a hawk. There is a strong smell of alcohol in the air, and her mother is hiding a panicked look with a smile as she talks to a group of older women.

"Yes, yes, the kids are just hyper. *Hyper*," she repeats, as if by saying this enough times it might be true.

I stand up to catch the waiter's attention. I wave my hands in the air but he whooshes right by me.

"Are you still going on about that money?" Basma grabs my suit and pulls me back down.

"It's a lot of money," I say as I plunk onto the seat.

"Let me deal with it." She sighs. She catches the eye of the fat waiter and with an authoritative flick of her wrist brings him over. She reels him in with one finger, like his chin is connected to her index finger with an invisible string. He leans down until his ear is inches away from her burgundy lips.

"Listen," she says, enunciating each word. "My friend here has been waiting for his change for an hour now. I don't care where it comes from and I don't want to hear whose fault it is, but if you don't get me that change in the next ten minutes I will make sure that you don't have a job by the end of the night."

The waiter nods and runs off. Five minutes later he is back with a wad of notes in his hand.

"That's how you do it," she says, stuffing the notes into my sweaty palm.

I look at the bills in my hand. I feel like I am going to vomit.

"Should I leave them a tip?" I ask Basma.

"After all this you want to tip them? The only tip they deserve is a shoe on their heads. You've spent too much time abroad, Rasa, you forgot how to speak to them."

In my ear Mimi is whispering furiously. "I'm in so much pain right now, you have no idea. I got laser lipo done the other day and I'm all bruised up. I know, I know, I know, I don't really need it, but it's just to get rid of those fatty areas that I've tried for years to diet away. I know my fat spots so I know it's not a matter of losing weight, you know? Please don't tell anyone."

Perhaps it is the alcohol that is doing the thinking on my behalf, having hijacked my actions like the Islamists hijacked our revolution, but I feel a sudden connection with Mimi and her secrets, and before I comprehend what I am doing I grab her gin and tonic and whisper in her ear, "My grandmother caught me in bed with Taymour last night."

I say this all in a rush, and then take a big gulp from her drink. Her face freezes for a moment, really only for a split second. Then, without saying anything, she turns her head and says not a word to me for the rest of the night. This is just as well as I am finally able to listen to the conversation taking place across the table.

"It's a question of public morality," Hamza is saying. "I mean, I'm not against gays. But there's a difference between the privacy of your own home and doing it in a public cinema."

"Are you talking about the cinema?" I ask.

"It's disgusting," Lulu says. "I believe in human rights, even gay rights if that's what they want. But do it in private for God's sake."

"But those people who go to the cinemas have nowhere else to go," I say.

"That doesn't make it acceptable to do this sort of thing in public," Hamza says. "What people do in the privacy of their own home is no one's business. But those men are perverts, using a public cinema as a sexual playground. This spreads diseases. Imagine if a young child had suddenly walked into the cinema."

"Everyone knew what that cinema was for. No one went there without knowing what was involved. And how is it public morality to beat them up and stick an egg in their ass?"

Hamza swats away my question with a wave of his hand. "Look, we need rules and regulations here. A public space is a public space. It's simple. That's what the morality law is for. They aren't there to prosecute the gays, they are there to prosecute perverts who want to have sex in public."

"Why is this bothering you so much, *ya zalameh*?" Dodi asks.

"It's not bothering me as much as it's bothering this guy," I point to Hamza. Basma kicks my leg under the table. "I'm telling you these men had no choice but to go there. They probably live in tiny one-bedroom apartments with wives and children and cousins and don't have any other escape. They don't have the luxury of a private space, of flights to Europe or America. Let's call this what it is, which is the government's attempt to distract us from the rising food prices and the protests. Let's arrest a dozen powerless slum dwellers that meet each other in a dirty old cinema."

"This has nothing to do with the economy or the terrorists," Hamza says. "The economy is doing great. Look around. You think we would have been able to have a beautiful wedding like this five or ten years ago? This government has liberalised our country. They've just built a brand-new highway that will lead directly from the western suburbs to the airport. No need to drive through downtown or any of those nasty places. The journey to the airport will be safer and more convenient. The project will be like a miracle, it will give a huge push to foreign investment."

"Open your eyes and see how the rest of the country lives. We are starving and can't even say a word about it."

"*Ya zalameh*, don't give me this communist shit." Hamza chuckles. "People always want to blame the government. You think you could be sitting here drinking gin and tonic if those terrorists came to power?"

"I was in the slums today," I yell, pointing my fork at him.

"I saw how people live. I saw the dirt and squalor. Just admit it, that we live in a police state that starves people."

"Change the subject," Basma orders the table.

"It's always too easy to blame the government," Hamza says, ignoring her. "*Ya zalameh*, let me tell you, the problem isn't the government. I work in the government. Those are good guys trying to make this country better. We're dealing with a population that does not value education . . . they are uneducated and don't want to do anything except quote the Quran and bomb innocent people. Look, imagine running a country is like running a giant company. Do the employees democratically elect the CEO? No, because they don't know what is needed to make the company profitable . . . and those crazy jihadis, they don't know how to run a country, they'll make a mess of it."

"This whole company analogy just isn't working for me," I mumble.

"Look at the president's wife and all the charity work she's done over the past ten years," Hamza says. "She was on the cover of *Vogue*. *Vogue*! *Ya zalameh*, she set up fifteen schools in the slums and she went there herself, but no one even bothers going to those schools. *Yaani*, they don't want to learn. That's our problem as a society. We don't want to learn."

"Give me a break," I say. "The First Lady's husband is stepping on the throats of the poor. The police are his militia, attacking anyone who dares to dissent. For most people, their only experience of the government is when the police come and beat them up. What will it take for you people to open your eyes? Must we dig up the bodies of those killed and sit them upright in the door of every house in this city so you will realise at what cost your stability comes?"

By now the tables next to us have gone quiet and people have shifted their gaze toward us.

"Look," Hamza says, his eyes flickering with the excitement of a fisherman who has just felt a heavy tug on his rod. "The uprisings may have started out well but they've degenerated into jihadis and terrorism."

"Oh, yes." I throw my hands in the air. "Jihadis and terrorism. Jihadis and terrorism. If you say it enough times maybe it will be true."

"Don't be a fool. The government here is good and fair, and the terrorism threats are real. It's not perfect but it's better than the alternatives. You say you've been to the slums, so you know the mind-set. It's a dangerous mind-set. Did you hear last week the Salafis came out from the slums with swords. It's like the Middle Ages. If you and some people like you want to be a bit theatrical about the government—you'll soon get over it."

My blood is boiling and I can feel my face turn red. Lulu starts talking but I am not hearing what she or anyone else is saying. I point at Hamza. "You're a regime prick. You're responsible for all the deaths that have happened. It's people like you!"

"I think you've had enough to drink," Basma says, grabbing the gin and tonic from my hand. "Maybe you should go home and get some sleep, Rasa. Things will seem less tragic in the morning."

"It won't make a difference. Day or night this thug will still make me sick. It'd be worse if I was sober." I clench my fists and feel the bills scrunch up in my palm.

"Relax," Lulu pleads. "Can we change the subject? None of this stuff matters—"

"Oh, shut up, you." I stand up and address the entire table. "It all matters. Don't you see that? It all fucking matters." I throw my napkin on the table and it drops into the glass of water, tipping the glass over my plate of food. The water swirls in the oil of the lamb and rice. People at the other tables begin to whisper to each other.

"Oh God, everyone's looking," I can hear Mimi say, holding her head in her hands. Her voice is far away now.

From the corner of my eye I see Leila shuffling toward me in her dress, teetering precariously on her heels. Behind her Taymour is staring at me, his jaw to the floor. Before I know what I am doing I walk around the table to where Hamza is sitting with a smug smirk on his face. He stands up but before he can say anything I push him hard. His legs fly up in the air as he trips backward over his chair and falls into the fountain with a splash.

"Immoral bastard," I say, watching him flail and splutter in the water. The music stops. I look around. Everyone is watching me. I run to the door, staggering drunkenly through the crowds of expensive dresses and black and white suits.

I am reaching for the door when a hand grabs my shoulder and spins me around. Taymour is looking at me, his eyes full of so many things. His hand on my shoulder moves up briefly, to touch the skin on my neck just above my shirt collar. Taymour and I are friends, good friends in fact. Wasn't it only natural that he would touch my neck lovingly on the night of his marriage? As our skin touches I see us together in bed, naked and laughing so hard we are in tears. I see myself shirtless, pulling down the shades in the bedroom, carefully, slat by creaking slat. I smell sweat and can hear the lazy strumming of a guitar. I see Taymour creep into his house as the sun rises and take off his clothes and slip into bed. I taste the strong black coffee we drank as we drove around the city, around and around, thinking and talking about what we could do, where we could go. Then I see Taymour and Leila, by the beach next to shimmering skyscrapers, pushing two boys on swings. I see Leila chopping onions at the kitchen table. I hear Taymour's voice humming in her ear as she lifts her arms to adjust her ponytail. Then the images blur into one another, like shuffling cards, and Taymour pulls his skin away from mine.

"You had something to give me?" he asks softly.

I lean over and kiss his cheek. "*Habibi*. I'm so sorry."

Taymour shakes his head. "You can't call me that here."

I smile. "But that's what you are. My *habibi*."

Taymour's mask begins to crack. "Please," he whispers. "I beg you to stop calling me that. Can't you see what it's doing to me?"

I look at his face. There are tears in his eyes. An unbearable silence settles between us. Finally, I turn around and walk away, from Taymour, from the silence. I take a few more steps toward the door. Before I leave I look back one last time, and realize that the man standing there did not betray me. The only person who betrayed me was myself.

I burst through the doors. They slam behind me, muffling the noise from the banquet hall. I'm underwater. My heart pounds in my chest, like the drumbeats of war or my very own *zaffeh*.

Even with all the alcohol coursing through my bloodstream I manage to hail a taxi outside the hotel and order him to take me home. I want nothing more than to fade like a shadow into the city before the reality of what I have done hits me. Hamza will get me for what I did. He will hunt me down and destroy me, like a cat that has caught a small bird. Even if he doesn't, there is no way I can show my face in those circles again.

"Don't go through the city centre, there's heavy traffic," I tell the driver.

"The centre is empty tonight," he says. "As of eleven o'clock the army closed it to all cars coming from the suburbs."

I look at my phone. It's just past midnight. I catch the driver's grey eyes in the rearview mirror. They look so familiar. I feel like I may have known him a long time ago.

"But what about people's businesses?" I ask, studying the driver's face.

"No businesses." He cracks his chewing gum between his teeth. "No one is allowed to leave their town and everyone should stay home."

It is the way his jaw clicks as he chews the gum that takes me back to that night. We have met before. The night after studying with Maj. The taxi driver in the red shirt. Is it really him? He's older now. His stomach has rounded and his temples are greying. Time has come and gone and the winds have brought us back together.

"Is the government attacking the eastern district?" I ask.

"There is no shelling," he says. "It is just clashes with terrorists."

"When I spoke to some people in al-Sharqiyeh today I did not see any terrorists. So the clashes are with the opposition?"

"Yes, yes," he says. "Some clashes, but only in the areas the terrorists have occupied."

I grab on to the back of his seat and lean in to him, so that we are almost cheek to cheek.

"But what about the women and children? You just said the army isn't allowing anyone to leave? What crime have they committed?"

"Well, they deserve it for allowing terrorists to live among them." He glances sideways at me with nervous eyes and cracks his chewing gum again.

"You're not answering me." I bang my palms against the back of the seat like a spoiled child. "What crime have women and children committed if someone has a gun in their neighbourhood?"

He is silent. We drive by a group of men protesting in support of the president, with signs saying the people and the regime are one hand. Army soldiers on nearby tanks wave their rifles in the air. The crowd cheers as we drive by. I turn back to the driver.

"You don't remember me, do you?"

He swallows hard. "I don't know what you're talking about."

"Is your family safe?"

"I took my wife and children out. Our house is in the area where the clashes are."

"So you're married?"

"With three girls," he says. The streetlights cast a hollow yellow glare on his tired face. We drive by a statue of the president, his right arm extending out toward the hills. Beside the statue two military men are patrolling the street.

"Is that what you wanted?"

He turns to face me, angry. "What do you think, that I'm *shaath*?"

"We're all some sort of *shaath*," I say. "We cannot accept that we might be different. But we're all different in our own way."

The man clutches the steering wheel tightly and says nothing. We drive along the deserted streets, across the bridges, and through the tunnels that coil under the city like snakes. It's time for decisions now, and everyone has made their choice: between state and terrorism, between honour and shame, between community and lies. I don't want to choose any more.

"So where are your wife and daughters now?" I whisper in his ear.

"They are staying with my wife's sister downtown."

"And what's your crime to lose your home? Will the government rebuild it?"

He is silent. Then, as if woken from a deep sleep, he yells, "They only give promises!"

My phone rings. It's Laura. I pick up.

"What story do you have for me now?" I yell. "Come on. Hit me with whatever you've got."

"Are you drunk?" Laura asks.

"Not just drunk, Laura, alive."

"Listen, I need you. The regime has just released photographs of Abdallah's body. Ahmed's son. From al-Sharqiyeh. He's been killed."

I think of Um Abdallah's face, the look in her eyes as she spoke of her son, the empty seat at their dinner table. "I can do a lot of things, Laura, but I can't bring back the dead. Trust me, I've tried."

"Rasa, listen to me," she snaps. "The opposition has declared an armed rebellion. This is war. The president is about to make an important speech. I need someone to get down here and help interview the crowds. I'll pay you double."

"Not double, not triple. Nothing. I want no part in any of this. Down with the president and the opposition! Down with all of society and their performances. Down with everything! Let everyone kill each other, and then when it's all gone we can start something new."

I hang up and take out the picture of Ahmed's son from my pocket. I slowly unfold the photograph, ironing out the creases that dissect the boy's face into squares. I look into Abdallah's eyes. I was right. There *is* sadness in his eyes, but it is not without hope. A glimmer of hope, yes, but hope nonetheless. I turn the photograph over, to the tiny black scribbles I wrote to Taymour earlier today. The lines are so close together, so desperate was I to fit everything in, that the white of the paper is barely visible. I tear the photograph apart, into smaller and smaller pieces and toss them out the window.

In the distance people are chanting. There's a faint whiff of burning tires in the air. I reach for my phone and call Maj. He picks up on the fifth ring.

"Rasa?" His voice is nearly drowned out by the familiar cacophony of cheers and thumping music. He's at Guapa.

"Yes, yes, it's me. Can you hear me?" I yell.

"Where are you?"

"Never mind where I am. Come to my house immediately. We have work to do."

A heavy wave of nausea grabs me and I tell the driver to stop the car. I open the door and do a sad little vomit on the pavement. When I am finished I wipe my mouth with my hand and settle back into the seat. There is a loud buzz in my ears. My eyes feel red and inflamed but the sickness has sobered me up. I feel better, less like death. The driver watches me through the rearview mirror with a worried look in his eyes. I wave at him to carry on and we are off again.

We speed through a tunnel. On the right-hand side someone has spray-painted "*Courage les Enfants*" on the brand-new concrete. All these new roads and tunnels would seem to suggest the city is somehow entering a new century with big ambitions. And yet these promises seem so cold and far away. I do not own any of this. I cannot touch it. I don't belong here. All I know is that I cannot step out of the car. The car is controllable. It is a small space, and the backseat is mine.

The voice of Oum Kalthoum meanders out of the crackling radio and permeates the air like a thick cloud of smoke. The song is *al-Atlal*, the same song that played in my room the first night I spent with Taymour.

Oh my heart, don't ask me where the love has gone

One night many years ago, at a time when life felt much simpler than it does today, Baba taught me how to listen to music. He was sitting in his favourite chair, its brown leather faded where he would rest his arms every night. With a glass of whisky in one hand and a shisha in the other, he would sit for hours listening to Oum Kalthoum. His eyes were closed and his head turned upward, gently swaying to her voice.

When he opened his eyes and saw that I was watching him, he motioned for me to come closer. I sat down beside him and he said, "You must wake up to Fairouz and fall asleep to Oum Kalthoum. Fairouz in the morning, Oum Kalthoum in the evening. Try it now. Come on, close your eyes."

I haven't forgotten you

He was right. In the morning, Fairouz's hopeful voice, like the trilling of a songbird, is fresh and cheery. Her melancholy lifts your spirits. In Fairouz's company the world is bright, and though sadness is always present, behind every word, her voice takes you to a lush hilltop under skies the sweetest blue. But the nights, especially nights like this, are for Oum Kalthoum. You only need one song, which lasts long enough to allow you to go deep, to descend into your memories. Best to do such nostalgic travelling at the end of the day, when you have the luxury to let your thoughts run away from you.

We drive through the darkness. To the right I can see the lights of the government buildings, the large interrogation room with its small windows that run across it. In the distance the shadows of al-Sharqiyeh loom on the eastern hill. I close my eyes and ride on the depth of Oum Kalthoum's voice like a cloud of cigarette smoke that takes me high. I imagine I am among the stars, looking down at myself crouching in the backseat of the old taxi.

The song on the radio is interrupted by a news bulletin.

"Breaking news," the presenter announces breathlessly. "We can confirm that the government will begin a raid in al-Sharqiyeh to clear the area of terrorists. Oh, you terrorists, we will crush you!" the presenter exclaims.

Silence falls in the car. The voice of Oum Kalthoum returns.

I've had it with this prison now that the world is mine

My phone lights up. Basma's name appears on the screen. I ignore it until it stops flashing and the phone goes dark again. The taxi brakes suddenly as a stray cat scampers across the road. I close my eyes and sink deeper into the seat. I've spent my life hunting for the silver lining in dark gutters, yearning for the unobtainable. My mother, Taymour, the revolution. What is this revolution I am looking for? This revolution exists only in my mind. The disfigured carcases of so many beautiful causes are scattered throughout history, battered by war and betrayal, their once hopeful spirit darkened and soured. Why should this cause be any different? For a single moment we seemed undefeatable. And now we've forgotten that we shared cigarettes as we marched, we no longer trust each other to throw Pepsi in each other's eyes to lessen the pain of the tear gas.

I wanted to prove that love conquers all, that love is stronger and more powerful than any other force in this world. But I could not even prove that with Taymour. We've captured our love and kept it hostage. I know now that I cannot love Taymour, or anyone else, except in complete frankness. What is the purpose of love if we cannot preserve its authenticity? Better we end it here and now, let us cut our losses and go our separate ways. But where would I go? My love for Taymour, for the revolution . . . that was my compass, steering me in the direction of what I felt was true. And my mother? Where is she now? For so long I missed my mother and father so much I wanted to die. I missed them and yet hated them for leaving me to pick up the pieces all alone. I am an explorer with a broken compass, with everyone pointing me in opposing directions. If I feel lost now I will feel worse tomorrow, and the day after, and the day after that.

If Taymour wants to live this way, to act out the role society wants of him, then who am I to tell him otherwise? Shall I wring his neck to force him to go one way when he wants to go another? If I did, I would be no better than the regime, no better than Teta or Hamza. There is no such thing as forcing someone to be free. My obligation is not to my love for him but rather to what this love represents. My obligation is only to myself. Like two parallel lines running alongside each other, Taymour and I could only ever come together if one of us were to break.

A few weeks after my father died, I was walking home from Maj's house late one evening. The roads were deserted, the midweek evening silent save for the chirping crickets. It was a ten-minute walk to my house, down the street and across an empty plot of land. I walked with my head down, looking at my white tennis shoes, trying to distract myself by focussing on avoiding the yellow stones on the sidewalk and only stepping on the pink ones. I hopped from one pink stone to the other, imagining the yellow stones were square pits of fire that would consume me if I fell in.

Headlights flooded the street behind me. I turned around. The lights were coming from a car parked in a dark driveway. The headlights switched off and then on again. The car was winking at me, acknowledging my presence. I turned around and walked, quicker now, the yellow stones coming at me faster.

The engine revved. The car drove toward me. I began to run. Chancing another look back at the car, I could just about make out the image of the driver through the glare of the head-lights. If what I saw was simply a hallucination, it appeared so vividly in my mind that to this day I swear that it was my father in that car. His eyes stared back at me from behind the wheel. I froze.

The car stalled in the middle of the road. The door opened, my father slowly stepped out. He walked to the front of the car and just stood there. With his figure silhouetted in the head-lights, his entire body appeared like it was on fire. He was looking at me and he was taller than I remembered, taller than any human could be. His legs stretched out so long that he was almost four times my height. His hands were by his sides, and when he lifted them there was a ball of fire in each of his palms. The flames licked his fingers and spread up his arms. He opened his mouth to speak, but no sound came out. His black mouth just stretched wider and wider, consuming his face like a photograph in flames.

I burst into a run. I ran to the end of the road and took a left, sprinting across the empty plot of land. At the end of the plot stood our house, a pale flickering light emanating from our living room. Teta watching television. As I ran, dry thistle and weeds scratched my ankles. The field was littered with Pepsi cans that sparkled in the moonlight like jagged blue glass. Behind me, my father's body was now ablaze. He chased after me, setting the weeds on fire until the entire plot was in flames. The heat from the fire burned the back of my neck.

My feet landed on the concrete sidewalk in front of our house. I stopped and turned around. The empty plot of land was cold and dark. Other than the sound of the wind rustling through the trees, the night was as dead as my father. I bent over and put my hands on my knees to catch my breath. Under the bright streetlights, I felt foolish for being scared of my own imagination. I began to laugh, like a maniac on the side of the road, watching the light from the television flicker in our window.

The house is dark and dancing with secrets. I walk to my bedroom, open the door that stood between us and Teta. Between us and the world. A flimsy wooden door. It was naïve to have believed that a plank of wood might be enough to protect Taymour and me. Then again nothing would have been strong enough to keep our secret.

Baba's old leather chair sits in the corner of my room. You see, our world stopped when Baba died. We still have the same rotting shelves, the same television, the same plates and chairs and knives and tables. We've been stuck in those times for too long now.

I sit in my father's chair and place my arms on the faded brown leather, as he might have done. I take a deep drag, and the red tip of my freshly lit cigarette blazes in the dark. There is the roar of a jet plane shooting across the sky, followed by the wail of an ambulance two streets away. The chair I am sitting in faces the open window, but there's not a whiff of breeze coming in. The room is stifling. Beads of sweat form on my forehead. Tonight is the hottest it's been all year.

The city is in the grips of a heat wave, and we are all trapped inside the furnace. Some choose to ignore the flames, hiding within a mirage of air-conditioned shopping malls, internationally certified hotels, expensive restaurants, and large plots of land awaiting construction, where if you're not careful the overgrown thistle conceals burning ghosts that chase you through your past. These lucky few build wedding cakes and towers of glass, concrete, and steel to shelter them from the flames. Meanwhile, inside imperial embassies protected by barbed wire and armed guards, fair-skinned men and women in flak jackets talk about fluctuating oil prices and counterinsurgency operations and stabilization projects and women's empowerment campaigns. And everyone is so self-important and self-deceiving and self-assured.

For the young men who are driven out of the slums of al-Sharqiyeh in search of a piece of bread and some work—even if the work involves slitting someone's throat on a hunch that it might please God—denial is a luxury they cannot afford. The city, ever so deceitful, lures these men deep into the desert in search of salvation and then traps them in prisons to roast in the fire. The flames grip these young men by the throat, and as the last drop of moisture evaporates from their parched lips, there is only silence.

But in the midst of this decaying, burning city, there are pockets of hope. It can be found in the tiny dark rooms in underground bars, where women with short hair cheer on men in dresses. It can be felt in the abandoned cinemas where anonymous strangers fall in love if only for a few moments, and in the living rooms where families crowd around, drinking sweet black tea and Skyping their homesick relatives so that together they can watch the long, rambling talk shows that go on all night. Despite the interrogation rooms where men in uniform crack clubs and electric wires on the naked body of someone's son or daughter, despite the prisons where men transform into sadistic killers for a dream and a paycheck, there are still pockets of hope in the streets of this city.

And it is in these decaying streets where the power lies. Street power: starry-eyed, raw, and foolish, like a hopeless romantic, used and torn this way and that by the politics of those living in palaces. For a moment we had the entire country in our hands. But then we flinched. And now street power has been torn down, its heart broken. We kicked the revolution's body to the curb and tried to walk away, not realizing that we buried ourselves in the process. And once one person is killed, then another and another, the deaths become so great that one life does not matter to anyone any more. You could be the queen of Guapa yet no one but your mother will weep over your corpse. But still, there are pockets of hope. And denial is no longer an option.

I look at the vines of jasmine that creep in through the window, embracing me with their fragrant flowers. Beyond them there's the kindergarten and behind it the minaret pokes out, its tip sparkling a bright green. In my tiredness the light appears to me as an exploding star in the sky. Up in that minaret the muezzin will soon clear his throat before calling this tormented city to prayer. Even with the windows shut and the shutters drawn tight, his calls are loud enough that it is as if he is right here in the room with me.

For many years it was me, Taymour, and the muezzin in this room. The muezzin's call to prayer was our alarm, warning us that Taymour needed to go home. I think of last night. Taymour had promised it wouldn't be our last. He swore we would find a way to stay together. Over the course of one day, one turn of the sun, all that has turned to dust.

Last night was also hot. The muezzin's microphone crackled. The sheets began to rustle as Taymour untangled himself from me. The rustling triggered that familiar sadness, the realization that we would not wake up beside each other this morning.

Taymour began to get dressed. I lay naked on my back watching him, aroused by the sight of his delicate muscles flexing as he pulled his underwear on. I looked at the chest of drawers, at the wooden frame that held the photo of Baba, which I had instinctively turned over when Taymour and I had come inside the room.

"Just a bit longer?" I asked.

Taymour smiled. He walked back to the bed and kissed my forehead. "I have to be up early. We're signing the marriage papers first thing in the morning."

"Are you sure this is what you want to do?" I asked. From now on he would be sleeping next to somebody else. I would have given up all the revolutions just so I could turn over every morning and find him there. I would press myself into his warm body and kiss his lips to taste his morning breath. It is strange that something so minuscule could mean so much, the act of waking up curled against the person you love.

He sat down on Baba's chair as he slid his feet into his socks. "This is the right decision, Rasa."

"It sounds like you're looking forward to it, then," I said. "That's great."

He looked up at me with concern. "I thought we discussed this. You know this doesn't change what we have."

I sighed and turned around. Taymour walked to the mirror and examined his reflection. He played with his hair, moving the part from the right to the left, then messing it all up again. In his eyes I could almost see him asking himself: How would society want my hair to appear?

Outside, the muezzin urged the city to get out of bed.

A scream shattered the air. It was more of a wail, the long hopeless wail of someone who had lost everything. Time stood still and Oum Kalthoum kept singing that note. Had it only been a moment, or did Oum Kalthoum really stretch out that note for hours? I had never noticed before.

Then came the banging.

"Open the door, Rasa! Open the door now!" Teta's voice boomed from behind the door.

The room began to shake. An earthquake, the walls caved in. I jumped out of bed, naked, and grabbed hold of Taymour to stop myself from falling. Neither of us said anything or even dared to breathe. I held on to Taymour and stared into his blazing eyes as they flitted back and forth between the door and me, naked and quivering.

The banging persisted. Words shot at us from behind the door, angry words that meant little when taken out of context or even when put together. The words were not important, but Teta flung them at us like flames shooting from her mouth. Her rage set fire to the bed, the door, the mirror, the flames engulfed us.

"Teta, what are you talking about?" I scrambled to pick up the clothes I had so carelessly thrown on the floor. I hurriedly dressed myself. First underwear, then jeans and T-shirt.

"Don't play this game with me, boy," Teta screamed. The banging got louder, angrier. I never knew an old woman could have such power in her fists, such fury. I felt that at any moment the ceiling might collapse or the mirror would crash to the floor.

Taymour grabbed me by the arms and shook me. "You have to let me out, Rasa," he pleaded with desperate eyes, all white and bulging. "I need to get out of here."

I closed my eyes and put my hands to my head. I felt that if I were to let go my head might explode. The banging on the door was louder now, like she was banging her fists on my head, breaking open the secret cage and letting the birds fly away.

"All right!" I yelled, opening my eyes. The banging

stopped. "All right I'll open the damn door. But you go to your room, Teta. You hear me? *Yalla!*"

Silence. Then Teta's footsteps echoed down the hall and there was a slamming of a door.

"Let me out," Taymour begged.

"Yes, yes," I muttered. I unlocked the door and peered into the empty hall. The doors to both Teta's and Doris's rooms were shut and the house was once again still. Teta had gone to her room as promised. Or had I imagined it all? I looked at Taymour. I had never seen a face so white. So filled with fear. He nodded, as if reading my mind. It had happened.

"Call me when this is done," he said as I walked him to the front door.

I held on to his hands. I didn't think I would ever be able to let go. For a moment I thought that perhaps we should just go back to my bedroom and lock ourselves in there. If we never set foot outside we could avoid the wedding and Teta and all of that nonsense. I could see Taymour and me curled up in my bed forever, feeding off scraps of food Doris might push through the keyhole.

"Call me when this is done," Taymour repeated.

"Promise me that I'll see you again," I said.

"I promise." He squeezed my hand one final time before letting go. He ran down the stairs and into the dark night without looking back.

When I could no longer see him I closed the door. Everything was quiet. If Teta's screams woke any of the neighbours, none had been curious enough to investigate.

I knocked on Teta's bedroom door. She opened it and followed me, wordlessly, into the kitchen. She took a seat at the table and stared into the middle distance. She did not look at me as I made her a cup of tea and sat across from her. The tea remained untouched on the table between us as we sat and smoked cigarettes in silence. I tried to form the sentences to explain but none of the words I had so diligently practiced in the bathroom mirror were welcome in the space between us. Had I been rehearsing those words, many years ago, for myself or for her?

"What did you see?" I asked. My throat clenched as I spoke, hoarse from the screams and tears that had been shocked back into hiding.

"I saw enough."

"Let me explain."

"I've seen him come before. At the time I thought you were doing drugs. It didn't even cross my mind . . . "

"Teta . . . "

"I know what your generation is like. I know that your generation doesn't look to marriage and is looking to experiment and try new things."

"Teta . . . "

"I don't ever want to see that boy in my house again, is that understood?"

I said nothing.

"Maybe it's my fault. Maybe I've been too easy, too open. Is it because I would stick almonds in your ass when you were constipated? You really were a constipated baby. There are so many girls dying over you. Why do you have to be with a man? That terrible boy must have seduced you. I could just sense that boy was no good."

I had never seen her like this before, speaking in runaway questions that dragged us into dead ends and tired circles. Finally she took a deep breath and sighed.

"We will have to keep quiet about this," she said in a practical tone, more to herself than to me. She stubbed her cigarette out in the ashtray and stood up. She patted down her cotton nightgown and walked out of the kitchen. I remained seated, listening as she shuffled to her bedroom and shut the door. Then I went to bed.

I still don't know what Teta saw when she looked through the keyhole. Did she see us kiss? Did she see us lying in bed together, forehead to forehead, alone in our thoughts? A few weeks ago Taymour and I had been in my bedroom when he stood up and walked to the door. He peered through the keyhole with the concentration of a scientist examining something in a microscope.

"People can see through the hole if the key is turned to the side," he remarked, turning the key back down so that it blocked the tiny space in the hole.

"Don't be paranoid." I sighed, pulling him back between the sheets.

We had been so careful. We had pulled the shutters down all the way, made sure the gaps between the slats were so tight not even the most curious eyes could peer in through the window. We had drawn the curtains and locked and bolted the door. We thought we had sealed our world airtight. But last night Teta managed to enter through the tiniest slip of a key in a lock.

I get up from Baba's chair and walk toward Teta's room, following the sounds of her heavy snores. When I was younger, like a mother fretting over a newborn, I worried that her snores would suddenly stop in the middle of the night. I was plagued by the thought that she would die and abandon me the way my mother and father had. Her snores, loud and rumbling through the thin walls separating our bedrooms, were how I made sure she was still alive. Tonight the snores are leading me to my final confrontation.

The door to her bedroom is ajar. She is asleep on her back under the covers. The deep creases on her face appear at ease as she sleeps. Her mind is elsewhere, in another world where last night never happened. Her mouth is open. The only evidence that this woman is Teta, strong and tough Teta, is in the imposing snores that boom from the back of her throat. One foot has escaped from under the white sheets, carefully manicured toes painted a simple red. The wooden furniture creaks gently in the night. It had been a long, hot day.

I stand by the bed and contemplate her. Study her, read her. Watching her sleep, I think of how much I love her. The love that I had for Mama and Baba I had put into her. Where should I put this love after tonight? And all the love Teta had for her son, which she deposited on to me, where is that love going to go? I would never again kiss those deep creases on her forehead, or the wrinkles that gently line her cheeks. I could probably trace the decay of this exhausted family in the wrinkles on her face. Would she even let me kiss those wrinkles now that she knows where my lips have been?

She's an old woman. She's had a long and difficult life. She's watched her only son die. And, as she never failed to remind me, there is nothing more painful than watching your only son die. Now her only grandson has died also. Worse than death, he's killed off the family name. He's dashed any hope of the family lineage continuing, of her son living through future generations.

My hands are shaking. I feel hollow and my nerves raw, as if I have just swallowed a vial of poison. I've let her down and brought her shame. I've dragged her along with me on this journey, this old woman who has been through enough in her life. I'm taking her on one last adventure.

A pillow lies on the ground by her bed. I pick it up. I feel the cool touch of the white cotton in my hands. She always stores the linen in the freezer to keep it cool during hot nights. If I place this cold pillow on her face, the soft cotton that smells of orange blossom detergent, and slowly press down, what would happen? They would chalk it up to an old woman who died in her sleep. I would have the house to myself. No one looking through keyholes, no questions about where I'm going or who I'm sharing a bed with. But would her ghost forever haunt me? Would her spirit still peer through keyholes?

Her eyes open. She looks at me with a certain fear. I drop the pillow. She sits up in bed and rubs her face.

"What are you doing standing there like a jinn?" she says.

I take a seat beside her. She burps, a fleshy, authoritative burp that lasts for a few long seconds.

"I shouldn't have eaten that damn cheese for dinner."

"What did you do tonight?" I ask her.

"Watched the shitty news, seeing how everyone's destroying this country. We live in a republic of shame. Where've you been all night?"

"I was at a wedding." I pause. My hands shake and I steady them on my knees. "It was the wedding of the man who was in my bed last night."

She glares at me and smacks her lips. "Have you no shame to discuss this openly with me?"

"I'm done with shame," I say. "I'm done with your rules about what is *eib* and what isn't. I have my own rules now."

"He has his own rules now," Teta says to the lampshade. She turns back to me. "And who else is following your rules, exactly? Tell me, who? Or is it just you? What will everyone else say about your rules?"

"They can say what they want."

"You think they will only talk about you?" She laughed. "What about me? Or do I not matter? And your father, God bless his soul. Does he deserve to have people talk about him?"

"Stop hanging Baba over me." I leap off the bed. "I have my own voice."

"What do you use your voice for? To seduce men to your bed? Is this a good use of your voice? Look around you. Look at this country. Look at what having a voice means. Having a voice, he says." She stops to take a breath. "Having a voice is worse than eating shit and being silent."

We take a break. She takes a sip of her water. I glance at my phone. It is therapeutic, the yelling. I feel better. And when there is silence, there is real silence. Not a stir in the house. Only Teta and me, battling it out.

Teta clears her throat. "Maybe you should go back to America with this voice of yours," she says.

"Would you even allow me to leave? If that was the case, you would have kicked me out last night. But no, you force me to live here, under your rules, under Baba's rules. If I were to leave I would be a heartless traitor."

"No, no, no." She shakes her head furiously like a stubborn child. "Your father is watching from the skies, boy, and there is no way I will let him think I accept you talking about him like this."

"Let's talk about Baba, then," I say. "What happened in those six months before he died?"

She is surprised by this question. So am I. The question escapes from a place within me that I did not know existed. Our fight had established a pattern, we had drawn a line and had come to an agreement over what was and wasn't acceptable to argue about. I don't trust these lines any more. As soon as a line is established it becomes necessary to cross it, if only to ensure the line doesn't become entrenched, to ensure it doesn't end up ruling us for another eternity.

"Where are my cigarettes?" Teta begins to get up but I block her path.

"Why didn't Baba go in for treatment?"

"Don't bring back the dead, Rasa."

"We've been living under the rules of the dead for fifteen years," I reply.

Teta takes another sip from the glass of water by her bedside table and turns on the lamp. In the glare I can see her eyelids are heavy and grey, as if she has been seeing what happened last night play out over and over again.

"What do you want to know?" she finally asks.

"Why didn't he go for treatment?"

"The treatment would never have worked, he would only have suffered more in his final few months," she says bitterly, pulling at her cotton nightgown. "The doctors said that even with treatment it was terminal. God wanted him and I wanted him, and I fought God for the life of my son, but in the end I lost."

"You let him die," I say.

"Don't you dare say that," Teta snaps. "All he wanted was to spend the last few months with me."

"And Mama?"

"Your mother was broken."

"She needed help. She still needs help."

"Your mother left because she knew what she was bringing to this family. For all her faults, your mother learned one thing from me: shame."

"You're lying. She couldn't have just forgotten about me. You made sure she would never find us again. You moved us away, cut us off until there was nothing left from our old life."

"Rasa, I was trying to protect you."

"But there was one thing left, wasn't there?" I say. "You overlooked one minor detail. The mailbox in the post office downtown. The same mailbox that you first rented out thirty years ago, when Baba left to university."

"Rasa, leave the past in the past."

"Did she send letters?" I grab her by the shoulders and begin to shake her. "Where are Mama's letters?"

She does not protest. She is content with being shaken like a rag doll. I stop and look at her. I try to imagine what she might be thinking. She does not actually care what people think of her, does she? What she cares about are those years before she lost her son, how fiercely she protected him and how suddenly he was taken from her. And for so long I was shielding her from losing the one thing she had left: me.

"Rasa, all I want is to make sure you're taken care of. If you . . . if you're with men, how will you live? Who will take care of you when you're old?"

"Give me the mailbox key now," I yell. I know the key must be somewhere in the house. My mother must have written to me. *My darling Rasa, I've missed you beyond words. I haven't stopped chopping onions since I left you with that witch.* I pull open the drawers of Teta's bedside table, digging past pills, a pair of stockings, and a stack of old photographs. I pull out the entire drawer and turn it upside down, emptying its contents on the floor. No key.

Teta is silent. She stares at the photo of Baba on her bedside table. It is a photo of him holding me as a newborn. In the photo Baba has a bushy mustache and a happy glimmer in his eyes. I move to her closet and rummage through her clothes, tossing them behind me as I search. When I've cleared her closet I begin to walk out the door. The key must be in the living room.

"You know, Rasa?" Teta says, as I walk out. I turn around to face her. "You're just like your father. He was like a gold coin. The more he aged the more beautiful he was. Even in his sickness, he was radiant."

I slam the door behind me and return to my bedroom. I turn on the lights, drag the chair toward the closet, and climb up, reaching for the shoe box hidden behind the books on the top shelf. I look through the various letters and postcards from Taymour I had stuffed in the shoe box earlier that morning, which seems a lifetime ago now. I pull out the only other thing in there: the photograph of Mama and me. I don't need to talk to Teta about last night. Once I find Mama's letters, any evidence of her existence, I'll talk to her. I'm her son, not Teta's.

I continue to search the house for any traces of my mother. I'm no longer afraid of making noise or waking anyone up. Let them all wake up and know that I am alive. In the living room

I grab Teta's bag and toss the contents on the floor. Her cigarettes, crusty tissues, glasses, chewing gum. All on the floor.

I turn to the walls. One by one, I tear the photos of Baba off the wall. I throw the framed picture of Teta and Baba on the floor, relishing the sound of the glass shattering. I tear out the photos and look inside the frame for the key.

For so long I had been so well behaved, the perfect grandson. I was protecting her just as much as she was protecting me. But at what cost?

"Where is she?" I yell, grabbing the cushions from the sofa and tearing at the seams until they unravel. No key. I toss the cushion across the room. It lands on the table and a glass ashtray falls to the floor. I run toward the bookcase and push the television off the shelf. I savour the thud it makes as it crashes on the carpet.

When there is nothing left to overturn, I stop and look at the room. I am panting like a madman. The room is covered in shattered glass and upturned furniture. There is no sign of Mama anywhere. For so long I had believed there was something of her here. I had held on to the hope that the house contained my mother somehow. But it was all in my head. She was never here. The only thing keeping her here was me.

I am crying as I go into the bathroom. It is as if the depth of my mother's pain has finally hit me. I am not just crying for my mother but also for myself, for the person I used to be, someone who believed they could change the world, who didn't feel so helpless about the thought of a young man from al-Sharqiyeh being tortured to death in prison, someone who could fall madly in love with no fear of the consequences. What am I going to do tomorrow? How will this new person fill his days?

I reach for the toothpaste and begin to brush my teeth. I take a good look at my face in the bathroom mirror. It is flushed and swollen. I move closer to my reflection, drawn by something familiar in my face. Red lines of burst blood vessels streak the area around my nostrils. As a child, I could always tell when my mother had vomited after drinking. She would throw herself into each heave with such intensity that blood vessels in her face would burst, leaving the area around her nose veiny and red. My eyes, bloodshot and exhausted, stare back at me. They are my mother's eyes. I look at her staring back at me in my reflection, at the demons she and I share, the deviance and otherness, and for the first time I am no longer alone.

But I am not just my mother, am I? This burning stubbornness to hold on to what is gone, to my mother, to Taymour, to the revolution, it is Teta who gave this to me. She raised me against all odds, this woman who thought her time of raising children was long gone. But after years of following her stubborn path, I learned something from her. I can only hope one day she will look back at this and admire me for carving out my own life.

Teta's door is still shut when I leave the bathroom. I walk to the living room and grab a pen and paper from the dusty drawer where she keeps her cards. I scratch out the numbers on the paper that list the score of an old game of bridge. I know how much Teta insists on saving paper by using every piece that remains blank.

I am like you. I scrawl on the page, between the hastily written numbers and calculations. I circle it to bring it to her attention and leave it on the table.

My phone vibrates in my pocket.

Come outside, the text from Maj reads.

There is a creak of a door opening.

"Sir?" Doris's voice drifts through the quiet house. I look into the corridor and see her head peeking out from her bedroom.

"Don't worry, everything is fine now," I say. I step into her room, which is dark save for a collection of candles that are burning by the nightstand, just under the painting Mama had done of Baba. It looks like a shrine, but who is it a shrine for— my mother or my father?

"Are you going out?" she whispers.

"Yes."

"Too much problems outside. My family called. They tell me to go back." She pauses and then pulls my wrist toward her and puts a small object in my palm.

It's a short, flat key.

"Don't tell Teta," she whispers, putting an index finger to her lips.

I step out of the apartment, close the front door, and walk down the steps and out of the building. On the empty street, the sun is rising in the east, bathing al-Sharqiyeh in reddish dawn. There are never any clouds this deep into summer, but this July morning, clouds of destruction hover over al-Sharqiyeh. Many citizens will be in their homes when they die today, and the smoke blooms that rise as the bombs drop will contain concrete, dust, furniture, bits of bodies, pulverised and floating above the ruins. On the horizon the slums are burning like a crazy carnival. They look so beautiful from far away and then they are gone, a smouldering ruin.

Maj is parked around the corner. When he sees me, he flashes his headlights twice.

"I'm sorry about tonight," he says when I get inside. He's wearing bright red lipstick, and has shaded the area around his eyes in dark kohl to blend out the bruises.

"I don't know if I can go on," I say.

He shrugs. "You'll go on."

"I'll go on." I nod. "And who will take care of us when we get old?"

He leans over and gives me a peck on the cheek. "You're

going to take care of me. I don't know who will take care of you."

I chuckle. I am tired and my head hurts. I don't know what tomorrow will bring, but I know it won't begin with shame.

"So what do you want to do?" Maj asks as we begin to drive.

"I don't know." I squeeze the key in my fist. But I do know what I want to do. I want to find my mother, to tell her that it's okay. That I'm okay. I turn to Maj. "Maybe we should go protest."

"Yes, yes. Great idea. Let's go protest. Against who?"

"Against everyone. Against everything."

"Sounds good," Maj says. "But first, maybe a drink or two at Guapa."

ACKNOWLEDGEMENTS

Mom, Dad, Sami, Nadeem, Amal, Mona: Thank you for the love and laughter.

My agent, Toby Eady, believed in me and the novel, and his encouragement and guidance throughout the process has been invaluable. My editors did wonders with a scrappy manuscript: Judith Gurewich—thank you for challenging me to think more clearly, more deeply, and more honestly; and Anjali Singh, for your early, unwavering belief in this story, your patience, guidance, kindness, and great Skype conversations. Thank you to Keenan McCracken, Lauren Shekari, Yvonne Cárdenas, and everyone else at Other Press for their help along the way.

I am indebted to Rowan Salim, Adam Barr, Muhammad El-Khairy, and Tim Ludford, who believed in this project from the very first kernel of an idea, and read countless drafts over the years. The four of you are jewels. Many others also took the time to read early drafts and offer detailed, thoughtful, and supportive feedback: Sami Haddad, Michael Round, Atiaf Alwazir, Nada Dalloul, Jamila El-Gizuli, Thoraya El-Rayyes, Raja Farah, Hannah Wright, Giuseppe Caruso, Ginny Hill, Nina Mufleh, Adrienne E. Treeby, Yazan Al-Saadi, Eliane Mazzawi, Danah Abdulla, Joshua Rogers, Tania Tabar, Yasmeen Tabbaa, Sarah Alhunaidi, and Jehan Bseiso. Djamila Issa, Becky Branford, Joud Abdel Majeid: thank you for opening your homes and hearts to me in Paris, London, and New York. I am grateful to *Kalimat* magazine for kindly publishing an early excerpt in their April 2014 issue.

Above all I thank Adam, my best friend and the love of my life. This book would not exist without your love and patience.

NOTES AND CREDITS

Song lyrics to Oum Kalthoum's "Al-Atlal" (The Ruins) were written by Ibrahim Nagy, and adapted from the translation produced by the Arabic Music Translation team (http://tinyurl.com/nogh49).

The character of the man playing the piano downtown was inspired by Ayham Ahmad, the "Piano Man" of Syria's besieged Yarmouk refugee camp. I came across a clip of Ayham playing a few years ago and was reduced to tears. I found it impossible not to write a character inspired by him. Ayham's story, and clips of his music, can be found here: http://tinyurl.com/p9cjfrm.